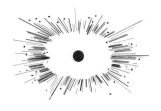

Tales of Old Earth

Tales of Old Earth

Michael Swanwick

Frog, Ltd.
Berkeley, California

Published by Frog, Ltd.

Frog, Ltd. books are distributed by
North Atlantic Books
P.O. Box 12327
Berkeley, California 94712

Book design by Treehouse Graphics

Printed in the United States of America

Library of Congress Cataloging-in-Publication Data

Swanwick, Michael.
    Tales of old earth / by Michael Swanwick.
        p.   cm.
    ISBN 1-58394-016-2 (alk. paper)
    1. Science fiction, American.   I. Title.

PS3569.W28 T35 2000
813'.54—dc21   99-087107

1 2 3 4 5 6 7 8 9 / 04 03 02 01 00

This book is dedicated to
Virginia Kidd, Deborah Beale,
Martha Millard, and Jennifer Brehl
——the Other Women in my life.

Contents

Foreword

The User's Guide to Michael Swanwick

Sometimes you have to step through the looking glass to get a proper look at someone standing next to you. During my science-fiction career, Michael Swanwick has been a hard guy to miss. He's steady, prolific, publishes all over the place, and, just like me, he has lost about a hundred awards.

But I didn't understand this guy's work at all properly until I went to Russia. I was at a science fiction convention in Saint Petersburg where they were having learned, earnest panels about Michael Swanwick. His novel *The Iron Dragon's Daughter* was the talk of the town.

This dragon book of Swanwick's is thoroughly unlike normal, tedious, off-the-rack dragon books. It's a world of magical elves and trolls where everybody's working in crappy, run-down factories, full of cruel backstabbing, many broken promises, strong-arm hustles, and pervasive despair. In other words, Russia. A shattered, rusty, "hard-fantasy" world, that is Russia to a T. I've spoken face-to-face to Russians, and they think I'm an interesting foreigner with some useful contacts outside their borders. But Michael Swanwick *really* speaks to Russians. They consider him a groundbreaking literary artist.

Then there is Swanwick the critic. I'm a critic myself, or I wouldn't be writing this introduction. I take this critical gibberish pretty seriously. I don't think an artist gets very far without a solid framework for objective understanding. You can sit there with a hammerlock on your muse, gushing prose under high pressure, and it may be pretty good stuff; but if you lack critical perspective, you'll become a toy of your own historical epoch. Your work will date quickly, because you are making way too many unconscious obeisances to the shibboleths of your own time.

Michael Swanwick, however, is a guy who has thoroughly got it down with the shibboleth and obeisance thing. Not only has he mastered this problem himself, he's quite good on the subject of other people's difficulties. Swanwick's "User's Guide to the Postmoderns" is the most important critical document about Cyberpunks and Humanists that ever came from a guy who was neither a cyberpunk nor a humanist. That article is, in fact, The Mythos. Swanwick definitively coined the Common Wisdom there. I very much doubt that a better assessment will ever be written.

At the time, one had to wonder why Swanwick had become the self-appointed arbiter of other people's quarrels. There certainly wasn't much that he could gain from this personally, and it predictably created a ow, much of it centered, with total injustice, on him, Michael Swanwick. But time has richly rewarded his courage and foresight. He did the field a genuine critical service. Science fiction is a better place for his efforts.

Not that I concur with everything Swanwick says, especially his painfully accurate assessment of my own motives. Agreement, maybe not. Respect, very definitely. I don't think that everything I write has to please Michael Swanwick. However, I would be very upset if he thought I was selling out or slacking off. Swanwick, a man and writer of firm integrity, has never sold out or slacked off. I cannot think of a single instance of this, ever, in the extensive Swanwick oeuvre. He is a strong, solid critic and he knows the evil smell of literary vices. Knowing that he's out there, sniffing—well, it keeps me to the grind.

Now we come to the matter of Swanwick being a "difficult writer." What's this allegation about? Well, let me be up-front here: he's not for mundane wimps. Forget about it. Terrible things happen in Swanwick fiction. People suffer, often gruesomely. Furthermore, it's a rare Swanwick work which does not include some mind-altering, meticulous instance of evil sex.

So, yes, by the blinkered standards of the Christian Coalition he is somewhat disgusting and obscene. However, the true core of the matter is the Swanwick is an inherently and intrinsically strange human being. Oh sure, he's married, has a child, pays his taxes, stays out of the slammer, but at his core he's a high-voltage visionary. He's not a professional writer dabbling in the sci-fi genre. He is that rarer and far more valuable thing, an inherently science-fictional thinker who has trained himself, through years of devoted effort, to speak fluently.

His approach to theme, plot, character, situation, are all completely orthogonal to the norm. When you start a Swanwick story, it's as if a guy had knocked on your door and come in walking on his hands. And not as a mere stunt either, for he proceeds to make himself entirely at home; he does the dishes with his feet, fetches a beer from the fridge with the crook of his knee, settles on the couch with the remote control in his toes and starts making sardonic comments. They're rather insightful, disturbing, off-the-wall assessments, replete with stick-to-your-skull images that demonstrate a lifetime of imaginative concentration. Your world is not the same when he leaves.

He's not always graceful or easy, he never caters or panders, but Michael Swanwick is the Real Thing. He is entirely authentic and in full command of his material. He's gone so far into science fiction that he's coming out the far side at high velocity. So, my task is done here: you're up to speed now, you have been warned. The rest is your own lookout.

I'm proud to call him my colleague.

Bruce Sterling
January 2000

The Very Pulse of the Machine

CLICK.

The radio came on.

"Hell."

Martha kept her eyes forward, concentrated on walking. Jupiter to one shoulder, Daedalus's plume to the other. Nothing to it. Just trudge, drag, trudge, drag. Piece of cake.

"Oh."

She chinned the radio off.

Click.

"Hell. Oh. Kiv. El. Sen."

"Shut up, shut up, shut up!" Martha gave the rope an angry jerk, making the sledge carrying Burton's body jump and bounce on the sulfur hardpan. "You're dead, Burton, I've checked, there's a hole in your faceplace big enough to stick a fist through, and I really don't want to crack up. I'm in kind of a tight spot here and I can't afford it, okay? So be nice and just shut the fuck up."

"Not. Bur. Ton."

"Do it anyway."

She chinned the radio off again.

1

Jupiter loomed low on the western horizon, big and bright and beautiful and, after two weeks on Io, easy to ignore. To her left, Daedalus was spewing sulfur and sulfur dioxide in a fan two hundred kilometers high. The plume caught the chill light from an unseen sun and her visor rendered it a pale and lovely blue. Most spectacular view in the universe, and she was in no mood to enjoy it.

Click.

Before the voice could speak again, Martha said, "I am not going crazy, you're just the voice of my subconscious, I don't have the time to waste trying to figure out what unresolved psychological conflicts gave rise to all this, and I am *not* going to listen to anything you have to say."

Silence.

THE MOON ROVER had flipped over at least five times before crashing sideways against a boulder the size of the Sydney Opera House. Martha Kivelsen, timid groundling that she was, was strapped into her seat so tightly that when the universe stopped tumbling, she'd had a hard time unlatching the restraints. Juliet Burton, tall and athletic, so sure of her own luck and agility that she hadn't bothered, had been thrown into a strut.

The vent-blizzard of sulfur dioxide snow was blinding, though. It was only when Martha had finally crawled out from under its raging whiteness that she was able to look at the suited body she'd dragged free of the wreckage.

She immediately turned away.

Whatever knob or flange had punched the hole in Burton's helmet had been equally ruthless with her head.

Where a fraction of the vent-blizzard—"lateral plumes" the planetary geologists called them—had been deflected by the boulder, a bank of sulfur dioxide snow had built up. Automatically, without thinking, Martha scooped up double-handfuls and packed them into the helmet. Really, it was a nonsensical thing to do; in a vacuum, the body wasn't about to rot. On the other hand, it hid that face.

Then Martha did some serious thinking.

For all the fury of the blizzard, there was no turbulence. Because there was no atmosphere to have turbulence *in*. The sulfur dioxide gushed out straight from the sudden crack that had opened in the rock, falling to the surface miles away in strict obedience to the laws of ballistics. Most of what struck the boulder they'd crashed against would simply stick to it, and the rest would be bounced down to the ground at its feet. So that—this was how she'd gotten out in the first place—it was possible to crawl *under* the near-horizontal spray and back to the ruins of the moon rover. If she went slowly, the helmet light and her sense of feel ought to be sufficient for a little judicious salvage.

Martha got down on her hands and knees. And as she did, just as quickly as the blizzard had begun—it stopped.

She stood, feeling strangely foolish.

Still, she couldn't rely on the blizzard staying quiescent. Better hurry, she admonished herself. It might be an intermittent.

Quickly, almost fearfully, picking through the rich litter of wreckage, Martha discovered that the mother tank they used to replenish their airpacks had ruptured. Terrific. That left her own pack, which was one-third empty, two fully-charged backup packs, and Burton's, also one-third empty. It was a ghoulish thing to strip Burton's suit of her airpack, but it had to be done. Sorry, Julie. That gave her enough oxygen to last, let's see, almost forty hours.

Then she took a curved section of what had been the moon rover's hull and a coil of nylon rope, and, with two pieces of scrap for makeshift hammer and punch, fashioned a sledge for Burton's body.

She'd be damned if she was going to leave it behind.

CLICK.

"This is. Better."

"Says you."

Ahead of her stretched the hard, cold sulfur plain. Smooth as glass. Brittle as frozen toffee. Cold as hell. She called up a visor-map and checked her progress. Only forty-five miles of mixed terrain to cross and she'd reach the lander. Then she'd be home free. No sweat, she thought.

Io was in tidal lock with Jupiter. So the Father of Planets would stay glued to one fixed spot in the sky. That was as good as a navigation beacon. Just keep Jupiter to your right shoulder, and Daedalus to your left. You'll come out fine.

"Sulfur is. Triboelectric."

"Don't hold it in. What are you really trying to say?"

"And now I see. With eye serene. The very. Pulse. Of the machine." A pause. "Wordsworth."

Which, except for the halting delivery, was so much like Burton, with her classical education and love of classical poets like Spencer and Ginsberg and Plath, that for a second Martha was taken aback. Burton was a terrible poetry bore, but her enthusiasm had been genuine, and now Martha was sorry for every time she'd met those quotations with rolled eyes or a flip remark. But there'd be time enough for grieving later. Right now she had to concentrate on the task at hand.

The colors of the plain were dim and brownish. With a few quick chin-taps, she cranked up their intensity. Her vision filled with yellows, oranges, reds—intense wax crayon colors. Martha decided she liked them best that way.

For all its Crayola vividness, this was the most desolate landscape in the universe. She was on her own here, small and weak in a harsh and unforgiving world. Burton was dead. There was nobody else on all of Io. Nobody to rely on but herself. Nobody to blame if she fucked up. Out of nowhere, she was filled with an elation as cold and bleak as the distant mountains. It was shameful how happy she felt.

After a minute, she said, "Know any songs?"

OH THE BEAR WENT over the mountain. The bear went over the mountain. The bear went over the mountain. To see what he could see.

"Wake. Up. Wake. Up."

To see what he could—

"Wake. Up. Wake. Up. Wake."

"Hah? What?"

"Crystal sulfur is orthorhombic."

She was in a field of sulfur flowers. They stretched as far as the eye could see, crystalline formations the size of her hand. Like the poppies of Flanders field. Or the ones in the Wizard of Oz. Behind her was a trail of broken flowers, some crushed by her feet or under the weight of the sledge, others simply exploded by exposure to her suit's waste heat. It was far from being a straight path. She had been walking on autopilot, and stumbled and turned and wandered upon striking the crystals.

Martha remembered how excited she and Burton had been when they first saw the fields of crystals. They had piled out of the moon rover with laughter and bounding leaps, and Burton had seized her by the waist and waltzed her around in a dance of jubilation. This was the big one, they'd thought, their chance at the history books. And even when they'd radioed Hols back in the orbiter and were somewhat condescendingly informed that there was no chance of this being a new lifeform, but only sulfide formations such as could be found in any mineralogy text ... even that had not killed their joy. It was still their first big discovery. They'd looked forward to many more.

Now, though, all she could think of was the fact that such crystal fields occurred in regions associated with sulfur geysers, lateral plumes, and volcanic hot spots.

Something funny was happening to the far edge of the field, though. She cranked up her helmet to extreme magnification and watched as the trail slowly erased itself. New flowers were rising up in place of those she had smashed, small but perfect and whole. And growing. She could not imagine by what process this could be happening. Electrodeposition? Molecular sulfur being drawn up from the soil in some kind of pseudocapillary action? Were the flowers somehow plucking sulfur ions from Io's almost nonexistent atmosphere?

Yesterday, the questions would have excited her. Now, she had no capacity for wonder whatsoever. Moreover, her instruments were back in the moon rover. Save for the suit's limited electronics, she had nothing to take measurements with. She had only herself, the sledge, the spare airpacks, and the corpse.

"Damn, damn, damn," she muttered. On the one hand, this was a dangerous place to stay in. On the other, she'd been awake almost twenty hours now and she was dead on her feet. Exhausted. So very, very tired.

"O sleep! It is a gentle thing. Beloved from pole to pole. Coleridge."

Which, God knows, was tempting. But the numbers were clear: no sleep. With several deft chin-taps, Martha overrode her suit's safeties and accessed its medical kit. At her command, it sent a hit of methamphetamine rushing down the drug/vitamin catheter.

There was a sudden explosion of clarity in her skull and her heart began pounding like a motherfucker. Yeah. That did it. She was full of energy now. Deep breath. Long stride. Let's go.

No rest for the wicked. She had things to do. She left the flowers rapidly behind. Good-bye, Oz.

FADE OUT. FADE IN. Hours had glided by. She was walking through a shadowy sculpture garden. Volcanic pillars (these were their second great discovery; they had no exact parallel on Earth) were scattered across the pyroclastic plain like so many isolated Lipschitz statues. They were all rounded and heaped, very much in the style of rapidly cooled magma. Martha remembered that Burton was dead, and cried quietly to herself for a few minutes.

Weeping, she passed through the eerie stone forms. The speed made them shift and move in her vision. As if they were dancing. They looked like women to her, tragic figures out of *The Bacchae* or, no, wait, *The Trojan Women* was the play she was thinking of. Desolate. Filled with anguish. Lonely as Lot's wife.

There was a light scattering of sulfur dioxide snow on the ground here. It sublimed at the touch of her boots, turning to white mist and scattering wildly, the steam disappearing with each stride and then being renewed with the next footfall. Which only made the experience all that much creepier.

Click.

"Io has a metallic core predominantly of iron and iron sulfide, overlain by a mantle of partially molten rock and crust."

"Are you still here?"

"Am trying. To communicate."

"Shut up."

She topped the ridge. The plains ahead were smooth and undulating. They reminded her of the Moon, in the transitional region between Mare Serenitatis and the foothills of the Caucasus Mountains, where she had undergone her surface training. Only without the impact craters. No impact craters on Io. Least cratered solid body in the Solar System. All that volcanic activity deposited a new surface one meter thick every millenium or so. The whole damned moon was being constantly repaved.

Her mind was rambling. She checked her gauges, and muttered, "Let's get this show on the road."

There was no reply.

Dawn would come—when? Let's work this out. Io's "year," the time it took to revolve about Jupiter, was roughly forty-two hours fifteen minutes. She'd been walking seven hours. During which Io would've moved roughly sixty degrees through its orbit. So it would be dawn soon. That would make Daedalus's plume less obvious, but with her helmet graphics that wouldn't be a worry. Martha swiveled her neck, making sure that Daedalus and Jupiter were where they ought to be, and kept on walking.

TRUDGE, TRUDGE, TRUDGE. Try not to throw the map up on the visor every five minutes. Hold off as long as you can, just one more hour, okay, that's good, and another two miles. Not too shabby.

The sun was getting high. It would be noon in another hour and a half. Which meant—well, it really didn't mean much of anything.

Rock up ahead. Probably a silicate. It was a solitary six meters high brought here by who knew what forces and waiting who knew how many thousands of years just for her to come along and need a place to rest. She found a flat spot where she could lean against it and, breathing heavily, sat down to rest. And think. And check the airpack. Four hours until she had to change it again. Bringing her down to two airpacks. She had slightly under twenty-four hours now. Thirty-five miles to go. That was less than two miles an hour. A snap. Might run a little tight on oxygen there toward the end, though. She'd have to take care she didn't fall asleep.

Oh, how her body ached.

It ached almost as much as it had in the '48 Olympics, when she'd taken the bronze in the women's marathon. Or that time in the internationals in Kenya she'd come up from behind to tie for second. Story of her life. Always in third place, fighting for second. Always flight crew and sometimes, maybe, landing crew, but never the commander. Never class president. Never king of the hill. Just once—once!—she wanted to be Neil Armstrong.

Click.

"The marble index of a mind forever. Voyaging through strange seas of thought, alone. Wordsworth."

"What?"

"Jupiter's magnetosphere is the largest thing in the solar system. If the human eye could see it, it would appear two and a half times wider in the sky than the sun does."

"I knew that," she said, irrationally annoyed.

"Quotation is. Easy. Speech is. Not."

"Don't speak, then."

"Trying. To communicate!"

She shrugged. "So go ahead—communicate."

Silence. Then, "What does. This. Sound like?"

"What does what sound like?"

"Io is a sulfur-rich, iron-cored moon in a circular orbit around Jupiter. What docs this. Sound like? Tidal forces from Jupiter and Ganymede pull and squeeze Io sufficiently to melt Tartarus, its subsurface sulfur ocean. Tartarus vents its excess energy with sulfur and sulfur dioxide volcanoes. What does. This sound like? Io's metallic core generates a magnetic field which punches a hole in Jupiter's magnetosphere, and also creates a high-energy ion flux tube connecting its own poles with the north and south poles of Jupiter. What. Does this sound like? Io sweeps up and absorbs all the electrons in the million-volt range. Its volcanoes pump out sulfur dioxide; its magnetic field breaks down a percentage of that into sulfur and oxygen ions; and these ions are pumped into the hole punched in the magnetosphere, creating a rotating field commonly called the Io torus. What does this sound like? Torus. Flux tube. Magnetosphere. Volcanoes. Sulfur ions. Molten ocean. Tidal heating. Circular orbit. What does this sound like?"

Against her will, Martha had found herself first listening, then intrigued, and finally involved. It was like a riddle or a word puzzle. There was a right answer to the question. Burton or Hols would have gotten it immediately. Martha had to think it through.

There was the faint hum of the radio's carrier beam. A patient, waiting noise.

At last, she cautiously said, "It sounds like a machine."

"Yes. Yes. Yes. Machine. Yes. Am machine. Am machine. Am machine. Yes. Yes. Machine. Yes."

"Wait. You're saying that Io is a machine? That you're a machine? That you're Io?"

"Sulfur is triboelectric. Sledge picks up charges. Burton's brain is intact. Language is data. Radio is medium. Am machine."

"I don't believe you."

TRUDGE, DRAG, TRUDGE, DRAG. The world doesn't stop for strangeness. Just because she'd gone loopy enough to think that Io was alive and a machine and talking to her didn't mean that Martha could stop walking. She had promises to keep, and miles to go before she slept. And speaking of sleep, it was time for another fast refresher—just a quarter-hit—of speed.

Wow. Let's go.

As she walked, she continued to carry on a dialogue with her hallucination or delusion or whatever it was. It was too boring otherwise.

Boring, and a tiny bit terrifying.

So she asked, "If you're a machine, then what is your function? Why were you made?"

"To know you. To love you. And to serve you."

Martha blinked. Then, remembering Burton's long reminiscences on her Catholic girlhood, she laughed. That was a paraphrase of the answer to the first question in the old Baltimore Catechism: *Why did God make man?* "If I keep on listening to you, I'm going to come down with delusions of grandeur."

"You are. Creator. Of machine."

"Not me."

She walked on without saying anything for a time. Then, because the silence was beginning to get to her again, "When was it I supposedly created you?"

"So many a million of ages have gone. To the making of man. Alfred, Lord Tennyson."

"That wasn't me, then. I'm only twenty-seven. You're obviously thinking of somebody else."

"It was. Mobile. Intelligent. Organic. Life. You are. Mobile. Intelligent. Organic. Life."

Something moved in the distance. Martha looked up, astounded. A horse. Pallid and ghostly white, it galloped soundlessly across the plains, tail and mane flying.

She squeezed her eyes tight and shook her head. When she opened her eyes again, the horse was gone. A hallucination. Like the voice of Burton/Io. She'd been thinking of ordering up another refresher of the meth, but now it seemed best to put it off as long as possible.

This was sad, though. Inflating Burton's memories until they were as large as Io. Freud would have a few things to say about *that*. He'd say she was magnifying her friend to a godlike status in order to justify the fact that she'd never been able to compete one-on-one with Burton and win. He'd say she couldn't deal with the reality that some people were simply better at things than she was.

Trudge, drag, trudge, drag.

So, okay, yes, she had an ego problem. She was an overambitious, self-centered bitch. So what? It had gotten her this far, where a more reasonable attitude would have left her back in the slums of greater Levittown. Making do with an eight-by-ten room with bathroom rights and a job as a dental assistant. Kelp and talapia every night, and rabbit on Sunday. The hell with that. She was alive and Burton wasn't—by any rational standard that made her the winner.

"Are you. Listening?"

"Not really, no."

She topped yet another rise. And stopped dead. Down below was a dark expanse of molten sulfur. It stretched, wide and black, across the streaked orange plains. A lake. Her helmet readouts ran a thermal topography from the negative 230°F at her feet to 65°F at the edge of the lava flow. Nice and balmy. The molten sulfur itself, of course, existed at higher ambient temperatures.

It lay dead in her way.

THEY'D NAMED IT LAKE STYX.

Martha spent half an hour muttering over her topo maps, trying to figure out how she'd gone so far astray. Not that it wasn't obvious. All that stumbling around. Little errors that she'd made, adding up. A tendency to favor one leg over the other. It had been an iffy thing from the beginning, trying to navigate by dead reckoning.

Finally, though, it all came together. Here she was. On the shores of Lake Styx. Not all that far off-course after all. Three miles, maybe, tops.

Despair filled her.

They'd named the lake during their first loop through the Galilean system, what the engineers had called the "mapping run." It was one of the largest features they'd seen that wasn't already on the maps from satellite probes or Earth-based reconnaissance. Hols had thought it might be a new phenomenon—a lake that had achieved its current size within the past ten years or so. Burton had thought it would be fun to check it out. And Martha hadn't cared, so long as she wasn't left behind. So they'd added the lake to their itinerary.

She had been so transparently eager to be in on the first landing, so afraid that she'd be left behind, that when she suggested they match fingers, odd man out, for who stayed, both Burton and Hols had laughed. "I'll play mother," Hols had said magnanimously, "for the first landing. Burton for Ganymede and then you for Europa. Fair enough?" And ruffled her hair.

She'd been so relieved, and so grateful, and so humiliated too. It was ironic. Now it looked like Hols—who would *never* have gotten so far off course as to go down the wrong side of the Styx—wasn't going to get to touch rock at all. Not this expedition.

"Stupid, stupid, stupid," Martha muttered, though she didn't know if she were condemning Hols or Burton or herself. Lake Styx was horseshoe-shaped and twelve miles long. And she was standing right at the inner toe of the horseshoe.

There was no way she could retrace her steps back around the lake and still get to the lander before her air ran out. The lake was dense enough that she could almost *swim* across it, if it weren't for the viscosity of the sulfur, which would coat her heat radiators and burn out her suit in no time flat. And the heat of the liquid. And whatever internal flows and undertows it might have. As it was, the experience would be like drowning in molasses. Slow and sticky.

She sat down and began to cry.

After a time she began to build up her nerve to grope for the snap-coupling to her airpack. There was a safety for it, but among those familiar with the rig it was an open secret that if you held the safety down with your thumb and yanked suddenly on the coupling, the whole thing would come undone, emptying the suit in less than a second. The gesture was so distinctive that hot young astronauts-in-training would mime it when one of their number said something particularly stupid. It was called the suicide flick.

There were worse ways of dying.

"Will build. Bridge. Have enough. Fine control of. Physical processes. To build. Bridge."

"Yeah, right, very nice, you do that," Martha said absently. If you can't be polite to your own hallucinations . . . She didn't bother finishing the thought. Little crawly things were creeping about on the surface of her skin. Best to ignore them.

"Wait. Here. Rest. Now."

She said nothing but only sat, not resting. Building up her courage. Thinking about everything and nothing. Clutching her knees and rocking back and forth.

Eventually, without meaning to, she fell asleep.

"Wake. Up. Wake. Up. Wake. Up."

"Uhh?"

Martha struggled up into awareness. Something was happening before her, out on the lake. Physical processes were at work. Things were moving.

As she watched, the white crust at the edge of the dark lake bulged outward, shooting out crystals, extending. Lacy as a snowflake. Pale as frost. Reaching across the molten blackness. Until there was a narrow white bridge stretching all the way to the far shore.

"You must. Wait," Io said. "Ten minutes and. You can. Walk across. It. With ease."

"Son of a bitch," Martha murmured. "I'm sane."

In wondering silence, she crossed the bridge that Io had enchanted across the dark lake. Once or twice the surface felt a little mushy underfoot, but it always held.

It was an exalting experience. Like passing over from Death into Life.

At the far side of the Styx, the pyroclastic plains rose gently toward a distant horizon. She stared up yet another long, crystal-flower-covered slope. Two in one day. What were the odds against that?

She struggled upward, flowers exploding as they were touched by her boots. At the top of the rise, the flowers gave way to sulfur hardpan again. Looking back, she could see the path she had crunched through the flowers begin to erase itself. For a long moment she stood still, venting heat. Crystals shattered soundlessly about her in a slowly expanding circle.

She was itching something awful now. Time to freshen up. Six quick taps brought up a message on her visor: *Warning: Continued use of this drug at current levels can result in paranoia, psychosis, hallucinations, misperceptions, and hypomania, as well as impaired judgment.*

Fuck that noise. Martha dealt herself another hit.

It took a few seconds. Then—whoops. She was feeling light and full of energy again. Best check the airpack reading. Man, *that* didn't look good. She had to giggle.

Which was downright scary.

Nothing could have sobered her up faster than that high little druggie laugh. It terrified her. Her life depended on her ability to maintain. She had to keep taking meth to keep going, but she also had to keep going under the drug. She couldn't let it start calling the shots. Focus. Time to switch over to the last airpack. Burton's airpack. "I've got eight hours of oxygen left. I've got twelve miles yet to go. It can be done. I'm going to do it now," she said grimly.

If only her skin weren't itching. If only her head weren't crawling. If only her brain weren't busily expanding in all directions.

TRUDGE, DRAG, TRUDGE, DRAG. All through the night. The trouble with repetitive labor was that it gave you time to think. Time to think when you were speeding also meant time to think about the quality of your own thought.

You don't dream in real-time, she'd been told. You get it all in one flash, just as you're about to wake up, and in that instant extrapolate a complex dream all in one whole. It feels as if you've been dreaming for hours. But you've only had one split second of intense nonreality.

Maybe that's what's happening here.

She had a job to do. She had to keep a clear head. It was important that she get back to the lander. People had to know. They weren't alone anymore. Damnit, she'd just made the biggest discovery since fire.

Either that, or she was so crazy she was hallucinating that Io was a gigantic alien machine. So crazy she'd lost herself within the convolutions of her own brain.

Which was another terrifying thing she wished she hadn't thought of. She'd been a loner as a child. Never made friends easily. Never had or been a best friend to anybody. Had spent half her girlhood buried in books. Solipsism terrified her—she'd lived right on the edge of it for too long. So it was vitally important that she determine whether the voice of Io had an objective, external reality. Or not.

Well, how could she test it?

Sulfur was triboelectric, Io had said. Implying that it was in some way an electrical phenomenon. If so, then it ought to be physically demonstrable.

Martha directed her helmet to show her the electrical charges within the sulfur plains. Crank it up to the max.

The land before her flickered once, then lit up in fairyland colors. Light! Pale oceans of light overlaying light, shifting between pastels, from faded rose to boreal blue, multilayered, labyrinthine, and all pulsing gently within the heart of the sulfur rock. It looked like thought made visual. It looked like something straight out of DisneyVirtual, and not one of the nature channels either—definitely DV-3.

"Damn," she muttered. Right under her nose. She'd had no idea.

Glowing lines veined the warping wings of subterranean electro-magnetic forces. Almost like circuit wires. They crisscrossed the plains in all directions, combining and then converging not upon her but in a nexus at the sled. Burton's corpse was lit up like neon. Her head, packed in sulfur dioxide snow, strobed and stuttered with light so rapidly that it shone like the sun.

Sulfur was triboelectric. Which meant that it built up a charge when rubbed.

She'd been dragging Burton's sledge over the sulfur surface of Io for how many hours? You could build up a hell of a charge that way.

So okay. There was a physical mechanism for what she was seeing. Assuming that Io really *was* a machine, a triboelectric alien device the size of Earth's moon, built eons ago for who knows what purpose by who knows what godlike monstrosities, then, yes, it might be able to communicate with her. A lot could be done with electricity.

Lesser, smaller, and dimmer "circuitry" reached for Martha as well. She looked down at her feet. When she lifted one from the surface, the contact was broken, and the lines of force collapsed. Other lines were born when she put her foot down again. Whatever slight contact might be made was being constantly broken. Whereas Burton's sledge was in constant contact with the sulfur surface of Io. That hole in Burton's skull would be a highway straight into her brain. And she'd packed it in solid SO_2 as well. Conductive *and* supercooled. She'd made things easy for Io.

She shifted back to augmented real-color. The DV-3 SFX faded away.

Accepting as a tentative hypothesis that the voice was a real rather than a psychological phenomenon. That Io was able to communicate with her. That it was a machine. That it had been built ...

Who, then, had built it?

Click.

"Io? Are you listening?"

"Calm on the listening ear of night. Come Heaven's melodious strains. Edmund Hamilton Sears."

"Yeah, wonderful, great. Listen, there's something I'd kinda like to know—who built you?"

"You. Did."

Slyly, Martha said, "So I'm your creator, right?"

"Yes."

"What do I look like when I'm at home?"

"Whatever. You wish. To."

"Do I breathe oxygen? Methane? Do I have antennae? Tentacles? Wings? How many legs do I have? How many eyes? How many heads?"

"If. You wish. As many as. You wish."

"How many of me are there?"

"One." A pause. "Now."

"I was here before, right? People like me. Mobile intelligent life forms. And I left. How long have I been gone?"

Silence. "How long—" she began again.

"Long time. Lonely. So very. Long time."

TRUDGE, DRAG. TRUDGE, DRAG. Trudge, drag. How many centuries had she been walking? Felt like a lot. It was night again. Her arms felt like they were going to fall out of their sockets.

Really, she ought to leave Burton behind. She'd never said anything to make Martha think she cared one way or the other where her body wound up. Probably would've thought a burial on Io was pretty damn nifty. But Martha wasn't doing this for her. She was doing it for herself. To prove that she wasn't entirely selfish. That she did too have feelings for others. That she was motivated by more than just the desire for fame and glory.

Which, of course, was a sign of selfishness in itself. The desire to be known as selfless. It was hopeless. You could nail yourself to a fucking cross and it would still be proof of your innate selfishness.

"You still there, Io?"

Click.

"Am. Listening."

"Tell me about this fine control of yours. How much do you have? Can you bring me to the lander faster than I'm going now? Can you bring the lander to me? Can you return me to the orbiter? Can you provide me with more oxygen?"

"Dead egg, I lie. Whole. On a whole world I cannot touch. Plath."

"You're not much use, then, are you?"

There was no answer. Not that she had expected one. Or needed it, either. She checked the topos and found herself another eighth-mile closer to the lander. She could even see it now under her helmet photomultipliers, a dim glint upon the horizon. Wonderful things, photomultipliers. The sun here provided about as much light as a full moon did back on Earth. Jupiter by itself provided even less. Yet crank up the magnification, and she could see the airlock awaiting the grateful touch of her gloved hand.

Trudge, drag, trudge. Martha ran and reran and rereran the math in her head. She had only three miles to go, and enough oxygen for as many hours. The lander had its own air supply. She was going to make it.

Maybe she wasn't the total loser she'd always thought she was. Maybe there was hope for her, after all.

Click.

"Brace. Yourself."

"What for?"

The ground rose up beneath her and knocked her off her feet.

WHEN THE SHAKING STOPPED, Martha clambered unsteadily to her feet again. The land before her was all a jumble, as if a careless deity had lifted the entire plain up a foot and then dropped it. The silvery glint of the lander on the horizon was gone. When she pushed her helmet's magnification to the max, she could see a metal leg rising crookedly from the rubbled ground.

Martha knew the shear strength of every bolt and failure point of every welding seam in the lander. She knew exactly how fragile it was. That was one device that was never going to fly again.

She stood motionless. Unblinking. Unseeing. Feeling nothing. Nothing at all.

Eventually she pulled herself together enough to think. Maybe it was time to admit it: She never *had* believed she was going to make it. Not really. Not Martha Kivelsen. All her life she'd been a loser. Sometimes—like when she qualified for the expedition—she lost at a higher level than usual. But she never got whatever it was she really wanted.

Why was that, she wondered? When had she ever desired anything bad? When you get right down to it, all she'd ever wanted was to kick God in the butt and get his attention. To be a big noise. To be the biggest fucking noise in the universe. Was that so unreasonable?

Now she was going to wind up as a footnote in the annals of humanity's expansion into space. A sad little cautionary tale for mommy astronauts to tell their baby astronauts on cold winter nights. Maybe Burton could've gotten back to the lander. Or Hols. But not her. It just wasn't in the cards.

Click.

"Io is the most volcanically active body in the Solar System."

"You fucking bastard! Why didn't you warn me?"

"Did. Not. Know."

Now her emotions returned to her in full force. She wanted to run and scream and break things. Only there wasn't anything in sight that hadn't already been broken. "You shithead!" she cried. "You idiot machine! What use are you? What goddamn use at all?"

"Can give you. Eternal life. Communion of the soul. Unlimited processing power. Can give Burton. Same."

"Hah?"

"After the first death. There is no other. Dylan Thomas."

"What do you mean by that?"

Silence.

"Damn you, you fucking machine! What are you trying to say?"

THEN THE DEVIL TOOK Jesus up into the holy city and set him on the highest point of the temple, and said to him, "If thou be the Son of God, cast thyself down: for it is written he shall give his angels charge concerning thee: and in their hands they shall bear thee up."

Burton wasn't the only one who could quote scripture. You didn't have to be Catholic, like her. Presbyterians could do it too.

Martha wasn't sure what you'd call this feature. A volcanic phenomenon of some sort. It wasn't very big. Maybe twenty meters across, not much higher. Call it a crater, and let be. She stood shivering at its lip. There was a black pool of molten sulfur at its bottom, just as she'd been told. Supposedly its roots reached all the way down to Tartarus.

Her head ached so badly.

Io claimed—had said—that if she threw herself in, it would be able to absorb her, duplicate her neural patterning, and so restore her to life. A transformed sort of life, but life nonetheless. "Throw Burton in," it had said. "Throw yourself in. Physical configuration will be. Destroyed. Neural configuration will be. Preserved. Maybe."

"Maybe?"

"Burton had limited. Biological training. Understanding of neural functions may be. Imperfect."

"Wonderful."

"Or. Maybe not."

"Gotcha."

Heat radiated up from the bottom of the crater. Even protected and shielded as she was by her suit's HVAC systems, she felt the difference between front and back. It was like standing in front of a fire on a very cold night.

They had talked, or maybe negotiated was a better word for it, for a long time. Finally Martha had said, "You savvy Morse code? You savvy orthodox spelling?"

"Whatever Burton. Understood. Is. Understood."

"Yes or no, damnit!"

"Savvy."

"Good. Then maybe we can make a deal."

SHE STARED UP INTO the night. The orbiter was out there somewhere, and she was sorry she couldn't talk directly to Hols, say good-bye and thanks for everything. But Io had said no. What she planned would raise volcanoes and level mountains. The devastation would dwarf that of the earthquake caused by the bridge across Lake Styx.

It couldn't guarantee two separate communications.

The ion flux tube arched from somewhere over the horizon in a great looping jump to the north pole of Jupiter. Augmented by her visor it was as bright as the sword of God.

As she watched, it began to sputter and jump, millions of watts of power dancing staccato in a message they'd be picking up on the surface of Earth. It would swamp every radio and drown out every broadcast in the Solar System.

THIS IS MARTHA KIVELSEN, SPEAKING FROM THE SURFACE OF IO ON BEHALF OF MYSELF, JULIET BURTON, DECEASED, AND JACOB HOLS, OF THE FIRST GALILEAN SATELLITES EXPLORATORY MISSION. WE HAVE MADE AN IMPORTANT DISCOVERY ...

Every electrical device in the System would *dance* to its song.

BURTON WENT FIRST. Martha gave the sledge a shove and out it flew, into empty space. It dwindled, hit, kicked up a bit of a splash. Then, with a disappointing lack of pyrotechnics, the corpse slowly sank into the black glop.

It didn't look very encouraging at all.

Still ...

"Okay," she said. "A deal's a deal." She dug in her toes and spread her arms. Took a deep breath. Maybe I am going to survive after all, she thought. It could be Burton was already halfway-merged into the oceanic mind of Io, and awaiting her to join in an alchemical marriage of personalities. Maybe I'm going to live forever. Who knows? Anything is possible.

Maybe.

There was a second and more likely possibility. All this could well be nothing more than a hallucination. Nothing but the sound of her brain short-circuiting and squirting bad chemicals in all directions. Madness. One last grandiose dream before dying. Martha had no way of judging.

Whatever the truth might be, though, there were no alternatives, and only one way to find out.

She jumped.

Briefly, she flew.

The Dead

THREE BOY ZOMBIES in matching red jackets bussed our table, bringing water, lighting candles, brushing away the crumbs between courses. Their eyes were dark, attentive, lifeless; their hands and faces so white as to be faintly luminous in the hushed light. I thought it in bad taste, but "This is Manhattan," Courtney said. "A certain studied offensiveness is fashionable here."

The blond brought menus and waited for our order.

We both ordered pheasant. "An excellent choice," the boy said in a clear, emotionless voice. He went away and came back a minute later with the freshly strangled birds, holding them up for our approval. He couldn't have been more than eleven when he died and his skin was of that sort connoisseurs call "milk glass," smooth, without blemish, and all but translucent. He must have cost a fortune.

As the boy was turning away, I impulsively touched his shoulder. He turned back. "What's your name, son?" I asked.

"Timothy." He might have been telling me the *specialite de maison*. The boy waited a breath to see if more was expected of him, then left.

Courtney gazed after him. "How lovely he would look," she murmured, "nude. Standing in the moonlight by a cliff. Definitely a cliff. Perhaps the very one where he met his death."

"He wouldn't look very lovely if he'd fallen off a cliff."

"Oh, don't be unpleasant."

The wine steward brought our bottle. "Chateau La Tour '17." I raised an eyebrow. The steward had the sort of old and complex face that Rembrandt would have enjoyed painting. He poured with pulseless ease and then dissolved into the gloom. "Good lord, Courtney, you *seduced* me on cheaper."

She flushed, not happily. Courtney had a better career going than I. She outpowered me. We both knew who was smarter, better connected, more likely to end up in a corner office with the historically significant antique desk. The only edge I had was that I was a male in a seller's market. It was enough.

"This is a business dinner, Donald," she said, "nothing more."

I favored her with an expression of polite disbelief I knew from experience she'd find infuriating. And, digging into my pheasant, murmured, "Of course." We didn't say much of consequence until dessert, when I finally asked, "So what's Loeb-Soffner up to these days?"

"Structuring a corporate expansion. Jim's putting together the financial side of the package, and I'm doing personnel. You're being headhunted, Donald." She favored me with that feral little flash of teeth she made when she saw something she wanted. Courtney wasn't a beautiful woman, far from it. But there was that fierceness to her, that sense of something primal being held under tight and precarious control that made her hot as hot to me. "You're talented, you're thuggish, and you're not too tightly nailed to your present position. Those are all qualities we're looking for."

She dumped her purse on the table, took out a single folded sheet of paper. "These are the terms I'm offering." She placed it by my plate, attacked her torte with gusto.

I unfolded the paper. "This is a lateral transfer."

"Unlimited opportunity for advancement," she said with her mouth full, "if you've got the stuff."

"Mmm." I did a line-by-line of the benefits, all comparable to what I was getting now. My current salary to the dollar—Ms. Soffner was showing off. And the stock options. "This can't be right. Not for a lateral."

There was that grin again, like a glimpse of shark in murky waters. "I knew you'd like it. We're going over the top with the options because we need your answer right away—tonight preferably. Tomorrow at the latest. No negotiations. We have to put the package together fast. There's going to be a shitstorm of publicity when this comes out. We want to have everything nailed down, present the fundies and bleeding hearts with a *fait accompli.*"

"My God, Courtney, what kind of monster do you have hold of now?"

"The biggest one in the world. Bigger than Apple. Bigger than Home Virtual. Bigger than HIVac-IV," she said with relish. "Have you ever heard of Koestler Biological?"

I put my fork down.

"Koestler? You're peddling corpses now?"

"Please. Postanthropic biological resources." She said it lightly, with just the right touch of irony. Still, I thought I detected a certain discomfort with the nature of her client's product.

"There's no money in it." I waved a hand toward our attentive waitstaff. "These guys must be—what?—maybe two percent of the annual turnover? Zombies are luxury goods: servants, reactor cleanups, Hollywood stunt deaths, exotic services"—we both knew what I meant—"a few hundred a year, maybe, tops. There's not the demand. The revulsion factor is too great."

"There's been a technological breakthrough." Courtney leaned forward. "They can install the infrasystem and controllers and offer the product for the factory-floor cost of a new subcompact. That's way below the economic threshold for blue-collar labor.

"Look at it from the viewpoint of a typical factory owner. He's already downsized to the bone and labor costs are bleeding him dry. How can he compete in a dwindling consumer market? Now let's imagine he buys into the program." She took out her Mont Blanc and began scribbling figures on the tablecloth. "No benefits. No liability suits. No sick pay. No pilferage. We're talking about cutting labor costs by at least two-thirds. Minimum! That's irresistible, I don't care how big your revulsion factor is. We project we can move five hundred thousand units in the first year."

"Five hundred thousand," I said. "That's crazy. Where the hell are you going to get the raw material for—?"

"Africa."

"Oh, God, Courtney." I was struck wordless by the cynicism it took to even consider turning the sub-Saharan tragedy to a profit, by the sheer, raw evil of channeling hard currency to the pocket Hitlers who ran the camps. Courtney only smiled and gave that quick little flip of her head that meant she was accessing the time on an optic chip.

"I think you're ready," she said, "to talk with Koestler."

At her gesture, the zombie boys erected projector lamps about us, fussed with the settings, turned them on. Interference patterns moired, clashed, meshed. Walls of darkness erected themselves about us. Courtney took out her flat and set it up on the table. Three taps of her nailed fingers and the round and hairless face of Marvin Koestler appeared on the screen. "Ah, Courtney!" he said in a pleased voice. "You're in—New York, yes? The San Moritz. With Donald." The slightest pause with each accessed bit of information. "Did you have the antelope medallions?" When we shook our heads, he kissed his fingertips. "Magnificent! They're ever so lightly braised and then smothered in buffalo mozzarella. Nobody makes them better. I had the same dish in Florence the other day, and there was simply no comparison."

I cleared my throat. "Is that where you are? Italy?"

"Let's leave out where I am." He made a dismissive gesture, as if it were a trifle. But Courtney's face darkened. Corporate kidnapping being the growth industry it is, I'd gaffed badly. "The question is—what do you think of my offer?"

"It's ... interesting. For a lateral."

"It's the start-up costs. We're leveraged up to our asses as it is. You'll make out better this way in the long run." He favored me with a sudden grin that went mean around the edges. Very much the financial buccaneer. Then he leaned forward, lowered his voice, maintained firm eye contact. Classic people-handling techniques. "You're not sold. You know you can trust Courtney to have checked out the finances. Still, you think: It won't work. To work, the product has to be irresistible, and it's not. It can't be."

"Yes, sir," I said. "Succinctly put."

He nodded to Courtney. "Let's sell this young man." And to me, "My stretch is downstairs."

He winked out.

KOESTLER WAS WAITING for us in the limo, a ghostly pink presence. His holo, rather, a genial if somewhat coarse-grained ghost afloat in golden light. He waved an expansive and insubstantial arm to take in the interior of the car and said, "Make yourselves at home."

The chauffeur wore combat-grade photomultipliers. They gave him a buggish, inhuman look. I wasn't sure if he was dead or not. "Take us to Heaven," Koestler said.

The doorman stepped out into the street, looked both ways, nodded to the chauffeur. Robot guns tracked our progress down the block.

"Courtney tells me you're getting the raw materials from Africa."

"Distasteful, but necessary. To begin with. We have to sell the idea first—no reason to make things rough on ourselves. Down the line, though, I don't see why we can't go domestic. Something along the lines of a reverse mortgage, perhaps, life insurance that pays off while you're still alive. It'd be a step towards getting the poor off our backs at last. Fuck 'em. They've been getting a goddamn free ride for too long; the least they can do is to die and provide us with servants."

I was pretty sure Koestler was joking. But I smiled and ducked my head, so I'd be covered in either case. "What's Heaven?" I asked, to move the conversation onto safer territory.

"A proving ground," Koestler said with great satisfaction, "for the future. Have you ever witnessed bare-knuckles fisticuffs?"

"No."

"Ah, now there's a sport for gentlemen! The sweet science at its sweetest. No rounds, no rules, no holds barred. It gives you the real measure of a man—not just of his strength but his character. How he handles himself, whether he keeps cool under pressure—how he stands up to pain. Security won't let me go to the clubs in person, but I've made arrangements."

HEAVEN WAS A CONVERTED movie theater in a rundown neighborhood in Queens. The chauffeur got out, disappeared briefly around the back, and returned with two zombie bodyguards. It was like a conjurer's trick. "You had these guys stashed in the *trunk?*" I asked as he opened the door for us.

"It's a new world," Courtney said. "Get used to it."

The place was mobbed. Two, maybe three hundred seats, standing room only. A mixed crowd, blacks and Irish and Koreans mostly, but with a smattering of uptown customers as well. You didn't have to be poor to need the occasional taste of vicarious potency. Nobody paid us any particular notice. We'd come in just as the fighters were being presented.

"Weighing two-five-oh, in black trunks with a red stripe," the ref was bawling, "tha gang-bang *gang*sta, tha bare-knuckle *brawla,* tha man with tha—"

Courtney and I went up a scummy set of back stairs. Bodyguard-us-bodyguard, as if we were a combat patrol out of some twentieth-century jungle war. A scrawny, potbellied old geezer with a damp cigar in his mouth unlocked the door to our box. Sticky floor, bad seats, a good view down on the ring. Grey plastic matting, billowing smoke.

Koestler was there, in a shiny new hologram shell. It reminded me of those plaster Madonnas in painted bathtubs that Catholics set out in their yards. "Your permanent box?" I asked.

"All of this is for your sake, Donald—you and a few others. We're pitting our product one-on-one against some of the local talent. By arrangement with the management. What you're going to see will settle your doubts once and for all."

"You'll like this," Courtney said. "I've been here five nights straight. Counting tonight." The bell rang, starting the fight. She leaned forward avidly, hooking her elbows on the railing.

The zombie was grey-skinned and modestly muscled, for a fighter. But it held up its hands alertly, was light on its feet, and had strangely calm and knowing eyes.

Its opponent was a real bruiser, a big black guy with classic African features twisted slightly out of true so that his mouth curled up in a kind of sneer on one side. He had gang scars on his chest and even uglier marks on his back that didn't look deliberate but like something he'd earned on the streets. His eyes burned with an intensity just this side of madness.

He came forward cautiously but not fearfully, and made a couple of quick jabs to get the measure of his opponent. They were blocked and countered.

They circled each other, looking for an opening.

For a minute or so, nothing much happened. Then the gangster feinted at the zombie's head, drawing up its guard. He drove through that opening with a slam to the zombie's nuts that made me wince.

No reaction.

The dead fighter responded with a flurry of punches, and got in a glancing blow to its opponent's cheek. They separated, engaged, circled around.

Then the big guy exploded in a combination of killer blows, connecting so solidly it seemed they would splinter every rib in the dead fighter's body. It brought the crowd to their feet, roaring their approval.

The zombie didn't even stagger.

A strange look came into the gangster's eyes, then, as the zombie counterattacked, driving him back into the ropes. I could only imagine what it must be like for a man who had always lived by his strength and his ability to absorb punishment to realize that he was facing an opponent to whom pain meant nothing. Fights were lost and won by flinches and hesitations. You won by keeping your head. You lost by getting rattled.

Despite his best blows, the zombie stayed methodical, serene, calm, relentless. That was its nature.

It must have been devastating.

The fight went on and on. It was a strange and alienating experience for me. After a while I couldn't stay focused on it. My thoughts kept slipping into a zone where I found myself studying the line of Courtney's jaw, thinking about later tonight. She liked her sex just a little bit sick. There was always a feeling, fucking her, that there was something truly repulsive that she *really* wanted to do but lacked the courage to bring up on her own.

So there was always this urge to get her to do something she didn't like. She was resistant; I never dared try more than one new thing per date. But I could always talk her into that one thing. Because when she was aroused, she got pliant. She could be talked into anything. She could be made to beg for it.

Courtney would've been amazed to learn that I was not proud of what I did with her—quite the opposite, in fact. But I was as obsessed with her as she was with whatever it was that obsessed her.

Suddenly Courtney was on her feet, yelling. The hologram showed Koestler on his feet as well. The big guy was on the ropes, being pummeled. Blood and spittle flew from his face with each blow. Then he was down; he'd never even had a chance. He must've known early on that it was hopeless, that he wasn't going to win, but he'd refused to take a fall. He had to be pounded into the ground. He went down raging, proud and uncomplaining. I had to admire that.

But he lost anyway.

That, I realized, was the message I was meant to take away from this. Not just that the product was robust. But that only those who backed it were going to win. I could see, even if the audience couldn't, that it was the end of an era. A man's body wasn't worth a damn anymore. There wasn't anything it could do that technology couldn't handle better. The number of losers in the world had just doubled, tripled, reached maximum. What the fools below were cheering for was the death of their futures.

I got up and cheered too.

IN THE STRETCH AFTERWARDS, Koestler said, "You've seen the light. You're a believer now."

"I haven't necessarily decided yet."

"Don't bullshit me," Koestler said. "I've done my homework, Mr. Nichols. Your current position is not exactly secure. Morton-Western is going down the tubes. The entire service sector is going down the tubes. Face it, the old economic order is as good as fucking gone. Of course you're going to take my offer. You don't have any other choice."

The fax outed sets of contracts. "A Certain Product," it said here and there. Corpses were never mentioned.

But when I opened my jacket to get a pen, Koestler said, "Wait. I've got a factory. Three thousand positions under me. I've got a motivated workforce. They'd walk through fire to keep their jobs. Pilferage is at zero. Sick time practically the same. Give me one advantage your product has over my current workforce. Sell me on it. I'll give you thirty seconds."

I wasn't in sales and the job had been explicitly promised me already. But by reaching for the pen, I had admitted I wanted the position. And we all knew whose hand carried the whip.

"They can be catheterized," I said—"no toilet breaks."

For a long instant Koestler just stared at me blankly. Then he exploded with laughter. "By God, that's a new one! You have a great future ahead of you, Donald. Welcome aboard."

He winked out.

We drove on in silence for a while, aimless, directionless. At last Courtney leaned forward and touched the chauffeur's shoulder.

"Take me home," she said.

RIDING THROUGH MANHATTAN I suffered from a waking hallucination that we were driving through a city of corpses. Grey faces, listless motions. Everyone looked dead in the headlights and sodium vapor streetlamps. Passing by the Children's Museum I saw a mother with a stroller through the glass doors. Two small children by her side. They all three stood motionless, gazing forward at nothing. We passed by a stop-and-go where zombies stood out on the sidewalk drinking forties in paper bags. Through upper-story windows I could see the sad rainbow trace of virtuals playing to empty eyes. There were zombies in the park, zombies smoking blunts, zombies driving taxies, zombies sitting on stoops and hanging out on street corners, all of them waiting for the years to pass and the flesh to fall from their bones.

I felt like the last man alive.

COURTNEY WAS STILL WIRED and sweaty from the fight. The pheromones came off her in great waves as I followed her down the hall to her apartment. She stank of lust. I found myself thinking of how she got just before orgasm, so desperate, so desirable. It was different after she came, she would fall into a state of calm assurance; the same sort of calm assurance she showed in her business life, the aplomb she sought so wildly during the act itself.

And when that desperation left her, so would I. Because even I could recognize that it was her desperation that drew me to her, that made me do the things she needed me to do. In all the years I'd known her, we'd never once had breakfast together.

I wished there was some way I could deal her out of the equation. I wished that her desperation were a liquid that I could drink down to the dregs. I wished I could drop her in a wine press and squeeze her dry.

At her apartment, Courtney unlocked her door and in one complicated movement twisted through and stood facing me from the inside. "Well," she said. "All in all, a productive evening. Good night, Donald."

"Good night? Aren't you going to invite me inside?"

"No."

"What do you mean, no?" She was beginning to piss me off. A blind man could've told she was in heat from across the street. A chimpanzee could've talked his way into her pants. "What kind of idiot game are you playing now?"

"You know what no means, Donald. You're not stupid."

"No I'm not, and neither are you. We both know the score. Now let me in, goddamnit."

"Enjoy your present," she said, and closed the door.

I FOUND COURTNEY'S PRESENT back in my suite. I was still seething from her treatment of me and stalked into the room, letting the door slam behind me. So that I was standing in near-total darkness. The only light was what little seeped through the draped windows at the far end of the room. I was just reaching for the light switch when there was a motion in the darkness.

'*Jackers!* I thought, and all in a panic lurched for the light switch, hoping to achieve I don't know what. Credit- jackers always work in trios, one to torture the security codes out of you, one to phone the numbers out of your accounts and into a fiscal trapdoor, a third to stand guard. Was turning the lights on supposed to make them scurry for darkness, like roaches? Nevertheless, I almost tripped over my own feet in my haste to reach the switch. But of course it was nothing like what I'd feared.

It was a woman.

She stood by the window in a white silk dress that could neither compete with nor distract from her ethereal beauty, her porcelain skin. When the lights came on, she turned toward me, eyes widening, lips parting slightly. Her breasts swayed ever so slightly as she gracefully raised a bare arm to offer me a lily. "Hello, Donald," she said huskily. "I'm yours for the night." She was absolutely beautiful.

And dead, of course.

NOT TWENTY MINUTES LATER I was hammering on Courtney's door. She came to the door in a Pierre Cardin dressing gown and from the way she was still cinching the sash and the disarray of her hair I gathered she hadn't been expecting me.

"I'm not alone," she said.

"I didn't come here for the dubious pleasures of your fair white body." I pushed my way into the room. (But couldn't help remembering that beautiful body of hers, not so exquisite as the dead whore's, and now the thoughts were inextricably mingled in my head, death and Courtney, sex and corpses, a Gordian knot I might never be able to untangle.)

"You didn't like my surprise?" She was smiling openly now, amused.

"No, I fucking did not!"

I took a step toward her. I was shaking. I couldn't stop fisting and unfisting my hands.

She fell back a step. But that confident, oddly expectant look didn't leave her face. "Bruno," she said lightly. "Would you come in here?"

A motion at the periphery of vision. Bruno stepped out of the shadows of her bedroom. He was a muscular brute, pumped, ripped, and as black as the fighter I'd seen go down earlier that night. He stood behind Courtney, totally naked, with slim hips and wide shoulders and the finest skin I'd ever seen.

And dead.

I saw it all in a flash.

"Oh, for God's sake, Courtney!" I said, disgusted. "I can't believe you. That you'd actually ... That thing's just an obedient body. There's nothing there—no passion, no connection, just ... physical presence."

Courtney made a kind of chewing motion through her smile, weighing the implications of what she was about to say. Nastiness won.

"We have equity now," she said.

I lost it then. I stepped forward, raising a hand, and I swear to God I intended to bounce the bitch's head off the back wall. But she didn't flinch—she didn't even look afraid. She merely moved aside, saying, "In the body, Bruno. He has to look good in a business suit."

A dead fist smashed into my ribs so hard I thought for an instant my heart had stopped. Then Bruno punched me in my stomach. I doubled over, gasping. Two, three, four more blows. I was on the ground now, rolling over, helpless and weeping with rage.

"That's enough, baby. Now put out the trash."

Bruno dumped me in the hallway.

I glared up at Courtney through my tears. She was not at all beautiful now. Not in the least. You're getting older, I wanted to tell her. But instead I heard my voice, angry and astonished, saying, "You ... you goddamn, fucking necrophile!"

"Cultivate a taste for it," Courtney said. Oh, she was purring! I doubted she'd ever find life quite this good again. "Half a million Brunos

are about to come on the market. You're going to find it a lot more difficult to pick up *living* women in not so very long."

I sent away the dead whore. Then I took a long shower that didn't
really make me feel any better. Naked, I walked into my unlit suite and
opened the curtains. For a long time I stared out over the glory and
darkness that was Manhattan.

I was afraid, more afraid than I'd ever been in my life.

The slums below me stretched to infinity. They were a vast necrop-
olis, a neverending city of the dead. I thought of the millions out there
who were never going to hold down a job again. I thought of how they
must hate me—me and my kind—and how helpless they were before
us. And yet. There were so many of them and so few of us. If they were
to all rise up at once, they'd be like a tsunami, irresistible. And if there
was so much as a spark of life left in them, then that was exactly what
they would do.

That was one possibility. There was one other, and that was that
nothing would happen. Nothing at all.

God help me, but I didn't know which one scared me more.

Scherzo with Tyrannosaur

A KEYBOARDIST WAS playing a selection of Scarlotti's harpsichord sonatas, brief pieces one to three minutes long, very complex and refined, while the *Hadrosaurus* herd streamed by the window. There were hundreds of the brutes, kicking up dust and honking that lovely flattened near-musical note they make. It was a spectacular sight.

But the *hors d'oeuvres* had just arrived: plesiosaur wrapped in kelp, beluga smeared over sliced maiasaur egg, little slivers of roast dodo on toast, a dozen delicacies more. So a stampede of common-as-dirt herbivores just couldn't compete.

Nobody was paying much attention.

Except for the kid. He was glued to the window, staring with an intensity remarkable even for a boy his age. I figured him to be about ten years old.

Snagging a glass of champagne from a passing tray, I went over to stand next to him. "Enjoying yourself, son?"

Without looking up, the kid said, "What do you think spooked them? Was it a—?" Then he saw the wranglers in their jeeps and his face fell. "Oh."

"We had to cheat a little to give the diners something to see." I gestured with the wine glass past the herd, toward the distant woods. "But there are plenty of predators lurking out there—troodons, dromaeosaurs . . . even old Satan."

He looked up at me in silent question.

"Satan is our nickname for an injured old bull rex that's been hanging around the station for about a month, raiding our garbage dump."

It was the wrong thing to say. The kid looked devastated. *T. rex* a scavenger! *Say it ain't so.*

"A tyrannosaur is an advantageous hunter," I said, "like a lion. When it chances upon something convenient, believe you me, it'll attack. And when a tyrannosaur is hurting, like old Satan is—well, that's about as savage and dangerous as any animal can be. It'll kill even when it's not hungry."

That satisfied him. "Good," he said. "I'm glad."

In companionable silence, we stared into the woods together, looking for moving shadows. Then the chime sounded for dinner to begin, and I sent the kid back to his table. The last hadrosaurs were gone by then.

He went with transparent reluctance.

The Cretaceous Ball was our big fund-raiser, a hundred thousand dollars a seat, and in addition to the silent auction before the meal and the dancing afterwards, everybody who bought an entire table for six was entitled to their very own paleontologist as a kind of party favor.

I used to be a paleontologist myself, before I was promoted. Now I patrolled the room in tux and cummerbund, making sure everything was running smoothly.

Waiters slipped in and out of existence. You'd see them hurry behind the screen hiding the entrance to the time funnel and then pop out immediately on the other side, carrying heavily-laden trays. *Styracosaurus* medallions in mastodon mozzarella for those who liked red meat. Archaeopteryx almondine for those who preferred white. Radicchio and fennel for the vegetarians.

All to the accompaniment of music, pleasant chitchat, and the best view in the universe.

Donald Hawkins had been assigned to the kid's table—the de Cherville Family. According to the seating plan the heavy, phlegmatic man was Gerard, the money-making *paterfamilias.* The woman beside him was Danielle, once his trophy wife, now aging gracefully. Beside them were two guests—the Cadigans—who looked a little overwhelmed by everything and were probably a favored employee and spouse. They didn't say much. A sullen daughter, Melusine, in a little black dress that casually displayed her perfect breasts. She looked bored and restless— trouble incarnate. And there was the kid, given name Philippe.

I kept a close eye on them because of Hawkins. He was new, and I wasn't expecting him to last long. But he charmed everyone at the table. Young, handsome, polite—he had it all. I noticed how Melusine slouched back in her chair, studying him through dark eyelashes, saying nothing. Hawkins, responding to something young Philippe had said, flashed a boyish, devil-may-care grin. I could feel the heat of the kid's hero-worship from across the room.

Then my silent beeper went off, and I had to duck out of the late Cretaceous and back into the kitchen, Home Base, year 2082.

THERE WAS A Time Safety Officer waiting for me. The main duty of a TSO is to make sure that no time paradoxes occur, so the Unchanging wouldn't take our time privileges away from us. Most people think that time travel was invented recently, and by human beings. That's because our sponsors don't want their presence advertised.

In the kitchen, everyone was in an uproar. One of the waiters was leaning, spraddle-legged and arms wide against the table, and another was lying on the floor clutching what looked to be a broken arm. The TSO covered them both with a gun.

The good news was that the Old Man wasn't there. If it had been something big and hairy—a Creationist bomb, or a message from a million years upline—he would have been.

When I showed up, everybody began talking at once.

"I didn't do *nothing,* man, this bastard—"

"—guilty of a Class Six violation—"

"—broke my fucking *arm,* man. He threw me to the ground!"

"—work to do. Get them out of my kitchen!"

It turned out to be a simple case of note-passing. One of the waiters had, in his old age, conspired with another recruited from a later period, to slip a list of hot investments to his younger self. Enough to make them both multibillionaires. We had surveillance devices planted in the kitchen, and a TSO saw the paper change hands. Now the perps were denying everything.

It wouldn't have worked anyway. The authorities keep strict tabs on the historical record. Wealth on the order of what they had planned would have stuck out like a sore thumb.

I fired both waiters, called the police to take them away, routed a call for two replacements several hours into the local past, and had them briefed and on duty without any lapse in service. Then I took the TSO aside and bawled him out good for calling me back real-time, instead of sending a memo back to me three days ago. Once something has happened, though, that's it. I'd been called, so I had to handle it in person.

It was your standard security glitch. No big deal.

But it was wearying. So when I went back down the funnel to Hilltop Station, I set the time for a couple hours after I had left. I arrived just as the tables were being cleared for dessert and coffee.

Somebody handed me a microphone, and I tapped it twice, for attention. I was standing before the window, a spectacular sunset to my back.

"Ladies and gentlemen," I said, "let me again welcome you to the Maastrichtian, the final age of the late Cretaceous. This is the last research station before the Age of Mammals. Don't worry, though—the meteor that put a final end to the dinosaurs is still several thousand years in the future." I paused for laughter, then continued.

"If you'll look outside, you'll see Jean, our dino wrangler, setting up a scent lure. Jean, wave for our diners."

Jean was fiddling with a short tripod. She waved cheerily, then bent back to work. With her blond ponytail and khaki shorts, she looked to be just your basic science babe. But Jean was slated to become one of the top saurian behaviorists in the world, and knew it too. Despite our best efforts, gossip slips through.

Now Jean backed up toward the station doors, unreeling fuse wire as she went. The windows were all on the second floor. The doors, on the ground floor, were all armored.

"Jean will be ducking inside for this demonstration," I said. "You wouldn't want to be outside unprotected when the lure goes off."

"What's in it?" somebody called out.

"Triceratops blood. We're hoping to call in a predator—maybe even the king of predator, *Tyrannosaurus rex* himself." There was an appreciative murmur from the diners. Everybody here had heard of *T. rex*. He had real star power. I switched easily into lecture mode. "If you dissect a tyrannosaur, you'll see that it has an extremely large olfactory lobe—larger in proportion to the rest of its brain than that of any other animal except the turkey vulture. Rex can sniff his prey"—carrion, usually, but I didn't say that—"from miles away. Watch."

The lure went off with a pop and a puff of pink mist.

I glanced over at the de Cherville table, and saw Melusine slip one foot out of her pump and run it up Hawkins' trouser leg. He colored.

Her father didn't notice. Her mother—her *step*mother, more likely—did, but didn't care. To her, this was simply what women did. I couldn't help notice what good legs Melusine had.

"This will take a few minutes. While we're waiting, I direct your attention to Chef Rupert's excellent pastries."

I faded back to polite applause, and began the round of table hopping. A joke here, a word of praise there. It's banana oil makes the world go round.

When I got to the de Chervilles, Hawkins' face was white.

"Sir!" He shot to his feet. "A word with you."

He almost dragged me away from the table.

When we were in private, he was so upset he was stuttering. "Th-that young woman, w-wants me t-to …"

"I know what she wants," I said coolly. "She's of legal age—make your own decision."

"You don't *understand!* I can't possibly go back to that table." Hawkins was genuinely anguished. I thought at first that he'd been hearing rumors, dark hints about his future career. Somehow, though, that didn't smell right. There was something else going on here.

"All right," I said. "Slip out now. But I don't like secrets. Record a full explanation and leave it in my office. No evasions, understand?"

"Yes, sir." A look of relief spread itself across his handsome young face. "Thank you, sir."

He started to leave.

"Oh, and one more thing," I said casually, hating myself. "Don't go anywhere near your tent until the fund-raiser's broken up."

THE DE CHERVILLES weren't exactly thrilled when I told them that Hawkins had fallen ill, and I'd be taking his place. But then I took a tyrannosaur tooth from my pocket and gave it to Philippe. It was just a shed—rexes drop a lot of teeth—but no need to mention that.

"It looks sharp," Mrs. de Cherville said, with a touch of alarm.

"Serrated, too. You might want to ask your mother if you can use it for a knife, next time you have steak," I suggested.

Which won him over completely. Kids are fickle. Philippe immediately forgot all about Hawkins.

Melusine, however, did not. Eyes flashing with anger, she stood, throwing her napkin to the floor. "I want to know," she began, "just *what* you think you're—"

Fortunately, that was when Satan arrived.

The tyrannosaur came running up the hillside at a speed you'd have to be an experienced paleontologist to know was less than optimal. Even a dying *T. rex* moves *fast.*

People gasped.

I took the microphone out of my pocket, and moved quickly to the front of the room. "Folks, we just got lucky. I'd like to inform those of you with tables by the window that the glass is rated at twenty tons per square inch. You're in no danger whatsoever. But you are in for quite a show. Those who are in the rear might want to get a little closer."

Young Philippe was off like a shot.

The creature was almost to us. "A tyrannosaur has a hyperacute sense of smell," I reminded them. "When it scents blood, its brain is overwhelmed. It goes into a feeding frenzy."

A few droplets of blood had spattered the window. Seeing us through the glass, Satan leaped and tried to smash through it.

Whoomp! The glass boomed and shivered with the impact. There were shrieks and screams from the diners, and several people started to their feet.

At my signal, the string quartet took up their instruments again, and began to play while Satan leaped and tore and snarled, a perfect avatar of rage and fury. They chose the scherzo from Shostokovich's piano quintet.

Scherzos are supposed to be funny, but most have a whirlwind, uninhibited quality that makes them particularly appropriate to nightmares and the madness of predatory dinosaurs.

Whoomp! That mighty head struck the window again and again and again. For a long time, Satan kept on frenziedly slashing at the window with his jaws, leaving long scratches in the glass.

Philippe pressed his body against the window with all his strength, trying to minimize the distance between himself and savage dino death. Shrieking with joyous laughter when that killer mouth tried to snatch him up. I felt for the kid, wanting to get as close to the action as he could. I could identify.

I was just like that myself when I was his age.

WHEN SATAN FINALLY wore himself out and went bad-humoredly away, I returned to the de Chervilles. Philippe had restored himself to the company of his family. The kid looked pale and happy.

So did his sister. I noticed that she was breathing shallowly. Satan does that to young women.

"You dropped your napkin." I handed it to Melusine. Inside was a postcard-sized promotional map, showing Hilltop Station and behind it Tent City, where the researchers lived. One of the tents was circled. Under it was written, *While the others are dancing.*

I had signed it *Don.*

"When I grow up I'm going to be a paleontologist," the kid said fervently. "A behavioral paleontologist, not an anatomist or a wrangler." Somebody had come to take him home. His folks were staying to dance. And Melusine was long gone, off to Hawkins' tent.

"Good for you," I said. I laid a hand on his shoulder. "Come see me when you've got the education. I'll be happy to show you the ropes."

The kid left.

He'd had a conversion experience. I knew exactly how it felt. I'd had mine standing in front of the Zallinger "Age of Reptiles" mural in the Peabody Museum in New Haven. That was before time travel, when paintings of dinosaurs were about as real as you could get. Nowadays I could point out a hundred inaccuracies in how the dinosaurs were depicted. But on that distant sun-dusty morning in the Atlantis of my youth, I just stood staring at those magnificent brutes, head filled with wonder, until my mother dragged me away.

It really was a pity. Philippe was so full of curiosity and enthusiasm. He'd make a great paleontologist. I could see that. He wasn't going to get to realize his dreams, though. His folks had too much money to allow *that*.

I knew because I'd glanced through the personnel records for the next hundred years and his name wasn't there anywhere.

It was possibly the least of the thousands of secrets I held within me, never to be shared. Still, it made me sad. For an instant I felt the weight of all my years, every petty accommodation, every unworthy expedience. Then I went up the funnel and back down again to an hour previous.

Unseen, I slipped out and went to wait for Melusine.

Maintaining the funnel is expensive. During normal operations—when we're not holding fund-raisers—we spend months at a time in the field. Hence the compound, with its army surplus platform tents and electrified perimeter to keep the monsters out.

It was dark when Melusine slipped into the tent.

"Donald?"

"Shhh." I put a finger to her lips, drew her close to me. One hand slid slowly down her naked back, over a scrap of crushed velvet, and then back up and under her skirt to squeeze that elegant little ass. She raised her mouth to mine and we kissed deeply, passionately.

Then I tumbled her to the cot, and we began undressing each other. She ripped off three buttons tearing my shirt from me.

Melusine made a lot of noise, for which I was grateful. She was a demanding, self-centered lay, who let you know when she didn't like what you were doing and wasn't at all shy about telling you what to do next. She required a lot of attention. For which I was also grateful.

I needed the distraction.

Because while I was in his tent, screwing the woman he didn't want, Hawkins was somewhere out there getting killed. According to the operational report that I'd write later tonight, and received a day ago, he was eaten alive by an old bull rex rendered irritable by a painful brain tumor. It was an ugly way to go. I didn't want to have to hear it. I did my best to not think about it.

Credit where credit is due—Melusine practically set the tent ablaze. So I was using her. So what? It was far from the worst of my crimes. It wasn't as if she loved Hawkins, or even knew him for that matter. She was just a spoiled little rich-bitch adventuress looking for a mental souvenir. One more notch on her diaphragm case. I know her type well. They're one of the perks of the business.

There was a freshly prepared triceratops skull by the head of the bed. It gleamed faintly, a pale, indistinct shape in the darkness. When Melusine came, she grabbed one of its horns so tightly the skull rattled against the floorboards.

Afterwards, she left, happily reeking of bone fixative and me. We'd each had our little thrill. I hadn't spoken a word during any of it, and she hadn't even noticed.

T. REX WASN'T MUCH of a predator. But then, it didn't take much skill to kill a man. Too slow to run, and too big to hide—we make perfect prey for a tyrannosaur.

When Hawkins' remains were found, the whole camp turned out in an uproar. I walked through it all on autopilot, perfunctorily giving orders to have Satan shot, to have the remains sent back uptime, to have the paperwork sent to my office. Then I gathered everybody together and gave them the Paradox Lecture. Nobody was to talk about what had just happened. Those who did would be summarily fired. Legal action would follow. Dire consequences. Penalties. Fines.

And so on.

It was two AM when I finally got back to my office, to write the day's operational report.

Hawkins's memo was there, waiting for me. I'd forgotten about that. I debated putting off reading it until tomorrow. But then I figured I was feeling as bad now as I was ever going to. Might as well get it over with.

I turned on the glow-pad. Hawkins' pale face appeared on the screen. Stiffly, as if he were confessing a crime, he said, "My folks didn't want me to become a scientist. I was supposed to stay home and manage the family money. Stay home and let my mind rot." His face twisted with private memories. "So that's the first thing you have to know—Donald Hawkins isn't my real name.

"My mother was kind of wild when she was young. I don't think she knew who my father was. So when she had me, it was hushed up. I was raised by my grandparents. They were getting a little old for child-rearing, so they shipped me back-time to when they were younger, and raised me alongside my mother. I was fifteen before I learned she wasn't really my sister.

"My real name is Philippe de Cherville. I swapped table assignments so I could meet my younger self. But then Melusine—my mother—started hitting on me. So I guess you can understand now—" he laughed embarrassedly—"why I didn't want to go the Oedipus route."

The pad flicked off, and then immediately back on again. He'd had an afterthought. "Oh yeah, I wanted to say . . . the things you said to me today—when I was young—the encouragement. And the tooth. Well, they meant a lot to me. So, uh . . . thanks."

It flicked off.

I put my head in my hands. Everything was throbbing, as if all the universe were contained within an infected tooth. Or maybe the brain tumor of a sick old dinosaur. I'm not stupid. I saw the implications immediately.

The kid—Philippe—was my son.

Hawkins was my son.

I hadn't even known I had a son, and now he was dead.

A BLEAK, BLANK time later, I set to work drawing time lines in the holographic workspace above my desk. A simple double-loop for Hawkins/Philippe. A rather more complex figure for myself. Then I factored in the TSOs, the waiters, the paleontologists, the musicians, the workmen who built the station in the first place and would salvage its fixtures when we were done with it . . . maybe a hundred representative individuals in all.

When I was done, I had a three-dimensional representation of Hilltop Station as a node of intersecting lives in time. It was one hell of a complex figure.

It looked like the Gordian knot.

Then I started crafting a memo back to my younger self. A carbon steel, razor-edged, Damascene sword of a memo. One that would slice Hilltop Station into a thousand spasming paradoxical fragments.

Hire him, fire her, strand a hundred young scientists, all fit and capable of breeding, one million years BC. Oh, and *don't* father any children.

It would bring our sponsors down upon us like so many angry hornets. The Unchanging would yank time travel out of human hands—retroactively. Everything connected to it would be looped out of reality and into the disintegrative medium of quantum uncertainty. Hilltop Station would dissolve into the realm of might-have-been. The research and findings of thousands of dedicated scientists would vanish from human knowing. My son would never have been conceived or born or sent callously to an unnecessary death.

Everything I had spent my life working to accomplish would be undone.

It sounded good to me.

When the memo was done, I marked it PRIORITY and MY EYES ONLY. Then I prepared to send it three months back in time.

The door opened behind me with a click. I spun around in my chair. In walked the one man in all existence who could possibly stop me.

"The kid got to enjoy twenty-four years of life before he died," the Old Man said. "Don't take that away from him."

I looked up into his eyes.

Into my own eyes.

Those eyes fascinated and repulsed me. They were deepest brown, and nested in a lifetime's accumulation of wrinkles. I've been working with my older self since I first signed up with Hilltop Station, and they were still a mystery to me, absolutely opaque. They made me feel like a mouse being stared down by a snake.

"It's not the kid," I said. "It's everything."

"I know."

"I only met him tonight—Philippe, I mean. Hawkins was just a new recruit. I barely knew him."

The Old Man capped the Glenlivet and put it back in the liquor cabinet. Until he did that, I hadn't even noticed I was drinking. "I keep forgetting how emotional I was when I was young," he said.

"I don't feel young."

"Wait until you're my age."

I'm not sure how old the Old Man is. There are longevity treatments available for those who play the game, and the Old Man has been playing this lousy game so long he practically runs it. All I know is that he and I are the same person.

My thoughts took a sudden swerve. "God damn that stupid kid!" I blurted. "What was he doing outside the compound in the first place?"

The Old Man shrugged. "He was curious. All scientists are. He saw something and went out to examine it. Leave it be, kid. What's done is done."

I glanced at the memo I'd written. "We'll find out."

He placed a second memo alongside mine. "I took the liberty of writing this for you. Thought I'd spare you the pain of having to compose it."

I picked up the memo, glanced at its contents. It was the one I'd received yesterday. "'Hawkins was attacked and killed by Satan shortly after local midnight today,'" I quoted. "'Take all necessary measures to control gossip.'" Overcome with loathing, I said, "This is exactly why I'm going to bust up this whole filthy system. You think I want to become the kind of man who can send his own son off to die? You think I want to become *you?*"

That hit home. For a long moment the Old Man did not speak. "Listen," he said at last. "You remember that day in the Peabody?"

"You know I do."

"I stood there in front of that mural wishing with all my heart— all *your* heart—that I could see a real, living dinosaur. But even then, even as an eight-year-old, I knew it wasn't going to happen. That some things could never be."

I said nothing.

"God hands you a miracle," he said, "you don't throw it back in his face."

Then he left.

I remained.

It was my call. Two possible futures lay side-by-side on my desk, and I could select either one. The universe is inherently unstable in every instant. If paradoxes weren't possible, nobody would waste their energy preventing them. The Old Man was trusting me to weigh all relevant factors, make the right decision, and live with the consequences.

It was the cruelest thing he had ever done to me.

Thinking of cruelty reminded me of the Old Man's eyes. Eyes so deep you could drown in them. Eyes so dark you couldn't tell how many corpses already lay submerged within them. After all these years working with him, I still couldn't tell if those were the eyes of a saint or of the most evil man in the world.

There were two memos in front of me. I reached for one, hesitated, withdrew my hand. Suddenly the choice didn't seem so easy.

The night was preternaturally still. It was as if all the world were holding its breath, waiting for me to make my decision.

I reached out for the memos.

I chose one.

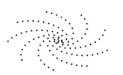

Ancient Engines

"Planning to live forever, Tiktok?"

The words cut through the bar's chatter and gab and silenced them. The silence reached out to touch infinity and then, "I believe you're talking to me?" a mech said.

The drunk laughed. "Ain't nobody else here sticking needles in his face, is there?"

The old man saw it all. He lightly touched the hand of the young woman sitting with him and said, "Watch."

Carefully the mech set down his syringe alongside a bottle of liquid collagen on a square of velvet cloth. He disconnected himself from the recharger, laying the jack beside the syringe. When he looked up again, his face was still and hard. He looked like a young lion.

The drunk grinned sneeringly.

The bar was located just around the corner from the local stepping stage. It was a quiet retreat from the aggravations of the street, all brass and mirrors and wood paneling, as cozy and snug as the inside of a walnut. Light shifted lazily about the room, creating a varying emphasis like clouds drifting overhead on a summer day, but far dimmer. The bar, the bottles behind the bar, and the shelves beneath the bottles behind the bar were all aggressively real. If there was anything virtual, it was set up high or far back, where it couldn't be touched. There was not a smart surface in the place.

"If that was a challenge," the mech said, "I'd be more than happy to meet you outside."

"Oh, noooooo," the drunk said, his expression putting the lie to his words. "I just saw you shooting up that goop into your face, oh so dainty, like an old lady pumping herself full of antioxidants. So I figured . . ." He weaved and put a hand down on a table to steady himself. ". . figured you was hoping to live forever."

The girl looked questioningly at the old man. He held a finger to his lips.

"Well, you're right. You're—what? Fifty years old? Just beginning to grow old and decay. Pretty soon your teeth will rot and fall out and your hair will melt away and your face will fold up in a million wrinkles. Your hearing and your eyesight will go and you won't be able to remember the last time you got it up. You'll be lucky if you don't need diapers before the end. But me—" he drew a dram of fluid into his syringe and tapped the barrel to draw the bubbles to the top—"anything that fails, I'll simply have it replaced. So, yes, I'm planning to live forever. While you, well, I suppose you're planning to die. Soon, I hope."

The drunk's face twisted, and with an incoherent roar of rage he attacked the mech.

In a motion too fast to be seen, the mech stood, seized the drunk, whirled him around, and lifted him above his head. One hand was closed around the man's throat so he couldn't speak. The other held both wrists tight behind the knees so that, struggle as he might, the drunk was helpless.

"I could snap your spine like *that*," he said coldly. "If I exerted myself, I could rupture every internal organ you've got. I'm two-point-eight times stronger than a flesh man, and three-point-five times faster. My reflexes are only slightly slower than the speed of light, and I've just had a tune-up. You could hardly have chosen a worse person to pick a fight with."

Then the drunk was flipped around and set back on his feet. He gasped for air.

"But since I'm also a merciful man, I'll simply ask nicely if you wouldn't rather leave." The mech spun the drunk around and gave him a gentle shove toward the door.

The man left at a stumbling run.

Everyone in the place—there were not many—had been watching. Now they remembered their drinks, and talk rose up to fill the room again. The bartender put something back under the bar and turned away.

Leaving his recharge incomplete, the mech folded up his lubrication kit and slipped it in a pocket. He swiped his hand over the credit swatch, and stood.

But as he was leaving, the old man swiveled around and said, "I heard you say you hope to live forever. Is that true?"

"Who doesn't?" the mech said curtly.

"Then sit down. Spend a few minutes out of the infinite swarm of centuries you've got ahead of you to humor an old man. What's so urgent that you can't spare the time?"

The mech hesitated. Then, as the young woman smiled at him, he sat.

"Thank you. My name is—"

"I know who you are, Mr. Brandt. There's nothing wrong with my eidetics."

Brandt smiled. "That's why I like you guys. I don't have to be all the time reminding you of things." He gestured to the woman sitting opposite him. "My granddaughter." The light intensified where she sat, making her red hair blaze. She dimpled prettily.

"Jack." The young man drew up a chair. "Chimaera Navigator-Fuego, model number—"

"Please. I founded Chimaera. Do you think I wouldn't recognize one of my own children?"

Jack flushed. "What is it you want to talk about, Mr. Brandt?" His voice was audibly less hostile now, as synthetic counterhormones damped down his emotions.

"Immortality. I found your ambition most intriguing."

"What's to say? I take care of myself, I invest carefully, I buy all the upgrades. I see no reason why I shouldn't live forever." Defiantly. "I hope that doesn't offend you."

"No, no, of course not. Why should it? Some men hope to achieve immortality through their works and others through their children. What could give me more joy than to do both? But tell me—do you *really* expect to live forever?"

The mech said nothing.

"I remember an incident happened to my late father-in-law, William Porter. He was a fine fellow, Bill was, and who remembers him anymore? Only me." The old man sighed. "He was a bit of a railroad buff, and one day he took a tour through a science museum that included a magnificent old steam locomotive. This was in the latter years of the last century. Well, he was listening admiringly to the guide extolling the virtues of this ancient engine when she mentioned its date of manufacture, and he realized that *he was older than it was.*" Brandt leaned forward. "This is the point where old Bill would laugh. But it's not really funny, is it?"

"No."

The granddaughter sat listening quietly, intently, eating little pretzels one by one from a bowl.

"How old are you, Jack?"

"Seven years."

"I'm eighty-three. How many machines do you know of that are as old as me? Eighty-three years old and still functioning?"

"I saw an automobile the other day," his granddaughter said. "A Dusenberg. It was red."

"How delightful. But it's not used for transportation anymore, is it? We have the stepping stages for that. I won an award once that had mounted on it a vacuum tube from Univac. That was the first real computer. Yet all its fame and historical importance couldn't keep it from the scrap heap."

"Univac," said the young man, "couldn't act on its own behalf. If it could, perhaps it would be alive today."

"Parts wear out."

"New ones can be bought."

"Yes, as long as there's the market. But there are only so many machine people of your make and model. A lot of you have risky occupations. There are accidents, and with every accident, the consumer market dwindles."

"You can buy antique parts. You can have them made."

"Yes, if you can afford them. And if not—?"

The young man fell silent.

"Son, you're not going to live *forever*. We've just established that. So now that you've admitted that you've got to die someday, you might as well admit that it's going to be sooner rather than later. Mechanical people are in their infancy. And nobody can upgrade a Model T into a stepping stage. Agreed?"

Jack dipped his head. "Yes."

"You knew it all along."

"Yes."

"That's why you behaved so badly toward that lush."

"Yes."

"I'm going to be brutal here, Jack—you probably won't live to be eighty-three. You don't have my advantages."

"Which are?"

"Good genes. I chose my ancestors well."

"Good genes," Jack said bitterly. "You received good genes and what did I get in their place? What the hell did I get?"

"Molybdenum joints where stainless steel would do. Ruby chips instead of zirconium. A number seventeen plastic seating for—hell, we did all right by you boys."

"But it's not enough."

"No. It's not. It was only the best we could do."

"What's the solution, then?" the granddaughter asked, smiling.

"I'd advise taking the long view. That's what I've done."

"Poppycock," the mech said. "You were an extensionist when you were young. I input your autobiography. It seems to me you wanted immortality as much as I do."

"Oh, yes, I was a charter member of the life-extension movement. You can't imagine the crap we put into our bodies! But eventually I wised up. The problem is, information degrades each time a human cell replenishes itself. Death is inherent in flesh people. It seems to be written into the basic program—a way, perhaps, of keeping the universe from filling up with old people."

"And old ideas," his granddaughter said maliciously.

"Touché. I saw that life-extension was a failure. So I decided that my children would succeed where I failed. That *you* would succeed. And—"

"You failed."

"But I haven't stopped trying!" The old man thumped the table in unison with his last three words. "You've obviously given this some thought. Let's discuss what I *should* have done. What would it take to make a true immortal? What instructions should I have given your design team? Let's design a mechanical man who's got a shot at living forever."

Carefully, the mech said, "Well, the obvious to begin with. He ought to be able to buy new parts and upgrades as they come available. There should be ports and connectors that would make it easy to adjust to shifts in technology. He should be capable of surviving extremes of heat, cold, and moisture. And—" he waved a hand at his own face—"he shouldn't look so goddamned pretty."

"I think you look nice," the granddaughter said.

"Yes, but I'd like to be able to pass for flesh."

"So our hypothetical immortal should be, one, infinitely upgradable; two, adaptable across a broad spectrum of conditions; and three, discreet. Anything else?"

"I think she should be charming," the granddaughter said.

"She?" the mech asked.

"Why not?"

"That's actually not a bad point," the old man said. "The organism that survives evolutionary forces is the one that's best adapted to its environmental niche. The environmental niche people live in is man-made. The single most useful trait a survivor can have is probably the ability to get along easily with other men. Or, if you'd rather, women."

"Oh," said the granddaughter, "he doesn't like *women*. I can tell by his body language."

The young man flushed.

"Don't be offended," said the old man. "You should never be offended by the truth. As for you—" he turned to face his granddaughter—"if you don't learn to treat people better, I won't take you places anymore."

She dipped her head. "Sorry."

"Apology accepted. Let's get back to task, shall we? Our hypothetical immortal would be a lot like flesh women, in many ways. Self-regenerating. Able to grow her own replacement parts. She could take in pretty much anything as fuel. A little carbon, a little water ..."

"Alcohol would be an excellent fuel," his granddaughter said.

"She'd have the ability to mimic the superficial effects of aging," the mech said. "Also, biological life evolves incrementally across generations. I'd want her to be able to evolve across upgrades."

"Fair enough. Only I'd do away with upgrades entirely, and give her total conscious control over her body. So she could change and evolve at will. She'll need that ability, if she's going to survive the collapse of civilization."

"The collapse of civilization? Do you think it likely?"

"In the long run? Of course. When you take the long view it seems inevitable. Everything seems inevitable. Forever is a long time, remember. Time enough for absolutely everything to happen."

For a moment nobody spoke.

Then the old man slapped his hands together. "Well, we've created our New Eve. Now let's wind her up and let her go. She can expect to live—how long?"

"Forever," said the mech.

"Forever's a long time. Let's break it down into smaller units. In the year 2500, she'll be doing what?"

"Holding down a job," the granddaughter said. "Designing art molecules, maybe, or scripting recreational hallucinations. She'll be deeply involved in the culture. She'll have lots of friends she cares about passionately, and maybe a husband or wife or two."

"Who will grow old," the mech said, "or wear out. Who will die."

"She'll mourn them, and move on."

"The year 3500. The collapse of civilization," the old man said with gusto. "What will she do then?"

"She'll have made preparations, of course. If there are radiation or toxins in the environment, she'll have made her systems immune from their effects. And she'll make herself useful to the survivors. In the seeming of an old woman she'll teach the healing arts. Now and then she might drop a hint about this and that. She'll have a data base squirreled away somewhere containing everything they'll have lost. Slowly, she'll guide them back to civilization. But a gentler one, this time. One less likely to tear itself apart."

"The year one million. Humanity evolves beyond anything we can currently imagine. How does she respond?"

"She mimics their evolution. No—she's been *shaping* their evolution. She wants a risk-free method of going to the stars, so she's been encouraging a type of being that would strongly desire such a thing. She isn't among the first to use it, though. She waits a few hundred generations for it to prove itself."

The mech, who had been listening in fascinated silence, now said, "Suppose that never happens? What if starflight will always remain difficult and perilous? What then?"

"It was once thought that people would never fly. So much that looks impossible becomes simple if you only wait."

"Four billion years. The sun uses up its hydrogen, its core collapses, helium fusion begins, and it balloons into a red giant. Earth is vaporized."

"Oh, she'll be somewhere else by then. That's easy."

"Five billion years. The Milky Way collides with the Andromeda Galaxy and the whole neighborhood is full of high-energy radiation and exploding stars."

"That's trickier. She's going to have to either prevent that or move a few million light years away to a friendlier galaxy. But she'll have time enough to prepare and to assemble the tools. I have faith that she'll prove equal to the task."

"One trillion years. The last stars gutter out. Only black holes remain."

"Black holes are a terrific source of energy. No problem."

"1.06 googol years."

"Googol?"

"That's ten raised to the hundredth power—one followed by a hundred zeros. The heat-death of the universe. How does she survive it?"

"She'll have seen it coming for a long time," the mech said. "When the last black holes dissolve, she'll have to do without a source of free energy. Maybe she could take and rewrite her personality into the physical constants of the dying universe. Would that be possible?"

"Oh, perhaps. But I really think that the lifetime of the universe is long enough for anyone," the granddaughter said. "Mustn't get greedy."

"Maybe so," the old man said thoughtfully. "Maybe so." Then, to the mech, "Well, there you have it: a glimpse into the future, and a brief biography of the first immortal, ending, alas, with her death. Now tell me. Knowing that you contributed something, however small, to that accomplishment—wouldn't that be enough?"

"No," Jack said. "No, it wouldn't."

Brandt made a face. "Well, you're young. Let me ask you this: Has it been a good life so far? All in all?"

"Not that good. Not good *enough.*"

For a long moment the old man was silent. Then, "Thank you," he said. "I valued our conversation." The interest went out of his eyes and he looked away.

Uncertainly Jack looked at the granddaughter, who smiled and shrugged. "He's like that, " she said apologetically. "He's old. His enthusiasms wax and wane with his chemical balances. I hope you don't mind."

"I see." The young man stood. Hesitantly, he made his way to the door.

At the door, he glanced back and saw the granddaughter tearing her linen napkin into little bits and eating the shreds, delicately washing them down with little sips of wine.

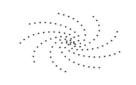

North of Diddy-Wah-Diddy

THE TRAIN TO HELL don't stop in New Jersey. It pulls out of Grand Central Station at midnight, moving slow at first but steadily picking up speed as it passes under the Bay, and by the time we hit the refineries, it's cannonballing. We don't stop for nothing. We don't stop for nobody. And if you step in our way expecting Old Goatfoot to apply the brakes, well, pardon me for saying it, but you're going to get exactly what's coming to you.

We don't stop and we don't slow down once that gleaming black-and-silver locomotive leaves the station. Not 'til we get to where we're going. Once we're rolling, there's no second chances. And no exceptions neither.

So that night the train *did* stop, I knew straight off that we were in for some serious trouble.

We were barreling through the Pine Barrens, shedding smoke and sulfur and sparks, when I heard the air brakes squeal. The train commenced to losing velocity. I was just about to open the snack bar, but right off I heard that sound, I flipped around the CLOSED sign, grabbed my cap, and skittered off to see what the matter was.

The damned were slumped in their seats. Some of them stared straight ahead of themselves at nothing in particular. Others peered listlessly out the windows or else at their own grey reflections in the glass. Our passengers are always a little subdued in the early stages of the trip.

"Oh, porter!" one of the damned called to me. She was a skinny little white woman with a worried-looking kind of pinched-in face. "Would it be all right of me to open the window just a crack, so I could get some air?"

I smiled gently into those big pleading eyes of hers and said, "Why, bless you, honey, you can do whatever you want. What difference could it possibly make now?"

She flinched back like I'd hit her.

But I reached over and took the window clips and slid it down two inches. "Don't go no further, I'm afraid. Some of the lost souls might take it into their heads to try and . . . you know?" I lowered my voice in a confidential manner.

Timidly, she nodded.

I got a pillow out of the overhead and fluffed it up for her. "Now you just let me slide this behind your head. There! Isn't that better? You relax now, and in a couple minutes the kitchen will be open. When I come back, I'll give you a menu. Got a nice selection of sandwiches and beverages. You rest up and have a comfy ride."

All the while I was talking, I was just about dying inside of curiosity. Through the window behind the old lady I could see that we'd stopped in a small clearing in the pines. We were miles from the nearest town. The only light here was what came from the moon and the greenish spill from the windows of the train itself. There were maybe half a dozen dim figures out there. I could see them hoist up a long crate of some kind. Somebody—and who else could it be but Billy Bones?— leaned out from the caboose with a lantern and waved them forward.

The damned stared out the windows with disinterest. Most likely they thought we were picking up more passengers. Only the crew knew different.

Still, I take pride in my work. I fussed over that little lady and by the time I left her she was actually smiling. It was only a tense little smile, but it was a smile still.

People can fool themselves into believing anything.

Soon as I got myself clear, I made straight for the baggage car. I had got me a real bad feeling about what was going on, and I intended to pry a few answers out of Billy Bones. But I didn't get beyond the door. When I tried to slide it back, it wouldn't budge. I seized it with both hands and applied some muscle. Nothing.

It was locked from inside.

I banged on the door. "Mister *Bones!*"

A silence, and then the peephole slide moved aside. A cadaverous slice of Billy Bones's face appeared. Flesh so tight it didn't hide the skull. Eyes as bright and glittery as a rat's. "What is it?"

"Don't you give me that what-is-it bullshit—why did we stop?" The pines made a dark, jagged line against the sky. I could smell them. If I wanted, I could step down off the train and walk into them. "Just what kind of unholy cargo have you taken on?"

Billy Bones looked me straight in the eye. "We ain't taken on no cargo."

"Now don't get me started," I said. "You open up and-"

He slammed that little slide-door right in my face.

I blinked. "Well!" I said. "You may think you've had the last word, Mister Billy Bones, but you have not, I assure you that!"

But I didn't feel nowhere near so brash as I made out. Billy Bones was a natural-born hustler down to his fingertips, the kind of man that could break you a quarter and short-change you a dollar in the process. Ain't nobody never outbluffed him. Ain't nobody never got nothing out of him that he didn't want to give. In my experience, what he didn't wish to say, I wasn't about to hear.

So back I strode, up the train, looking for Sugar. My old stomach ulcer was starting to act up.

"DIDDY-WAH-DIDDY!" Sugar bawled. He strolled briskly through the car, clacking his ticket punch. "Diddy-Wah-Diddy, Ginny Gall, WEST Hell, Hell, and BeluthaHATCHie! Have your tickets ready."

I gave him the high sign. But a portly gent in a pinstripe suit laid hold of his sleeve and launched into a long complaint about his ticket, so I had to hold back and wait. Sugar listened patiently to the man for a time, then leaned over him like a purple storm cloud. The man cringed away. He's big, is Sugar, and every ounce of him is pure intimidation.

"I tell you what, sir," he said in a low and menacing way. "Why don't you take a spoon and jab it in your eye? Stir it around good. See how clean you can scrape out the socket." He punched the ticket. "I guarantee you that a week from now you gone look back upon the experience with nostalgia."

The man turned grey and for an instant I thought he was going to rise up out of his seat. But Sugar smiled in a way that bulged up every muscle in his face and neck and the man subsided. Sugar stuck the ticket stub in the seat clip. Then, shaking his head, he came and joined me between cars.

His bulk filled what space there was pretty good. "Make it brief, Malcolm. I got things to do."

"You know anything 'bout why we stopped?" Those dim people were trudging away into the pines. None of them looked back, not even once. They just dissolved into the shadows. "I saw Billy Bones take on a crate and when I asked him about it, he clammed right up."

Sugar stared at me with those boogieman eyes of his. In all the three-four years he'd been on the train, I don't recall ever seeing him blink. "You ain't seen nothing," he said.

I put my hands on my hips. "Now, don't *you* start in on me! I was a porter on this train back when your mama was sucking tittie."

Sugar seemed to swell up then, a great black mountain with two pinpricks of hellfire dancing in his eyes. "You watch what you say about my mother."

The hairs on the back of my neck prickled. But I didn't back down. "Just what you intending to do?" I shook my finger in his face. "You know the regs. If you so much as touch me, you're off the train. And they don't let you out in Manhattan, neither!"

"Can't say I much care." He put those enormous hands on my shoulders. His voice was small and dreamy. "After this run, I don't much care whether I keep this job or not."

All the while he spoke, those hands kept kneading my shoulders. He laid one huge thumb alongside my face and shoved my head to the side. I didn't much doubt he could crush my bones and snap my spine, if he wanted to. He was that strong. And I could see that he'd enjoy it.

"I ain't said nothing!" I was terrified. "I ain't said nothing about your mama."

Sugar considered this for a long time, that sleepy little smile floating on his face. At last he said, "See that you don't."

And he turned away.

I exhaled. I can't say I knew Sugar at all well. He was a recent addition to the crew; the conductor before him took to visiting the juke joints and gambling dens of Ginny Gall during stopovers and lost his precariously-held spiritual balance. But if ever anyone was meant to be a badman, it was Sugar. He was born just naturally brimming-over with anger. They say when the midwife slapped his bottom, the rage in his voice and the look on his face were so awful that straightaway she threw him down on the floor. He was born with a strangler's hands and a murderer's eyes. The rest of him, the size and bulk of him, just grew, so's to have a package big enough and mean enough to contain all the temper there inside.

And they also say that when the midwife lifted up her foot to crush Sugar to death, his mama rose up off of the bed and thrashed her within an inch of her life. She was one of those tiny little women too, but her love for her baby was that strong. She threw that midwife right out of the room and down the stairs, broken bones and all. Then she picked up Sugar and put him to her breast and cooed at him and sang to him until he fell asleep. That's the kind of blood flowed in Sugar's veins, the kind of stuff he was made from.

There was a sudden lurch and the train started to move again. Whatever was going down, it was too late to stop it now.

With Billy Bones and Sugar refusing to talk to me, there wasn't any chance none of the girls would either. They were all three union, and Billy was their shop steward. Me, I was union too, but in a different shop.

The only remaining possible source of information was Old Goat-foot. I headed back for the concession stand to fetch a bottle of rye. I had it in a paper bag under one arm and was passing through the sleeper cars when a door slid open and a long slim hand crooked a red-nailed finger.

I stepped into the compartment. A ginger-colored woman closed the door and slid between me and it. For an instant we just stood there looking at each other. At last she said, "Porter."

"Yes'm?"

She smiled in a sly kind of way. "I want to show you something." She unbuttoned her blouse, thrusting her chest forward. She was wearing one of those black lacy kinds of bras that squeeze the breasts together and up. It was something to behold.

"If you'll excuse me, ma'am," I said uncomfortably. "I have to get back to work."

"I got work for you right here," she said, grabbing at me. I reached for the doorknob, but she was tugging at my jacket, trying to get it open. I grabbed her by the wrists, afraid of losing a button.

"Please, ma'am." I was just about dying of embarrassment.

"Don't you please ma'am me, boy! You know I got what you want and we both know I ain't got long to use it." She was rubbing herself against me and at the same time trying to shove my head down into her bosom. Somehow her brassiere had come undone and her breasts were slapping me in the face. It was awful. I was thrashing around, struggling to get free, and she was all over me.

Then I managed to slip out of her grip and straight-arm her so that she fell on her back onto the bunk. For a second she lay there looking rumpled and expectant.

I used that second to open the door and step out into the hall. Keeping a wary eye on the woman, I began to tug my uniform back into place.

When she realized I wasn't going to stay, her face twisted, and she spat out a nasty word.

"Cocksucker!"

It hurt. I'm not saying it didn't. But she was under a lot of pressure, and it wouldn't have been professional for me to let my feelings show. So I simply said, "Yes'm. That's so. But I'm sure there are plenty of men on board this train who would be extremely interested in what you got to offer. The dining room opens soon. You might take a stroll up that way and see what sort of gents are available."

I slipped away.

Back when I died, men like me called ourselves "queers." That's how long ago it was. And back then, if you were queer and had the misfortune to die, you were automatically damned. It was a mortal sin just being one of us, never mind that you didn't have any say in the matter. The Stonewall Riots changed all that. After them, if you'd lived a good life you qualified for the other place. There's still a lot of bitterness in certain circles of Hell over this, but what are you going to do? The Man in charge don't take complaints.

It was my misfortune to die several decades too early. I was beat to death in Athens, Georgia. A couple of cops caught me in the back seat of a late-model Rambler necking with a white boy name of Danny. I don't guess they actually meant to kill me. They just forgot to stop in time. That sort of thing went on a lot back then.

First thing I died, I was taken to this little room with two bored-looking angels. One of them sat hunched over a desk, scribbling on a whole heap of papers. "What's this one?" he asked without looking up.

The second angel was lounging against a filing cabinet. He had a kindly sort of face, very tired-looking, like he'd seen the worst humanity had to offer and knew he was going to keep on seeing it until the last trump. It was a genuine kindness, too, because out of all the things he could've called me, he said, "A kid with bad luck."

The first angel glanced up and said, "Oh." Then went back to his work.

"Have a seat, son," the kindly angel said. "This will take a while."

I obeyed. "What's going to become of me?" I asked.

"You're fucked," the first angel muttered.

I looked to the other.

He colored a little. "That's it," he said. "There just plain flat-out ain't no way you're going to beat this rap. You're a faggot and faggots go to Hell." He kind of coughed into his hand then and said, "I'll tell you what, though. It's not official yet, but I happen to know that the two yahoos who rousted you are going to be passing through this office soon. Moonshining incident."

He pulled open a file drawer and took out a big fat folder overflowing with papers. "These are the Schedule C damnations in here. Boiling maggots, rains of molten lead, the whole lot. You look through them, pick out a couple of juicy ones. I'll see that your buddies get them."

"Nossir," I said. "I'd rather not."

"Eh?" He pushed his specs down his nose and peered over them at me. "What's that?"

"If it's all the same to you, I don't want to do nothing to them."

"Why, they're just two bull-neck crackers! Rednecks! White-trash peckerwoods!" He pointed the file at me. "They beat you to death for the fun of it!"

"I don't suppose they were exactly good men," I said. "I reckon the world will be better off without them. But I don't bear them any malice. Maybe I can't find it in me to wish them well, and maybe I wasn't what you'd call a regular churchgoer. But I know that we're supposed to forgive our trespassers, to whatever degree our natures allow. And, well, I'd appreciate it if you didn't do any of those things to them."

The second angel was staring at me in disbelief, and his expression wasn't at all kindly anymore. The first angel had stopped scribbling and was gawking at me too.

"Shit," he said.

THREE DAYS THEY spent bickering over me.

I presented something of a political problem for those who decide these matters, because of course they couldn't just let me go Upstairs. It would have created a precedent.

The upshot of it was that I got a new job. They gave me a brass-button uniform and two weeks' training, and told me to keep out of trouble. And so far, I had.

Only now, I was beginning to think my lucky streak was over.

OLD GOATFOOT LOOKED over his shoulder with a snarl when I entered the cab of the locomotive. Of all the crew only he had never been human. He was a devil from the git-go, or maybe an angel once if you believe Mister Milton. I pulled the bag off of the bottle of rye and let the wind whip it away, and his expression changed. He wrapped a clawed hand around the bottle and took a swig that made a good quarter of its contents disappear.

He let out this great rumbling sigh then, part howl and part belch, like no sound that had ever known a human throat. I shuddered, but it was just his way of showing satisfaction. In a burnt-out cinder of a voice, Old Goatfoot said, "Trouble's brewing."

"That so?" I said cautiously.

"Always is." He stared out across the wastelands. A band of centaurs, each one taller than a ten-story building, struggled through waist-high muck in the distance. Nasty stuff it was—smelled worse than the Fresh Kill landfill over to New Jersey. "This time, though." He shook his head and said, "Ain't never seen nothing like it. All the buggers of Hell are out."

He passed me back the bottle.

I passed my hand over the mouth, still hot from his lips, and took a gingerly little sip. Just to be companionable. "How come?"

He shrugged. "Dunno. They're looking for something, but fuck if I can make out what."

Just then a leather-winged monster larger than a storm cloud lifted over the horizon. With a roar and a flapping sound like canvas in the wind, it was upon us. The creature was so huge that it covered half the sky, and it left a stench behind that I knew would linger for hours, even at the speeds we were going. "That's one ugly brute," I remarked.

Old Goatfoot laughed scornfully and knocked back another third of the bottle. "You worried about a little thing like that?" He leaned his head out the window, closed one nostril with a finger, and shot a stream of snot into the night. "Shitfire, boy, I've seen Archangels flying over us."

Now I was genuinely frightened. Because I had no doubt that whatever the powers that be were looking for, it was somewhere on our train. And this last meant that all of Heaven and Hell were arrayed against us. Now, you might think that Hell was worry enough for anybody, but consider this—they *lost.* Forget what folks say. The other side are mean mothers, and don't let nobody tell you different.

Old Goatfoot finished off the bottle and ate the glass. Then, keeping one hand on the throttle all the while, he unbuttoned his breeches, hauled out his ugly old thing, and began pissing into the firebox. There were two firemen standing barefoot in the burning coals, shoveling like madmen. They dropped their shovels and scrambled to catch as much of the spray as they could, clambering all over each other in their anxiousness for a respite, however partial, however brief, from their suffering. They were black as carbon and little blue flames burned in their hair. Old Goatfoot's piss sizzled and steamed where it hit the coals.

Damned souls though they were, I found it a distressing sight.

"Y'all have to excuse me," I said uneasily. "They'll be opening the casino round about now. I got work to do."

Old Goatfoot farted. "Eat shit and die," he said genially.

Back in the casino car, Billy Bones had set up his wheel, and folks that on an ordinary day gambled like there was no tomorrow had pulled out all the stops. They were whooping and laughing, talking that big talk, and slapping down paper money by the fistful. Nobody cared that it was a crooked game. It was their last chance to show a little style.

Billy Bones was in his element, his skull-face grinning with avarice. He spun the wheel with one hand and rested the other on the haunch of a honey in smoke-grey stockings and a skirt so short you could see all the way to Cincinnati. She had one hand on Billy's shoulder and a martini and a clove cigarette both in the other, and you could see she was game for anything he might happen to have in mind. But so far as

Billy was concerned, she was just a prop, a flash bit of glamour to help keep the money rolling in.

LaBelle, Afreya, and Sally breezed by with their trays of cigarettes, heroin, and *hors d'oeuvres.* They were all good girls, and how they got here was—well, I guess we all know how good girls get in trouble. They fall for the wrong man. They wore white gloves and their uniforms were tight-cut but austere, for they none of them were exactly eager to be confused with the damned. Sally gave me a bit of a smile, sympathetic but guarded.

We had some good musicians died for this trip, and they were putting in some hot licks. Maybe they sensed that with the caliber of competition Down Below, they were going to be a long time between gigs. But they sure were cooking.

Everybody was having a high old time.

This was the jolly part of the trip, and normally I enjoyed it. Not today.

Sugar stood by the rear door, surrounded by a bevy of the finest honeys imaginable. This was nothing new. It was always a sight how they flocked to him on the southbound platform at Grand Central Station, elegantly dressed women who weren't even dead yet, rolling their eyes and wriggling their behinds something outrageous. Sooner or later one would ask, "You ever seen . . . him?" and then, when he squinted at her like he couldn't quite make out what she was getting at, "You know—Lucifer? The Devil."

At which point Sugar would say, "Seen him? Why, just this last run, I had a private audience with His Satanic Majesty. Sugar, he says to me, You been talking mighty big of late, I guess it's time to remind you who's boss."

"What did you say?" They would all hold their breaths and bend close.

"I said, Drop your pants and bend over, motherfucker. *I'm* driving now."

They'd shriek then, scandalized and delighted. And when Sugar opened his arms, two of the honeys would slide in under them neat as you please.

Business was brisk at the bar. I tried not to let my thoughts show, but I must've made a bad job of it, for I was just thrusting one of those little paper umbrellas into a frozen daiquiri when a hand closed upon my shoulder.

I whirled around, right into the most knowing smile I'd ever seen. It was a smart-dressed lady, all in red. She had on a bowler hat and she smoked a cigar. Her skirt went all the way to the ground, but there was a slit up one side and you could see the silver derringer stuck into her garter.

"You look worried," she said. "I wouldn't think the crew had much of anything to worry about."

"We're human, ma'am. Subject to the thousand natural shocks the flesh is heir to." I sighed. "And I will confess that if I weren't obliged to be here behind the bar—well. What's your pleasure?"

For a long moment she studied me.

"You interest me," she said at last, and vanished into the crowd.

Not much later she was back, steering a shy little porcelain doll of a girl by the elbow. "Missy can tend bar," she said. She slipped one hand between the girl's legs and the other behind her shoulder blades and hoisted her clear over the bar. It was an astonishing display of strength and she did it with no special emphasis, as if it were the most natural thing in the world. "She's had more than sufficient experience."

"Now hold on," I said. "I can't just—"

"Missy doesn't mind. Do you, little sweet?"

The girl, wide-eyed, shook her head no.

"Wait for me here." The lady leaned down and kissed her full on the mouth—full, and deep too. Nobody paid any mind. The festivities had reached that rowdy stage. "You come with me."

I didn't have much choice but to follow.

Her name, she said, was Jackie. And, when I'd introduced myself, "I'm going to help you, Malcolm."

"Why?"

"I have observed," she said, "that other people are often willing to accept whatever events may chance to happen to them, rather than take an active part in their unfolding. That's not me." She glanced scorn-fully back at the casino car. "I am no gambler. All my pleasure lies in direct action. Tell me your problem. Make it interesting."

When I'd told my story, Jackie took the cigar out of her mouth and stared at it thoughtfully. "Your friend's attention is currently given over entirely to the pursuit of money. Can't you just go back to the baggage car now and look?"

I shook my head. "Not with Sugar standing by the rear door."

We were in the space between the casino and the next car forward, with the rails flashing by underneath and the cars twisting and rattling about us. Jackie put a hand on the bottommost rung of the access lad-der and said, "Then we'll go over the roof."

"Now, just a minute!"

"No delays." She frowned down at her skirt. "As soon as I can arrange a change of clothing."

Up the sleeper car she strode, opening doors, glancing within, slam-ming them shut again. Fifth one she tried, there was a skinny man in nothing but a white shirt working away on top of his lady-love. He looked up angrily. "Hey! What the fuck do you-"

Jackie pressed her derringer against his forehead and nodded toward a neatly folded bundle of clothing. "May I?"

The man froze. He couldn't die here, but that didn't mean he'd rel-ish a bullet through his skull. "They're yours."

"You're a gent." Jackie scooped up the bundle. Just before closing the door, she paused and smiled down at the terrified face of the woman underneath her victim.

"Pray," she said, "continue."

In the hallway she whipped off her skirt, stepped into the slacks, and zipped them up before I had the chance to look away. The jacket she tossed aside. She buttoned the vest over her blouse and tentatively tried on one of the man's wing tips. "They fit!"

I WENT UP THE rungs first. The wind was rushing over the top of the train something fierce. Gingerly, I began crawling across the roof of the casino car. I was scared out of my wits and making no fast progress, when I felt a tap on my shoulder. I looked back.

My heart about failed me. Jackie was standing straight up, oblivious to the furious rattling speed of the train. She reached down and hauled me to my feet. "Let's dance!" she shouted into my ear.

"What?" I shouted back, disbelieving. The wind buffeted us wildly. It whipped off Jackie's bowler hat and sent it tumbling away. She laughed.

"*Dance!* You've heard of dancing, haven't you?"

Without waiting for a reply, she seized me by the waist and whirled me around, and we were dancing. She led and I followed, fearful that the least misstep would tumble us from the train and land us broken and lost in the marshes of Styx. It was the single most frightening and exhilarating experience of my entire existence, moreso even than my first time with that traveling man out by the gravel quarry at the edge of town.

I was so frightened by now that it no longer mattered. I danced, hesitantly at first, and then with abandon. Jackie spun me dizzily around and around. The wind snatched sparks from her cigar and spangled the night with stars. Madness filled me and I danced, I danced, I danced.

At last Jackie released me. She looked flushed and satisfied. "That's better. No more crawling, Malcolm. You and I aren't made for it. Like as not, all our strivings will come to nothing in the end; we must celebrate our triumph now, while yet we can." And somehow I knew precisely how she felt and agreed with it too.

Then she glanced off to the side. The dark wastelands were zipping past. A ghastly kind of corpse-fire was crawling over the muck and filth to either side of the tracks. "A person might jump off here with no more damage than a broken arm, maybe a couple of ribs. We can't be more than—what?—two hundred fifty, three hundred miles south of New Jersey? It would not be difficult for a determined and spirited individual to follow the tracks back and escape."

"Nobody escapes," I said. "Please don't think of it."

A flicker of sadness passed over her face then, and she said, "No, of course not." Then, brisk again, "Come. We have work to do. Quickly. If anybody heard us stomping about up here, they'll know what we're up to."

We came down between cars at the front of the baggage car. There was a tool closet there I had the key to, and inside it a pry bar. I had just busted open the padlock when LaBelle suddenly slammed through the door from the front of the train, wild-eyed and sweaty.

"Malcolm," she said breathlessly, "don't!"

From somewhere about her person—don't ask me where—Jackie produced a wicked-looking knife. "Do not try to stop us," she said softly.

"You don't understand," LaBelle cried. "There's a *hound* on board!"

I heard it coming then.

The hounds of Hell aren't like the Earthly sort: They're bigger than the biggest mastiffs and they bear a considerable resemblance to rats. Their smell is loathsome beyond description and their disposition even worse.

LaBelle shrieked and shrank aside as the hound came bounding down the aisle.

With something between a howl and a scream, it was upon us.

"Go!" Jackie shoved me through the doorway. "I'll handle this. You do your part now."

She slammed the door shut.

Silence wrapped itself about me. It was ghastly. For all I could hear, the hound didn't even exist.

I flicked on the electric and in its swaying light took a look around. All the usual baggage: cases of fine French wines and satin sheets for the Lords of Hell, crates of shovels and rubber hip boots and balky manual typewriters for the rest. But to the rear of the car there was one thing more.

A coffin.

It was a long, slow walk to the coffin. I thought of all the folks I'd known who'd died and gone where I'd never see them again. I thought of all those things it might contain. It seemed to me then like Pandora's box, filled with nameless dread and the forbidden powers of Old Night. There was nothing I wanted to do less than to open it.

I took a deep breath and jammed the edge of the pry bar into the coffin. Nails screamed, and I flung the top back.

The woman inside opened her eyes.

I stood frozen with horror. She had a wrinkled little face, brown as a nut, and you could tell just by looking at it that she'd led a hard life. There was that firmness about the corners of her mouth, that unblinking quality about the eyes. She was a scrawny thing, all bones and no flesh, and her arms were crossed over her flat chest. Light played about her face and lit up the coffin around her head. I looked at her and I was just flat-out afraid of what was going to happen to Sugar and to me and to all of us when word of this got out.

"Well, young man?" she said in a peppery sort of way. "Aren't you going to help me up?"

"Ma'am?" I gaped for an instant before gathering myself together. "Oh! Yes, ma'am. Right away, ma'am." I offered her my hand and helped her sit up. The little shimmer of light followed her head up. Oh, sweet Heaven, I thought. She's one of the Saved.

I OPENED THE DOOR from the baggage compartment reluctantly, fearful of the hound that must surely wait just outside. Still, what other choice did I have?

There was Jackie, spattered from head to foot with shit and gore, and her clothes all in tatters. She stood with her legs braced, a cocky smile on her face, and the butt-end of her cigar still clenched in her teeth. LaBelle crouched by her feet—she shakily stood up when I emerged—staring at something in the distant marshes. Away off behind us, a howl of pain and rage like nothing I'd ever heard before dwindled to nothing.

The hound was nowhere to be seen.

First thing the old woman said then was, "Young lady. Do you think it seemly to be walking about dressed as a man?"

Jackie took the cigar butt out of her mouth.

"Get rid of that filthy thing too."

For an instant, I thought there was going to be trouble. But then Jackie laughed and flung the cigar out into the night. It was still lit and

I could see by the way the old lady frowned that she'd noticed that too.

I offered her my arm again and we made our way slowly up the train.

She was Sugar's mother. I never had any doubt about that. As we walked up the train, she questioned LaBelle and me about her son, whether he was well, was he behaving himself, did he have a special lady-friend yet, and what exactly did he have in mind for her and him?

LaBelle was all in a lather to tell us how Sugar had arranged things. He'd kept in regular touch with the folks back home. So he'd been informed how his mother had spent her life just waiting and praying for the fullness of time so that she could die and get to see her baby boy again. Nobody'd had the heart to tell her about his new job. Sugar and his relations figured that since Divine Providence wasn't going to bring them together, it was up to him.

"He got it all worked out. He saved all his money," LaBelle said, "enough to set himself up in a little place on the outskirts of Ginny Gall. You'll like it there," she assured the old lady. "People say it's not half bad. It's where the folks in Hell go for a big Saturday night."

The old lady said nothing. Something about the way her jaw clenched, though, gave me an uneasy feeling.

THE CASINO CAR FELL silent when we entered.

"*Mama!*" Sugar cried. He ran to her side and hugged her. They were both crying, and so were the girls. Even Billy-B had a strange kind of twisted smile on his face.

Mrs. Selma Green took a long, slow look around the car and its inhabitants. She did not look content. "Sugar, what are you doing in such raffish company? What bad thing have you done to bring you to such a pass? I thought I'd watched over you better than that."

Sugar drew himself up proudly. "I never did a cruel or evil thing in all my life, Mama. You know that. I never did nothing you'd've disapproved of." His eyes swept the room disdainfully, and to the damned and the crew alike he said, "Not because I much cared, one way or the other. But because I knew what you expected of me. There was bad company, at times, tried to mislead me. Wicked women urged wicked things upon me. But never was a man big enough or a woman sweet enough to make me go against your teachings."

Personally, I believed it. A man like Sugar—what need had he of violence? People just naturally made room for him. And those who wouldn't, well, that was only self-defense, wasn't it?

But his mother did not look convinced. "What, then, are you doing *here?*" And there is absolutely no way I could do justice to the scorn with which she said that last word.

Sugar looked abashed. "I dunno," he mumbled. "They just didn't like my looks, I guess."

"The truth, boy!"

"I, uh, kind of mouthed off to the Recording Angel, Mama. That's how I wound up here." He grew angry at the memory; you could see it still rankled. "You oughta be grateful we're letting a roughneck like you squeak by, he said. Don't bend no rules for me, I told him. I'd expect a little more gratitude than you're showing, he says. Ain't grateful to man nor angel, says I, for something I earned on my own right. Oh, that angel was mad enough to spit nails! He wanted me to bow and truckle to him. But I got my pride. I told him I wouldn't play nigger for nobody. And I guess that's what brought me here."

"We don't use that word," Mrs. Green said smartly. Her son looked puzzled. "The N-word."

"No, Mama," he said, all contrite.

"That's better. You're a good boy, Sugar, only sometimes you forget yourself." She allowed herself a small, austere smile. "You've got your-self in another fix, and I guess it's up to me to see you right again."

She yanked the emergency brake cord.

With a scream of brakes that could be heard all the way to Diddy-Wah-Diddy, the train ground toward a halt. In the blackness of the night I heard monstrous things struggling toward us through the shit and filth of the marshes of Styx. I heard the sound of dangerous wings.

"Oh, Mama!" Sugar wailed. "What have you done?"

"Deceit don't cure nothing. We're going to have it all out, and bring everything into the open," she said. "Stand up straight."

So there it was.

The trial was held up front in the locomotive, with two Judges towering over the engine, and the damned crowded into the front cars, climbing up on each other's shoulders and passing every word back so those in the rear could follow. To one side of the engine crouched Bagamothezth, Lord of Maggots. Two long, sagging pink paps hung limply down over his hairy belly, and living filth dropped continually from his mouth. A rank wind blew off of his foul body. To look upon his squirmily tentacled eyelids and idiot gaze was to court despair.

The other judge was an Archangel. He shone whiter than house paint and brighter than an incandescent bulb, and to look upon him ... Well. You know that awful feeling you get when you look through a telescope at some little fuzzy bit of light that's maybe not even visible to the naked eye? Only there it is, resolved into a million billion stars, cold and clear and distinct, and you and the Earth and everything you've ever known or thought about just dwindles down to insignificance? That's what the Archangel was like, only infinitely worse.

I found myself staring at first one Judge and then the other, back and forth, repulsed by the one, repelled by the majesty of the other, but unable to look away. They were neither of them something you could turn your back on.

Bagamothezth spoke in a voice shockingly sweet, even cloying. "We have no claim upon the sanctified Mrs. Selma Green. I presume you are declaring an immediate writ of sainthood upon her?"

The Archangel nodded. And with that the old lady was wrapped in blazing light and shot up into the night, dwindling like a falling star in reverse. For a second you could see her shouting and gesturing, and then she was gone.

"Sugar Green," Bagamothezth said. "How do you plead?"

Sugar stood up before the Judges, leaning forward a little as if into a great wind. His jaw was set and his eyes blazed. He wasn't about to give in an inch. "I just wanted to be with my-"

Bagamothezth clucked his tongue warningly.

"I just—"

"*Silence!*" the Archangel roared; his voice shook the train and rattled the tracks. My innards felt scrambled. Him and Sugar locked eyes. For a minute they stood thus, longer than I would've believed any individual could've stood up to such a being. At last Sugar slowly, angrily bowed his head and stared down at the ground. "How do you plead?"

"Guilty, I guess," he mumbled. "I only-"

"William Meredith Bones," the Archangel said. "How do you plead?"

Billy-B squared his shoulders and spoke up more briskly than I would've expected him to. "All my life," he said, "I have followed the dollar. It has been my North Star. It has proved comprehensible to me in ways that men and women were not. It has fetched me here where human company would have brought me to a worse place. To the best of my lights I have remained true to it." He spread his arms. "Sugar offered me money to smuggle his mother on board. What was I to do? I couldn't turn him down. Not and be true to my principles. I had no choice."

"How much," asked the Archangel in a dangerously quiet voice, "were you paid?"

Billy Bones lifted his jaw defiantly. "Forty-five dollars."

Those of us who knew Billy roared. We couldn't help it. We whooped and hollered with laughter until tears ran down our cheeks. The thought of Billy inconveniencing himself for so paltry a sum was flat-out ludicrous. He blushed angrily.

"So you did not do it for the money," said Bagamothezth.

"No," he muttered, "I guess not."

One by one, LaBelle, Afreya, and Sally were called upon to testify and acknowledge their guilt. Then I was called forward.

"Malcolm Reynolds," the Archangel said. "Your fellows have attested that, out of regard for your spiritual welfare, they did not involve you in this plot. Do you nevertheless wish to share their judgment?"

Something inside of me snapped. "No, no!" I cried. I couldn't help noticing the disgusted expression that twisted up Billy Bones' lips and the pitying looks that the girls threw my way, but I didn't care. I'd been through a lot and whatever strength I had in me was used up. Then too, I had seen what goes on in Diddy-Wah-Diddy and points south and I wanted no part of any of it. "It was all them—I had nothing to do with any of it! I swear if I'd known, I would've turned them all in before I would've let this happen!"

The Judges looked at one another. Then one of them, and for the life of me I can't remember which, cleared his throat and passed judgment.

WE GOT A NEW crew now. Only me and Goatfoot are left over from the old outfit. The train goes on. The Judges ruled that Sugar's love for his mother, and the fact that he was willing to voluntarily undergo damnation in order to be with her, was enough to justify his transfer to a better place, where his mama could keep an eye on him. LaBelle and Afreya and Sally, and Billy Bones too, were deemed to have destroyed the perfect balance of their souls that kept them shackled to the railroad. They were promoted Upstairs as well.

Me, I'd cooked my own goose. They accepted my plea of noninvolvement, and here I remained. The girls were pretty broken up about it, and to tell the truth, so was I, for a time. But there it was. Once these things been decided, there ain't no court of appeal.

I could've done without Billy-B's smirk when they handed him his halo and wings, like he'd outsmarted all the world one more time. But it was a pure and simple treat to see LaBelle, Afreya, and Sally transformed. They were good girls. They deserved the best.

With all the fuss, we were all the way to the end of the line in Beluthahatchie before anybody noticed that Jackie had taken advantage of the train being stopped for the trial to slip over the side. She believed, apparently, that it would be possible to backtrack through three hundred eighty miles of black-water marshes, evade the myriad creatures that dwell therein, the least of which is enough to freeze the marrow in your bones, cross the Acheron trestle bridge, which is half a mile high and has no place to hide when the trains cross over, and so pass undetected back to New Jersey.

It made me sad to think on it.

And that's all there is to tell. Except for one last thing.

I got a postcard, just the other day, from Chicago. It was kind of battered and worn like it'd been kicking around in the mails a long time.
No return address. Just a picture of a Bar-B-Q hut which, however, I
don't expect would be any too difficult for a determined individual to
locate. And the message:

> If one boundary is so ill-protected, then how
> difficult can the other be? I have a scheme
> going that should reap great profit with only
> moderate risk. Interested?
>
> J.
>
> P.S. Bring your uniform.

So it seems I'm going to Heaven. And why not?
I've surely seen my share of Hell.

The Mask

THIS IS A STORY they tell in the Communes: That one evening the Lady Nakashima paused atop the Rialto to admire the view, her cloak billowing as if in a breeze, and was accosted by a drunken German.

Holographic dragons curled in the air over the gondolas and vaporetti, winking in and out of existence as unseen technicians tuned their projectors for some minor festival. A bison, the lions of Saint Mark, the author of the *Commedia*. The Lady Nakashima let them fade from her consciousness. She had much to think about. ZeissOptik had filed a logo-infringement suit against one of Nakashima Commune's subsidiaries. An instability in the currency markets was holding up a planned expansion into Brazilian farm biologicals. Just that afternoon Household had discovered Yoshio, her youngest, accessing Malaysian cockfighting magazines. Something would have to be done and quickly to nip this unhealthy appetite in the bud. She also had a business dinner to plan.

"*Fuorisola* witch!" A heavy-set man gripped her arm. "I've found you at last."

"You mistake me."

Her voice was as cool and emotionless as the smooth white mask all corporate chiefs wore in public to thwart kidnappers. But the man would not let go of her, would not listen. "Betrayed!" he sobbed. "How could I have been so stupid? What a fool I was to believe you!" His breath stank of Scotch and grappa.

Four hundred eighty six gigaK of interactivity were woven into the Lady Nakashima's cloak. She was not afraid of the man's obvious strength. "In what way have you been betrayed?" Her mask relayed sub-vocalized commands to her security forces along with an image of his red face and close-cropped head.

He is the engineer Gerhardt Betelheimer, they told her, a defector from Green Hamburg, sponsored for citizenship by the Ritter Commune.

"I have lost family, friends, and homeland, all for the love of you."

"Who do you think I am?"

"Bitch! I know you all right."

"I am not she."

He carried a fragmentation pistol; her mask showed his hand, thrust deep within his overcoat, clutching it convulsively. Her political section said he had been recruited by the Lady Christiaana, her ally and some-times rival in many enterprises. Security directed her to keep him talk-ing. "Were you not well paid?" she asked.

Betelheimer shook his head bullishly. "I never wanted money."

"Everybody wants money."

The rhythm of the passing crowds changed ever so slightly as her people eased into position. Maria Delgado had often boasted that her antiterrorist unit was the best on the continent. Now she was proving it. The day-officer urged the Lady Nakashima to draw free of her accoster; her cloak was too subtle a defense to protect her from his crude weapon.

She stood her ground. "If not money," she insisted, "then what is it you want? A position, perhaps? The chance to employ your talents to the fullest?"

Betelheimer stared stupidly at her. His heart rate, perspiration, and mental indices soared. A squat woman with a thin, greasy mustache paused nearby and reached casually into her shopping bag. The Lady Nakashima silently warned her away. "All I ever asked of you was one night. Not even that—an hour! I traded all I had for a taste of something you never meant to give." He began to pull the gun from his pocket. "Now you can watch me die!"

An artist by the canal took down his canvas and folded the easel, pointing it casually toward the bridge; three schoolgirls ran laughing through the crowd, silver glints in their hands; an enormously fat African nobody could ever have felt threatened by lumbered up smiling.

Stand clear! the day-officer cried.

But the Lady Nakashima did not stand clear, but rather stilled the German's hand, saying, "I will keep my word."

He looked at her long and hard. "Not fucking likely," he said at last.

"Release me," she commanded. "Take my arm as a gentleman would. There is a pensione not far from here which we maintain for visiting dignitaries. I will take you there."

His hand slowly unclenched. He rocked on his heels with doubt and suspicion. But his instant of resolution had passed. There was nothing for him to do but go along.

The Lady Nakashima led him away from the Grand Canal and through the narrow calles and sottoportegas of San Polo. Night was falling. For all the people in the streets, she could hear the wind over the rooftops and the chirping of sparrows. One by one the church bells began to chime. She crossed herself.

Betelheimer snorted derisively.

"I am constantly amazed by you Continentals," she said with a touch of asperity. "When your pious, horrified-by-profit representatives come here to negotiate contracts, the first thing they do is visit the casinos. They bet more money than they can afford to lose, and they indulge in drugs they would never tolerate in their own territories. They hire prostitutes of the basest sort. It never occurs to one of you to attend Mass."

Political reported that Betelheimer had been involved in power-plant design. He had defected a month ago, leaving behind a wiped laboratory core and many angry colleagues. The Lady Christiaana had completed a tour of vassal corporations in the German Green States and Denmark shortly before. Her people had filed seven related patents since. Industrial espionage with seduction was deemed all but certain.

How valuable are these patents? she asked.

The question was kicked over to Jean-Luc Chicouenne in Marketing Analysis. So-so, he said with a Gallic curl of the lips that she could hear in his voice. A few technical flourishes. A useful twist or two.

"I don't give a damn about your Papist superstitions," the German said.

"The more fool you, then."

Espionage was considered sharp practice among the *fuorisoli* but nothing more, a minor vice that everyone dabbled in from time to time. And the Lady Christiaana was notorious for her flirtations. Most likely she had turned Gerhardt Betelheimer out of simple boredom.

They entered a courtyard where a Noguchi fountain, acquired at enormous cost from a bankrupt government collective in Duluth, sent sweet water laughing into the air. Sixth-generation filtration systems were the single greatest contribution the new era had given the city and as a result fountains were popular endowments. Down a calle no wider than a doorway was the home of one of the Commune's junior vice-presidents. His family had been removed, she was told. The rooms had been swept and secured. She was to go up the stairs and to the left. Her people had arranged fresh sheets and flowers.

"I WANT YOU NAKED," Betelheimer growled. He was only dimly visible in the gloom. The springs groaned when he fell onto the bed. He pulled off his clothes quickly, angrily, throwing his boots noisily across the room. The Lady Nakashima undressed more slowly, more deliberately.

"May I retain my mask?"

"I don't give a shit if I never see your face again."

With a whisper of silk, the last of her clothing slipped to the floor. Against Security's objections, she put the cloak aside. She powered down her mask; it was only a mask now. Betelheimer grinned nastily as she knelt down on the bed.

"That's more like—" Reaching for her, he clumsily knocked a framed picture from the end table. Petit bourgeois reflexes kicked in and he leaned over to retrieve it. It was a steelpoint portrait of Dante Alighieri.

Betelheimer's brows knitted. "It's that damned allegorist again. His fucking picture is everywhere in this town. Why?" She said nothing. "I asked you a question, whore! He never lived here—he was a goddamned Florentine. What is he to you?"

"He was a *fuoruscito*," the Lady Nakashima said quietly. "An exile. His political enemies had expelled him from his own city. He was a man who understood the pain of loss. Like us."

Something in her voice burned through the German's haze of alcohol and self-pity. Brusquely, he swung up a hand to trip a switch beam. Light flared.

The Lady Nakashima was of a height with the Lady Christiaana, but that was all. The light revealed her ten-years-older breasts, her softening belly, her heavier thighs, her shorter legs. Sober, Gerhardt Betelheimer could never have confused the two.

He stared up in horror. "You're not her!"

"So I told you."

She looked down at his stocky torso, his round and pinkish stomach, with mingled compassion and disdain. His face was a parody of remorse; he was capable only of the extremes of emotion, it seemed, anger or anguish but nothing in between. His hands tried to cover his erect penis. It bounced free of them, like a ridiculous rubber toy. "You're not her," he repeated. "Oh God. Oh God. Forgive me, I—I mistook you for somebody else."

She touched his lips with one cool finger.

"Your lady made a promise. I will keep it for her." A gesture dimmed the lights, returning the mask of twilight to the room. Reaching into darkness, she moved his hands to her hips.

"But why?" he asked.

"What binds one of us," she said, "binds us all."

And she did for him as had been promised.

For this was the Lady Nakashima honored in the boardrooms and palazzos, and by her husband as well. Gerhardt Betelheimer found work with the Bache-Rockefeller Commune, and in later years rose high in the councils of Venice. The Lady Christiaana was censured for her part in the affair, a setback that took her most of a decade to recover from.

THIS IS A STORY the *fuorisoli* tell and here is the lesson they wish you to take away from it: They lost Manhattan; they lost Japan; they lost Britain and Hong Kong and Taiwan out of the folly of their arrogance. When anticorporate ideologies first swept the globe they relied entirely on hirelings and employees to fight their battles. They did not accept responsibility. They enjoyed the fruit that others had planted and thus it was taken away from them. But this final island they would not lose.

Here they would make their stand.

Mother Grasshopper

IN THE YEAR ONE, we came in an armada of a million spacecraft to settle upon, colonize, and claim for our homeland this giant grasshopper on which we now dwell.

We dared not land upon the wings for, though the cube-square rule held true and their most rapid motions would be imperceptible on a historic scale, random nerve firings resulted in pre-movement tremors measured at Richter 11. So we opted to build in the eyes, in the faceted mirrorlands that reflected infinities of flatness, a shimmering Iowa, the architecture of home.

It was an impossible project and one, perhaps, that was doomed from the start. But such things are obvious only in retrospect. We were a young and vigorous race then. Everything seemed possible.

Using shaped temporal fields, we force-grew trees which we cut down to build our cabins. We planted sod and wheat and buffalo. In one vivid and unforgettable night of technology we created a layer of limestone bedrock half a mile deep upon which to build our towns. And when our work was done, we held hoe-downs in a thousand county seats all across the eye-lands.

We created new seasons, including Snow, after the patterns of those we had known in antiquity, but the night sky we left unaltered, for this was to be our home ... now and forever. The unfamiliar constellations would grow their own legends over the ages; there would be time. Generations passed, and cities grew with whorls of suburbs like the arms of spiral galaxies around them, for we were lonely, as were the thousands and millions we decanted who grew like the trees of the cisocellar plains that were as thick as the ancient Black Forest.

I was a young man, newly bearded, hardly much more than a shirt-tail child, on that Harvest day when the stranger walked into town.

This was so unusual an event (and for you to whom a town of ten thousand necessarily means that there *will be strangers*, I despair of explaining) that children came out to shout and run at his heels, while we older citizens, conscious of our dignity, stood in the doorways of our shops, factories, and co-ops to gaze ponderously in his general direction. Not quite *at* him, you understand, but over his shoulder, into the flat, mesmeric plains and the infinite white skies beyond.

He claimed to have come all the way from the equatorial abdomen, where gravity is three times eye-normal, and this was easy enough to believe, for he was ungodly strong. With my own eyes I once saw him take a dollar coin between thumb and forefinger and bend it in half—and a steel dollar at that! He also claimed to have walked the entire distance, which nobody believed, not even me.

"If you'd walked even half that far," I said, "I reckon you'd be the most remarkable man as ever lived."

He laughed at that and ruffled my hair. "Well, maybe I am," he said. "Maybe I am."

I flushed and took a step backwards, hand on the bandersnatch-skin hilt of my fighting knife. I was as feisty as a bantam rooster in those days, and twice as quick to take offense. "Mister, I'm afraid I'm going to have to ask you to step outside."

The stranger looked at me. Then he reached out and, without the slightest hint of fear or anger or even regret, touched my arm just below the shoulder. He did it with no particular speed and yet somehow I could not react fast enough to stop him. And that touch, light though it was, paralyzed my arm, leaving it withered and useless, even as it is today.

He put his drink down on the bar, and said, "Pick up my knapsack."

I did.

"Follow me."

So it was that without a word of farewell to my family or even a backward glance, I left New Auschwitz forever.

THAT NIGHT, OVER A campfire of eel grass and dried buffalo chips, we ate a dinner of refried beans and fatback bacon. It was a new and clumsy experience for me, eating one-handed. For a long time, neither one of us spoke. Finally I said, "Are you a magician?"

The stranger sighed. "Maybe so," he said. "Maybe I am."

"You have a name?"

"No."

"What do we do now?"

"Business." He pushed his plate toward me. "I cooked. It's your turn to wash."

Our business entailed constant travel. We went to Brinkerton with cholera and to Roxborough with typhus. We passed through Denver and Venice and Saint Petersburg and left behind fleas, rats, and plague. In Upper Black Eddy, it was ebola. We never stayed long enough to see the results of our work, but I read the newspapers afterwards, and it was about what you would expect.

Still, *on the whole,* humanity prospered. Where one city was decimated, another was expanding. The overspilling hospitals of one county created a market for the goods of a dozen others. The survivors had babies.

We walked to Tylersburg, Rutledge, and Uniontown and took wagons to Shoemakersville, Confluence, and South Gibson. Booked onto steam trains for Mount Lebanon, Mount Bethel, Mount Aetna, and Mount Nebo and diesel trains to McKeesport, Reinholds Station, and Broomall. Boarded buses to Carbondale, Feasterville, June Bug, and Lincoln Falls. Caught commuter flights to Paradise, Nickel Mines, Niantic, and Zion. The time passed quickly.

Then one shocking day my magician announced that he was going home.

"Home?" I said. "What about your work?"

"*Our* work, Daniel," he said gently. "I expect you'll do as good a job as ever I did." He finished packing his few possessions into a carpet bag.

"You can't!" I cried.

With a wink and a sad smile, he slipped out the door.

For a time—long or short, I don't know—I sat motionless, unthinking, unseeing. Then I leaped to my feet, threw open the door, and looked up and down the empty street. Blocks away, toward the train station, was a scurrying black speck.

Leaving the door open behind me, I ran after it.

I just missed the afternoon express to Lackawanna. I asked the stationmaster when was the next train after it. He said tomorrow. Had he seen a tall man carrying a carpetbag, looking thus and so? Yes, he had. Where was he? On the train to Lackawanna. Nothing more heading that way today. Did he know where I could rent a car? Yes, he did. Place just down the road.

Maybe I'd've caught the magician if I hadn't gone back to the room to pick up my bags. Most likely not. At Lackawanna station I found he'd taken the bus to Johnstown. In Johnstown, he'd moved on to Erie and there the trail ran cold. It took me three days' hard questioning to pick it up again.

For a week I pursued him thus, like a man possessed.

Then I awoke one morning and my panic was gone. I knew I wasn't going to catch my magician anytime soon. I took stock of my resources, counted up what little cash-money I had, and laid out a strategy. Then I went shopping. Finally, I hit the road. I'd have to be patient, dogged, wily, but I knew that, given enough time, I'd find him.

Find him, and kill him too.

The trail led me to Harper's Ferry, at the very edge of the oculus. Behind was civilization. Ahead was nothing but thousands of miles of empty chitin-lands.

People said he'd gone south, off the lens entirely.

Back at my boarding house, I was approached by one of the lodgers. He was a skinny man with a big mustache and sleeveless white t-shirt that hung from his skinny shoulders like wet laundry on a muggy Sunday.

"What you got in that bag?"

"Black death," I said, "infectious meningitis, tuberculosis. You name it."

He thought for a bit. "I got this wife," he said at last. "I don't suppose you could . . ."

"I'll take a look at her," I said, and hoisted the bag.

We went upstairs to his room.

She lay in the bed, eyes closed. There was an IV needle in her arm, hooked up to a drip feed. She looked young, but of course that meant nothing. Her hair, neatly brushed and combed, lay across the coverlet almost to her waist, was white—white as snow, as death, as finest bone china.

"How long has she been like this?" I asked.

"Ohhhh . . ." He blew out his cheeks. "Forty-seven, maybe fifty years?"

"You her father?"

"Husband. Was, anyhow. Not sure how long the vows were meant to hold up under these conditions: can't say I've kept 'em any too well. You got something that bag for her?" He said it as casual as he could, but his eyes were big and spooked-looking.

I made my decision. "Tell you what," I said. "I'll give you forty dollars for her."

"The sheriff wouldn't think much of what you just said," the man said low and quiet.

"No. But then, I suppose I'll be off of the eye-lands entirely before he knows a word of it."

I picked up my syringe.

"Well? Is it a deal or not?"

HER NAME WAS VICTORIA. We were a good three days march into the chitin before she came out of the trance state characteristic of the interim zombie stage of Recovery. I'd fitted her with a pack, walking shoes, and a good stout stick, and she strode along head up, eyes blank, speaking in the tongues of angels afloat between the stars.

"—cisgalactic phase intercept," she said. "Do you read? Das Uber-raumboot zuruckgegenerinnernte. Verstehen? Anadaemonic mesotechnological conflict strategizing. Drei tausenden Affen mit Laseren! Hello? Is anybody—"

Then she stumbled over a rock, cried out in pain, and said, "Where am I?"

I stopped, spread a map on the ground, and got out my pocket gravitometer. It was a simple thing: a glass cylinder filled with aerogel and a bright orange ceramic bead. The casing was tin, with a compressor screw at the top, a calibrated scale along the side, and the words "Flynn & Co." at the bottom. I flipped it over, watched the bead slowly fall. I tightened the screw a notch, then two, then three, increasing the aerogel's density. At five, the bead stopped. I read the gauge, squinted up at the sun, and then jabbed a finger on an isobar to one edge of the map.

"Right here," I said. "Just off the lens. See?"

"I don't—" She was trembling with panic. Her dilated eyes shifted wildly from one part of the empty horizon to another. Then suddenly, sourcelessly, she burst into tears.

Embarrassed, I looked away. When she was done crying, I patted the ground. "Sit." Sniffling, she obeyed. "How old are you, Victoria?"

"How old am . . . ? Sixteen?" she said tentatively. "Seventeen?" Then, "Is that really my name?"

"It was. The woman you were grew tired of life, and injected herself with a drug that destroys the ego and with it all trace of personal history." I sighed. "So in one sense you're still Victoria, and in another sense you're not. What she did was illegal, though; you can never go back to the oculus. You'd be locked into jail for the rest of your life."

She looked at me through eyes newly young, almost childlike in their experience, and still wet with tears. I was prepared for hysteria, grief, rage. But all she said was, "Are you a magician?"

That rocked me back on my heels. "Well—yes," I said. "I suppose I am."

She considered that silently for a moment. "So what happens to me now?"

"Your job is to carry that pack. We also go turn-on-turn with the dishes." I straightened, folding the map. "Come on. We've got a far way yet to go."

We commenced marching, in silence at first. But then, not many miles down the road and to my complete astonishment, Victoria began to *sing!*

WE FOLLOWED THE faintest of paths—less a trail than the memory of a dream of the idea of one—across the chitin. Alongside it grew an occasional patch of grass. A lot of wind-blown loess had swept across the chitin-lands over the centuries. It caught in cracks in the carapace and gave purchase to fortuitous seeds. Once I even saw a rabbit. But before I could point it out to Victoria, I saw something else. Up ahead, in a place where the shell had powdered and a rare rainstorm had turned the powder briefly to mud, were two overlapping tire prints. A motorbike had been by here, and recently.

I stared at the tracks for a long time, clenching and unclenching my good hand.

The very next day we came upon a settlement.

It was a hardscrabble place. Just a windmill to run the pump that brought up a trickle of ichor from a miles-deep well, a refinery to process the stuff edible, and a handful of unpainted clapboard buildings and Quonset huts. Several battered old pickup trucks sat rusting under the limitless sky.

A gaunt man stood by the gate, waiting for us. His jaw was hard, his backbone straight and his hands empty. But I noted here and there a shiver of movement in a window or from the open door of a shed, and I made no mistake but that there were weapons trained upon us.

"Name's Rivera," the man said when we came up to him.

I swept off my bowler hat. "Daniel. This's Miss Victoria, my ward."

"Passing through?"

"Yessir, I am, and I see no reason I should ever pass this way again.

If you have food for sale, I'll pay you market rates. But if not, why, with your permission, we'll just keep on moving on."

"Fair spoken." From somewhere Rivera produced a cup of water, and handed it to us. I drank half, handed the rest to Victoria. She shivered as it went down.

"Right good," I said. "And cold too."

"We have a heat pump," Rivera said with grudging pride. "C'mon inside. Let's see what the women have made us to eat."

Then the children came running out, whooping and hollering, too many to count, and the adult people behind them, whom I made out to be twenty in number. They made us welcome.

They were good people, if outlaws, and as hungry for news and gossip as anybody can be. I told them about a stump speech I had heard made by Tyler B. Morris, who was running for governor of the Northern Department, and they spent all of dinnertime discussing it. The food was good, too—ham and biscuits with red-eye gravy, sweet yams with butter, and apple cobbler to boot. If I hadn't seen their chemical complex, I'd've never guessed it for synthetic. There were lace curtains in the window, brittle-old but clean, and I noted how carefully the leftovers were stored away for later.

After we'd eaten, Rivera caught my eye and gestured with his chin. We went outside, and he led me to a shed out back. He unpadlocked the door and we stepped within. A line of ten people lay unmoving on plain-built beds. They were each catheterized to a drip-bag of processed ichor. Light from the door caught their hair, ten white haloes in the gloom.

"We brought them with us," Rivera said. "Thought we'd be doing well enough to make a go of it. Lately, though, I don't know, maybe it's the drought, but the blood's been running thin, and it's not like we have the money to have a new well drilled."

"I understand." Then, because it seemed a good time to ask, "There was a man came by this way probably less'n a week ago. Tall, riding a—"

"He wouldn't help," Harry said. "Said it wasn't his responsibility. Then, before he drove off, the sonofabitch tried to buy some of our food." He turned and spat. "He told us you and the woman would be coming along. We been waiting."

"Wait. He told you I'd have a woman with me?"

"It's not just us we have to think of!" he said with sudden vehemence. "There's the young fellers, too. They come along and all a man's stiff-necked talk about obligations and morality goes right out the window. Sometimes I think how I could come out here with a length of iron pipe and—well." He shook his head and then, almost pleadingly, said, "Can't you do something?"

"I think so." A faint creaking noise made me turn then. Victoria stood frozen in the doorway. The light through her hair made of it a white flare. I closed my eyes, wishing she hadn't stumbled across this thing. In a neutral voice I said, "Get my bag."

Then Rivera and I set to haggling out a price.

WE LEFT THE SETTLEMENT with a goodly store of food and driving their third-best pickup truck. It was a pathetic old thing and the shocks were scarce more than a memory. We bumped and jolted toward the south.

For a long time Victoria did not speak. Then she turned to me and angrily blurted, "You *killed* them!"

"It was what they wanted."

"How can you say that?" She twisted in the seat and punched me in the shoulder. Hard. "How can you sit there and ... *say* that?"

"Look," I said testily. "It's simple mathematics. You could make an equation out of it. They can only drill so much ichor. That ichor makes only so much food. Divide that by the number of mouths there are to feed and hold up the result against what it takes to keep one alive. So much food, so many people. If the one's smaller than the other, you starve. And the children wanted to live. The folks in the shed didn't."

"They could go back! Nobody *has* to live out in the middle of nowhere trying to scratch food out of nothing!"

"I counted one suicide for every two waking adults. Just how welcome do you think they'd be, back to the oculus, with so many suicides living among them? More than likely that's what drove them out here in the first place."

"Well ... nobody would be starving if they didn't insist on having so many damn children."

"How can you stop people from having children?" I asked.

There was no possible answer to that and we both knew it. Victoria leaned her head against the cab window, eyes squeezed tight shut, as far from me as she could get. "You could have woken them up! But no, you had your bag of goodies and you wanted to play. I'm surprised you didn't kill *me* when you had the chance."

"Vickie ..."

"Don't speak to me!"

She started to weep.

I wanted to hug her and comfort her, she was so miserable. But I was driving, and I only had the one good arm. So I didn't. Nor did I explain to her why it was that nobody chose to simply wake the suicides up.

THAT EVENING, AS USUAL, I got out the hatchet and splintered enough chitin for a campfire. I was sitting by it, silent, when Victoria got out the jug of rough liquor the settlement folks had brewed from ichor. "You be careful with that stuff," I said. "It sneaks up on you. Don't forget, whatever experience you've had drinking got left behind in your first life."

"Then *you* drink!" she said, thrusting a cup at me. "I'll follow your lead. When you stop, I'll stop."

I swear I never suspected what she had in mind. And it had been a long while since I'd tasted alcohol. So, like a fool, I took her intent at face value. I had a drink. And then another.

Time passed.

We talked some, we laughed some. Maybe we sang a song or two.

Then, somehow, Victoria had shucked off her blouse and was dancing. She whirled around the campfire, her long skirts lifting up above her knees and occasionally flirting through the flames so that the hem browned and smoked but never quite caught fire.

This wildness seemed to come out of nowhere. I watched her, alarmed and aroused, too drunk to think clearly, too entranced even to move.

Finally she collapsed gracefully at my feet. The firelight was red on her naked back, shifting with each gasping breath she took. She looked up at me through her long, sweat-tangled hair, and her eyes were like amber, dark as cypress swamp water, brown and bottomless. Eyes a man could drown in.

I pulled her toward me. Laughing, she surged forward, collapsing upon me, tumbling me over backwards, fumbling with my belt and then the fly of my jeans. Then she had my cock out and stiff and I'd pushed her skirt up above her waist so that it seemed she was wearing nothing but a thick red sash. And I rolled her over on her back and she was reaching down between her legs to guide me in and she was smiling and lovely.

I plunged deep, deep, deep into her, and oh god but it felt fine. Like that eye-opening shock you get when you plunge into a cold lake for the first time on a hot summer's day and the water wraps itself around you and feels so impossibly good. Only this was warm and slippery-slick and a thousand times better. Then I was telling her things, telling her I needed her, I wanted her, I loved her, over and over again.

I AWOKE THE NEXT morning with a raging hangover. Victoria was sitting in the cab of the pickup, brushing her long white hair in the rearview mirror and humming to herself.

"Well," she said, amused. "Look what the cat dragged in. There's water in the jerrycans. Have yourself a drink. I expect we could also spare a cup for you to wash your face with."

"Look," I said. "I'm sorry about last night."

"No you're not."

"I maybe said some foolish things, but——"

Her eyes flashed storm-cloud dark. "You weren't speaking near so foolish then as you are now. You meant every damn word, and I'm holding you to them." Then she laughed. "You'd best get at that water. You look hideous."

So I dragged myself off.

Overnight, Victoria had changed. Her whole manner, the way she held herself, even the way she phrased her words, told me that she wasn't a child anymore. She was a woman.

The thing I'd been dreading had begun.

"RESISTANCE IS USELESS," Victoria read. "For mine is the might and power of the Cosmos Itself!" She'd found a comic book stuck back under the seat and gone through it three times, chuckling to herself, while the truck rattled down that near-nonexistent road. Now she put it down. "Tell me something," she said. "How do you know your magician came by this way?"

"I just know is all," I said curtly. I'd given myself a shot of B-complex vitamins, but my head and gut still felt pretty ragged. Nor was it particularly soothing having to drive this idiot truck one-armed. And, anyway, I couldn't say just how I knew. It was a feeling I had, a certainty.

"I had a dream last night. After we, ummmm, danced."

I didn't look at her.

"I was on a flat platform, like a railroad station, only enormous. It stretched halfway to infinity. There were stars all around me, thicker and more colorful than I'd ever imagined them. Bright enough to make your eyes ache. Enormous machines were everywhere, golden, spaceships I suppose. They were taking off and landing with delicate little puffs of air, like it was the easiest thing imaginable to do. My body was so light I felt like I was going to float up among them. You ever hear of a place like that?"

"No."

"There was a man waiting for me there. He had the saddest smile, but cold, cruel eyes. Hello, Victoria, he said, and How did you know my name, I asked. Oh, I keep a close eye on Daniel, he said, I'm grooming him for an important job. Then he showed me a syringe. Do you know what's in here? he asked me. The liquid in it was so blue it shone." She fell silent.

"What did you say?"

"I just shook my head. Mortality, he said. It's an improved version of the drug you shot yourself up with fifty years ago. Tell Daniel it'll be waiting for him at Sky Terminus, where the great ships come and go. That was all. You think it means anything?"

I shook my head.

She picked up the comic book, flipped it open again. "Well, anyway, it was a strange dream."

THAT NIGHT, AFTER doing the dishes, I went and sat down on the pickup's sideboard and stared into the fire, thinking. Victoria came and sat down beside me. She put a hand on my leg. It was the lightest of touches, but it sent all my blood rushing to my cock.

She smiled at that and looked up into my eyes. "Resistance is useless," she said.

Afterwards we lay together between blankets on the ground. Looking up at the night sky. It came to me then that being taken away from normal life young as I had been, all my experience with love had come before the event and all my experience with sex after, and that I'd therefore never before known them both together. So that in this situation I was as naive and unprepared for what was happening to us as Victoria was.

Which was how I admitted to myself I loved Victoria. At the time it seemed the worst possible thing that could've happened to me.

WE SAW IT FOR the first time that next afternoon. It began as a giddy feeling, like a mild case of vertigo, and a vague thickening at the center of the sky as if it were going dark from the inside out. This was accompanied by a bulging up of the horizon, as if God Himself had placed hands flat on either edge and leaned forward, bowing it upward.

Then my inner ear *knew* that the land which had been flat as flat for all these many miles was now slanting downhill all the way to the horizon. That was the gravitational influence of all that mass before us. Late into the day it just appeared. It was like a conjuring trick. One moment it wasn't there at all and then, with the slightest of perceptual shifts, it dominated the vision. It was so distant that it took on the milky backscatter color of the sky and it went up so high you literally couldn't see the top. It was—I knew this now—our destination:

The antenna.

Even driving the pickup truck, it took three days after first sighting to reach its base.

On the morning of one of those days, Victoria suddenly pushed aside her breakfast and ran for the far side of the truck. That being the only privacy to be had for hundreds of miles around.

I listened to her retching. Knowing there was only one thing it could be.

She came back, pale and shaken. I got a plastic collection cup out of my bag. "Pee into this," I told her. When she had, I ran a quick diagnostic. It came up positive.

"Victoria," I said. "I've got an admission to make. I haven't been exactly straight with you about the medical consequences of your . . . condition."

It was the only time I ever saw her afraid. "My God," she said, "What is it? Tell me! What's happening to me?"

"Well, to begin with, you're pregnant."

THERE WERE NO ROADS to the terminus, for all that it was visible from miles off. It lay nestled at the base of the antenna, and to look at the empty and trackless plains about it, you'd think there was neither reason for its existence nor possibility of any significant traffic there.

Yet the closer we got, the more people we saw approaching it. They appeared out of the everywhere and nothingness like hydrogen atoms being pulled into existence in the stressed spaces between galaxies, or like shards of ice crystallizing at random in supercooled superpure water. You'd see one far to your left, maybe strolling along with a walking stick slung casually over one shoulder and a gait that just told you she was whistling. Then beyond her in the distance a puff of dust from what could only be a half-track. And to the right, a man in a wide-brimmed hat sitting ramrod-straight in the saddle of a native parasite larger than any elephant. With every hour a different configuration, and all converging.

Roads materialized underfoot. By the time we arrived at the terminus, they were thronged with people.

The terminal building itself was as large as a city, all gleaming white marble arches and colonnades and parapets and towers. Pennants snapped in the wind. Welcoming musicians played at the feet of the columns. An enormous holographic banner dopplering slowly through the rainbow from infrared to ultraviolet and back again, read:

BYZANTIUM PORT AUTHORITY
MAGNETIC-LEVITATION MASS TRANSIT DIVISION
GROUND TERMINUS

Somebody later told me it provided employment for a hundred thousand people, and I believed him.

Victoria and I parked the truck by the front steps. I opened the door for her and helped her gingerly out. Her belly was enormous by then, and her sense of balance was off. We started up the steps. Behind us, a uniformed lackey got in the pickup and drove it away.

The space within was grander than could have been supported had the terminus not been located at the cusp of antenna and forehead, where the proximate masses each canceled out much of the other's attraction. There were countless ticket windows, all of carved mahogany. I settled Victoria down on a bench—her feet were tender—and went to stand in line. When I got to the front, the ticket-taker glanced at a computer screen and said, "May I help you, sir?"

"Two tickets, first-class. Up."

He tapped at the keyboard and a little device spat out two crisp pasteboard tickets. He slid them across the polished brass counter, and I reached for my wallet. "How much?" I said.

He glanced at his computer and shook his head. "No charge for you, Mister Daniel. Professional courtesy."

"How did you know my name?"

"You're expected." Then, before I could ask any more questions,

"That's all I can tell you, sir. I can neither speak nor understand your language. It is impossible for me to converse with you."

"Then what the hell," I said testily, "are we doing now?"

He flipped the screen around for me to see. On it was a verbatim transcript of our conversation. The last line was: I SIMPLY READ WHAT'S ON THE SCREEN, SIR.

Then he turned it back toward himself and said, "I simply read what's—"

"Yeah, yeah, I know," I said. And went back to Victoria.

EVEN AT MAG-LEV speeds, it took two days to travel the full length of the antenna. To amuse myself, I periodically took out my gravitometer and made readings. You'd think the figures would diminish exponentially as we climbed out of the gravity well. But because the antennae swept backward, over the bulk of the grasshopper, rather than forward and away, the gravitational gradient of our journey was quite complex. It lessened rapidly at first, grew temporarily stronger, and then lessened again, in the complex and lovely flattening sine-wave known as a Sheffield curve. You could see it reflected in the size of the magnetic rings we flashed through, three per minute, how they grew skinnier then fatter and finally skinnier still as we flew upward.

On the second day, Victoria gave birth. It was a beautiful child, a boy. I wanted to name him Hector, after my father, but Victoria was set on Jonathan, and as usual I gave in to her.

Afterwards, though, I studied her features. There were crow's-feet at the corners of her eyes, or maybe "laugh lines" is more appropriate, given Victoria's personality. The lines to either side of her mouth had deepened. Her whole face had a haggard cast to it. Looking at her, I felt a sadness so large and pervasive it seemed to fill the universe.

She was aging along her own exponential curve. The process was accelerating now, and I was not at all certain she would make it to Sky Terminus. It would be a close thing in either case.

I could see that Victoria knew it too. But she was happy as she hugged our child. "It's been a good life," she said. "I wish you could have grown with me—don't pout, you're so solemn, Daniel!—but other than that I have no complaints."

I looked out the window for a minute. I had known her for only— what?—a week, maybe. But in that brief time she had picked me up, shaken me off, and turned my life around. She had changed everything. When I looked back, I was crying.

"Death is the price we pay for children, isn't it?" she said. "Down below, they've made death illegal. But they're only fooling themselves. They think it's possible to live forever. They think there are no limits to growth. But everything dies—people, stars, the universe. And once it's over, all lives are the same length."

"I guess I'm just not so philosophical as you. It's a damned hard thing to lose your wife."

"Well, at least you figured that one out."

"What one?

"That I'm your wife." She was silent a moment. Then she said, "I had another dream. About your magician. And he explained about the drug. The one he called mortality."

"Huh," I said. Not really caring.

"The drug I took, you wake up and you burn through your life in a matter of days. With the new version, you wake up with a normal human lifespan, the length people had before the immortality treatments. One hundred fifty, two hundred years—that's not so immediate. The suicides are kept alive because their deaths come on so soon; it's too shocking to the survivors' sensibilities. The new version shows its effects too slowly to be stopped."

I stroked her long white hair. So fine. So very, very brittle. "Let's not talk about any of this."

Her eyes blazed "Let's *do!* Don't pretend to be a fool, Daniel. People multiply. There's only so much food, water, space. If nobody dies, there'll come a time when everybody dies." Then she smiled again, fondly, the way you might at a petulant but still promising child. "You know what's required of you, Daniel. And I'm proud of you for being worthy of it."

Sky Terminus was enormous, dazzling, beyond description. It was exactly like in Vickie's dream. I helped her out onto the platform. She could barely stand by then, but her eyes were bright and curious. Jonathan was asleep against my chest in a baby-sling.

Whatever held the atmosphere to the platform, it offered no resistance to the glittering, brilliantly articulated ships that rose and descended from all parts. Strange cargoes were unloaded by even stranger longshoremen.

"I'm not as excited by all this as I would've been when I was younger," Victoria murmured. "But somehow I find it more satisfying. Does that make sense to you?"

I began to say something. But then, abruptly, the light went out of her eyes. Stiffening, she stared straight ahead of herself into nothing that I could see. There was no emotion in her face whatsoever.

"Vickie?" I said.

Slowly, she tumbled to the ground.

It was then, while I stood stunned and unbelieving, that the magician came walking up to me.

In my imagination I'd run through this scene a thousand times: Leaving my bag behind, I stumbled off the train, toward him. He made no move to escape. I flipped open my jacket with a shrug of the shoulder, drew out the revolver with my good hand, and fired.

Now, though ...

He looked sadly down at Victoria's body and put an arm around my shoulders.

"God," he said, "don't they just break your heart?"

I stayed on a month at the Sky Terminus to watch my son grow up. Jonathan died without offspring and was given an orbital burial. His coffin circled the grasshopper seven times before the orbit decayed and it scratched a bright meteoric line down into the night. The flare lasted about as long as would a struck sulfur match.

He'd been a good man, with a wicked sense of humor that never came from my side of the family.

So now I wander the world. Civilizations rise and fall about me. Only I remain unchanged. Where things haven't gotten too bad, I scatter mortality. Where they have I unleash disease.

I go where I go and I do my job. The generations rise up like wheat before me, and like a harvester I mow them down. Sometimes—not often—I go off by myself, to think and remember. Then I stare up into the night, into the colonized universe, until the tears rise up in my sight and drown the swarming stars.

I am Death and this is my story.

Riding the Giganotosaur

"HOW DOES IT FEEL?"

"It feels *great!*"

The physical therapist lifted one of George Weskowski's arms and flexed it, to check its range of motion. It took all of her strength to do so, even though George wasn't resisting. She frowned. "No need to roar," she chided.

"Sorry."

"There's a transmitter chip connected to your speech centers. Just subvocalize, and I can pick up what you're saying on this radio. Tell me how your head feels."

He considered. "Fine. Just fine."

"No aches, itches, irritation around the sutures?"

"No."

"Dizziness, nausea, hallucinations, phantom sounds or smells, mood swings, loss of appetite?"

"I could eat a horse!"

The therapist held up a mirror. "Now look at yourself."

His skin was green, mottled with yellow, and covered with pebbly scales. His eyes were small, beady, homicidal. His arms, massive compared to what he had once possessed but puny compared to the rest of his new body, ended in three scimitar-taloned fingers. His legs were enormous. So was his tail. Opening his mouth revealed a murderous array of razor-sharp teeth.

"Oh yes," he cried rapturously. "Yes, oh my goodness, yes, absolutely, yes, yes."

"You like it?"

"It's everything I ever dreamed of being."

"The appearance doesn't bother you?"

"I look terrific!"

He did, too. *Giganotosaurus* was the biggest, baddest predator ever to walk the Earth—larger, heavier, and more fearsome even than the old record-holder, *Tyrannosaurus rex.* "The king is dead," George whispered to himself. "Long live the king."

"What was that?"

"I said I'm eager to begin therapy, Dr. Alvarez."

"Good. Then let's try standing up."

This, however, was nowhere near so satisfactory. George lurched eagerly to his knees and promptly overbalanced. He leaned against the side of the barn, making the wood creak, to ease his descent to the straw-covered ground. "Damn!"

"Careful—you weigh over eight tons now. And your leg bones are hollow—like a bird's. You could easily break one doing that."

"I'll remember."

"Good. Now your problem is that you're *pushing* it. It's only your forebrain we've grafted atop the existing brain, remember, and it isn't familiar with the body. However, the hindbrain knows what to do. All the motor skills are already fully functional. Don't intellectualize. Just picture what you want. The original brain has no defenses against you; it accepts your thoughts as its own. What you have to do is learn to *ride* it."

"I'll try," he said humbly.

"Excellent. We'll begin by ..."

SIX HOURS LATER, George was walking easily around and around the corral. He had even essayed a few brief sprints, with varied results. As he walked, he breathed deeply of the Cretaceous air, savoring the intoxicating mix of greenery and resins, the dark, heady undersmell of decay.

Old Patagonia Station was located on a flood plain, with a fern prairie to one side, and a forest of towering conifers to the other. There was a stream nearby—he could smell it—and the glint of a lake far off in the distance. It was a fresh, wondrous, unexplored world, and he was anxious to be off and into it.

"When can I begin field work?" he asked.

Dr. Alvarez pursed her lips. "You're still recovering from the surgery. We won't be making that decision for a few weeks."

"But . . ." He waved a futile little paw outward, toward the lands that stretched to a misty blue horizon and beyond, unspoiled, virginal, his for the taking. He'd have to travel clear around the world to encounter a man-made structure. All the way back to the time station and its outbuildings behind him—and once they were gone, there wouldn't be anything more like them for another ninety million years. "I thought I could get in some hunting before nightfall."

"That reminds me." The therapist went back into the barn and returned, dragging a heavy sack behind her. With a grunt, she hoisted it up and emptied it into a trough.

"What's that?"

"A specially-formulated blend of protein, roughage, and vitamins. The wranglers call it dino chow." She paused. "That's our little joke."

"You expect me to eat *kibble?*" he asked, horrified.

The prairie to one side of Old Patagonia Station had been browsed clear by the migratory herds of titanosaurs, rebbachisaurs, and andesaurs that dominated the local ecology. The forest, though, with its close-thronged trees, presented the colossal herbivores with an impenetrable barrier. They could feed on the leaves at its border, but nothing more. The interior was forbidden them.

But not George.

Large as he was, he was slim enough to slip between the trees—just. He ran, leaped over the fence with a bound, and was gone into the woods. It was a beautiful, sunshiny day, and his greenish-yellow skin blended with the foliage perfectly.

THAT EVENING HE made his first kill.

He experienced his new life in three distinct phases. There was the initial heady rush of freedom, when he ran as far and fast as his powerful new body would take him, wild with animal joy. Then he settled down into a happy daze. No more bosses! No more networking, no more memos, no more meetings! He'd never see the inside of an office again, sweat out another cold sell, face down another IRS audit. He sauntered along aimlessly, occasionally letting out a roar, just to watch the bright flocks of birds with taloned wings take flight in fear. This phase lasted him about an hour.

Then his stomach rumbled, and suddenly he discovered what a frustrating time and place the Patagonian Cretaceous could be.

The problem was that he hadn't the slightest idea of how to hunt, and he was too impatient to simply sit back and let the giganotosaur's old brain take over.

He tried. Twice he saw herbivores in the distance, and his body trembled with blood-lust and began striding toward them. But then—he couldn't help it—he'd bellowed with hunger and bravado, and charged. Each time, the creatures spooked and ran, too fast for him to catch up with them. Those suckers could move! They ran a lot faster than anything that size had any right to run.

He, in turn, was a sprinter—capable of the short, shocking dash that could do the job *if* he were close enough to overtake his target in the first mad rush of his attack. Before the creature could get its unwieldy bulk moving. Then, briefly, he was the fastest animal in existence. But he could only maintain that insane spurt of speed for a few minutes. More than that, his energy would give out, and his prey would escape every time.

So he realized he would have to stalk the brutes.

Running lightly along the fringe between forest and prairie, George saw in the distance a number of black specks. As he came closer, the specks resolved themselves into long-necked giants feeding upon the tall trees at the edge of the prairie.

Titanosaurs. They were immense things, averaging some twenty-five to thirty meters in length. It was hard to see how they managed to eat enough to keep such tremendous bodies fed. Even a small one would rot long before George could eat it all.

Slyly, he slipped into the forest.

With a stealthy ease that both pleased and astonished him, he sped quietly between the dark trees. It was a climax forest, so there was plenty of room between the trunks. The ground was covered with a litter of decomposing leaves, which deadened the sound of his footfalls. He was able to get so close to the titanosaurs that he could hear them chomping down on leaves and branches, and smell the stinking mounds of dung they left behind.

Cautiously, he drew closer.

Slanting rays of dusty yellow sunshine pierced the green canopy overhead and descended like beams of grace to its dark floor. Birds with toothed beaks flitted through the beams, like painted angels briefly glimpsed in the glory of early morning. George waited for his eyes to adapt, then crept into the new growth at the verge of the forest. He looked up at the nearest titanosaur. Its neck stretched up into the trees, taller than any giraffe's.

God, he thought. Look at the size of that monster.

For an instant—only an instant—his spirit quailed. Then he gathered all his strength and, with a scream, ran straight at the nearest giant, intending to leap up at its soft, undefended throat, and tear it open.

But it didn't quite work out that way.

The instant the titanosaur became aware of him, it shifted its weight onto its hind legs and wheeled about. That slender, endless tail came slashing around like a whip, straight at George.

For an instant he could not think. His mind went completely blank with astonishment.

That instant was the saving of him.

While George was mentally paralyzed, his giganotosaur reflexes took over, skidding his body to a stop, ducking frantically down, and scrabbling desperately with legs and stubby little arms to get away from the gigantic sauropod.

The tail came crashing down and dealt him a glancing blow. He received the merest fraction of its force, but that was enough. It knocked him over and sent him tumbling back into the small trees and cycads at the verge of the forest. And it *stung*. It stung like blue blazes.

By the time George had gathered himself together and stood again, aching but unbroken, the titanosaur was gone. It had ambled away, further down the forest line, and its fellows with it, to look for some food that wasn't infested with impertinent little predators.

George burned with humiliation.

This wasn't what he'd paid for. This wasn't what he'd spent a lifetime slaving away in the financial markets in order to buy. He'd wanted to be a carnivore, goddamnit, a killer in fact as well as in spirit. The ballbusting and competitor-breaking aspects of the business world had their satisfactions. But he'd wanted to experience competition in its purest form, murderous and merciless, as Nature had intended.

It was obvious to him now that no predator, not even the mighty giganotosaur, was meant to prey upon the giant sauropods. They were protected by their size, their bulk, their mass. It had been folly to think he could hunt down and kill a titanosaur.

This was a disappointment, but one he would have to live with. He was just going to have to scale down his expectations a bit. Someday, perhaps, he would know enough to take out one of those big bastards. But in the meantime, he had to get himself fed.

While he was preoccupied with his thoughts, the giganotosaur had gotten itself up and crept back to the verge of the forest. It found a place where it could crouch, hidden by the new growth, and there it waited.

By the time George was able to focus outward again, his body had found what it wanted for supper.

He didn't know what the creature was called. It was small for a dinosaur, about the size of a large boar, and went about on four legs, rooting in the dirt among the ferns and low bushes of the prairie.

George watched it, motionless, from the edge of the forest. His binocular vision was excellent—better than what his human eyes had enjoyed for a decade. His body knew what to do. It quivered with tension, anxious to attack. But he held it back, with forced patience. He wanted his first kill to be a clean one.

The creature moved a little closer to him, a little further away, a little closer again. It was oblivious to his presence.

Finally, he let slip the leash. His body charged forward, almost silently, head low and close to the ground. The creature looked up, saw him, and squealed. But before it could turn and run, he was upon it. His massive jaws closed upon its neck with a snap. Blood spurted, warm and sticky. He shook his head twice, to snap the beast's spine. And it was dead.

He crunched it down to nothing in a matter of minutes.

AFTERWARDS, HE SOUGHT out a stream and drank until his thirst was slaked. The water was warm and brown. It tasted great.

When he'd had his fill, he lay on his stomach in the ferns above the bank. Dragonflies came and hovered in the air before him like small helicopters.

He stared dreamily out into the western sky, where the setting sun was painting the clouds gold and orange and red, and took stock. Since this morning he had experienced pride, anger, gluttony, and—now—sloth. Four of the seven deadly sins in the course of a few hours.

By God, that was the way to spend a day.

This was the life for a man.

THEY CAUGHT UP with him a week later. He was tearing away great hunks of flesh from the side of an australotopsian he had killed, when he heard the growl of an internal combustion engine in the distance. He ignored it, crunching ribs and pushing his muzzle into the cavity thus opened in search of the heart.

He liked the heart best. It made him feel more of a predator to eat an animal's heart while it was still warm. How many times had he wished he could do this to one of his competitors? Countless times. Now he could.

The Land Rover pulled up. Two figures got out.

"Having fun?"

George lifted his head from his prey. His muzzle was wet with blood. His eyes, surely, glittered with the savage joy of the kill. He knew that he must look the perfect image of Satanic fury. He grinned.

"I sure am, Dr. Alvarez."

The man standing behind Alvarez involuntarily drew back a step. But she stood her ground. "Well, fun time's over. You've got work to do. I've come to take you back to the station."

He'd noticed the trailer behind the Land Rover, and suspected what it was for. But the australotops was the biggest thing he had killed so far, and he was glad to have witnesses.

"I've got an idea of how a giganotosaur could take out a titanosaur, doctor. If I were to charge it from the side, leap up, and then cling to it with my forearms—they're certainly strong enough; I could use them like grappling hooks—then I could kick quite a gash into its side with my powerful hind limbs. All I'd have to do then is drop off and follow the titanosaur from a safe distance. Even if it didn't die from loss of blood, the wound would be sure to get infected. *Voila*—a year's supply of hamburger!"

"Mr. Weskowski, nobody is interested in what hunting strategies a dinosaur with a human brain could come up with. We want to learn what hunting strategies it *has*. We want to learn how a giganotosaur really operates. And for that, we need you to come back, cooperate, and apply yourself to your studies."

George threw his head back and laughed. His auditors put their hands over their ears.

"Let me talk to him," the man said then. He was a slender little fellow, with a thin mustache.

"And who are you?" George asked. "I don't believe we've been introduced."

"My name is Ramon Delgado. I'm a doctor of paleontological transition psychology."

"I don't need a psychologist. Especially one with a specialty so new that I'm its only possible subject."

"Mr. Weskowski, please listen to me. You've gone directly from an aged, cancer-ridden body to one that's strong and extremely physical—it makes sense that you'd feel a certain exuberance. A sense of personal invulnerability. But you can't simply break all ties with humankind. Strong as you are, big as you are, you can't exist on your own."

"When I was a kid," George said, "the Speaker of the House was a man named Newt Gingrich. This was back in the United States, you understand, and at that time the Speaker of the House was an extremely powerful man.

"Now, old Newt decided he wanted something to brighten up his office. So he strolled over to the Smithsonian, picked out a *Tyrannosaurus rex* skull from their collection, and took it with him. Oh boy, how the curators hated him for that! But there was nothing they could do about it. Because he had the power. And they were just a bunch of scientists."

"I fail to see the point of your parable," Dr. Delgado said carefully.

"It's simply that there are people who have to do what they're told to do, and people who don't. I'm one of the latter. All my life, I was a renegade, a rule-breaker. Did you know that I was a pioneer in lawsuit futures?"

"I'm afraid I'm not familiar with the term."

"It's like junk bonds. You find a potentially profitable lawsuit like, oh let's say, against automobile manufacturers for making a product that kills tens of thousands of people a year. Now, normally a suit like that, against a multibillion-dollar industry, with countless lawyers and the willingness to spend decades in litigation, isn't worth pursuing. Who can afford to wait that long for the payoff? But here's the beauty part. We made up bonds selling a fixed fraction of the eventual settlement, enough to raise a war chest of several hundred million dollars. And, win or lose, we turned an immediate profit. Suddenly, the most unlikely lawsuits are doable!"

"This worked?" Delgado said dubiously.

"We unleashed a *flood* of lawsuits! The United States of America was paralyzed! The GNP took a nose dive! They had to pass laws against what we were doing to prevent the collapse of their entire economic system. But of course by then, I'd already made my bundle."

Dr. Delgado looked sick. "You may have made a lot of money," he said. "But at what cost in human suffering? For what?"

"Why, for *this!*" George dipped down to rip off another five-hundred-pound chunk of carcass. He swallowed it down whole, distending his throat grotesquely, then continued, "This is my retirement plan. Half my money went into a trust for the grandkids. The other half went to pay for this."

Alvarez stepped forward, her eyes flashing. "No, it only went part-way toward paying for this. A great deal of the cost of this project came out of Argentina's science research budget. That's why you had to sign those contracts agreeing to pay us back with your labor as a researcher."

"Too bad," George said complacently. "Looks to me like you negotiated yourself a raw deal."

"We negotiated in good faith, Mr. Weskowski."

"You forgot to make it enforceable. You forgot to come up with a way to make Mr. *Giganotosaurus* give a damn."

He winked and was gone.

TIME PASSED—a season, perhaps less. A cloudy day came when George was ambling moodily across the prairie, moving from stream to stream, watering hole to watering hole, just to see what terror he could stir up among the herbivores. He was feeling rather lonely. More and more, of late, he was feeling lonely. He was contemplating returning to the station, just to see how things were going. He wasn't about to give up his freedom and go to work for them, of course. But he'd learned a lot about being a giganotosaur. Maybe he could barter a bit of information in exchange for some companionship.

It was precisely then that he experienced something unlike anything he had ever felt before.

One instant, everything was normal, and the next all was changed, changed absolutely. He smelled something! His head whipped around, seemingly of its own volition. Something alluring.

Without understanding why, George found himself running. What's happening to me? he wondered. His mind felt dazed and confused, helplessly out of control, and at the same time strangely joyous. But the body knew what it wanted, and it knew, too, what to do.

He crashed through the thin fringe of cycads along a stream, and splashed through the water and up the other bank. Leafy branches whipped away from his enormous body, and then he was face to face with the source of his new emotions:

It was another giganotosaur.

But this one was a female, a queen. He could tell by her scent. And she was waiting for him.

He could tell that by her scent too.

Their eyes locked. Mincingly, with coquettish little steps, the queen turned away from him, lowering her head, and raising her tail. Her eyes never left his.

He would have thought that the bulge where the top of his skull had been removed and replaced with a ceramic cap to protect his human forebrain would have made him unattractive to a female giganotosaur. Particularly since the skin that had been force-grown over it was still new and pinkish. But it was obvious that this queen thought him a wholly proper giganotosaur.

She raised her head and made a warbling noise.

George felt a strange surging sensation down below, in his cloaca and penile nubs. Distantly, the human part of him felt a kind of repulsed horror. This is bestiality, it babbled, it's sinful, it's wrong, it's disgusting. But that was mere intellectualization. Waves of chemicals swept up from the brain stem and overwhelmed his thoughts, tumbling and drowning them in wild tides of a lust more pure and primitive than anything he'd ever felt before.

He made a deep sound in the back of his throat.

She answered him.

He moved toward her.

She did not retreat.

They screwed right there in the open. The mechanics of it were awkward. They involved him getting alongside her and slowly forcing her to the ground, and then throwing one leg over her stiff tail, while she twisted around toward him, so their private parts could connect. It wasn't easy. But connect they did, and with a roar of triumph he entered her.

It didn't last nearly as long as human sex did. Once they had forced their cloacae together, the act was half-done. But the experience was beyond words. It was the apotheosis of physical contact, all need and urgent selfishness, with not a thought for the pleasure or comfort of his partner. It was rutting, pure and simple.

And it felt great.

Once, the queen moved as if to disengage. Quick as a flash, he seized her throat with his sharp-taloned little arms—now he knew what they were good for!—and didn't let go until he'd gotten everything he wanted out of her.

I have another data point for you, Dr. Alvarez, he thought fleetingly. Dino sex is terrific sex. He'd been to Thailand and he'd been to the Philippines, and wherever he'd gone, he'd bought the best. This was better.

Afterwards he lay sprawled on his back in the ferns, one foot dangling up in the air, like a tabby rolling in a catnip patch. Maybe I'll get a bumper sticker made up and stick it on my ass, he thought: *Giganotosaurs Do It With Genitalia Bigger Than Your Entire Body.*

He had his eyes closed and was savoring the heat of the sun on their lids when something thumped on the ground beside him.

George opened his eyes. It was a juvenile sauropod leg, torn from a carcass that was, by the smell of it, still reasonably fresh. Above it loomed his queen. Obviously a girl who knew how to take care of her guy.

Then he looked beyond her, and rolled over and up on his feet in astonishment. There were two more giganotosaurs standing behind her!

They were both female as well.

George smiled inwardly. Take a number, ladies, he thought, and we'll see what I can do.

THUS BEGAN THE BEST period of his life. The queens filled his days with sex and companionship, hunting with him when he felt the urge, and hunting *for* him when he did not. The vague notion he had been incubating of returning to Old Patagonia Station faded to nothing, like the mists that dissolved each morning with the rising of the Mesozoic sun.

The world was his. He filled it. It existed for him and him alone. He inhabited it in all its aspects.

In George's universe, all that mattered was him and his three queens. They were his posse. They were the street gang he'd never belonged to as a kid. They were the outlaws he'd always wanted be one of, but never dared approach. They were the bad boys, the bullies, the kids from the wrong side of the track, whose lives had always looked so alluring and dangerous from the vantage point of his staid middle-class upbringing. They took what they wanted, fucked whom they wished, did whatever entered their heads, and never asked anyone for permission or forgiveness.

Eat. Fuck. Kill. It was a relationship he could understand. It was life pared down to its essence. And—for a while—life was good.

THEN, ONE DAY, they turned on him.

It caught him by surprise. The queens had been moody and restless all morning, but what of that? They were dinosaurs. They were carnivores. They were *supposed* to have an attitude.

He was stalking in the lead position when one of his queens, the largest of the three and the one he had known first (Eve, he had named her, and the other two were Slut and Scarface, though they would none of them ever know it), lengthened her stride and came up alongside him. He didn't turn to look. There was an australotopsian up ahead—he could smell the fragile life within it, warm and appetizing—and George was hungry. All his attention was focused on his unwary prey.

The queen matched strides with him. Her head twisted to face his.

Suddenly, without warning, she lunged. Her great jaws came crunching down on the side of his face. Those nightmare teeth pierced skin and flesh in a dozen places and, with a hideous grating noise, ground against the bones of his jaw and skull.

Jesus fucking Christ—that *hurt!* The pain was blinding. George jerked away, feeling his tough skin rip like paper as the queen's teeth slid free from his face. She lunged at him again.

He veered clumsily away, only to find that Scarface had come up on his other side, blood-lust in her eyes. Then Slut screamed behind him, and he knew that he had neither friend nor ally in all the world.

He ran.

Blind with panic, he fled. Like furies, the queens pursued him across the rolling prairie. He let them chase him where they would, turning aside when a lake loomed up before him, and then up along a creek that fed into that lake. A stand of cycads forced him into the water, splashing frantically up the sandy stream bed, and then he had neither time nor the presence of mind to climb out. He had no choice but to go upstream, away from the lake.

They hunted him as a team—one queen on each bank, and Eve noisily splashing in the stream behind him.

The banks rose to either side, which was all to the good, for it meant that only the one queen was an immediate danger to him. But sooner or later the stream would narrow, which was disastrous, for he knew that if ever Scarface and Slut got into a position to jump on him from above, they would do it.

He had seen them practice such hunting maneuvers before.

He ran in abject terror, leaping the fallen logs that formed dams and bridges across the water, slipping on the layers of wet leaves that gathered at the bottom of the creek's still pools, stumbling on sudden changes in texture of the creek bed. How many times had he run down game with them in this exact same manner? A dozen? A hundred? It hardly mattered.

Now it was his turn.

Ravening, the giganotosaurs harried him up the stream.

So this is what terror feels like, he thought crazily. The water smashed underfoot and branches whipped his face. His legs ached and his lungs burned, and yet the queens—who could have been no less exhausted—did not fall back. They could smell his blood, and having smelled blood were mad for the kill. They screamed like harpies.

It made no sense, damn it. It wasn't rational! What did the bitches want from him? If they meant to drive him away—then, yes, he would go, and happily, and never once look back, damn them. They didn't need to keep chasing him! But if they were hungry, there was a world full of game that could be run down with a fraction the effort they were expending now. Anyway, he was a carnivore—no animal killed a carnivore for food unless it was literally starving. His flesh simply wouldn't taste good!

It didn't make sense. It just wasn't fair.

Why couldn't they see that?

Coming around a curve he saw that the stream ahead ran straight and true, and for an instant his heart lifted, for he dared hope that he could put on a burst of speed here that would discourage and leave behind his pursuers. But then he raised his sight to the next bend, and all hope died within him.

A great mound of dead trees and branches, twice his height, clogged the bed there. The shallow stream as it was now could never have held such a load. This tangle had been deposited here by a spring flood that had swollen the creek far beyond its present banks, and then, subsiding, left its burden of debris behind.

There was no way around the thing—not without climbing up into the waiting jaws of either Scarface or Slut.

He would have to climb over it.

It was not at all certain that he *could* climb over it, though. The near uselessness of his tiny forelimbs would make it extremely difficult. As would the three raging queens snapping at his heels, ready to leap upon him should he fall. There had to be some alternative.

Frantically he wracked his brain. Wildly, he looked around for some way—any way!—out of this predicament.

There was none.

So when he came to the tangle, he tried to run straight up it. His tremendous foot landed solid on one of the logs. He twisted his body and leaped for a second. That seized, he leaned his body forward, chest sliding against the branches, and surged upward. His feet scrabbled for purchase. He was now his own height above the streambed, and still climbing. He tried to fight his way yet higher.

And failed.

A log rolled under his feet, and simultaneously Eve arrived at the log jam to find him out of her reach. Furiously she rammed her head into the tangle like a powerful hammer. The combination of his weight and her force set everything into motion.

The other two queens, meanwhile, had jumped down from the bank and were trying to reach him from either side. Screaming in rage, they leaped upon the overtoppling deadwood, splintering branches and further destabilizing the entire mass.

All the world shifted underfoot. George fell over backwards, and the pile on top of him. Logs tumbled and rolled over onto his chest.

A roaring confusion of noise filled his ears. He felt a leg *snap* between two tree trunks.

Through a haze of pain, he saw logs settling down over him.

The queens had leaped away when the deadwood began to slide. Now they returned to see if they could get at him. Once! Twice! Three times they rammed their massive heads against the pile, trying to force a way to George's still body.

They could not. George was pinned down at the bottom of the pile, and no application of giganotosaur strength would suffice to dig him free. He was there permanently.

Finally, they left him for dead.

He was not dead, though. He only wished he were. Lying half in and half out of the water, with the crushing weight of the logs pressing down upon him, George rested his head against the cool, cool mud, and prayed for an end to his pain.

It did not come.

After a time he noticed a protorat staring at him from deep within the tangled wood, its eyes glittery with terror. Looking back, he remembered a time not many days ago when for amusement he had stood spraddle-legged and motionless for almost an hour by the burrow of one of this creature's small mammalian kinsfolk. Waiting ... waiting with dinosaur patience for the beastie to emerge, blinking and optimistic, into the dawn of an age that would soon, within another few tens of millions of years, end with the extinction of the dinosaurs and the opportunistic rise of this insignificant vermin's offspring.

His patience had been rewarded. At last the creature had come forth, a small, hairy, and undistinguished animal, and quite possibly the direct ancestor of Man.

The timid little thing reared up on its hind legs directly in front of George's stupendous body. Wee ancestor, George thought, you've just won the grand prize in the Evolution's Clearing House Sweepstakes. When I and my kind are gone, your descendants will get to rule everything.

Then he had pissed on it.

How many gallons of urine had he drenched the little bastard with? Impossible to say. It was a lot, anyway. Battered and hysterical, the mammal had fled back into the ground. George had roared with laughter then, over and over, startling and confusing his queens and shocking the prairie into fearful silence.

"Come to get your revenge, have you?" George muttered. "Going to defend the honor of your kind by gnawing on my bones?"

But there was no radio anywhere near to receive his words, and even if the protorat could have heard them, it wouldn't've understood. In any event, it did not move. Its chest trembled with panicky breath and its dread-filled eyes jerked every time George shifted his gaze, but otherwise it was motionless.

"Well, you're in luck," George continued. "I'm trapped, I'm in pain, and I don't think I'm ever going to get out of here." Those marcasite eyes jerked again, and George scowled. "Why are you still here? If you're so afraid of me, why haven't you run?"

He focused all his attention on the beast and discovered what he had missed before: That its tail was caught between two logs. It was as trapped as he was.

There was irony here, if he only knew how to read it. Here he was, the biggest, meanest bruiser ever to walk the Earth—helpless. He was as irrevocably trapped as the weak, fearful creature quivering before him. They were one in their dilemma.

Well, these past few months excepted, when *hadn't* he been trapped? Caught up in his work, entangled in a marriage that had slowly turned grey and joyless, sandbagged by a detective with a camera in a hotel room in Albany and subsequently shafted in the divorce settlement, and finally, at age seventy-two, painted into a corner by his firm's mandatory retirement policy.

And what did he have to show for it all?

Now that he was going to die, what was he leaving behind? One very wealthy ex, three kids who didn't particularly care for him (not that he blamed them), and four of the sweetest grandchildren anybody had ever laid eyes on. The grandchildren, anyway, were good. The rest was not.

He'd made a pot of money over a long lifetime running with the wolves in the financial markets, and spent it all on a much shorter lifetime running with the giganotosaurs in the wild. And in the end everybody—humans and dinosaurs alike—he'd trusted had turned on him.

It only confirmed what he'd learned long ago. There was no loyalty in this world. Every man lived alone, and he died alone as well. That was simply the way it was.

Something squeaked.

It was a very small sound, but it brought his attention back, with a start, to the trapped protorat.

The animal's tail was caught in the junction of two logs, the uppermost of which also lay across the top of his own head and shoulder. He could not hope to free himself from the woodpile. But if he summoned all his strength, he could shift the logs a little. Not enough to do him any good. But maybe enough to free the terrified mammal.

"I *could* do it," George said, "but I'm not going to. If I have to die, then so do you."

The protorat stared at him uncomprehendingly, still afraid.

For a long moment he said nothing.

Then:

"All right, you sonofabitch," he rumbled, "live."

He heaved his shoulder and the logs parted for an instant, freeing the protorat's tail.

In a flash, it was gone.

"Didn't even ... stay around long enough to say ... thanks, did you?" George said. This last, pointless expenditure of energy had just about used him up. He didn't have any more reserves of strength to draw on. "Your descendants ... are going to be ... just like you."

Still—and inexplicably, for what use was a protorat's life to anyone, even itself?—it made him feel better knowing that if he had to die, he could at least postpone the experience for something else.

Just as his eyes were closing for what he was convinced was the last time, he heard a throbbing noise, like the warm and beating heart of the world opening to him, to share with him some desperately important revelation. Lying with his face half in the water, he listened. And in the instant before the darkness closed around him, he penetrated the secret of that sound, and knew it for what it was:

A helicopter.

Greyness wrapped itself about him then, like a thick wool blanket, and he fell into a troubled, painful sleep. Once he heard somebody say, "Oh, man, this is going to take a *lot* of antibiotics," and then no more.

"WELL, IF IT ISN'T Peter Pan!"

"Dr. Alvarez," George mumbled. He did not meet her eyes. "And Dr. Delgado, too. It's good to see you."

"You're lucky we've been monitoring your vital signs," Alvarez said. "Otherwise, you'd be dead."

"I know," George said meekly. Then, "You ... had a chip in me? You knew where I was all the time?"

"It was in your contract. Surely you read it through."

"Oh, yeah. I remember now." George was hanging from the center of the barn in a kind of makeshift sling-and-traction arrangement. One leg was plastered into a cast. There were bandages everywhere, and wide strips of tape wrapped tightly around his chest. He'd been told some ribs were broken.

"So what happened?"

"My queens attacked me." George felt a great emptiness, a bottomless sense of betrayal. "For no reason! One minute everything was great, the next minute—*bam!* Dr. Alvarez, why did they do that? Why?"

"Your queens were in heat when you met them. Giganotosaurs, like every other theropod we know of, are only periodically interested in sex. Once the mating season was over they weren't interested in having you around anymore. You can't blame them for this—male giganoto-saurs will eat their young if given the chance. We would have told you this, if you'd only listened."

"Oh."

He'd been a fool. Vast landscapes of his self-delusion opened up before him. Tears filled his great eyes. He hadn't known that dinosaurs could cry.

Dr. Alvarez snorted disdainfully. "This is what you wanted, Mr. Weskowski—nature red in fang and claw, right? Only, in reality life in the wild is usually solitary, poor, nasty, brutish, and short."

He made an unhappy noise in his throat.

But now Dr. Delgado stepped forward. "Please, Maria," he said admonishingly. "You're not helping. Go away." And to George: "I want to read something to you. I got this out of the library when I heard you were being airlifted back to the station. It's from a sermon by John Donne, and I think you're capable of understanding it now." He got out a small brown leather-jacketed book from his pocket, adjusted his glasses, smoothed down his mustache with two nervous strokes of a long, lean finger, and began to read:

> "No man is an island, entire of itself. Every man is a piece of the continent, a part of the main. If a clod be washed away by the sea, Europe is the less, as well as if a promontory were, as well as if a manor of thy friends or of thine own were. Any man's death diminishes me, because I am involved in Mankind. And therefore never send to know for whom the bell tolls. It tolls for thee."

He looked up again, a serious expression on his narrow intellectual face. "You tried to declare independence from humanity, and for several reasons it didn't work. Some of these reasons are pragmatic—access to decent medical care being one of them. Others, though, are matters of the soul. You never *were* a giganotosaur, you know. Only a man riding on top of one."

For a second time, George's eyes filled with tears.

"Well, Mr. Weskowski," Delgado said. "Are you ready to rejoin the human race?"

It was a bright Cretaceous morn.

Claw-winged archaeopteryxes were singing in the trees. The gently mournful cry of the rebbachisaur sounded over the prairie. Dawn mice were scuttling furtively about, harvesting seed from the flowering plants that flourished in the shade of the woods. George ignored them. He stood waiting, as still and motionless as a billboard.

He'd been working for weeks following a small herd of titanosaurs, studying their behavior, their eating patterns, their rudimentary social structure. He could do that, for his smell was familiar and unthreatening to the titanosaurs, where that of humans was not. Every night, after they'd bedded down, he'd transmitted his findings back to Old Patagonia Station.

An engine sounded in the distance.

This was not the first, but only the most recent of many such studies. He'd proven himself time after time as a capable and hard-working researcher. Now he was waiting for his reward.

The engine noise grew steadily louder. It peaked and crescendoed. Almost here. George found himself trembling with excitement.

A jeep came up over the rise, and slowed to a noisy stop. Alvarez was in the driver's seat. She cut the engine and slammed open a door. "Everybody out!" she shouted.

The children came tumbling out of the jeep, laughing and shouting. They fell silent when they saw George.

He stretched out his arms toward them. "Come on, kids!" he cried joyfully. "Let Grampa give you a ride on his back!"

Wild Minds

I MET HER AT A businesspersons' orgy in London. The room was in the back of a pub that was all brass and beveled glass, nostalgia and dark oak. The doorkeeper hesitated when it saw how many times I'd attended in the last month. But then I suggested it scroll up my travel schedule, and it saw that I wasn't acting out a sex-addiction script, but properly maintaining my forebrain and hindbrain balances. So it let me in.

Inside, the light was dimly textured and occasionally mirrored. Friendly hands helped me off with my clothing. "I'm Thom," I murmured, and "Annalouise . . . Enoch . . . Abdul . . . Magdalena . . . Claire," those nearest quietly replied. Time passed.

I noticed Hellene not because she was beautiful—who pays attention to beauty, after the first hour?—but because it took her so long to find release. By the time she was done, there was a whole new crowd; only she and I remained of all who had been in the room when I entered.

In the halfway room, we talked.

"My assemblers and sorters got into a hierarchic conflict," I told her. "Too many new faces, too many interchangeable cities."

She nodded. "I've been under a lot of stress myself. My neural mediator has become unreliable. And since I'm scheduled for an upgrade,

126

it's not worth it running a purge. I had to offline the mediator, and take the week off from work."

"What do you do?" I asked. I'd already spotted her as being optimized.

She worked in human resources, she said. When I heard that, I asked, "Is there any hope for people like me? Those who won't accept optimization, I mean."

"Wild minds?" Hellene looked thoughtful. "Five years ago I'd've said no, open-and-shut, end of story. Period. Zero rez. Today, though ..."

"Yes?"

"I don't know," she said in an anguished voice. "I simply don't know."

I could sense something significant occurring within myself, intuit some emotional sea-change organizing itself deep on the unseen levels—the planners building new concept-language, the shunts and blocks being rearranged. Of course I had no way of knowing what it was. I hadn't been optimized. Still—

"Can I walk you home?" I asked.

She looked at me for a long and silent second. "I live in Prague."

"Oh."

"We could go to your place, if it's not too far."

WE TOOK THE HYPERMETRO to Glasgow. Got off at the Queen Street Station and walked up to my flat in Renfrew Street. We talked a little on the train, but Hellene fell silent when we hit the street.

They don't like the old places, the new people, cluttered with seedy pubs and street corner hangouts, the niches where shabby men sit slumped over their whisky in paper bags, the balconies from which old women watch over the street. It unnerves them, this stench of accommodation and human dirt. It frightens them that it works so well, when it so obviously shouldn't.

"You're a Catholic," she said.

She was looking at my icon, a molecular reproduction of Ad Reinhardt's "For T.M." It's one of his black paintings, his first, and modestly small. At first it seems unvaryingly colorless; you have to stare at it for some time to see the subtle differences in the black, the thick cross that quarters and dominates that small lightless universe. He painted it for Thomas Merton, who was a monk.

My copy is a duplicate as exact as human technology can make it; more exact than human perception can distinguish. I use it as a focus for meditation. Opposite it is a Charles Rennie MacIntosh chair, high-backed. An original because it was made to his directions. Sometimes I'll sit in the one and stare at the other, thinking about distinctions, authenticity, and duplicity.

"You wouldn't need meditation if you were optimized."

"No. But the Church considers it a mortal sin, you see."

"The Church can't possibly approve of your attending orgies."

"Oh. Well. It's winked at." I shrugged. "As long as you go to confession before you take Communion ..."

"What do you see when you meditate?"

"Sometimes I see comfort there; other times I see suffering."

"I don't like ambiguity. It's an artifact of the old world." She turned away from the picture. She had those chill Scandinavian features that don't show emotions well. She was beautiful, I realized with a mental start. And, almost at the same instant but twice as startling, I realized that she reminded me of Sophia.

Out of nowhere, without transition, Hellene said, "I must return to Prague. I haven't seen my children in two weeks."

"They'll be glad to see you."

"Glad? I doubt it. No more than I will be to see them," she said in the manner of one totally unable to lie to herself. "I've spun off three partials that they like considerably more than they do me. And I signed them up with Sterling International for full optimization when they were eight."

I said nothing.

"Do you think that makes me a bad mother?"

"I wanted children, too," I said. "But it didn't work out."

"You're evading the question."

I thought for a second. Then, because there was no way around it short of a lie, I said, "Yes. Yes, I do." And, "I'm going to put a kettle on. Would you like a cup?"

MY GRANDFATHER USED TO talk about the value of a good education. His generation was obsessed with the idea. But when the workings of the human brain were finally and completely understood—largely as a result of the NAFTA "virtual genome" project—mere learning became so easy that most corporations simply educated their workforce themselves to whatever standards were currently needed. Anybody could become a doctor, a lawyer, a physicist, provided they could spare the month it took to absorb the technical skills.

With knowledge so cheap, the only thing workers had to sell was their character: their integrity, prudence, willingness to work, and hard-headed lack of sentiment. Which is when it was discovered that a dozen spiderweb-thin wires and a neural mediator the size of a pinhead would make anybody as disciplined and thrifty as they desired. Fifty cents worth of materials and an hour on the operating table would render anybody eminently employable.

The ambitious latched onto optimization as if it were a kite string that could snatch them right up into the sky. Which, in practical terms, it was. Acquiring a neural mediator was as good as a Harvard degree used to be. And—because it was new, and most people were afraid of it—optimization created a new elite.

Sophia and I used to argue about this all the time. She wanted to climb that kite string right into the future. I pointed out that it was the road to excommunication. Which shows just what a hypocrite I was. Back then I was not at all a religious man. I didn't need the comfort of religion the way I do now.

But you take your arguments where you can get them. Wild minds don't know from rational discourse. They only care about winning. Sophia was the same. We yelled at each other for hour upon hour, evening after evening. Sometimes we broke things.

Hellene drank her tea unsweetened, with milk.

WE TALKED THROUGH the night. Hellene, of course, didn't need sleep. Normally I did, but not tonight. Something was happening within me;

I could feel my components buzzing and spinning. The secondary chemical effects were enough to keep me alert. Those, and the tea.

"You seem an intelligent enough man," she said at one point, and, gesturing at the wooden floors and glass windows, "How can you live in such primitive squalor? Why reject what science has revealed about the workings of the brain?"

"I have no complaints about the knowledge *per se.*" I used to have a terrible temper. I was a violent, intemperate man. Or so it seems to me now. "Learning the structural basis of emotions, and how to master them before they flush the body with adrenaline, has been a great benefit to me."

"So why haven't you been optimized?"

"I was afraid of losing myself."

"Self is an illusion. The single unified ego you mistake for your 'self' is just a fairy tale that your assemblers, sorters, and functional transients tell one another."

"I know that. But still . . ."

She put her cup down. "Let me show you something."

From her purse she took out a box of old-fashioned wooden matches. She removed five, aligned them all together in a bundle, and then clenched them in her hand, sulfur side down, with just the tips of the wood ends sticking out.

"Control over involuntary functions, including localized body heat," she said.

There was a gout of flame between her fingers. She opened her hand. The matches were ablaze.

"The ability to block pain."

This wasn't a trick. I could smell her flesh burning.

When the matches had burned out, she dumped them in her saucer, and showed me the blackened skin where they had been. The flesh by its edges was red and puffy, already starting to blister.

"Accelerated regenerative ability."

For five minutes she held her hand out, flat and steady. For five minutes I watched. And at the end of that five minutes, it was pink and healed. Unblackened. Unblistered.

Hellene spooned sugar into her teacup, returning to the sugar bowl at least six times before she was done. She drank down the sweet, syrupy mess with a small moue of distaste. "These are only the crude physical manifestations of what optimization makes possible. Mentally—there are hardly the words. Absolute clarity of thought, even during emergencies. Freedom from prejudice and superstition. Freedom from the tyranny of emotion."

There was a smooth, practiced quality to her words. She'd said she was in human resources—now I knew she was a corporate recruiter. One salesman can always recognize another.

"Sometimes," I said carefully, "I enjoy my emotions."

"So do I—when I have them under control," Hellene said with a touch of asperity. "You mustn't judge the experience by a malfunctioning mediator."

"I don't."

"It would be like judging ecological restoration by the Sitnikov Tundra incident."

"Of course."

"Or seeing a junked suborbital and deciding that rocket flight was impossible."

"I understand completely."

Abruptly, Hellene burst into tears.

"Oh God—no. Please," she said when I tried to hold her and comfort her. "It's just that I'm not used to functioning without the mediator and so I get these damned emotional transients. All my chemical balances are out of whack."

"When will your new mediator be—?"

"Tuesday."

"Less than three days, then. That's not so bad."

"It wouldn't be, if I didn't need to see my children."

I waited while she got herself under control again. Then, because the question had been nagging at me for hours, I said, "I don't understand why you had children in the first place."

"Blame it on Berne. The Bureau des Normalisations et Habitudes was afraid not enough people were signing up for optimization. It was discovered that optimized people weren't having children, so they crafted a regulation giving serious career preference to those who did."

"Why?"

"Because people like me are necessary. Do you have any idea how complicated the world has gotten? Unaugmented minds couldn't begin to run it. There'd be famines, wars . . ."

She was crying again. This time when I put my arms around her, she did not protest. Her face turned to bury itself in my shoulder. Her tears soaked a damp rectangle through my shirt. I could feel their moisture on my skin.

Holding her like that, stroking her infinitely fine hair, thinking of her austere face, those pale, pale eyes, I felt the shunts and blocks shifting within me. All my emotional components wheeled about the still instant, ready to collapse into a new paradigmatic state at the least provocation. The touch of a hand, the merest ghost of a smile, the right word. I could have fallen in love with her then and there.

Which is the price one pays for having a wild mind. You're constantly at the mercy of forces you don't fully understand. For the moment I felt like a feral child standing on the twilight lands between the cultivated fields and the wolf-haunted forests, unable to choose between them.

THEN, AS QUICKLY AS IT BEGAN, it was over. Hellene pushed herself away from me, once again in control of her emotions. "Let me show you something," she said. "Have you got home virtual?"

"I don't use it much."

She took a small device out of her purse. "This is an adapter for your set. Very simple, very safe. Give it a try."

"What does it do?"

"It's a prototype recruitment device, and it's intended for people like you. For the space of fifteen seconds, you'll know how it feels to be optimized. Just so you can see there's nothing to be afraid of."

"Will it change me?"

"All experience changes you. But this is only a magnetic resonance simulacrum. When the show's over, the lights come up and the curtains go down. There you are in your seat, just as before."

"I'll do it," I said, "if you'll agree to try out something for me afterwards."

Wordlessly, she handed me the adapter.

I PUT ON THE WRAPAROUNDS. At my nod, Hellene flicked the switch. I sucked in my breath.

It was as if I had shrugged off an enormous burden. I felt myself straighten. My pulse strengthened and I breathed in deep, savoring the smells of my apartment; they were a symphony of minor and major keys, information that a second ago I had ignored or repressed. Wood polish and hair mousse. A hint of machine oil from the robot floor-cleaner hiding under my bed, which only came out while I was away. Boiled cabbage from a hundred bachelor dinners. And underneath it all, near-microscopic traces of lilac soap and herbal shampoo, of *Ambrosie* and *Pas de Regret,* of ginger candies and Trinidadian rum, the olfactory ghost of Sophia no amount of scrubbing could exorcise.

The visuals were minimal. I was standing in an empty room. Everything—windows, doorknob, floor—had been painted a uniform white. But mentally, the experience was wonderful. Like standing upon a mountain top facing into a thin, chill wind. Like diving naked into an ice-cold lake at dawn. I closed my eyes and savored the blessed clarity that filled my being.

For the first time in as long as I could remember, I felt just fine.

There were any number of mental exercises I could try out. The adapter presented me with a menu of them. But I dismissed it out of hand. Forget that nonsense.

I just wanted to stand there, not feeling guilty about Sophia. Not missing her. Not regretting a thing. I knew it wasn't my fault. Nothing was my fault, and if it had been that wouldn't have bothered me either. If I'd been told that the entire human race would be killed five seconds after I died a natural death, I would've found it vaguely interesting, like something you see on a nature program. But it wouldn't have troubled me.

Then it was over.

For a long instant I just sat there. All I could think was that if this thing had been around four years ago, Sophia would be here with me now. She'd never have chosen optimization knowing it would be like *that*. Then I took off the wraparounds.

Hellene was smiling. "Well?" she said. She just didn't get it.

"Now it's your turn to do something for me."

For a flicker of an instant she looked disappointed. But it didn't last. "What is it?"

"It'll be morning soon," I said. "I want you to come to Mass with me."

Hellene looked at me as if I'd invited her to wallow in feces. Then she laughed. "Will I have to eat human flesh?"

It was like a breath of wind on a playing-card castle. All the emotional structures my assemblers had been putting together collapsed into nothingness. I didn't know whether I should be glad or sad. But I knew now that I would never—*could* never—love this woman.

Something of this must have showed in my expression, for Hellene quickly said, "Forgive me, that was unspeakably rude." One hand fluttered by the side of her skull. "I've grown so used to having a mediator that without it I simply blurt out whatever enters my head." She unplugged the adapter and put it back in her purse. "But I don't indulge in superstitions. Good God, what would be the point?"

"So you think religion is just a superstition?"

"It was the first thing to go, after I was optimized."

Sophia had said much the same thing, the day of her optimization. It was an outpatient operation, in by three, out by six, no more complicated than getting your kidneys regrown. So she was still working things out when she came home. By seven she'd seen through God, prayer, and the Catholic Church. By eight she had discarded her plans to have children and a lifelong love of music. By nine she'd outgrown me.

Hellene cocked her head to the side in that mannered little gesture optimized businesspeople use to let you know they've just accessed the time. "It's been lovely," she said. "Thank you, you've been so very kind. But now if you'll excuse me, I really must go. My children—"

"I understand."

"I face a severe fine if I don't see them at least twice a month. It's happened three times so far this year and quite frankly my bank account can't take it."

On the way out, Hellene noticed the portrait of Sophia by the door. "Your wife?" she asked.

"Yes."

"She's exquisite."

"Yes," I said. "She is." I didn't add that I'd killed her. Nor that a panel of neuroanalysts had found me innocent by virtue of a faulty transition function and, after minor chemical adjustments and a two-day course on anger control techniques, had released me onto the street without prejudice.

Or hope.

That was when I discovered the consolation of religion. Catholics do not believe in faulty transition functions. According to the Church, I had sinned. I had sinned, and therefore I must repent, confess, and atone.

I performed an act of true contrition, and received absolution. God has forgiven me.

Mind you, I have not forgiven *myself*. Still, I have hope.

Which is why I'll never be optimized. The thought that a silicon-doped biochip could make me accept Sophia's death as an unfortunate accident of neurochemistry and nothing more, turns my stomach.

"Good-bye," I said.

Hellene waved a hand in the air without turning around. She disappeared in the direction of Queen Street Station. I shut the door.

From Hill Street, which runs the height of Glasgow's Old City, you can stand at an intersection and look down on one side upon Charing Cross and on the other upon Cowcaddens. The logic of the city is laid clear there and although the buildings are largely Victorian (save for those areas cleared by enemy bombings in World War II, which are old modern), the logic is essentially medieval: The streets have grown as they will, in a rough sort of grid, and narrow enough that most are now fit for one-way traffic only.

But if you look beyond Cowcaddens, the ruins of the M8 Motorway cut through the city, wide and out of scale, long unused but still fringed by derelict buildings, still blighting the neighborhoods it was meant to serve. A dead road, fringed by the dead flesh of abandoned buildings.

Beyond, by the horizon, were the shimmering planes and uncertain surfaces of the buildings where the new people lived, buildings that could never have been designed without mental optimization, all tensengricity and interactive film. I'd been in those bright and fast habitats. The air *sings* within their perfect corridors. Nobody could deny this.

Still, I preferred the terraces and too-narrow streets and obsolete people you find in the old city. The new people don't claim to be human, and I don't claim that being human is any longer essential. But I cling to the human condition anyway, out of nostalgia perhaps but also, possibly, because it contains something of genuine value.

I sat in the straight-backed Charles Rennie MacIntosh and stared at the icon. It was all there, if only I could comprehend it: the dark dimensions of the human mind. Such depths it holds!

Such riches.

10

The Raggle Taggle Gypsy-O

Among twenty snowy mountains, the only moving thing was the eye of Crow. The sky was blue, and the air was cold. His beard was rimed with frost. The tangled road behind was black and dry and empty.

At last, satisfied that there was nobody coming after them, he put down his binoculars. The way down to the road was steep. He fell three times as he half pushed and half swam his way through the drifts. His truck waited for him, idling. He stamped his feet on the tarmac to clear the boot treads and climbed up on the cab.

Annie looked up as he opened the door. Her smile was warm and welcoming, but with just that little glint of man-fear first, brief as the green flash at sunset, gone so quickly you wouldn't see it if you didn't know to look. *That wasn't me, babe,* he wanted to tell her. *Nobody's ever going to hit you again.* But he said nothing. You could tell the goddamnedest lies, and who was there to stop you? Let her judge him by his deeds. Crow didn't much believe in words.

He sat down heavily, slamming the door. "Cold as hell out there," he commented. Then, "How are they doing?"

Annie shrugged. "They're hungry again."

"They're always hungry." But Crow pulled the wicker picnic hamper out from under the seat anyway. He took out a dead puppy and pulled back the slide window at the rear of the cab. Then, with a snap of his wrist, he tossed the morsel into the van.

The monsters in the back began fighting over the puppy, slamming each other against the walls, roaring in mindless rage.

"Competitive buggers." He yanked the brake and put the truck into gear.

They had the heat cranked up high for the sake of their cargo, and after a few minutes he began to sweat. He pulled off his gloves, biting the fingertips and jerking back his head, and laid them on the dash, alongside his wool cap. Then he unbuttoned his coat.

"Gimme a hand here, willya?" Annie held the sleeve so he could draw out his arm. He leaned forward and she pulled the coat free and tossed it aside. "Thanks," he said.

Annie said nothing. Her hands went to his lap and unzipped his pants. Crow felt his pecker harden. She undid his belt and yanked down his BVDs. Her mouth closed upon him. The truck rattled underneath them.

"Hey, babe, that ain't really safe."

"Safe." Her hand squeezed him so hard he almost asked her to stop. But thought better of it. "I didn't hook up with a thug like you so I could be *safe*."

She ran her tongue down his shaft and begun sucking on his nuts. Crow drew in his breath. What the hell, he figured, might as well go along for the ride. Only he'd still better keep an eye on the road. They were going down a series of switchbacks. Easy way to die.

He downshifted, and downshifted again.

It didn't take long before he spurted.

He came and groaned and stretched and felt inordinately happy. Annie's head came up from his lap. She was smiling impishly. He grinned back at her.

Then she mashed her face into his and was kissing him deeply, passionately, his jism salty on her tongue and her tongue sticky in his mouth, and he *couldn't see!* Terrified, he slammed his foot on the brake.

He was blind and out of control on one of the twistiest and most dangerous roads in the universe. The tires screamed.

He pushed Annie away from him so hard the back of her head bounced off the rider-side window. The truck's front wheels went off the road. Empty sky swung up to fill the windshield. In a frenzy, he swung the wheel so sharply he thought for a second they were going to overturn. There was a hideous *crunch* that sounded like part of the frame hitting rock, and then they were jolting safely down the road again.

"God damn," Crow said flatly. "Don't you ever do that again." He was shaking. "You're fucking crazy!" he added, more emphatically.

"Your fly is unzipped," Annie said, amused.

He hastily tucked himself in. "Crazy."

"You want crazy? You so much as look at another woman and I'll show you crazy." She opened the glove compartment and dug out her packet of Kents. "I'm just the girl for you, boyo, and don't you forget it." She lit up and then opened the window a crack for ventilation. Mentholated smoke filled the cabin.

In a companionable wordlessness they drove on through the snow and the blinding sunlight, the cab warm, the motor humming, and the monsters screaming at their back.

For maybe fifty miles he drove, while Annie drowsed in the seat beside him. Then the steering got stiff and the wheel began to moan under his hands whenever he turned it. It was a long, low, mournful sound like whale-song.

Without opening her eyes, Annie said, "What kind of weird-shit station are you listening to? Can't you get us something better?"

"Ain't no radio out here, babe. Remember where we are."

She opened her eyes. "So what is it, then?"

"Steering fluid's low. I think maybe we sprung a leak back down the road, when we almost went off."

"What are we going to do about it?"

"I'm not sure there's much we *can* do."

At which exact moment they turned a bend in the road and saw a gas station ahead. Two sets of pumps, diesel, air, a Mini-Mart, and a garage. Various machines of dubious functionality rusting out back.

Crow slammed on the brakes. "*That* shouldn't be there." He knew that for a fact. Last time he'd been through, the road had been empty all the way through to Troy.

Annie finally opened her eyes. They were the greenest things Crow had ever seen. They reminded him of sunlight through jungle leaves, of moss-covered cathedrals, of a stone city he'd once been to, sunk in the shallow waters of the Caribbean. That had been a dangerous place, but no more dangerous than this slim and lovely lady beside him. After a minute, she simply said, "Ask if they do repairs."

CROW PULLED UP IN FRONT of the garage and honked the horn a few times. A hound-lean mechanic came out, wiping his hands on a rag. "Yah?"

"Lissen, Ace, we got us a situation here with our steering column. Think you can fix us up?"

The mechanic stared at him, unblinking, and said, "We're all out of fluid. I'll take a look at your underside, though."

While the man was on a creeper under the truck, Crow went to the crapper. Then he ambled around back of the garage. There was a window there. He snapped the latch, climbed in, and poked around.

When he strolled up front again, the mechanic was out from under the truck and Annie was leaning against one of the pumps, flirting with him. He liked it, Crow could tell. Hell, even faggots liked it when Annie flirted at them.

Annie went off to the ladies' when he walked up, and by the time she came back the mechanic was inside again. She raised her eyebrows and Crow said, "Bastard says he can't fix the leak and ain't got no fluid. Only I boosted two cases out a window and stashed 'em in a junker out back. Go in and distract him, while I get them into the truck."

Annie thrust her hands deep into the pockets of her leather jacket and twisted slightly from foot to foot. "I've got a better thought," she said quietly. "Kill him."

"Say what?"

"He's one of Eric's people."

"You sure of that?"

"Ninety percent sure. He's here. What else could he be?"

"Yeah, well, there's still that other ten percent."

Her face was a mask. "Why take chances?"

"Jesus." Crow shook his head. "Babe, sometimes you give me the creeps. I don't mind admitting that you do."

"Do you love me? Then kill him."

"Hey. Forget that bullshit. We been together long enough, you must know what I'm like, okay? I ain't killing nobody today. Now go into the convenience there and buy us ten minutes, eh? Distract the man."

He turned her around and gave her a shove toward the Mini-Mart. Her shoulders were stiff with anger, her bottom big and round in those tight leather pants. God, but he loved the way she looked in those things! His hand ached to give her a swat on the rump, just to see her scamper. Couldn't do that with Annie, though. Not now, not never. Just one more thing that bastard Eric had spoiled for others.

He had the truck loaded and the steering column topped up by the time Annie strode out of the Mini-Mart with a boom box and a stack of CDs. The mechanic trotted after her, toting up prices on a little pad. When he presented her with the total, she simply said, "Send the bill to my husband," and climbed into the cab.

With a curt, wordless nod, the man turned back toward the store.

"Got any more doubts?" Annie asked coldly.

Crow cursed. He'd killed men in his time, but it wasn't anything he was proud of. And never what you'd call murder. He slammed down the back of the seat, to access the storage compartment. All his few possessions were in there, and little enough they were for such a hard life as he'd led. Some spare clothes. A basket of trinkets he'd picked up along the way. His guns.

Forty miles down the road, Annie was still fuming. Abruptly, she turned and slammed Crow in the side with her fist. Hard. She had a good punch for a woman. Keeping one hand on the wheel, he half-turned and tried to seize her hands in one enormous fist. She continued hitting him in the chest and face until he managed to nab them both.

"What?" he demanded, angrily.

"You should have killed him."

"Three handfuls of gold nuggets, babe. I dug 'em out of the Yukon with my own mitts. That's enough money to keep anybody's mouth shut."

"Oh mercy God! Not one of Eric's men. Depend upon it, yon whoreson caitiff was on the phone the very instant you were out of his sight."

"You don't know that kind of cheap-jack hustler the way I do—" Crow began. Which was—he knew it the instant the words left his mouth—exactly the wrong thing to say to Annie. Her lips went thin and her eyes went hard. Her words were bitter and curt. Before he knew it, they were yelling at each other.

Finally he had no choice but to pull over, put the truck in park, and settle things right there on the front seat.

Afterwards, she put on a CD she liked, old ballads and shit, and kept on playing it over and over. One in particular made her smile at him, eyes sultry and full of love, whenever it came on.

> *It was upstairs downstairs the lady went*
> *Put on her suit of leather-o*
> *And there was a cry from around the door*
> *She's away wi' the raggle taggle gypsy-o*

To tell the truth, the music wasn't exactly to his taste. But that was what they liked back where Annie came from. She couldn't stand his music. Said it was just noise. But when he felt that smile and those eyes on him it was better than three nights in Tijuana with any other woman he'd ever met. So he didn't see any point in making a big thing out of it.

The wheel was starting to freeze up on them again. Crow was looking for a good place to pull off and dump in a few cans of fluid, when suddenly Annie shivered and sat up straight. She stared off into the distance, over the eternal mountains. "What is it?" he asked.

"I have a premonition."

"Of what?" He didn't much like her premonitions. They always came true.

"Something. Over there." She lifted her arm and pointed.

Two Basilisks lifted up over the mountains.

"Shit!"

He stepped on the gas. "Hold tight, babe. We're almost there. I think we can outrun 'em."

THEY CAME DOWN the exit ramp with the steering column moaning and howling like a banshee. Crow had to put all his weight on the wheel to make it turn. Braking, he left the timeless lands.

And came out in Rome.

One instant they were on the exit ramp surrounded by lifeless mountains. The next they were pushing through narrow roads choked with donkey carts and toga-clad pedestrians. Crow brought the truck to a stop, and got out to add fluid.

The truck took up most of the road. People cursed and spat at him for being in their way. But nobody seemed to find anything unusual in the fact that he was driving an internal-combustion engine. They all took it in their stride.

It was wonderful how the timelines protected themselves against anachronisms by simply ignoring them. A theoretical physicist Crow had befriended in Babylon had called it "robust integrity." You could introduce the printing press into dynastic Egypt and six months later the device would be discarded and forgotten. Machine-gun the infant Charlemagne and within the year those who had been there would remember him having been stabbed. A century later every detail of his career as Emperor would be chronicled, documented, and revered, down to his dotage and death.

It hadn't made a lot of sense to Crow, but, "Live with it," the physicist had said, and staggered off in search of his great-great-five-hundred-times-great-grandmother with silver in his pocket and a demented gleam in his eye. So there it was.

Not an hour later, they arrived at the Coliseum and were sent around back to the tradesmen's entrance.

"*Ave,*" Crow said to the guard there. "I want to talk to one of the—hey, Annie, what's Latin for animal-wrangler?"

"Bestiarius."

"Yeah, that's it. Fella name of Carpophorus."

CARPOPHORUS WAS DELIGHTED with his new pets. He watched eagerly as the truck was backed up to the cage. Two sparsores with grappling-hooks unlatched the truck doors and leaped back as eleven nightmares poured out of the truck. They were all teeth and claws and savage quickness. One of their number lay dead on the floor of the truck. Not bad for such a long haul.

"What are they?" Carpophorus asked, entranced.

"Deinonychi."

" 'Terrible-claws,' eh? Well, they fit the bill, all right." He thrust an arm between the bars, and then leaped back, chuckling, as two of the lithe young carnivores sprang at it. "Fast, too. Oh, Marcus *will* be pleased!"

"I'm glad you like 'em. Listen, we got a little trouble here with our steering column ..."

"Down that ramp, to the right. Follow the signs. Tell Flamma I sent you." He turned back to the deinonychi, and musingly said, "Should they fight hoplomachi? Or maybe dimachaeri?" Crow knew the terms; the former were warriors who fought in armor, the latter with two knives.

"Horses would be nice," a sparsore commented. "If you used andabatae, they'd be able to strike from above."

Carpophorus shook his head. "I have it! Those Norse bear-sarkers I've been saving for something special—what could be more special than this?"

It was a regular labyrinth under the Coliseum. They had everything down there: workshops, brothels, training rooms, even a garage. At the mention of Carpophorus' name, a mechanic dropped everything to check out their truck. They sat in the stands, munching on a head of lettuce and watching the gladiators practice. An hour later a slave came up to tell them it was fixed.

THEY BOUGHT A ROOM at a tavern that evening and ordered the best meal in the house. Which turned out to be sow's udders stuffed with fried baby mice. They washed it down with a wine that tasted like turpentine and got drunk and screwed and fell asleep. At least, Annie did. Crow sat up for a time, thinking.

Was she going to wake up some morning in a cold barn or on a piss-stained mattress and miss her goose-down comforters, her satin sheets, and her liveried servants? She'd been nobility, after all, and the wife of a demiurge ...

He hadn't meant to run off with anybody's wife. But when he and some buddies had showed up at Lord Eric's estates, intent upon their own plans, there Annie was. No man that liked women could look upon Annie and not want her. And Crow couldn't want something without trying to get it. Such was his nature—he couldn't alter it.

He'd met her in the gardens out by Lord Eric's menagerie. A minor tweak of the weather had been made, so that the drifts of snow were held back to make room for bright mounds of prehistoric orchids. "Th'art a ragged fellow indeed, sirrah," she'd said with cool amusement.

He'd come under guise of a musician at a time when Lord Eric was away for a few years monkeying with the physical constants of the universe or some such bullshit. The dinosaurs had been his target from the first, though he wasn't above boffing the boss's lady on the way out. But something about her made him want her for more than just the night. Then and there he swore to himself that he'd win her, fair and without deceit, and on his own terms. "These ain't rags, babe," he'd said, hooking his thumbs into his belt. "They're my colors."

THEY STAYED IN ROME for a week, and they didn't go to watch the games, though Annie—who was born in an era whose idea of entertainment included public executions and bear-baitings—wanted to. But the deinonychi were by all accounts a hit. Afterwards, they collected their reward in the form of silver bars, "as many," Carpophorus gleefully quoted his sponsor, Marcus, as saying, "as the suspension of their truck will bear."

Marcus was a rich man from a good family and had political ambitions. Crow happened to know he'd be dead within the month, but he didn't bother mentioning the fact. Leave well enough alone, was his motto.

"Why did we wait around," Annie wanted to know afterwards, "if we weren't going to watch?"

"To make sure it actually happened. Eric can't come in now and snatch back his dinos without creating a serious line paradox. As I read it, that's considered bad form for a Lord of Creation." They were on the streets of Rome again, slowed to a crawl by the density of human traffic. Crow leaned on the horn again and again.

They made a right turn and then another, and then the traffic was gone. Crow threw the transmission into second and stepped on the accelerator. They were back among the Mountains of Eternity. From here they could reach any historical era and even, should they wish, the vast stretches of time that came before and after. All the roads were clear, and there was nothing in their way.

LESS THAN A MONTH LATER, subjective time, they were biking down that same road, arguing. Annie was lobbying for him to get her a sidecar and Crow didn't think much of that idea at all.

"This here's my *hog,* goddamnit!" he explained. "I chopped her myself—you put a sidecar on it, it'll be all the fuck out of balance."

"Yeah, well, I hope you enjoy jerking off. Because my fucking ass is so goddamn sore that ..."

He'd opened up the throttle to drown out what she was about to say when suddenly Annie was pounding on his back, screaming, "Pull over!"

Crow was still braking the Harley when she leaned over to the side and began to puke.

When she was done, Crow dug a Schlitz out of the saddlebags and popped the tab. Shakily, she accepted it. "What was it?" he asked.

Annie gargled and spat out the beer. "Another premonition—a muckle bad one, I trow." Then, "Hey. Who do I have to fuck to get a smoke around here?"

Crow lit up a Kent for her.

Midway through the cigarette, she shuddered again and went rigid. Her pupils shrank to pinpricks, and her eyes turned up in their sockets, so they were almost entirely white. The sort of thing that would've gotten her burned for a witch, back in good old sixteenth-c England.

She raised a hand, pointing. "Incoming. Five of them."

THEY WERE UGLY FUCKERS, the Basilisks were: black, unornamented two-rotor jobs, and noisy too. You could hear them miles off.

Luckily, Annie's foresight had given Crow the time to pick out a good defensive position. Cliff face to their back, rocks to crouch behind, enough of an overhang they couldn't try anything from above. Enough room to stash the bike, just in case they came out of this one alive. There was a long, empty slope before them. Their pursuers would have to come running up it.

The formation of Basilisks thundered closer.

"Pay attention, babe," Crow said. "I'm gonna teach you a little guerrilla warfare."

He got out his rifle from its saddle sheath. It was a Savage 110 Tactical. Good sniper rifle. He knew this gun. He'd packed the shells himself. It was a reliable piece of machinery.

"This here's a trick I learned in a little jungle war you probably ain't never heard of. Hold out your thumb at arm's length, okay? Now you wait until the helicopter's as big as the thumb. That's when it's close enough you can shoot it down."

"Will that work?" she asked nervously.

"Hell, if the Cong could do it, so can I."

HE TOOK OUT THREE Basilisks before the others could sweep up and around and out of range again. It was damned fine shooting if he did say so himself. But then the survivors set down in the distant snow and disgorged at least thirty armed men. Which changed the odds somewhat.

Annie counted soldiers, and quietly said, "Crow . . ."

Crow held a finger to her lips.

"Don't you worry none about *me*. I'm a trickster, babe. I'm archetypal. Ain't none of them can touch the Man."

Annie kissed his finger and squeezed his hand. But by the look in her eyes, he could tell she knew he was lying. "They can make you suffer, though," she said. "Eric has an old enemy staked to a rock back at his estates. Vultures come and eat his intestines."

"That's his brother, actually." It was an ugly story, and he was just as glad when she didn't ask him to elaborate. "Hunker down, now. Here they come."

The troops came scattershot up the slope, running raggedly from cover to cover. Very professional. Crow settled himself down on his elbows, and raised his rifle. Not much wind. On a day like today, he ought to be able to hit a man at five hundred yards ten times out of ten. "Kiss your asses good-bye," he muttered.

He figured he'd take out half of them before they got close enough to throw a stasis grenade.

LORD ERIC WAS A well-made man, tall and full of grace. He had the glint of power to him, was bold and fair of face. A touch of lace was at his wrist. His shirt was finest silk.

"Lady Anne," he said.

"Lord Eric."

"I have come to restore you to your home and station: to your lands, estates, gracious powers, and wide holdings. As well as to the bed of your devoted husband." His chariot rested in the snow behind him; he'd waited until all the dirty work was done before showing up.

"You are no longer my husband. I have cast my fortune with a better man than thou."

"That gypsy?" He afforded Crow the briefest and most dismissive of glances. "'Tis no more than a common thief, scarce worth the hemp to hang him, the wood to burn him, the water to drown him, nor the earth to bury him. Yet he has made free with a someat trifle that is mine and mine alone to depose—I speak of your honor. So he must die. He must die, and thou be brought to heel, as obedient to my hand as my hawk, my hound, or my horse."

She spat at his feet. "Eat shit, asshole."

Lord Eric's elegant face went white. He drew back his fist to strike her.

Crow's hands were cuffed behind his back, and he couldn't free them. So he lurched suddenly forward, catching his captors and Eric by surprise, and took the blow on his own face. That sucker hurt, but he didn't let it show. With the biggest, meanest grin he could manage, he said, "See, there's the difference between you and me. You couldn't stop yourself from hurting her. I could."

"Think you so?" Lord Eric gestured and one of his men handed him a pair of grey kid gloves of finest Spanish leather. "I raised a mortal above her state. Four hundred years was she my consort. No more."

Fear entered Annie's eyes for the first time, though nobody who knew her less well than Crow could have told.

"I will strangle her myself," Eric said, pulling on the gloves. "She deserves no less honor, for she was once my wife."

The tiger cage was set up on a low dais, one focus of the large, oval room. Crow knew from tiger cages, but he'd never thought he'd wind up in one. Especially not in the middle of somebody's party.

Especially not at Annie's wake.

The living room was filled with demiurges and light laughter, cocaine and gin. Old Tezcatlipoca, who had been as good as a father to Crow in his time, seeing him, grimaced and shook his head. Now Crow regretted ever getting involved with Spaniards, however sensible an idea it had seemed at the time.

The powers and godlings who orbited the party, cocktails in hand, solitary and aloof as planets, included Lady Dale, who bestowed riches with one hand and lightnings from the other, and had a grudge against Crow for stealing her distaff; Lord Aubrey of the short and happy lives, who hated him for the sake of a friend; Lady Siff of the flames, whose attentions he had once scorned; and Reverend Wednesday, old father death himself, in clerical collar, stiff with disapproval at Crow's libertine ways.

He had no allies anywhere in this room.

Over there was Lord Taleisin, the demiurge of music, who, possibly alone of all this glittering assemblage, bore Crow no ill will. Crow figured it was because Tal had never learned the truth behind that business back in Crete.

He figured, too, there must be some way to turn that to his advantage.

"You look away from me every time I go by," Lord Taleisin said. "Yet I know of no offense you have given me, or I you."

"Just wanted to get your attention is all," Crow said. "Without any of the others suspecting it." His brow was set in angry lines but his words were soft and mild. "I been thinking about how I came to be. I mean, you guys are simply *there,* a part of the natural order of things. But us archetypes are created out of a million years of campfire tales and wishful lies. We're thrown up out of the collective unconscious. I got to wondering what would happen if somebody with access to that unconscious—you, for example—was to plant a few songs here and there."

"It could be done, possibly. Nothing's certain. But what would be the point?"

"How'd you like your brother's heart in a box?"

Lord Tal smiled urbanely. "Eric and I may not see eye to eye on everything, yet I cannot claim to hate him so as to wish the physical universe rendered uninhabitable."

"Not him. Your other brother."

Tal involuntarily glanced over his shoulder, toward the distant mountain, where a small dark figure lay tormented by vultures. The house had been built here with just that view in mind. "If it could be done, don't you think I'd've done it?" Leaving unsaid but understood: *How could you succeed where I have failed?*

"I'm the trickster, babe—remember? I'm the wild card, the unpredictable element, the unexpected event. I'm the blackfly under the saddle. I'm the ice on the O-rings. I am the *only* one who could do this for you."

Very quietly, Lord Taleisin said, "What sureties do you require?"

"Your word's good enough for me, pal. Just don't forget to spit in my face before you leave. It'll look better."

"HAVE FUN," LORD ERIC said, and left the room.

Eric's men worked Crow over good. They broke his ribs and kicked in his face. A couple of times they had to stop to get their breath back, they were laboring so hard. He had to give them credit, they put their backs into the work. But, like Crow himself, the entertainment was too boorish for its audience. Long before it was done, most of the partyers had left in boredom or disgust.

At last he groaned, and he died.

Well, what was a little thing like death to somebody like Crow? He was archetypal—the universe demanded that he exist. Kill him here-and-now and he'd be reborn there-and-then. It wouldn't be long before he was up and around again.

But not Annie.

No, that was the bitch of the thing. Annie was dead, and the odds were good she wasn't coming back.

AMONG TWENTY SMOG-CHOKED cities, the only still thing was the eye of Crow. He leaned back, arms crossed, in the saddle of his Harley, staring at a certain door so hard he was almost surprised his gaze didn't burn a hole in it.

A martlet flew down from the sky and perched on the handlebars. It was a little bird, round-headed and short-beaked, with long sharp wings. Its eyes were two stars shining. "Hail!" it said.

"Hail, fire, and damnation," Crow growled. "Any results?"

"Lord Taleisin has done as you required, and salted the timelines with songs. In London, Nashville, and Azul-Tlon do they praise her beauty, and the steadfastness of her love. In a hundred guises and a thousand names is she exalted. From mammoth-bone medicine lodges to MTVirtual, they sing of Lady Anne, of the love that sacrifices all comfort, and of the price she gladly paid for it."

Still the door did not open.

"That's not what I asked, shit-for-brains. Did it work?"

"Perhaps." The bird cocked its head. "Perhaps not. I was told to caution you: Even at best, you will only have a now-and-again lady. Archetypes don't travel in pairs. If it works, your meetings will be like solar eclipses—primal, powerful, rare, and brief."

"Yeah, yeah."

The creature hesitated, and if a bird could be said to look abashed, then it looked strangely abashed. "I was also told that you would have something for me."

Without looking, Crow unstrapped his saddlebag and rummaged within. He removed a wooden heart-shaped box, tied up in string. "Here."

With a glorious burst of unearthly song, the martlet seized the string in its talons and, wings whirring, flew straight up into the sky. Crow did not look after it. He waited.

He waited until he was sure that the door would never open. Then he waited some more.

The door opened.

Out she came, in faded Levis, leather flight jacket, and a black halter top, sucking on a Kent menthol. She was looking as beautiful as the morning and as hard as nails. The sidewalk cringed under her high-heeled boots.

"Hey, babe," Crow said casually. "I got you a sidecar. See? It's lined with velvet and everything."

"Fuck that noise," Annie said and, climbing on behind him, hugged him so hard that his ribs creaked.

He kick-started the Harley and with a roar they pulled out into traffic. Crow cranked up the engine and popped a wheelie. Off they sped, down the road that leads everywhere and nowhere, to the past and the future, Tokyo and Short Pump, infinity and the corner store, with Annie laughing and unafraid, and Crow flying the black flag of himself.

Microcosmic Dog

ELLEN GILLESPIE LIVED in a world of her own. It looked much the way New York City would had it been wrapped around an asteroid and then turned inside out. Sitting on her balcony she could see a sky full of buildings that curved overhead and warped back down again somewhere behind her back. Ellen had lived in this world so long that it seemed absolutely normal to her.

She was happy there.

Each morning, she cabbed down to the Village for Turkish coffee and bagels with cream cheese and lox at Kuscazk's, a sidewalk café not far from the White Horse Saloon where Dylan Thomas had so famously drunk himself to death. Lunch varied. It might be a salad *vinaigrette* with a glass of white wine at the MoMA or then again it might be a hot dog and a Coke bought from a vendor and eaten in Central Park at the foot of the Alice statue, where she could watch the little children launch their toy boats out on the sailing pond. It depended entirely upon her mood. Suppers—unless she had a date—she ate at Lutèce.

It was a good life for a single woman with an income. Her apartment was large enough for the occasional dinner party, and even though she had designated one room her library and set aside another for a darkroom, there was still space enough to work at home on days when she simply couldn't face going to the office. She loved everything about New York—its neverending variety, the sunshine that daily welled up from its many rivers, the fact that it never slept. Sometimes she took a close friend and the futon out onto the balcony at night and they would make love there, illumined only by the splendor of a thousand neon signs and a million starry windows arching overhead.

She was in her study one day, going over photo proofs for a spread that *Vogue* had commissioned, when her girlfriend Stasi walked in— Ellen never bothered to lock her door—with an enormous sheep dog at her heels and announced that she was going away.

"Away? Away where?"

"Oh, you know." Stasi waved a hand vaguely. "Away."

"Well, when are you coming back?"

"*Dear* child." Stasi was a model and had once come within a whisper of supermodeldom. The experience had left its mark on her diction. "I'm not coming back. None of us are. Ever."

A chill ran through Ellen. "What do you mean? You don't mean that."

"I just dropped by to ask if you'd take my dog." Stasi's hand was on the door now. "Don't let it beg at the table. Two meals a day is plenty."

"Wait!" Ellen cried. Stasi's eyes, when she looked back, were paler than pale—coldly, unblinkingly fixed upon death. It was terrifying. All Ellen's questions, objections, arguments, died on her tongue. "What's the dog's name?"

"Dog."

"Dog? Just Dog?"

"Dog."

"Why Dog?"

Stasi shrugged. "That's its name."

"Oh. Well, that makes sense. I guess."

And then she was gone.

Ellen closed the door. "Well, Dog, I guess it's just you and me, then. I'd better send out for some dog food. I wonder what you like to eat."

"Alpo will do fine," Dog said.

"You can talk!"

"Yes. I'm a talking Dog." It walked to a corner, turned around three times, then lay down and promptly fell asleep.

Ellen was astonished, of course. But no more so than by the behavior of certain other roommates she had lived with in her time. New York was full of surprises. One either grew used to them or went back home to Idaho or New Jersey or wherever it was that one came from.

She called down to the concierge for a case of Alpo and, for the moment, that was that.

THERE SEEMED TO BE fewer people than usual out on the street the next day. But Manhattan was a chaotic system, full of strange rhythms and unpredictable effects. You never knew what to expect.

Kuscazk's was almost empty, but Conrad said they were out of her coffee anyway, so Ellen had to settle for a mocha latte. Dog lay by her feet, gnawing at a plate of sausages that Conrad had placed there at her direction. "You really lead a charmed existence," it remarked.

"You should talk," Ellen said a little nervously. She still wasn't sure how she felt about sharing her life—her secrets—with a talking dog. "I mean, there you are with your sausages and all the Alpo you could possibly want and somebody to see that you're properly groomed and you don't even have to hold down a job. Some people would say you've got it made."

"You wouldn't trade places with me, though."

"No, I guess not."

She paid with her American Express, left a cash tip, and took a cab to the office.

Rudolfo was waiting for her with a stack of black-and-white glossies he wanted her approval on. They were, as expected, technically brilliant, but— "Rudy, these are perverse! What happened to this woman's fingers? They're deformed. My God, all these people are missing things! Ears and legs and— this is supposed to be a fashion shoot, not a wallow in the gutter."

Rudolfo drew himself up haughtily. He was tall and thin and young and black; disdain looked good on him. "Perversity sells, daarling. Anyway, these are the best we can get. Every physically whole model in Manhattan has gone away."

She came to a photo of a woman with part of her skull missing and put a hand over it so she wouldn't have to see. "What about the agency in Soho? The one that made that big presentation last week."

"Out of business. I went there yesterday and it was gone. Vacated. *Tout perdu.* Models gone, the building torn down, and the street packed up into vans and shipped away."

"Now that's ridic—"

Dog, lying motionless on a sheepskin rug, suddenly said, "A singularity engine requires a black hole no more than a yard across of at least 0.00023 Solar mass embedded within a curdled self-generated matrix of electromagnetic flux. It is capable of generating and maintaining a wavefront reality at a complexity of 86 million polygons per second. A single engine—"

"*What,*" Ellen snapped, "are you talking about?"

Dog snorted, and twitched, and gracelessly stood—a process similar to watching the film of an avalanche being run backwards. "I'm sorry, I must have been talking in my sleep."

"You were saying something about black holes and polygons. And numbers—there were a lot of numbers involved."

"Was I?"

"Excuse me," Rudolfo said. "What's with the mutt?"

"Its name is Dog. It can talk."

"Typical. Here I am, trying to hold a serious conversation about something important and you're off in Never-Never Land, talking to the animals as if you were Eliza Doolittle."

"Eliza Doolittle did not—oh, what's the point? Rudolfo, why are you being so *difficult* today?" She stopped. "Did you have a fight with Gregor?"

"Who?"

"Gregor. Your boyfriend!"

Rudolfo looked blank.

"The guy you've been living with for the past three years. The one with the dimples and a thing for Quentin Tarantino movies. The one who did the cute trick with the cheese omelet that I told you I'd have to strangle you if you told me about it one more time. *That* Gregor!"

"I honestly don't know what you're talking about."

"Take out your wallet," Ellen said. "Look in the card holder. You'll find a photo of the two of you together, behind your driver's license."

Rudolfo obeyed. He slid out the photograph and stared wordlessly at it for a long time. Finally he said, "He's gorgeous."

"Well, that's what I've always said." Ellen smiled.

"But I have no memory of him whatsoever," he said in a troubled voice. "Or of any other boyfriends, for that matter. I can't remember my mother. I can't remember my childhood. I don't even believe I had one."

"Now I don't know what *you're* talking about."

Rudolfo sank to the floor, put his head in his hands, and began to cry. Alarmed, Ellen crouched down beside him and put an arm over his shoulder. "Don't cry, Rudy. Whatever the trouble is, it's not that bad."

"It is!" Rudolfo raised his tear-stained face from his hands. "I've lost my past, I've lost my memories, I've lost this boyfriend you tell me I had ... Dear God, what's happening to me?"

"I don't know," Ellen said fearfully. "But it's time we found out. We'll start by talking to Gregor." She lifted the phone and hit speed dial. But the line was dead. She tried clicking the receiver like people did in the movies. Nothing. "Okay, then, we'll go over in person. Where is it you guys live, anyway?"

"In Brooklyn," Dog answered for him.

Determination filled Ellen. "Come on," she said to Rudolfo, "we're going to get to the bottom of this thing."

There was a roadblock at the Brooklyn Bridge. All the cars were being turned back. "Keep moving, keep moving!" the traffic cop shouted.

Ellen shoved Dog aside and stuck her head out the window. "What's going on?"

"Brooklyn is closed."

"What are you talking about? Brooklyn can't be closed. It's a borough, for cripes sake."

"It's closed," the cop repeated, "for repairs." To the cabbie he said, "Now clear out before I yank your license!"

So they left. "Did you hear what he said?" Ellen asked, a little hysterically. "He said that Brooklyn was closed for repairs!"

"Does a cinnamon bun taste the same to you as it does for me?" Rudolfo asked in a lifeless monotone. "Do you experience its texture in more detail? Is it buttered? Are there raisins?"

"Rudolfo, you're not making any sense." Ellen stared at the passing buildings. They all looked alike. Had they always been so drab? So ... unornamented?

"What is it like to live a complete life? One that's continuous, and detailed across the full bandwidth for every physical sense? One in which nothing is experienced in synopsis? I can't imagine how glorious your existence must be."

"What *are* you talking about?"

There was no reply.

When Ellen turned to look, she was—save for Dog—alone in the back seat. "Where'd he go?" she asked in astonishment. "What happened to Rudolfo?"

"I ate him," Dog said.

"Very funny." Ellen shivered and settled back in her seat. This was creepy and then some. Something was seriously wrong.

In silence they rode back uptown.

Rockefeller Center was clogged with people. The cabbie leaned on his horn and tried to force a way through, without success. So Ellen paid and got out.

"What's going on?" she asked a stranger.

"They're dedicating a statue." He pointed to where Prometheus used to be. It had been replaced by a new sculpture. Down the avenue she could see parts of the old statue being hauled away, the head, a leg, an enormous bronze hand.

From this angle, the new statue looked like a cutaway model of New York City. Ellen could see all the tiny buildings lining its interior, the skyscrapers like stalactites and stalagmites pointing toward the central axis. Looked at from the outside and seen all at once, it was obviously in the shape of a human figure, legs together and arms outflung. The torso, she supposed, was Manhattan, with the Village down in the crotch.

A vertiginous wave of unreality washed through Ellen. It was true, she thought. The city *was* formed in the shape of a person. It was so obvious. How could she have never noticed it before?

"Well?" Dog said. "Aren't you going to go around to the front and see who it's of?"

With a bound, it was running ahead of her, barking joyfully. People hurried out of its way, making a path through the crowd which she followed effortlessly around to the front of the statue.

It was her. It was a statue of Ellen Gillespie in a space suit.

Ellen shivered. "This is bizarre."

"Think of it as a wake-up call."

"Hah?" Ellen stared down at the shaggy creature beside her. "What do you mean?"

"How obvious do I have to be?" asked Dog. There was a distinct edge in its voice. "Do I have to spell it out for you?"

Ellen looked directly into the animal's eyes. They were hard and cold. Suddenly she was afraid. Suddenly it didn't seem a soft and fluffy and lovable Dog at all.

As casually as she could—and continually fighting the urge to run— Ellen pushed her way out of the crowd and across Forty-eighth to Fifth Avenue, and stuck out her arm. A cab pulled up and she leaped inside, slamming the door before Dog could follow her.

"Where to?" the cabbie asked.

"I don't know—out. Away. Queens."

"Closed."

"The Bronx Zoo."

"Not there any more."

"The Whitney!"

The cabbie flipped the flag on the meter.

Behind her, she saw Dog raise a paw to hail another cab.

THE WHITNEY WAS HOLDING a Bill Viola retrospective. The place should have been thronged. But it was so completely deserted that there wasn't even anybody there to take her money. Her footsteps echoed noisily in the empty galleries. She was pretty sure she'd given her canine pursuer the slip. Now that she had, however, she had no idea what her next move should be.

In bleak desolation, Ellen wandered from installation to installation. In one room she saw her own image, reflected upside down in a drop of water and thrown up on a wall, shimmer and swell and then disappear as the drop fell with a soft *boom* onto a miked tambourine. Under ordinary circumstances, it was exactly the kind of art she liked best. Now it only filled her with dread.

A new drop of water was projected upon the wall. Within it, she saw Dog loom up behind her.

Briefly, she closed her eyes. Then she turned.

"All right," she said. "What's going on?"

"New York City is being deconstructed."

"Why?"

"You've been living in the past," Dog said. "Now it's time to pull yourself together and resume your real life."

With a pedantic wave of a paw, it directed her attention to the wall.

The projected water drop was gone, replaced by a space suit caught up in a tangle of machinery adrift in vacuum. Alongside the suit floated a featureless black sphere. Tendrils of energy flowed between suit and sphere. "The year is 2870. A starfreighter was ferrying a singularity engine to Beta Comae Berenices for the colony on New Amsterdam when the engines blew. Everybody died except for one person. The supercargo. You."

"I'm blue collar?" Ellen cried, horrified.

"Supercargo is a perfectly respectable profession." Dog turned toward the screen again. Now it showed a starship breaking up. Atomic fires flared. Bulkheads peeled away. "And you were a good spacer. You kept your head. With only seconds in which to act, you accessed the singularity and gave it a series of commands."

Words flowed across the wall: SEND FOR HELP. KEEP ME ALIVE. KEEP ME SAFE. KEEP ME HEALTHY AND SANE.

"The singularity did what it could. It disassembled what bits of the ship remained to build the sub-space distress beacon. That didn't leave much to keep you alive with. So it used what it had: Your suit. And your body.

"It took you apart, and with your elements built a microscopic version of ancient Manhattan inside your space suit. Then it reconstructed you, with appropriate memories, inside that environment. I think you'll agree that it interpreted your commands well."

"I don't have to listen to this," Ellen said wildly. "I won't!"

She turned her back and walked away. Dog did not follow.

But there was no exit.

There was nothing but the Whitney, with its two and a half floors of video installations, its half-floor of abstract expressionism, its gift shop, and its rather basic ground-floor *patisserie*. The doors no longer existed, and all the windows looked out upon anymore was human blood and tissue.

All that was left of New York City was this one small bubble of space suspended within a world of her own flesh.

SHE FOUND DOG WAITING for her in the *patisserie*. Almost in tears, she demanded, "Why are you *doing* this to me?"

"The rescue ship has come," it replied. "New York is no longer needed, so it's being dismantled."

"That's what's become of Stasi, then? And Rudolfo and Gregor and everybody else? They've been destroyed?"

"They never were real. Only you were real. And now it's time for you to rejoin the outer world." Dog lowered its voice persuasively. "That's why I'm here. To ease the way for you."

"Ease the way?"

"It's your turn now." Where a pastry cart had been was now a couch with brocaded red-and-green roses. "I want you to lie down and close your eyes. This won't take a minute."

"Hey, wait. Hold on here. What if I don't want to?"

"Relax. This won't hurt a bit. You have my word on it."

Ellen thought she detected a trace of unctuousness in Dog's voice. But she wasn't sure. To focus herself, she picked up a bread stick and carefully buttered it on one side, thinking only of the task at hand and how good it would taste. She was about to eat it, in spite of her diet, when a thought came to her.

She put the bread stick, untasted, down on a plate.

"Not so fast," Ellen said slowly. "I said to keep me safe, and I said to call for help, but I didn't say anything about what to do when help came. Your orders didn't say anything about reconstructing me. So if I don't cooperate, I don't have to leave."

For a long moment Dog was silent. Finally it said, "I was hoping you wouldn't realize that."

"Well, I do. And I'm not cooperating!"

"Ellen, the singularity can't look after you and serve the needs of the New Amsterdam colony as well. It's needed there. They've reached the critical population mass where human beings alone can't run the society without wars and economic disasters. There are people dying for lack of what you're selfishly refusing to share."

"I don't care," Ellen said harshly. "Put it back. I want my life just the way it was—Rudy, the Village, my job, everything. You have to keep me healthy and sane, right? Well, this is making me feel distinctly unhealthy. I am definitely having unbalanced thoughts."

Dog sighed. "As you wish," it said. "So be it."

EVERYTHING WAS BACK TO NORMAL.

To celebrate, Ellen held a party. She told the caterers from Too Cute to Cook to set out beluga on crackers, raw tuna wrapped in kelp, and crudites for the vegetarians, and to keep the Perignon flowing. Then she invited all her very best friends, and a few celebrities from the literary world, with a seasoning of strangers just to keep the mix from getting predictable.

It was fun. For a while.

But there came a moment ... when Stasi was doing her impression of Richard Nixon voguing at the Rubber Club, and Rudolfo and Gregor were camping it up and exchanging desperate little kisses in the guise of making fun of themselves, and Tom Disch and Joyce Carol Oates were analyzing the latest John Grisham novel with delicate mockery, and a handsome stranger—a stockbroker who had come in with Esme and then high-handedly abandoned her—was giving Ellen the eye from the far side of the room ... that she realized how empty it all felt.

None of it really mattered. None of them was real.

It was like finding herself trapped inside a television sitcom. Everybody was manic. Everybody was funny. They were all doing their damnedest to amuse her. And it had all the charm of canned laughter.

Meat puppets, she thought. They're all nothing more than meat puppets.

The handsome young stockbroker chose that moment to make his move. He strolled over to Ellen's chair and, putting one hand on its back, leaned over to murmur a cynical witticism in her ear. As he did, the other hand lightly clenched her knee.

Revolted, she pushed him away.

She shoved him so hard that the stockbroker fell over backward, right on his Armani-clad ass. Then Ellen stood and shouted, "Get out!"

The party fell silent. Everybody looked at her, shocked.

"Get out, get out, get out! You're not real, any of you! Why should I pretend you are?" And then, as mouths opened in protest, "Don't look hurt either!"

Mouths closed. Faces blank, her guests obediently filed out. In less than a minute the room was empty.

Ellen began to cry.

"Hell," somebody said, "is no other people."

Ellen looked up. Dog stood in the doorway. "Had enough?" it asked.

She nodded wearily.

"Good." Taking her by the hand, Dog gently led Ellen to her bedroom. It sat her down on the bed. Through the open window, she could hear the city noises—traffic, sirens, saxophones—one by one shut themselves off.

Silence enfolded the universe.

At Dog's direction, Ellen kicked off her shoes and lay on her back. The mattress was soft and comforting. She crossed her hands on her chest. "What do I do now?"

"Close your eyes," Dog said.

"I'm afraid."

"There'll be an instant of darkness. Then you'll wake up in the larger world—the real world."

A sudden spasm of doubt hit Ellen then, as cold and hard as a cupronickel asteroid in a decades-long orbit around a dead star. "Suppose I don't wake up? What if I just cease to be like all my fr—all the people I thought were my friends? I don't want that to happen to me."

"Your rescuers are scrambling out of their airlock," Dog said soothingly. "They're desperate to save you. They're coming just as fast as they can."

"But I only have your word for that!"

"Now they can see your suit. Their hearts are filled with joy and hope. They're flying toward you with arms extended."

A silk-soft paw brushed lightly over her face from forehead to chin. Reflexively, her eyelids fluttered shut.

"Have faith," Dog said.

The darkness closed about her like a mouth.

In Concert

THE POSTERS HAD BEEN plastered all over Sevastopol for a month, huge black-and-red things with only two words on them:

IN CONCERT

Nothing else. Just those two words and the harsh profile of a face so familiar to Tex that it sometimes seemed hard-wired into his neural structure, the outward expression of a truth encoded in his genes from birth. Time, place, and price had been omitted so the same posters could be used in every city of the tour. Everybody knew no tickets would ever reach the box office. Favors would be called in, backs scratched, envelopes stuffed with American currency exchanged. For weeks, the pasteboards had described complex orbits between the black market and the highest reaches of the Party hierarchy, each one being traded again and again, multiplying in value, greasing the wheels, the perfect bribe, the surest way of getting anything from a new Sony Walkman to a preferred position on the waiting lists for a bigger apartment.

Tonight they would all—tickets, favors, bribes—come to rest.

"Get up, you hooligan!"

Tex squinted up into the face of the squattest, ugliest woman he had ever seen. Shapeless dress, shapeless body, a red babushka from which dry wisps of grey hair struggled to escape. Twin lines from the corners of her mouth framed her chin, giving her the jaws of a turtle. Maybe she was a gnome.

"Hah?" He had been sitting at the bottom of a long flight of public steps, staring idly through the fumes and traffic at a lot across the prospekt. A makeshift market had been built there, where vendors sold vegetables, hot coffee, and flowers from small kiosks. He was working on a song. Trying to come up with a rhyme for "oblivion."

"Don't sprawl like that! Shame on you! Who do you think you are to block everybody's passage?"

The steps rose past the white-walled city offices, and though it was not yet quitting time all the apparatchiks had left early to avoid the weekend crush of traffic to their country dachas. The buildings were empty and so were the stairs. Without saying a word, Tex put his guitar back into its case and closed the snaps. Swiping at the seat of his cheap Bulgarian jeans, he stood and smiled at her. She sniffed and turned away.

The No. 10 trolleybus arrived then, and Tex got on. A couple of people were ahead of him at the punch, so he didn't bother to cancel his ticket. He found a seat near the back and, gripping his guitar case between his knees, stared glumly out a scratched and dirty window, trying to imagine himself on stage, electric guitar slung low at the hip, and in the audience girls in punk leather screaming ecstatically. The old woman perversely took the seat beside him, though there were others available.

With a lurch and a harsh clatter of gears, the trolleybus started off. A year ago it would have run soundlessly. Next year it might not run at all. Thank you, Comrade Gorbachev.

More posters floated by, singly and in groups. On the blind side of an old warehouse they had been plastered up four-by-three, like a video array set to multiply the same static image over and over.

IN CONCERT IN CONCERT IN CONCERT IN CONCERT
IN CONCERT IN CONCERT IN CONCERT IN CONCERT
IN CONCERT IN CONCERT IN CONCERT IN CONCERT

Somebody had defaced each and every poster with the circle-and-A anarchy symbol.

"Vandals!" The turtle woman jabbed a bony finger in Tex's ribs. "That's a disgusting way to treat the People's property! These hoodlums probably go to the same school as you—why don't you and your friends do something about them? Band together, show some solidarity, teach them respect. Sevastopol is such a beautiful city, after all, don't you agree?"

"Sevastopol is a shithole." Tex turned away from the outraged O of her mouth and stared out the window again. They were going by a park; wrought-iron bandstands, couples out strolling hand in hand. It was very nineteenth-century. He sighed.

He didn't even know why he was bothering.

Both Boris and Andrei had sneered when he asked if they wanted to come along. It was pointless, they said. The little he could hear from outside wasn't going to be worth listening to. Anyway, the Boss was old stuff, little more than a walking cadaver kept alive by cryonics, morphine, and bimonthly whole-blood changes. Three surgeons traveled as part of his road crew and a team of paramedics waited on standby alert backstage whenever he performed.

Then Andrei had said that if Tex wanted to take in some real music, he had the new Butthole Surfers bootleg, which his sister's boyfriend, who worked a Black Sea merchanter, had copped in a greymarket bazaar in Turkey. They could maybe score some hashish from one of the Afghan War vets who hung around the servicemen's club, and go out behind the skating rink and get stoned and drunk and break things.

Tex had replied that he was sick to death of hardcore and that it was just an excuse for no-talents who could scream but couldn't sing to avoid learning how to finger bar chords. That hadn't pleased Boris, who had just settled on the stage name of Misha Cyberpunk and was thinking of shaving his head. He'd asked if that meant they were going to work up yet *another* version of "Mustang Sally." At which point Andrei had had to step in to prevent a fight.

So he was going alone.

Worse, his friends had a point. This trip was a perfect example of what his teachers called "the cult of personality" whenever the bastards got onto the subject of their students' taste in music. He was being a jerk. No question about that.

But still. This was more than just another appearance by just another guitar hero. This was more than just another one-night stand by one of the founding fathers of rock and roll. So what if he had to listen from outside the hall? It was the last chance he was ever going to have to get even that close to the man.

It was the Boss's farewell tour.

FORTY MINUTES LATER the trolleybus let him off at the concert hall.

The Fisherman's Palace of Culture stood above Kamyshovaya Bay, surrounded by gently sloping grass lawns. It was a great four-story square building, all glass and concrete, with seating for two thousand spectators and half again that many more if they decided to pack the aisles. They could have booked the act into the soccer stadium and filled every seat; but the Boss preferred concert halls. The acoustics were more to his liking.

It was late afternoon. A salt breeze blew up from the water, and he could look down on the fishing craft at anchor in the bay. The lawns were heroically large, muscular Social Realist landscaping intended to proclaim the glory and triumph of the Soviet sod and fertilizer industries. The effect was badly undercut by the line of totalitarian grey highrises across the roadway, concrete monsters identical down to their water stains. Some of their hard-faced denizens had set up card tables by the parking lot and were offering packs of Winstons and Belgian beer at thirty rubles a can. A surprisingly large number of people were standing casually about the concert hall grounds, trying not to look conspicuous.

A fisherman reclined on the grass, cap on his knee and a brown paper bag in his hand. His trousers were dirty and his sweater torn. "Comrade musician! Come, have a swig." He waggled the bag invitingly.

Tex shrugged and awkwardly sat down beside him. Inside, though, he felt a wonderful warmth. For this one moment, everything was okay. Sitting above the bay, sharing a bottle with a real fisherman, was an authentic experience, an unquestionably cool thing to be doing. He accepted the bottle and drank. The vodka was warm and tasted of fusel oil.

He took too large a mouthful, choked, gasped, and forced a smile. "Good stuff," he said.

"American!" The fisherman sounded pleased. He held out a hand. "It is good to meet a fine young American boy like you. My name is Yuri."

He took the proffered hand and shook his head. "I've been a citizen for years. My father's a researcher for the Institute of Oceanography." He was sick of the questions everyone asked when they heard his accent and he hated his parents for bringing him here. There were times when even the beatings the kids back in Austin gave him for being a Commie pinko creep would be a small price to pay if he could return home. He wasn't treated all that much better here anyway.

"The guys at school call me Tex."

He managed to make it sound as if they'd never meant it as an insult.

Yuri grinned broadly, showing steel teeth and hideous gums. "Play some music. Something romantic, maybe it will draw in some pretty girls."

"Uh, well . . ." He unlatched the case, drew out the guitar, began tuning the strings. "Actually, I'm not as good as I'd like to be. I've got this band together," presuming that Andrei and good old Misha Cyberpunk hadn't dismantled Chernobyl in his absence, "but it's hard to find a place to practice." He strummed a C chord, shifted to an F and then a B. Finally he settled on a slow version he'd worked up of "I Am the Walrus," singing the words in English and crooning the "yellow matter custard" line with exaggerated sweetness.

"You are another Vladimir Vysotsky," the fisherman said admiringly. A couple of art students—the boy was dressed in black and had dyed his hair an unnatural red—wandered within range of Yuri's bellow, and he waved them over. "Comrade artists! Come join us, have a swig!"

"YOU KNOW WHY I'M HERE?" Yuri asked two hours later. The No. 7 bus had just pulled up to the front of the hall, and the latest load of ticket-holders was getting off. They were chatting happily, eagerly, the pampered offspring of Party officials, most of them, with a few low-ranking Red Army or Black Sea Fleet officers scattered here and there for flavoring. Many were vacationers from the bathing resorts, dressed in Benetton fashions. They pooled and flowed elegantly up the twin stairways to the second-floor entrance. In addition to the art students, Yuri had drawn in a young grocery clerk, a locksmith, and a scruffy blond girl who said she was a truck driver, though nobody believed her. "Do you know why?"

Smiling, they shook their heads.

"I am here because of *them*. All those guys walking up the steps into the Fisherman's Palace of Culture. I thought, how embarrassed they must be at not having a single fisherman in the Fisherman's Palace. So here I am. You're welcome!" he shouted to a cluster of apparatchiks climbing out of their Mercedes.

They pointedly ignored him.

"Ahh, I love those bastards, and they know it."

"You may be here," said the redheaded art student, "but you couldn't get inside that building tonight to save your life."

"Who said that?" Yuri sat up straight and stared around him incredulously. "Of course I could get in. There is always a way in for a man like me."

The student laughed uneasily, like someone who is trying to be pleasant but is not sure he understands the joke.

"You don't believe me? I'll show you. I'll get in, and I'll get all of you in with me." He lurched to his feet. "Come on, it's my treat!"

"THIS IS CRAZY," Tex said. They had circled the building three times, trying all the side doors and sizing up security—very tight—at the loading dock out back where the equipment trucks were parked. Now they were back at the first door they had checked.

"It couldn't hurt to try." Yuri knocked. Nothing happened. He tried again, louder. Still nothing. Balling his hand into a fist he pounded at the door until it echoed and boomed.

After a minute, the door opened slightly. A beefy militiaman stood within, a big mustache all but hiding his mouth. "What do you want?" He glared at them. Tex could see he was holding the door from the inside so it couldn't be grabbed away from him. Yuri smiled ingratiatingly and said, "Comrade! Look at us. I have the honor to be an honest fisherman. My friend here"—he nodded at Tex—"is a factory worker and himself a talented musician. This young man in black is a student who spent the last harvest digging potatoes on a cooperative. This fine young woman—"

The guard started to close the door, and Yuri grabbed at the edge.

"Listen to me! We are the Masses, we are the People, we are the Revolution! Those well-dressed people in there"—he pointed scornfully—"who are they? The privileged class, I say this not angrily but in sad truth. Why are they inside and we without? This is a betrayal of the principles of—"

"Fifty dollars American," said the militiaman, "and I'll let six of you in. No more. If you get the money together come back to this door and knock."

He slammed it in their faces.

But when they pooled their resources it turned out they were all of them paupers. All together they had only eighty-nine rubles and three American singles. "Anyway," the grocer grumbled, "even if we had the rubles, where would we find somebody with the hard currency to sell?"

The locksmith glanced significantly at the scraggly line of card tables by the lot but said nothing.

"Don't be downcast," Yuri said. He gathered the paper notes together, arranging them in his fist so they made an untidy mass with the greenbacks on the outside. "Looks pretty good, eh? I'll wave these in fatso's face, and when he makes a grab at them, Tex will yank open the door and we'll all push forward. We'll overwhelm the little prick."

They went back to the door. "I can't believe we're doing this." The female art student hugged herself and shivered.

Yuri raised a hand. "Are we all in place? Tex—stand right there, be ready for action."

Tex positioned himself, setting his guitar case by his feet to free his hands. Their little group was drawing attention now. Three or four loiterers joined them to see what was up. Yuri banged on the door. "Hey in there! Get off your thumb and open up!"

The door opened a cautious crack. "Let me count—" the militiaman said suspiciously, and "*Now!*" Yuri shouted.

Eight hands seized the door, and it flew open with a crash. Scooping up his guitar, Tex joined the others as they surged forward. The guard fell back in angry astonishment, pulling a truncheon from his belt.

All was confusion. Tex was running wildly down the hallway when a sudden *crack* made him turn his head. Yuri was sinking to his knees, face a glistening red. Drops of blood flew from the billy club. It was paralyzing, unbelievable. Tex stopped, the art students flashing by hand in hand, and stared.

"Run!" Yuri gasped.

Then the fat militiaman was coming directly toward him, with an expression so cold and violent that Tex panicked. He fled blindly, guitar case knocking against his side. What am I doing here? he wondered. He no longer had the slightest interest in seeing the show.

He pushed through a crowded corridor. People were running, shouting, struggling. There was a militiaman kneeling atop the little truck driver's chest. She was trying to bite his arm. Tex turned a corner, ran up a concrete and steel stairway. Heavy footsteps pounded behind him.

He ran like the wind, through corridors and empty rehearsal halls, without shaking his pursuer. His mind was blank with fear. He was hopelessly lost.

The militiaman caught up to Tex in the doorway of a dressing room and knocked him to the ground. The guitar case skittered away. A boot smashed into his ribs, and in the sudden crystalline clarity of the pain, he found himself looking up into the goateed face of a man who had swiveled in his seat from a makeup mirror to see what the fuss was about. It was a heartbreakingly familiar face.

It was the Boss himself—Vladimir Ilyich Ulyanov, idol of millions, the man known to his countless fans as Nikolai Lenin.

In that agonized instant there was time enough to take in everything and yet no time in which to act. He saw Lenin's calm, dispassionate face looking thoughtfully down at him, and heard the sadistic chuckle of the guard as he reached down to grab Tex's collar. He saw the knick-knacks on the dresser top, a framed autographed picture of Karl Marx holding his saxophone, a silver hairbrush, a pack of Salems. Half sunk in shadow, the objects seemed freighted with awful significance.

Lenin watched silently as the militiaman hauled Tex up and smashed him in the face with his brutal fist. Tex felt a wondering sense of betrayal and then he was slammed against the cinder-block wall and his vision whited out.

When sight returned, he saw the guard raising a booted foot over his guitar case.

"No!" he croaked. "Not my axe!"

For the first time, a spark of interest animated Lenin's face. He raised an index finger and the militiaman froze, foot in air.

"So," Lenin said. "A fellow musician?"

Tex nodded warily.

"Sit down." Lenin gestured to a chair, and Tex collapsed into it. His body felt bruised, aching, ugly.

"My friends . . ."

"You can do nothing for them." The militiaman, Tex noted, had not left but merely drawn back against the wall where he stood, arms folded, watching everything with avid eye.

Lenin stood, walked over to the guitar case, and brought it back to his chair. Resting it across his knees, he undid the snaps. "A Martin." He held it up, admiring its shape and heft. "Not bad, for an acoustic. How did you come by it?"

"I brought it with me from Austin."

Tex waited for the usual questions, but Lenin surprised him by merely remarking, "You should paint the front like the Lone Star flag. It would be good theater." He ran a thumb over the strings, coaxing a sigh from its twelve-stringed throat. "You like it here in Sevastopol?"

"Sevastopol is——" He stopped. "It's a beautiful city. But I miss Texas."

An inattentive nod. Lenin put the Martin down. "What kind of music do you play? Thrash, reggae, acid house?"

"No way! I only play good ol' rock and roll."

Lenin snorted. "Rock is dead. The bloodsuckers and moneymakers have drained it dry. There's nothing left but the carcass. Word just hasn't gotten out to the street yet." He was silent for a long moment. "There was real excitement to it in the old days. It was raw, it was impolite, it was everything your parents hated. It said to them: You cannot control us. You can't lock us in, hold us back, keep us down. We're free and we know it and there's nothing you can do about it. The future is ours.

"Now? Pfaugh! It's been bought and sold, homogenized, pasteurized, processed, and packaged, like so many waxed-paper cartons of yogurt."

"But not your music," Tex said eagerly. "Your music is——"

"*Look at me!*" Lenin slammed his fists on the dresser. Shocked, Tex for the first time actually looked at him critically, and saw how haggard his appearance was. There were purple circles under his eyes, and the skin hung loose and white and dry from his skull. He was more corpse than man. "I'm a fucking zombie. I've been on the road so long I can't remember anything else. Doesn't it seem to you that there's something obscene about a man my age strutting and posturing on stage, acting out juvenile fantasies of power and rebelliousness? It's a farce. It's——"

An officious little man with a clipboard stuck his head in the door and barked, "Fifteen minutes."

"Yes, yes." The life went out of Lenin's face. Wearily, he picked up a makeup brush. His eyes lifted to the glass and met Tex's in the reflection.

"Take him out," Lenin said. His face was a mask. In the mirror, the fat militiaman smiled. A cold sizzle ran up Tex's side as he realized that anything could happen to him now. One word from Lenin, and he would be led to the basement and beaten to death. No one would ever know. The Boss stared at him for a long time, enigmatic, unreadable. Then, as if he had just now come to a decision, he added, "Give him a seat in the hall."

TEX FOUND HIMSELF dazedly sitting third row center as the roadies slouched about the stage, hooking together the amps and running sound checks. Without fanfare the band came on, one by one, and picked up their instruments. Ignoring the applause, they tightened snares, checked the tuning of their guitars, slid a finger up and down the keyboard. Familiar faces all, but nameless. Somebody threw a spot on the empty mike at the center of the stage. The Boss did not appear.

The audience began to clap in rhythm. "Len-in, Len-in, Len-in!" they chanted. The noise filled the hall, pounding, urgent, desperate, and climaxed in an explosion of screams and cheers when a sudden spotlight alerted them to curtains parting to stage left.

Lenin.

He strode briskly, almost angrily, on stage, while the applause went on and on and on. Light bounced from the shiny tips of his shoes. The crease in his grey trousers was sharp as a knife. When he reached the center of the stage a roadie scuttled up to hand him his Stratocaster and a second patched in the jack. They faded quickly back as, looping the guitar strap over his head, he stood up to the mike. The audience was still applauding madly.

He held up a hand for quiet.

The crowd hushed. He cleared his throat. The stage lights brought out the circles under his eyes, the gaunt appearance, the fatigue lying just under the skin. In an unaccented, emotionless voice, he said, "The Workers Control the Means of Production," then turned to give the band the downbeat.

The band was a little ragged on the first number. The applause at its conclusion was loud but not really enthusiastic, more dutiful than heartfelt. Lenin stared down at his shoes, then up again and said, "Religion is the Opiate of the Masses." He struck a chord.

Listening, Tex experienced a dismay so complete that he could feel it down in the soles of his feet. Again, the music was uninspired. There was nothing fresh there; it was all the same chops, the same licks, the same words delivered with exactly the same phrasing as they had been twenty-forty-sixty million years ago when Lenin was young and the songs were new, and people still believed that rock and roll could change the world. All the energy, all the significance was gone, transformed to mere nostalgia.

And so it went, for song after song.

This was horrible. One side of his face was swelling up, and Tex wanted to cry. If he hadn't been given so prominent a seat, he would have stood up and slipped away—he could hear a faint rustling off to the edges of the crowd that might be people doing just that. But it would be too noticeable if he left. It would be a slap in the Boss's face.

He had no choice but to stick it out.

Tex glanced to either side of him. The naval officer to his right was looking down at his watch. A moon-faced girl to his other side looked puzzled, like there was something wrong but she didn't think herself smart enough to understand what. He wondered what had become of Yuri and his other friends from the assault on the door. Their sufferings seemed grotesquely wasted now.

But gradually then an odd thing began to happen. With each number, Lenin seemed to gain strength from the crowd, energy from their gathering enthusiasm, power from their applause. The band pulled together behind him. The music got tighter.

Midway through "Rural Electrification," it all came together. The band went into the break, organ soaring and bass like thunder. They were really cooking now. With sudden vigor, Lenin shucked out of his grey jacket and stood in shirt and vest.

A roadie materialized from the gloom to take away the jacket, but the guitarist ignored him. He ran to the edge of the stage and held the jacket out at arm's length, above the waving, grasping hands, and began to tease the fans. He dipped it down almost within their reach, then yanked it back again, and danced to center stage.

Again Lenin dangled the jacket, his eyes flashing with dark amusement. And though Tex knew it was an illusion, that with the lights in his eyes Lenin couldn't distinguish one audience member from another, he felt an electric spark of contact. He leaped for the jacket, as mad as any of them to snatch the prize.

Suddenly Lenin jerked back. He whirled the jacket around his head three times, then skimmed it out into the crowd. While those nearest to where it came down fought frenziedly for a scrap, he snatched up his guitar again and, spontaneously abandoning the song midway through, shouted, "Red October!"

It was one of his best numbers, a real rabble-rouser, and the first chords brought all the auditorium to their feet.

How long that number lasted, no one could say. He stretched it out, working changes and playing variants no other musician would even have attempted. He wrung every last drop of sweat there was to be had from it. He drove his listeners wild.

Then, without pausing, he segued into his signature anthem, "Workers of the World, Unite!"

The audience *roared*. They were standing on their chairs now, clapping their hands over their heads, dancing in the aisles. And when he came to the chorus, everyone joined in, without exception, all voices raised to sing along, one voice, united:

You have nothing to lose!
You have nothing to lose!
You have nothing to lose . . .
But your chains.

The guitars soared and snarled. The drummer was going crazy. The noise was thunderous, the stressed-concrete roof billowed outward into the starry night to make room for it, and still it grew. Tex was jumping—jumping!—up and down atop his chair, wild with joy, ecstatic, singing along. Caught up in the music, for the first time since leaving Austin he felt not alone, but among friends. A great wave of solidarity took the crowd and made them all one, united, a part of something great.

You have nothing to lose . . .
But your chains.

Now people were linking arms, Red Army with Black Sea Fleet, doctors with bureaucrats with factory workers, forming chains that stretched clear across the hall, swaying in time to the music and singing along. Up in the balcony too, everybody was singing, so great a flood of song that the Boss's voice was lost in it. Tears were rolling down Tex's cheeks. He felt such a joy as would be impossible to describe. They were all, every one of them, brave and selfless and free. They were all one.

It could have gone on forever.

Radiant Doors

THE DOORS BEGAN OPENING on a Tuesday in early March. Only a few at first—flickering and uncertain because they were operating at the extreme end of their temporal range—and those few from the earliest days of the exodus, releasing fugitives who were unstarved and healthy, the privileged scientists and technicians who had created or appropriated the devices that made their escape possible. We processed about a hundred a week, in comfortable isolation and relative secrecy. There were videocams taping everything, and our own best people madly scribbling notes and holding seminars and teleconferences where they debated the revelations.

Those were, in retrospect, the good old days.

In April the floodgates swung wide. Radiant doors opened everywhere, disgorging torrents of ragged and fearful refugees.

There were millions of them and they had, every one, to the least and smallest child, been horribly, horribly abused. The stories they told were enough to sicken anyone. I know.

We did what we could. We set up camps. We dug latrines. We ladled out soup. It was a terrible financial burden to the host governments, but what else could they do? The refugees were our descendants. In a very real sense, they were our children.

Throughout that spring and summer, the flow of refugees continued to grow. As the cumulative worldwide total ran up into the tens of millions, the authorities were beginning to panic—was this going to go on forever, a plague of human locusts that would double and triple and quadruple the population, overrunning the land and devouring all the food? What measures might we be forced to take if this kept up? The planet was within a lifetime of its loading capacity as it was. It couldn't take much more. Then in August the doors simply ceased. Somebody up in the future had put an absolute and final end to them.

It didn't bear thinking what became of those who hadn't made it through.

"MORE TALES FROM THE burn ward," Shriver said, ducking through the door flap. That was what he called atrocity stories. He dumped the files on my desk and leaned forward so he could leer down my blouse. I scowled him back a step.

"Anything useful in them?"

"Not a scrap. But that's not my determination, is it? You have to read each and every word in each and every report so that you can swear and attest that they contain nothing the Commission needs to know."

"Right." I ran a scanner over the universals for each of the files, and dumped the lot in the circular file. Touched a thumb to one of the new pads—better security devices were the very first benefit we'd gotten from all that influx of future tech—and said, "Done."

Then I linked my hands behind my neck and leaned back in the chair. The air smelled of canvas. Sometimes it seemed that the entire universe smelled of canvas. "So how are things with you?"

"About what you'd expect. I spent the morning interviewing vics."

"Better you than me. I'm applying for a transfer to Publications. Out of these tents, out of the camps, into a nice little editorship somewhere, writing press releases and articles for the Sunday magazines.

Cushy job, my very own cubby, and the satisfaction of knowing I'm doing some good for a change."

"It won't work," Shriver said. "All these stories simply blunt the capacity for feeling. There's even a term for it. It's called compassion fatigue. After a certain point you begin to blame the vic for making you hear about it."

I wriggled in the chair, as if trying to make myself more comfortable, and stuck out my breasts a little bit more. Shriver sucked in his breath. Quietly, though—I'm absolutely sure he thought I didn't notice. I said, "Hadn't you better get back to work?"

Shriver exhaled. "Yeah, yeah, I hear you." Looking unhappy, he ducked under the flap out into the corridor. A second later his head popped back in, grinning. "Oh, hey, Ginny—almost forgot. Huong is on sick roster. Gevorkian said to tell you you're covering for her this afternoon, debriefing vics."

"Bastard!"

He chuckled, and was gone.

I SAT INTERVIEWING A WOMAN whose face was a mask etched with the aftermath of horror. She was absolutely cooperative. They all were. Terrifyingly so. They were grateful for anything and everything. Sometimes I wanted to strike the poor bastards in the face, just to see if I could get a human reaction out of them. But they'd probably kiss my hand for not doing anything worse.

"What do you know about midpoint-based engineering? Gnat relays? Sub-local mathematics?"

Down this week's checklist I went, and with each item she shook her head. "Prigogine engines? SVAT trance status? Lepton soliloquies?" Nothing, nothing, nothing. "Phlenaria? The Toledo incident? 'Third Martyr' theory? Science Investigatory Group G?"

"They took my daughter," she said to this last. "They did things to her."

"I didn't ask you that. If you know anything about their military

organization, their machines, their drugs, their research techniques—
fine. But I don't want to hear about people."

"They did things." Her dead eyes bored into mine. "They—"

"Don't tell me."

"—returned her to us midway through. They said they were under-
staffed. They sterilized our kitchen and gave us a list of more things to
do to her. Terrible things. And a checklist like yours to write down her
reactions."

"Please."

"We didn't want to, but they left a device so we'd obey. Her father
killed himself. He wanted to kill her too, but the device wouldn't let
him. After he died, they changed the settings so I couldn't kill myself
too. I tried."

"God damn." This was something new. I tapped my pen twice, acti-
vating its piezochronic function, so that it began recording fifteen seconds earlier. "Do you remember anything about this device? How large
was it? What did the controls look like?" Knowing how unlikely it was
that she'd give us anything usable. The average refugee knew no more
about their technology than the average here-and-now citizen knows
about television and computers. You turn them on and they do things.
They break down and you buy a new one.

Still, my job was to probe for clues. Every little bit contributed to
the big picture. Eventually they'd add up. That was the theory, anyway.
"Did it have an internal or external power source? Did you ever see anybody servicing it?"

"I brought it with me," the woman said. She reached into her filthy
clothing and removed a fist-sized chunk of quicksilver with small, multicolored highlights. "Here."

She dumped it in my lap.

IT WAS AUTOMATION THAT did it or, rather, hyperautomation. That old
bugaboo of fifty years ago had finally come to fruition. People were no
longer needed to mine, farm, or manufacture. Machines made better
administrators, more attentive servants. Only a very small elite—the

vics called them simply their Owners—was required to order and ordain. Which left a lot of people who were just taking up space.

There had to be *something* to do with them.

As it turned out, there was.

That's my theory, anyway. Or, rather, one of them. I've got a million: Hyperautomation. Cumulative hardening of the collective conscience. Circular determinism. The implicitly aggressive nature of hierarchic structures. Compassion fatigue. The banality of evil.

Maybe people are just no damn good. That's what Shriver would have said.

The next day I went zombie, pretty much. Going through the motions, connecting the dots. LaShana in Requisitions noticed it right away. "You ought to take the day off," she said, when I dropped by to see about getting a replacement PzC(15)/pencorder. "Get away from here, take a walk in the woods, maybe play a little golf."

"Golf," I said. It seemed the most alien thing in the universe, hitting a ball with a stick. I couldn't see the point of it.

"Don't say it like that. You love golf. You've told me so a hundred times."

"I guess I have." I swung my purse up on the desk, slid my hand inside, and gently stroked the device. It was cool to the touch and vibrated ever so faintly under my fingers. I withdrew my hand. "Not today, though."

LaShana noticed. "What's that you have in there?"

"Nothing." I whipped the purse away from her. "Nothing at all." Then, a little too loud, a little too blustery, "So how about that pencorder?"

"It's yours." She got out the device, activated it, and let me pick it up. Now only I could operate the thing. Wonderful how fast we were picking up the technology. "How'd you lose your old one, anyway?"

"I stepped on it. By accident." I could see that LaShana wasn't buying it. "Damn it, it was an accident! It could have happened to anyone."

I fled from LaShana's alarmed, concerned face.

NOT TWENTY MINUTES LATER, Gevorkian came sleazing into my office. She smiled, and leaned lazily back against the file cabinet when I said hi. Arms folded. Eyes sad and cynical. That big plain face of hers, tolerant and worldly-wise. Wearing her skirt just a *smidge* tighter, a *touch* shorter than was strictly correct for an office environment.

"Virginia," she said.

"Linda."

We did the waiting thing. Eventually, because I'd been here so long I honestly didn't give a shit, Gevorkian spoke first. "I hear you've been experiencing a little disgruntlement."

"Eh?"

"Mind if I check your purse?"

Without taking her eyes off me for an instant, she hoisted my purse, slid a hand inside, and stirred up the contents. She did it so slowly and dreamily that, I swear to God, I half expected her to smell her fingers afterwards. Then, when she didn't find the expected gun, she said, "You're not planning on going postal on us, are you?"

I snorted.

"So what is it?"

"What is it?" I said in disbelief. I went to the window. Zip zip zip, down came a rectangle of cloth. Through the scrim of mosquito netting the camp revealed itself: canvas as far as the eye could see. There was nothing down there as fancy as our labyrinthine government office complex at the top of the hill—what we laughingly called the Tentagon—with its canvas air-conditioning ducts and modular laboratories and cafeterias. They were all army surplus, and what wasn't army surplus was Boy Scout hand-me-downs. "Take a look. Take a goddamn fucking look. That's the future out there, and it's barreling down on you at the rate of sixty seconds per minute. You can *see* it and still ask me that question?"

She came and stood beside me. Off in the distance, a baby began to wail. The sound went on and on. "Virginia," she said quietly. "Ginny, I understand how you feel. Believe me, I do. Maybe the universe *is* deterministic. Maybe there's no way we can change what's coming. But that's not proven yet. And until it is, we've got to soldier on."

"Why?"

"Because of *them*." She nodded her chin toward the slow- moving revenants of things to come. "They're the living proof of everything we hate and fear. They are witness and testimony to the fact that absolute evil exists. So long as there's the least chance, we've got to try to ward it off."

I looked at her for a long, silent moment. Then, in a voice as cold and calmly modulated as I could make it, I said, "Take your goddamned hand off my ass."

She did so.

I stared after her as, without another word, she left.

This went beyond self-destructive. All I could think was that Gevorkian wanted out but couldn't bring herself to quit. Maybe she was bucking for a sexual harassment suit. But then again, there's definitely an erotic quality to the death of hope. A sense of license. A nicely edgy feeling that since nothing means anything anymore, we might as well have our little flings. That they may well be all we're going to get.

And all the time I was thinking this, in a drawer in my desk the device quietly sat. Humming to itself.

PEOPLE KEEP HAVING CHILDREN. It seems such a terrible thing to do. I can't understand it at all, and don't talk to me about instinct. The first thing I did, after I realized the enormity of what lay ahead, was get my tubes tied. I never thought of myself as a breeder, but I'd wanted to have the option in case I ever changed my mind. Now I knew I would not.

It had been one hell of a day, so I decided I was entitled to quit work early. I was cutting through the camp toward the civ/noncom parking lot when I ran across Shriver. He was coming out of the vic latrines. Least romantic place on Earth. Canvas stretching forever and dispirited people shuffling in and out. And the smell! Imagine the accumulated stench of all the sick shit in the world, and you've just about got it right.

Shriver was carrying a bottle of Spanish champagne under his arm. The bottle had a red bow on it.

"What's the occasion?" I asked.

He grinned like Kali and slid an arm through mine. "My divorce finally came through. Wanna help me celebrate?"

Under the circumstances, it was the single most stupid thing I could possibly do. "Sure," I said. "Why not?"

Later, in his tent, as he was taking off my clothes, I asked, "Just why did your wife divorce you, Shriver?"

"Mental cruelty," he said, smiling.

Then he laid me down across his cot and I let him hurt me. I needed it. I needed to be punished for being so happy and well fed and unbrutalized while all about me ...

"Harder, God damn you," I said, punching him, biting him, clawing up blood. "Make me pay."

CAUSE AND EFFECT. Is the universe deterministic or not? If everything inevitably follows what came before, tickety-tock, like gigantic, all-inclusive clockwork, then there is no hope. The refugees came from a future that cannot be turned away. If, on the other hand, time is quanticized and uncertain, unstable at every point, constantly prepared to collapse in any direction in response to totally random influences, then all that suffering that came pouring in on us over the course of six long and rainy months might be nothing more than a phantom. Just an artifact of a rejected future.

Our future might be downright pleasant.

We had a million scientists working in every possible discipline, trying to make it so. Biologists, chaoticists, physicists of every shape and description. Fabulously dedicated people. Driven. Motivated. All trying to hold out a hand before what must be and say "Stop!"

How they'd love to get their mitts on what I had stowed in my desk.

I hadn't decided yet whether I was going to hand it over, though. I wasn't at all sure what was the right thing to do. Or the smart thing, for that matter.

Gevorkian questioned me on Tuesday. Thursday, I came into my office to discover three UN soldiers with hand-held detectors, running a search.

I shifted my purse back on my shoulder to make me look more strack, and said, "What the hell is going on here?"

"Random check, ma'am." A dark-eyed Indian soldier young enough to be if not my son then my little brother politely touched fingers to forehead in a kind of salute. "For up-time contraband." A sewn tag over one pocket proclaimed his name to be PATHAK. "It is purely standard, I assure you."

I counted the stripes on his arm, compared them to my civilian GS-rating and determined that by the convoluted UN protocols under which we operated, I outranked him.

"Sergeant Major Pathak. You and I both know that all foreign nationals operate on American soil under sufferance, and the strict understanding that you have no authority whatsoever over native civilians."

"Oh, but this was cleared with your Mr.—"

"I don't give a good goddamn if you cleared it with the fucking Dalai Lama! This is my office—your authority ends at the door. You have no more right to be here than I have to finger-search your goddamn rectum. Do you follow me?"

He flushed angrily, but said nothing.

All the while, his fellows were running their detectors over the file cabinet, the storage closets, my desk. Little lights on each flashed red red red. Negative negative negative. The soldiers kept their eyes averted from me. Pretending they couldn't hear a word.

I reamed their Sergeant major out but good. Then, when the office had been thoroughly scanned and the two noncoms were standing about uneasily, wondering how long they'd be kept here, I dismissed the lot. They were all three so grateful to get away from me that nobody asked to examine my purse. Which was, of course, where I had the device.

After they left, I thought about young Sergeant Major Pathak. I wondered what he would have done if I'd put my hand on his crotch and made a crude suggestion. No, make that an order. He looked to be a real straight arrow. He'd squirm for sure. It was an alarmingly pleasant fantasy.

I thought it through several times in detail, all the while holding the gizmo in my lap and stroking it like a cat.

THE NEXT MORNING, there was an incident at Food Processing. One of the women started screaming when they tried to inject an micro-miniaturized identi-chip under the skin of her forehead. It was a new system they'd come up with that was supposed to save a per-unit of thirteen cents a week in tracking costs. You walked through a smart doorway, it registered your presence, you picked up your food, and a second doorway checked you off on the way out. There was nothing in it to get upset about.

But the woman began screaming and crying and—this happened right by the kitchens—snatched up a cooking knife and began stabbing herself, over and over. She managed to make nine whacking big holes in herself before the thing was wrestled away from her. The orderlies took her to Intensive, where the doctors said it would be a close thing either way.

After word of that got around, none of the refugees would allow themselves to be identi-chipped. Which really pissed off the UN peacekeepers assigned to the camp, because earlier a couple hundred vics had accepted the chips without so much as a murmur. The Indian troops thought the refugees were willfully trying to make their job more difficult. There were complaints of racism, and rumors of planned retaliation.

I spent the morning doing my bit to calm things down—hopeless—and the afternoon writing up reports that everyone upstream wanted to receive ASAP and would probably file without reading. So I didn't have time to think about the device at all.

But I did. Constantly.

It was getting to be a burden.

For health class, one year in high school, I was given a ten-pound sack of flour, which I had to name and then carry around for a month, as if it were a baby. Bippy couldn't be left unattended; I had to carry it everywhere or else find somebody willing to baby-sit it. The exercise was supposed to teach us responsibility and scare us off of sex. The first thing I did when the month was over was to steal my father's .45, put Bippy in the back yard, and empty the clip into it, shot after shot. Until all that was left of the little bastard was a cloud of white dust.

The machine from the future was like that. Just another bippy. I had it, and dared not get rid of it. It was obviously valuable. It was equally obviously dangerous. Did I really want the government to get hold of something that could compel people to act against their own wishes? Did I honestly trust them not to immediately turn themselves into everything that we were supposedly fighting to prevent?

I'd been asking myself the same questions for—what?—four days. I'd thought I'd have some answers by now.

I took the bippy out from my purse. It felt cool and smooth in my hand, like melting ice. No, warm. It felt both warm *and* cool. I ran my hand over and over it, for the comfort of the thing.

After a minute, I got up, zipped shut the flap to my office, and secured it with a twist tie. Then I went back to my desk, sat down, and unbuttoned my blouse. I rubbed the bippy all over my body: up my neck, and over my breasts, and around and around on my belly. I kicked off my shoes and clumsily shucked off my pantyhose. Down along the outside of my calves it went, and up the insides of my thighs. Between my legs. It made me feel filthy. It made me feel a little less like killing myself.

How it happened was, I got lost. How I got lost was, I went into the camp after dark.

Nobody goes into the camp after dark, unless they have to. Not even the Indian troops. That's when the refugees hold their entertainments. They had no compassion for each other, you see—that was our dirty little secret. I saw a toddler fall into a campfire once. There were vics all around, but if it hadn't been for me, the child would have died. I snatched it from the flames before it got too badly hurt, but nobody else made a move to help it. They just stood there looking. And laughing.

"In Dachau, when they opened the gas chambers, they'd find a pyramid of human bodies by the door," Shriver told me once. "As the gas started to work, the Jews panicked and climbed over each other, in a futile attempt to escape. That was deliberate. It was designed into the system. The Nazis didn't just want them dead—they wanted to be able to feel morally superior to their victims afterwards."

So I shouldn't have been there. But I was unlatching the door to my trailer when it suddenly came to me that my purse felt wrong. Light. And I realized that I'd left the bippy in the top drawer of my office desk. I hadn't even locked it.

My stomach twisted at the thought of somebody else finding the thing. In a panic, I drove back to the camp. It was a twenty-minute drive from the trailer park, and by the time I got there I wasn't thinking straight. The civ/noncom parking lot was a good quarter-way around the camp from the Tentagon. I thought it would be a simple thing to cut through. So, flashing my DOD/Future History Division ID at the guard as I went through the gate, I did.

Which was how I came to be lost.

THERE ARE NEIGHBORHOODS in the camp. People have a natural tendency to sort themselves out by the nature of their suffering. The twitchers, who were victims of paralogical reprogramming, stay in one part of the camp, and the mods, those with functional normative modifications, stay in another. I found myself wandering through crowds of people who had been "healed" of limbs, ears, and even internal organs— there seemed no sensible pattern. Sometimes our doctors could effect a partial correction. But our primitive surgery was, of course, nothing like that available in their miraculous age.

I'd taken a wrong turn trying to evade an eyeless, noseless woman who kept grabbing at my blouse and demanding money, and gotten all turned around in the process when, without noticing me, Gevorkian went striding purposefully by.

Which was so unexpected that, after an instant's shock, I up and followed her. It didn't occur to me not to. There was something strange about the way she held herself, about her expression, her posture. Something unfamiliar.

She didn't even *walk* like herself.

The vics had dismantled several tents to make a large open space surrounded by canvas. Propane lights, hung from tall poles, blazed in a ring about it. I saw Gevorkian slip between two canvas sheets and, after a moment's hesitation, I followed her.

It was a rat fight.

The way a rat fight works, I learned that night, is that first you catch a whole bunch of Norwegian rats. Big mean mothers. Then you get them in a bad mood, probably by not feeding them, but there are any number of other methods that could be used. Anyway, they're feeling feisty. You put a dozen of them in a big pit you've dug in the ground. Then you dump in your contestant. A big guy with a shaven head and his hands tied behind his back. His genitals are bound up in a little bit of cloth, but other than that he's naked.

Then you let them fight it out. The rats leap and jump and bite and the big guy tries to trample them underfoot or crush them with his knees, his chest, his head—whatever he can bash them with.

The whole thing was lit up bright as day, and all the area around the pit was crammed with vics. Some shouted and urged on one side or the other. Others simply watched intently. The rats squealed. The human fighter bared his teeth in a hideous rictus and fought in silence.

It was the creepiest thing I'd seen in a long time.

Gevorkian watched it coolly, without any particular interest or aversion. After a while it was obvious to me that she was waiting for someone.

Finally that someone arrived. He was a lean man, tall, with keen, hatchetlike features. None of the vics noticed. Their eyes were directed inward, toward the pit. He nodded once to Gevorkian, then backed through the canvas again.

She followed him.

I followed her.

They went to a near-lightless area near the edge of the camp. There was nothing there but trash, the backs of tents, the razor-wire fence, and a gate padlocked for the night.

It was perfectly easy to trail them from a distance. The stranger held himself proudly, chin up, eyes bright. He walked with a sure stride. He was nothing at all like the vics.

It was obvious to me that he was an Owner.

Gevorkian too. When she was with him that inhuman arrogance glowed in her face as well. It was as if a mask had been removed. The fire that burned in his face was reflected in hers.

I crouched low to the ground in the shadow of a tent and listened as the stranger said, "Why hasn't she turned it in?"

"She's unstable," Gevorkian said. "They all are."

"We don't dare prompt her. She has to turn it in herself."

"She will. Give her time."

"Time," the man repeated. They both laughed in a way that sounded to me distinctly unpleasant. Then, "She'd better. There's a lot went into this operation. There's a lot riding on it."

"She will."

I stood watching as they shook hands and parted ways. Gevorkian turned and disappeared back into the tent city. The stranger opened a radiant door and was gone.

CAUSE AND EFFECT. They'd done ... *whatever* it was they'd done to that woman's daughter just so they could plant the bippy with me. They wanted me to turn it in. They wanted our government to have possession of a device that would guarantee obedience. They wanted to give us a good taste of what it was like to be them.

Suddenly I had no doubt at all what I should do. I started out at a determined stride, but inside of nine paces I was *running*. Vics scurried to get out of my way. If they didn't move fast enough, I shoved them aside.

I had to get back to the bippy and destroy it.

WHICH WAS STUPID, stupid, stupid. If I'd kept my head down and walked slowly, I would have been invisible. Invisible and safe. The way I did it, though, cursing and screaming, I made a lot of noise and caused a lot of fuss. Inevitably, I drew attention to myself.

Inevitably, Gevorkian stepped into my path.

I stumbled to a halt.

"Gevorkian," I said feebly. "Linda. I—"

All the lies I was about to utter died in my throat when I saw her face. Her expression. Those eyes. Gevorkian reached for me. I skipped back in utter panic, turned—and fled. Anybody else would have done the same.

It was a nightmare. The crowds slowed me. I stumbled. I had no idea where I was going. And all the time, this monster was right on my heels.

Nobody goes into the camp after dark, unless they have to. But that doesn't mean that nobody goes in after dark. By sheer good luck, Gevorkian chased me into the one part of the camp that had something that outsiders could find nowhere else—the sex-for-hire district.

There was nothing subtle about the way the vics sold themselves. The trampled-grass street I found myself in was lined with stacks of cages like the ones they use in dog kennels. They were festooned with strings of Christmas lights, and each one contained a crouched boy. Naked, to best display those mods and deformities that some found attractive. Off-duty soldiers strolled up and down the cages, checking out the possibilities. I recognized one of them.

"Sergeant Major Pathak!" I cried. He looked up, startled and guilty. "Help me! Kill her—please! Kill her now!"

Give him credit, the Sergeant major was a game little fellow. I can't imagine what we looked like to him, one harridan chasing the other down the streets of Hell. But he took the situation in at a glance, unholstered his sidearm, and stepped forward. "Please," he said. "You will both stand where you are. You will place your hands upon the top of your head. You will—"

Gevorkian flicked her fingers at the young soldier. He screamed, and clutched his freshly-crushed shoulder. She turned away from him, dismissively. The other soldiers had fled at the first sign of trouble. All her attention was on me, trembling in her sight like a winded doe. "*Sweet little vic,*" she purred. "If you won't play the part we had planned for you, you'll simply have to be silenced."

"No," I whispered.

She touched my wrist. I was helpless to stop her. "You and I are going to go to my office now. We'll have fun there. Hours and hours of fun."

"Leave her be."

As sudden and inexplicable as an apparition of the Virgin, Shriver stepped out of the darkness. He looked small and grim.

Gevorkian laughed, and gestured.

But Shriver's hand reached up to intercept hers, and where they met, there was an electric blue flash. Gevorkian stared down, stunned, at her hand. Bits of tangled metal fell away from it. She looked up at Shriver.

He struck her down.

She fell with a brief harsh cry, like that of a sea gull. Shriver kicked her, three times, hard: In the ribs. In the stomach. In the head. Then, when she looked like she might yet regain her feet, "It's one of *them!*" he shouted. "Look at her! She's a spy for the Owners! She's from the future! Owner! Look! Owner!"

The refugees came tumbling out of the tents and climbing down out of their cages. They looked more alive than I'd ever seen them before. They were red-faced and screaming. Their eyes were wide with hysteria. For the first time in my life, I was genuinely afraid of them. They came running. They swarmed like insects.

They seized Gevorkian and began tearing her apart.

I saw her struggle up and halfway out of their grips, saw one arm rise up above the sea of clutching hands, like that of a woman drowning.

Shriver seized my elbow and steered me away before I could see any more. I saw enough, though.

I saw too much.

"Where are we going?" I asked when I'd recovered my wits.

"Where do you think we're going?"

He led me to my office.

THERE WAS A STRANGER waiting there. He took out a hand-held detector like Sergeant Major Pathak and his men had used earlier and touched it to himself, to Shriver, and to me. Three times it flashed red, negative. "You travel through time, you pick up a residual charge," Shriver explained. "It never goes away. We've known about Gevorkian for a long time."

"U.S. Special Security," the stranger said, and flipped open his ID. It meant diddle-all to me. There was a badge. It could have read Captain Crunch for all I knew or cared. But I didn't doubt for an instant that he was SS. He had that look. To Shriver he said, "The neutralizer."

Shriver unstrapped something glittery from his wrist—the device he'd used to undo Gevorkian's weapon—and, in a silent bit of comic bureaucratic punctilio, exchanged it for a written receipt. The security officer touched the thing with his detector. It flashed green. He put both devices away in interior pockets.

All the time, Shriver stood in the background, watching. He wasn't told to go away.

Finally, Captain Crunch turned his attention to me again. "Where's the snark?"

"Snark?"

The man removed a thin scrap of cloth from an inside jacket pocket and shook it out. With elaborate care, he pulled it over his left hand. An inertial glove. Seeing by my expression that I recognized it, he said, "Don't make me use this."

I swallowed. For an instant I thought crazily of defying him, of simply refusing to tell him where the bippy was. But I'd seen an inertial glove in action before, when a lone guard had broken up a camp riot. He'd been a little man. I'd seen him crush heads like watermelons.

Anyway, the bippy was in my desk. They'd be sure to look there.

I opened the drawer, produced the device. Handed it over. "It's a plant," I said. "They want us to have this."

Captain Crunch gave me a look that told me clear as words exactly how stupid he thought I was. "We understand more than you think we do. There are circles and circles. We have informants up in the future, and some of them are more highly placed than you'd think. Not everything that's known is made public."

"Damn it, this sucker is *evil*."

A snake's eyes would look warmer than his. "Understand this: We're fighting for our survival here. Extinction is null-value. You can have all the moral crises you want when the war is won."

"It should be suppressed. The technology. If it's used, it'll just help bring about ..."

He wasn't listening.

I'd worked for the government long enough to know when I was wasting my breath. So I shut up.

WHEN THE CAPTAIN LEFT with the bippy, Shriver still remained, looking ironically after him. "People get the kind of future they deserve," he observed.

"But that's what I'm saying. Gevorkian came back from the future in order to help bring it about. That means that time isn't deterministic." Maybe I was getting a little weepy. I'd had a rough day. "The other guy said there was a lot riding on this operation. They didn't know how it was going to turn out. They didn't *know*."

Shriver grunted, not at all interested.

I plowed ahead unheeding. "If it's not deterministic—if they're working so hard to bring it about—then all our effort isn't futile at all. This future can be prevented."

Shriver looked up at last. There was a strangely triumphant gleam in his eye. He flashed that roguish ain't-this-fun grin of his, and said, "I don't know about you, but some of us are working like hell to *achieve* it."

With a jaunty wink, he was gone.

Ice Age

IT WAS EARLY AFTERNOON when Rob carried the last carton into their new apartment and was—finally, officially—moved in. He was setting it down atop a stack of crated books to be unpacked later when Gail said something from the kitchen. "What's that?" he shouted.

She poked her head into the hallway. "I *said*—Hey, the landlord left the old refrigerator in."

Rob sauntered to the kitchen. The counters were cluttered with boxes of half-unpacked cooking utensils. "Probably too much trouble to remove it."

The refrigerator, yellowed to a grimy antique ivory, was welded immovably into the corner of the kitchen by decades' worth of petrified crud. Its top, the motor housing, rose like an art deco pagoda, in three tiers of streamlined vents. This made the refrigerator look vaguely futuristic—the future of the 1930s, though, not of the present.

Rob patted the motor housing. "This is actually very good design," he said. "In modern refrigerators the motor is set underneath and the waste heat from it rises up into the refrigerator. Then the heat has to be pumped out by the same motor that produced it, generating yet more waste heat. It's a vicious cycle. But with the modern machines they're after consumer gloss, so the motor is set down there anyway."

Gail pulled a bottle of zinfandel out of a cardboard box and set the now-empty box under the kitchen sink. "Trash goes there," she said. "You want some wine?"

The refrigerator hummed lightly, a friendly, reassuring sound. "Sure. The landlord left the refrigerator on; there's probably even some ice left."

"That's what I like about you. You ain't got no couth at all."

Rob shrugged. "I'm a barbarian." He opened the freezer compartment and found it almost overgrown with old ice. It had already swallowed up two ice cube trays and an ancient package of frozen peas. One tray, though, was almost free, and by hammering on it with the heel of his hand he could get it loose. He cracked the tray and carried a handful of ice back to the table.

"Plenty extra," he offered. Gail curled a lip. But she set out a goblet for him anyway, and poured wine in it.

Rob leaned back and swirled his drink, listening to the ice clink. He took a sip.

And stopped. Was that a *bug* in the one ice cube? He fished it out with two fingers and held it up to the light.

The cube was heavily frosted across one surface where condensate from the freezer had formed, though that was already beginning to melt from the wine. Within the cube were swirls of tiny bubbles, too small to notice if you didn't look closely. And beyond them, deep in the center, was a large black speck, a creature the size of a horsefly trapped in the ice's pellucid depths. He peered closer.

There was a wooly mammoth in his ice cube.

It was dark and shaggy, with a head that tapered down to a long, filament-sized trunk. Two all but invisible tusks twisted from its mouth. Its legs were folded in against the body. Its fur was a deep auburn red. A small and perfect wooly mammoth, no larger than a bread crumb.

Rob didn't move. The ice was cold and stung his hand, but he didn't shift it. All he could think of were the Saturday afternoon movies that began with someone finding an ancient animal frozen in ice. Though usually those ended with the animal eating Tokyo, he reminded himself.

"Hey," Gail said. "What're you staring at so intently?"

Rob opened his mouth, shut it again. Gently he lowered the ice cube to the tabletop. Drops of water appeared on its side, oozed down to the Formica, and began to form a micropuddle.

"Gail," he said carefully, "I want you to look inside this ice cube and tell me what you see."

Following his example, Gail placed her hands flat on the table and leaned forward. "Wow," she whispered. "That's—Rob, that's *beautiful.*"

The creature was fractionally easier to see now. Its tusks, long for its size—was that an indicator of age?—were yellowed and one was broken at its tip. Its eyes, frozen open and almost too small to be seen, were blue. The fur was badly matted, and there were a couple of tiny bare patches.

Gail jumped up and began running water in the sink. She returned with a bowl that steamed gently. "Here," she said, "let's thaw it out." With infinite care she eased the ice cube into the water.

After a while Rob said, "Ice melts slowly doesn't it?" and then, reluctantly, "Maybe we should call the Smithsonian or something."

"If you could convince them to look at this," Gail pointed out, "which I doubt, they'd only take it away from us."

"There is that," Rob agreed, relieved that Gail too felt no obligation to give the mammoth away.

At last the ice melted. Rob fished out the wee mammoth with a spoon. It was still and tiny in his hand. Suddenly, he felt very close to tears. Against all logic, he had hoped it would thaw out alive. "Here," he said, and let the beast fall from his hand to Gail's.

By dumping the contents of every carton in the house onto the floor, Gail had managed to find a magnifying glass. Now she squinted through it. "That's a wooly mammoth all right," she said. "Would you look at those eyes! And—guess what—the toe leathers are pink!" Her voice fell to a mutter then rose again: "Hey, are those *spear points* in its side?"

Rob's momentary *tristesse* melted in the heat of Gail's excitement. He leaned over her shoulder, trying to see. "I wonder how you'd go about getting something like this preserved in Lucite," Gail mused. Then she straightened and turned to face him. "Maybe there's more of these in the freezer!"

Gail took the lead. She opened the refrigerator and peered into the freezer. Nudging the ice cube tray with a finger, she squinted at the ice around it. Then, gingerly, she pulled out the tray and, after examining it briefly, stared through the small space that was not yet swallowed up by the slow, devouring ice. She whistled softly.

"What?" Rob said.

She shook her head, still staring into the freezer.

"What? *Tell* me."

"I think you'd better look for yourself."

Rob put an arm around her waist and laid his head beside hers so they could both peer within. The light inside was dim but serviceable, the land beyond the ice half-lit by some unseen source. He stared past the rime into a tiny, mountainous country. Off to one side, a small glacier was partially visible. To the foreground, a trickle of water—a river in miniature—meandered through a dark, Nordic pine forest.

Huddled by the river was a town, stone and wood buildings all in a jumble and surrounded by high stone walls.

"My God," Rob breathed. "*There's a lost civilization in my refrigerator.*"

They stared at each other for a moment, eyes wide, then returned, wonderingly, to the freezer.

It was dark in the back reaches. Silently cursing the gloom, Rob strained to see. The town was laid out on a semicircular plan against the water, though the streets were a hopeless maze. Clearly they had been built haphazardly, at random.

Atop a hill near the center of town stood a cathedral, squat and heavy, but still recognizable as such. It dominated the town. By the river's edge stood a castle. All the other buildings radiated from these two loci. The town walls were clearly anachronistic remnants, though, for slum buildings—hovels, actually—had been built up against them. In places the walls were actually breached, the stones carted away for building materials. Several roads ran from the town through the pine forest, and one—a major one—ran along the river.

Finally Gail stepped back and said, "You know, this doesn't make any sense at all."

"That so?" Rob did not look up from the freezer.

"I mean, this is clearly an early medieval city. Wooly mammoths died out sometime in the neolithic."

Rob looked at her. Cold air seeped from the refrigerator. Placing a hand on his arm, Gail tugged him away from the freezer and softly closed the door. "Let's have some coffee," she suggested.

ROB BREWED THE COFFEE while Gail dumped the already-poured wine down the sink. They brooded over mugs of Kenyan in silence. Gail touched the tiny mammoth with the tip of her fingernail. It was not in good shape; putrefaction was setting in, as if time were catching up with the long ages it had lain frozen in the ice. She crooked an eyebrow at Rob, and he nodded agreement.

While Rob unhooked the spider plant from its new position over the kitchen window, Gail wrapped the mammoth in a corner of white tissue paper.

They dug a small hole in the soil under the plant with an old fork, and buried the creature with full military honors.

Rob solemnly placed the plant back on its hook.

Without saying a word, they both turned to the refrigerator.

THEY OPENED THE FREEZER compartment together. Rob took one look, and his mouth fell open.

The town was still there. But it had changed and grown while they were away. It had evolved. The stone walls were down, and the cathedral had been rebuilt in the soaring, Gothic style. It no longer dominated the town, though; now it was one large building among many. The streets were wider, too, and the town had expanded out of sight behind the left-hand ice. It was a city now.

The details were harder to make out than before, though, for it seemed that the industrial revolution was in full swing. Bristling forests of smokestacks belched thick black smoke into the wintry sky. The riverside was choked with hundreds of tiny docks, the castle torn down to make room for them, and impossibly thin railroad tracks crawled through the depleted pine forests, past the glacier's edge, and over the snow-capped mountains to some unseen destination.

The town had evolved into a city in a matter of minutes. Even as they watched, buildings appeared and disappeared. Roads shifted position instantaneously. Entire sections of the city were rebuilt in the twinkling of an eye. "The time rate in there must be fantastic," Rob said. "I'll bet that years—decades—are going by as we stand here."

The city pulsed with movement. Its people were invisible, as were their vehicles and beasts of burden, for they all moved too quickly to be seen, but traffic patterns were shimmering gray uncertainties in the streets, dark where traffic was heavy, and pale where light.

The buildings were growing larger and taller. They exploded into the air as steel-beam construction was discovered. The sky to the far side of the city began flickering darkly, and it took an instant to realize that they were seeing the airlanes from an exurban airport hidden behind the ice.

"I think we've reached the present," Gail said.

Rob leaned forward to get a better look, and was caught in the wash of the first thermonuclear blast.

There was an instantaneous *flash* and pure white light flooded his skull. Needles of pain lanced through his eyes, and he staggered backwards from the freezer, a hand over his face.

"*Rob!*" Gail cried in a panicky voice, and from her tone he could tell that she had blinked or glanced away at the crucial instant. She was okay then, and knowing that gave him the presence of mind to slam the refrigerator door shut as he fell over backwards.

Afterimages burned in his mind: A quadrant of the city disappearing into sudden crater, a transcendentally bright mushroom cloud that was gone before it was there, subliminal traces of fire and smoke, and blast zones where all traffic and life abruptly ceased. The pictures jumbled one on top of another.

"Rob, are you okay? Say something!"

He was lying on his back, his head in Gail's lap. "I'm ... I'm okay," he managed to say. And even as he said it, it began to come true. Through the bright wash of nothingness, the kitchen started to seep through.

The details were vague and tentative at first, then stronger. It was like being blinded by a flashbulb, except that the afterimage was a small mushroom cloud.

"Gail," he croaked. "They're fighting a nuclear war in there."

"There now, don't get excited," she said soothingly.

He struggled to sit up. "They're using tac-nukes in my refrigerator and you're telling me to *calm down?*"

"It's good advice anyway," she insisted. Then she giggled. "Boy, you should see your face!"

"Why? What's the matter with it?" But she simply shook her head, too full of laughter to respond. He stalked off to the bathroom and numbly stared into the mirror. His face was bright red from the primary radiation. "Oboy," he said. "That's going to be a bad sunburn in the morning."

Back in the kitchen, he eyed the refrigerator with trepidation. "Let me," Gail said. Gingerly, being careful to keep her head averted, she opened the door the tiniest possible crack.

A dozen flashes of light flickered in and out of existence, like a badly out of synch strobe. The reflected brilliance off the walls dazzled both Gail and Rob; clearly there had been an escalation in megatonnage. Gail slammed the door shut.

Rob sighed. "Well, I guess it was too much to expect them to outgrow war over the course of two minutes." He looked helplessly at Gail. "But what do we do now?"

"Send out for a pizza?" she suggested.

THE SUN HAD SET, leaving only a faint golden smear in the sky by the time they had finished the pizza. Rob ate the last, nearly-cold piece, and Gail dumped box and crusts in the cardboard box under the sink.

"It's been over two hours," Rob said. "They must've had time to rebuild by now."

Gail touched his arm, squeezed tenderly. "They may have killed themselves off, Rob. We have to face up to that possibility."

"Yeah." Rob pushed back his chair and stood. Feeling like John

Wayne, he advanced on the refrigerator. "Let's go for it," he said, and jerked the door open a sliver. Nothing happened. He opened it all the way.

The freezer was still intact. There was a black smear across one corner of the ice, but that was all. Cautiously, they stared in.

The city was still there, between glacier and icy river. It had not been destroyed in the nuclear spasm wars of late afternoon. But it had changed.

The skyscrapers had continued to grow and to evolve. They had become tall, delicate fronds that gleamed soft gold and green. Skywalks appeared between the fairy towers. "Look." Rob pointed to threadlike structures that wove intricate patterns through the city. "Monorails!"

Flickermotes appeared in the air between the towers. Were they flying cars, Rob wondered, or possibly personal jetpacks? There was no way of knowing. And what were those shimmering domes that sprang up like mushrooms after a rain on the outskirts of town?

"It looks like the Emerald City of Oz," Gail said. "Only not just green." Rob nodded agreement. Some new technology was invented then, and the city changed again. Now the buildings seemed to be made of curdled light, or possibly crystals of glowing fog. Whatever they were, they weren't entirely solid. They receded into dimensions that weren't there.

"I think the time rate is accelerating," Gail said in a small voice.

The city pulsed and danced to some unearthly syncopation. It sent out blossoms and shoots, and exploded into the sky in firework structures of color and essence, and joyous, whimsical light. It was a strangely *playful* city.

There was some kind of leakage from the freezer too. Some kind of broadcast. Rob and Gail picked up flashes of color and quick, incomprehensible messages, broadcast directly to their brains, maybe, or their nerve webs or possibly even to each individual cell of their bodies. They could understand none of it. Then there was another shift of technology, and the impressions cut off.

But the city was still changing, and the rate of change still accelerating. Now the unsubstantial towers swayed like fronds of seaweed lashed by a hurricane. Faster. Now the radius of the city exploded outward and imploded inward again. Again it happened and again, like circles of light pulsing outward. Giant machines throbbed in the air and were gone. Highways of light moved out and up into the night. Too quick to be seen, leaving behind only an impression of incredible bulk, *something* stooped over the city.

The changes were coming still faster now—as if the city were searching for something, trying out and rejecting alternate configurations in pursuit of some specific goal. The buildings became piles of orange diamonds, matrixes of multicolored spheres, a vast tangle of organic vines. The city was a honeycomb, a featureless monolith, a surrealistic birthday cake.

This search lasted a full five minutes. Then, for an instant, the city reached a kind of crystalline perfection, and all change, all motion ceased. It stood poised on the numinous edge between instant and infinity. For that brief, eternal second, nothing happened.

Then the city exploded.

Beams and lattices of light, like playful twisted lasers, shot into the air, between the masses of ice and out into the kitchen. Massively ornate constructs of color and nothing else flickered into existence over the sink and oven. They phased out of being, then halfway in again, and then were gone. The city rose into the air, and separated out into component planes and solids. Very briefly, it *sang.* Very briefly, it existed both in the refrigerator and in the kitchen, as if its presence were too large for any one location.

And then it went away. It did not move in any direction they could comprehend. It just went ... away.

They stood blinking. After the lights and bright colors of the city, the freezer compartment seemed dark and still. Gail shook her head wonderingly. Rob gently touched the ice. Where the city had stood was nothing but a few dead walls, a handful of ancient ruins half-buried in drifting snow.

Even as they watched, these last traces of civilization crumbled into dust, destroyed by the relentless onslaught of time.

"I wonder where they've gone to." Rob closed the refrigerator door. "Some other dimension?"

Gail did not respond immediately. Then she said, "I doubt that *we* could understand." She was wide-eyed and solemn.

Nevertheless, she didn't object when Rob went around to the back of the refrigerator and pulled the plug. They stood looking at it in silence for a while.

"We'll clean it out with ammonia before we turn it on again," Rob said.

Gail took his hand. "C'mon, kid. Let's go to bed."

ROB WOKE UP THE NEXT morning, sleepy-eyed and sunburnt. He stumbled to the kitchen and, after brewing coffee, automatically pulled open the refrigerator to get some milk.

The inside of the refrigerator smelled rich and moist, with the acrid tang of food starting to rot. Rob wrinkled his nose and started to close the door. But on impulse—just to be safe—he peered into the freezer compartment.

The interior of the freezer was green and steamy. A brontosaurus no longer than his thumb raised its head ponderously above the jungle growth and blinked.

Walking Out

TERRY BISSEL WOKE UP one morning knowing he had to get out of the city. Take a jitney up Broadway and keep on going forever. Travel so far and so fast that if someone were to shine a flashlight after him, by the time the beam caught up it would've dissipated to nothingness. "I don't want to live here anymore," he said aloud without opening his eyes. It was true. For a long time he lay motionless, simply savoring the thought. A strange elation dawned within him. "I want to live in the country."

His wife was in the kitchen, humming to herself. The blender growled briefly. She was grinding beans for coffee. There was the sizzle of eggs and ham in the skillet. Kris was a lark. Eight months pregnant, and she still got up first.

He pulled on his slacks and rolled up the futon. In the doorway, he paused briefly to watch Kris waft lightly from sink to counter. Then he said, "Let's move to New England."

Kris stood very still at the counter. She didn't turn around.

"C'mon, babe, you know you hate it here. Too much noise, too many people, hardly enough room to fucking turn around in. I want to live in Connecticut—no, Vermont! I want a big, rambling house where you can see meadows out the kitchen window and woods beyond them. And mountains! Snow in the winter and fresh apples in the fall. I want the kind of place where sometimes you get up before dawn to watch the deer crossing the lawn."

"Terry," Kris said warningly.

Down on the street, the recyclers were rattling the bins of cans and bottles, slamming bales of paper and bags of digestibles into the various bellies of their truck. They were in a good mood, to judge by the loud, yakyakking sound of their voices. "Yo, Nee-C! You still seeing that old fool, Benjy?" And: "He got better stuff than you do, Maaaalcolm." And: "You don't know till you try, babe! I got stuff I ain't never used." The crew was laughing uproariously at this exchange. "I heard that," said the woman. "Fact is, I heard you ain't had the opportunity to use none of it!"

"Listen to that." Terry snorted. "That's exactly the kind of crap I'm talking about. Hey—you ever see a moose?"

"No."

"I did once when I was young. My folks took us kids to this little bed-and-breakfast outside of Montpelier and—hey, the woman that runs it must be getting pretty old by now. Maybe she'd like to sell. What do you think? Wanna run a B and B? It couldn't hurt to ask."

Kris whirled abruptly. "We need more coffee," she said in a choked voice. "We're out."

"I thought I heard the grinder."

"That was ... decaffeinated. I put it in by accident." With harsh, choppy motions, she unscrewed the grinder and slammed its contents into the disposal. "Go across the street, why don't you, and get us some beans?"

"You're the boss." He grabbed up Kris in both arms, lifted her to the ceiling and whirled her around. "You and the little Creature from the Black Lagoon." He kissed her belly, set her down, and ducked into the cubby to throw on robe and slippers. Then he headed out, leaving his wife weeping behind him.

It was a wonderful morning!

On the elevator, Mrs. Jacinto from two floors up smiled and said hello. Her husband, Herb, was a municipal gardener, as tall as she was fat, and a dab hand at cribbage. Terry had played him a few times and the man was definitely a shark. "How are you doing this lovely morning, Mr. Bissel?"

"Couldn't be better—we're going to move."

"Well, isn't that nice? I expected you children would, now that you have the little one on the way. Oh, and that reminds me. Tell that pretty wife of yours I have some morning sickness tea that I'm bringing up later on; I know you'll think it's foolishness, but tell her to give it a try, it really does work. Are you moving Downtown?"

"We're leaving the city altogether, Mrs. Jacinto. We're moving to the country."

The smile froze on her face. "Well," she said. "Well, well."

The doors opened for the ground floor and she skittered away.

It was a quick hop-skip-and-jump across the street to the Java Tree. On the way back, Terry plucked a daisy—perhaps one of Herb's—from the street turf. He opened the top of the coffee sack and buried the stem in the beans.

"You'll be going to the Housing Authority today, won't you?" Kris asked when he got back. She accepted the coffee, filled a glass with water for the daisy, and put it up on the window sill without comment. Ignoring their earlier conversation entirely, pretending it had never happened. "Like you promised?"

Well, getting out was a new idea. It would probably take her a while to adjust to it. "Why not?" Terry said, playing along. "If we want a bigger apartment, we'll have to move, right? And if we want to move, one of us is going to have to go stand in line. That's just the way it is. Doesn't matter what you want, you've got to stand in line." He winked jauntily.

"I'd go myself," Kris said in a strained voice. "I don't mind. It's just that—" She looked down at the Creature.

"Hey, hey. I didn't say I wouldn't, did I?"

Tight-lipped, she shook her head.

"Then it's settled." Terry ducked into the bedroom and opened the closet. Silk jacket, snakeclone shoes. On the way out, he paused in the doorway. "Hey. What about Maine? Maybe we could find a place outside of Portland, nice and convenient to your Mom, wouldn't that be nice?"

As he left, he heard Kris beginning to cry again. Pregnant women were emotional. He understood that.

THEIR FLAT WAS IN the heart of Midtown, at the foot of one of the giant condenser stacks that drew current out of the flux and into the power grid. The building was wrapped around the tower's anchor pier, and even though the engineers swore it was perfectly shielded from any harmful radiation, this fact had kept the rents low. No question but a new flat was going to give them sticker shock. Maybe that was all to the good, though. When Krissie saw the bottom line, she might well change her mind about New England. The law gave them a three-month cooling off period; it would be easy to break the lease.

Kris wanted to move Downtown to be closer to her sister. Maybe he could talk Robin into moving as well. They could get adjacent farms and raise llamas.

It was another beautiful morning. The Municipal Weather Authority had programmed a crisp autumnal tang into the air. Light breezes stirred the little trees on the building tops. They looked just fine outlined against the dome.

A paper bag blew past Terry's feet and automatically he started after it. But then a street urchin appeared out of nowhere, a skinny black kid in an oversized basketball jersey, and snatched it up. He leaped high, tucking in his knees for a double somersault, and slam-dunked the bag into a recycling can. With a flourish, he swiped his bank card through the slot to pick up the credit.

Terry applauded lightly.

"WATCHES!" THE SHABBY MAN SANG. He was only a step away from being a beggar. His jacket was shiny and his shoes weren't. One side of his face was scarred from old radiation burns. That and a blackwork Luna

Rangers tattoo marked him as a vet. The watches flew in great loops and figure eights, blinking and goggling whimsically.

"This sort of post-capitalist consumer faddism is only a form of denial, you know," Terry told him.

"Hah? What're you talking about?"

"Think about it. Your devices consume three times their own weight in time and labor for their design, manufacture, and—now—sales. But what do they accomplish? A moment's diversion from the sad fact of existence. It's a measure of our desperation that we'd devote so much energy in order to generate a respite, however brief, from our very real problems."

"What are you, some kinda nut? Get out of here!" the vendor said angrily.

Terry stuck his hands in his pockets. "The truth hurts, eh?"

Without answering, the shabby man called his watches in. They came swooping down on him, finding safe harbor in his many pockets. He turned and hobbled away.

"It's called denial!" Terry shouted after him. "Therapists have known about it for centuries!"

It was rush hour in the subway. The crowds were so thick that people were constantly losing their hold on the platform grab bars and being jostled up in the air. If it weren't for friendly hands to pull them down, they'd be in serious trouble.

The peoplemover "Spirit of Leningrad" pulled in. Seats filled up fast, and there were six or seven people left standing when it left the station. A teenager in an orange leather jacket studded with video pins sat down next to Terry, then offered his chair to an old woman. A dozen pop songs clashed faintly from his pins. The crone smiled at him, sat down, adjusted her seat.

"I'm moving to New England," Terry told her. "Maybe this month."

She glared at him and turned her chair away.

City dwellers were rude. Terry was used to it. He sighed, and flicked on his paper.

HOUSING SHORTAGE SHAKES CITY said the *Times.* Just another reason to get out. WORST SITUATION SINCE WAR. There were people, it seemed, who'd been waiting weeks for a suitable upgrade. Of course the *Times* was an opposition paper—it had to put a bad face on everything. JOBLESS RATE HITS 35% said the *News.* The *News* was an establishment rag; somewhere in the article would be statistics justifying the situation. But the way Terry saw it, the figures spoke for themselves. With a third of the working population on sabbatical at any given time, that meant almost three percent were between jobs, pounding the pavement, making do with three-quarters normal salary and benefits. Times were tough.

Terry hit Midtown before the Authority office opened, so he stopped in a diner for brunch. It was a Polynesian joint with thatched roofs over the tables and white sand covering the floor. He ordered the papaya-breadfruit surprise and two eggs that had never been inside a chicken. He didn't bother with the orange juice. It never tasted like the stuff he used to drink when he was a kid. The way he figured it, if they didn't have it down by now, they never would. You simply couldn't get oranges like they had back then anymore.

He picked at his food, thinking about Krissie. Pregnancy was tough. Kris had less than a year's leave for it. And the neighborhood maternity center—well, he guessed it was okay. Just last night the nurse-midwife had come by for the weekly and she'd said Krissie was doing fine. Still, you couldn't help but worry.

What kind of a place was this to bring up a kid in, anyway? Children needed to run wild, enough room so they could stretch out and grow, woods they could disappear into for hours and days at a time.

"A penny for your thoughts," the waitress said when she brought the bill and a thumbpad.

Terry waved a hand toward the dugout canoe that hung from the rafters in the back of the diner over a small turquoise waterfall. "That thing's Malaysian, you know that? This whole place is about as Polynesian as I am. I mean, you can talk about cultural preservation all you want, but let's be honest here. It's pointless to pretend you can preserve a culture you've never experienced first-hand. You wind up with the

MGM-Disney fantasy version of something that never existed in the first place. You get where I'm coming from?"

He jabbed his thumb on the pad and left without even picking up his complimentary breath mint.

DOWNTOWN WASN'T SO BAD as Midtown if you had kids. But of course—all this urban bureaucracy!—you couldn't do anything so simple as just *move* there. You had to stand in line. Flats were assigned according to a complicated formula. So many points from the monthly lottery (one ticket for paying rent; extra for civic service or orbital work) and so many for need (about one room per family member, plus kitchen and bath). Plug in the neighborhood stats—quality-of-life, environmental health, access to schools, clinics, entertainment—and out pops the number. They'd drawn a high number last month, thanks in part to the Black Lagooner being on its way, so they'd decided it was now or never.

He spent half an hour sitting on a gut-sprung sofa before the government lady called him in. She rose to shake his hand. "Mr. Bissel. Thank you for your patience." He took a chair and she sank back down behind her desk. "Where exactly were you thinking of moving?"

"New Hampshire."

She looked up.

Terry laughed. "Just a joke. Right now, today, I'm interested in something Downtown. Quiet. Spacious. Suitable for a newborn."

"I—see." The government lady touched three spots on her desk and it spat out a hardcopy of three addresses. But she didn't hand them over. "Mr. Bissel, I note that you're monolingual."

"Yeah? So?"

"No crafts or hobbies. You don't play any musical instruments." She frowned. "Your cultural preservation ratings are distinctly below the mean."

"Aw, c'mon, you know as well as I do, that stuff's all bullshit."

The woman's eyes flared. "I most certainly do *not!* Multidiversity—"

"—is a crock. Look, if you want to preserve our goddamn priceless ethnic and cultural heritages, then just hand out rifles. What do you think ethnicity is all about, if it's not hating the people in the next county? Molotov cocktails for everybody in the bar! Kill the lot and let God sort 'em out! The plain and simple truth is that instead of trying to preserve our tribal identifications, we ought to be doing everything we can to obliterate them. You want to prevent the next war? Burn the family albums!"

Her mouth opened and shut. She said nothing.

Terry picked up the hardcopy. On the way out, he grinned and said, "Never mind me. I'm Irish on my mother's side, and 'tis like me Mither always sez: The only thing the Irish like better than an argument is a good fight."

THE FIRST APARTMENT was in Chinatown, overlooking the Canal. There were some kids jigging crabs on the stairs out front. Little goats were running around on the roof. Terry liked water well enough, but he didn't like sky goats all that much. Supposedly they helped keep the city clean by eating trash. He couldn't see it.

The manager of the building was a fat Mongolian who was more interested in his saxophone than in showing the flat. Terry stood, hands behind his back, looking at the Buddhist woodcuts on the wall while the man finished a snatch from *Rhapsody in Blue*. Then he sighed and put down his instrument. Lumbering, he led the way to the fourth floor.

The present tenant was, according to the hardcopy, a high-wire artist who was joining an Uptown circus. He squatted on the floor, greasing parts of a disassembled unicycle. He didn't even look up from his work, but just grunted.

"Most of building is squatters," the super said, with an expansive gesture. "Only this guy is movers. No face canal, si? No face canal."

"No face canal is right," Terry muttered. He stared out the window into a filthy airshaft with a few vegetable gardens down below. Some kids were playing wall ball. They had those garish knee and elbow grips that were all the craze nowadays, and were swarming up the walls three and four floors. One of them made a face at him.

He smiled back at her. I'm leaving the city, little girl, and you're *not*.

One look was enough, though. The super was obviously glad to get back to his music. He called an absentminded "Adios, good buddy amigo" after Terry. There was a strong Hispanic component in this neighborhood; he probably thought he was speaking English.

Off to prospect number two in Little America.

Little America was as motley a place as its namesake. The prospect was a two-bedroom flat that had been created by knocking out the walls between two pre-War flats. It faced the street, and between the clash of bicycle bells and street musicians, fishmongers, vegetable-carvers, poetry slammings (Terry had signed a petition against slamming once, but the Street Poets Union had power and a popular argument that they were a "humanizing influence" on the city), and people laughing, he would never've gotten any sleep.

The super was ethnic Kenyan, with skin as purple as a plum. She had an overprecise New Oxford accent and said she was working on an interactive software history cycle. "You and half the universe," Terry said, and she cheerily agreed. But when he suggested she look into someplace outside the city, where rents were cheaper, her expression changed to one of offended *hauteur.* "Look at the apartment. Rent it or don't," she snapped. "Be quick about it. I haven't the time for any nonsense from the likes of you."

In the actual case, there wasn't any real choice. The baby would never get any sleep in this bedlam. And Krissie might like this sort of neigborhood, but as far as Terry was concerned it was exactly the sort of overcrowded chaos that he wanted to get away from.

"I'll pass," he said.

THIRD TIME WAS the charm. The apartment was on the top floor, windows on three sides, with solid oak floors. They hadn't learned how to grow oak by the plank until ten years ago, so he could only imagine how much it had cost new. There was a modern kitchen with a tap-line to the local shops so he wouldn't have to be trotting all the way across the street whenever the wife got one of her cravings. There were kids playing wall ball outside, but they weren't going any higher than the third floor, so the noise was tolerable.

The clincher was that the surrounding buildings opened up in a way that gave him a completely unobstructed view of Jupiter through the city dome. Terry was a sucker for cloudgazing. He could sit and watch the planet's slow-swirling weather fronts endlessly shifting from pattern to pattern for hours.

IT WAS EVENING when Terry finally got home, and all the city lights were blue-shifting into twilight. He felt weary but virtuous. Krissie, he knew, would be pleased, and that was all that really mattered.

There were two strangers in the flat when he came in. A slender woman and a real bruiser of a man. From the quiet neutrality of their dress, Terry guessed they were counselors or therapists of some sort.

"Hello," he said pleasantly. "What's going on?"

"Terry," his wife said. "A woman called from the Housing Authority. She told me how you behaved and I—" She looked helplessly about her. "And I—"

"Mr. Bissel," the woman said. "You've been telling people that you plan to move out of the city."

"Yeah, so? That's not a crime. I mean, look around you. It's a perfectly rational response to an intolerable situation." Krissie was crying again.

"You want to move to ... New England, is it?"

"Look." He spread his hands in bafflement. "What is all this?"

Kris stepped close to him. Through angry tears she said, "The War, Terry—remember the War? There *is* no New England, not anymore. Three weeks the asteroids fell. Three weeks! The clouds covered the skies for years!" She was hysterical now, babbling. "Everything was destroyed—Earth, Mars, all the colonies. The cities. My mother. All of them." She began punching him on the chest. "My brother Allen! Mrs. Kressner! Jamal Hardessy! Angela Hughes!"

The burly man slid himself between them. Gently he placed his enormous hands on Terry's arms. It was like being gripped by a mountain. "Don't bother, Mrs. Bissel," he said. "We get a lot of these cases. More every year. They never listen."

The woman opened the door. "He'll be taken care of," she said.

"Where are you taking him?" Kris asked fearfully.

"Someplace pleasant," the man said. "You'll be informed when he's ready for visitors."

"But you can't. I need him here. My God, there's a baby on the way!"

"Mrs. Bissel. We cannot allow your husband to wander about loose. His illness—it's like a virus. It could infect others. He's a threat to the survival of the city."

"Oh, not my husband. You don't know Terry. He's a good man. He—"

Harshly, the woman said, "It may not show ordinarily. But we're all precariously balanced. This exaggerated kindness we show each other, our horror of conflict, the cult of preservation—these are signs of denial. All our society is an extreme reaction to ... to what happened. We're none of us totally sane, you know. We're all of us at risk."

They escorted him into the hall.

"Terry!" his wife cried. "Try to concentrate. Try to concentrate. You can't leave the city. We're the only surviving colony—the last habitat that humanity has left. There is nowhere else to go."

"Oh no," Terry said happily as they shut the door behind him. "I know where I'm going. I'm going to the country!"

The Changeling's Tale

FILL THE PIPE AGAIN. If I'm to tell this story properly, I'll need its help. That's good. No, the fire doesn't need a new log. Let it die. There are worse things than darkness.

How the tavern creaks and groans in its sleep! 'Tis naught but the settling of its bones and stones, and yet never a wraith made so lonesome a sound. It's late, the door is bolted, and the gates to either end of the Bridge are closed. The fire burns low. In all the world only you and I are awake. This is no fit tale for such young ears as yours, but—oh, don't scowl so! You'll make me laugh, and that's no fit beginning to so sad a tale as mine. All right, then.

Let us pull our stools closer to the embers and I'll tell you all.

I MUST BEGIN TWENTY years ago, on a day in early summer. The Ogre was dead. Our armies had returned, much shrunken, from their desperate adventures in the south and the survivors were once again plying their trades. The land was at peace at last, and trade was good. The tavern was often full.

The elves began crossing Long Bridge at dawn.

I was awakened by the sound of their wagons, the wheels rumbling, the silver bells singing from atop the high poles where they had been set to catch the wind. All in a frenzy I dressed and tumbled down from the chimney-loft and out the door. The wagons were painted with bright sigils and sinuous overlapping runes, potent with magic I could neither decipher nor hope to understand. The white oxen that pulled them spoke gently in their own language, one to the other. Music floated over the march, drums and cymbals mingling with the mournful call of the long curling horn named Serpentine. But the elves themselves, tall and proud, were silent behind their white masks.

One warrior turned to look at me as he passed, his eyes cold and unfriendly as a spearpoint. I shivered, and the warrior was gone.

But I had *known* him. I was sure of it. His name was ... A hand clasped my shoulder. It was my uncle. "A stirring sight, innit? Those are the very last, the final elven tribe. When they are passed over Long Bridge, there will be none of their kind left anywhere south of the Awen."

He spoke with an awful, alien sadness. In all the years Black Gabe had been my master—and being newborn when my father had marched away to the Defeat of Blackwater, I had known no other—I had never seen him in such a mood before. Thinking back, I see that it was at that instant I first realized in a way so sure I could feel it in my gut that he would someday die and be forgotten, and after him me. Then, though, I was content simply to stand motionless with the man, sharing this strangely companionable sense of loss.

"How can they tell each other apart?" I asked, marveling at how similar were their richly decorated robes and plain, unfeatured masks.

"They—"

A fire-drake curled in the air, the morning rocket set off to mark the instant when the sun's disk cleared the horizon, and my eyes traveled up to watch it explode. When they came down again, my uncle was gone. I never saw him again.

EH? FORGIVE ME. I was lost in thought. Black Gabe was a good master, though I didn't think so then, who didn't beat me half so often as I deserved. You want to know about my scars? There is nothing special about them—they are such markings as all the *am'rta skandayaksa* have. Some are for deeds of particular merit. Others indicate allegiance. The triple slashes across my cheeks mean that I was sworn to the Lord Cakaravartin, a war-leader whose name means "great wheel turning king." That is a name of significance, though I have forgotten exactly what, much as I have forgotten the manner and appearance of the great wheel-turner himself, though there was a time when I would happily have died for him. The squiggle across my forehead means I slew a dragon.

Yes, of course you would. What youth your age would not? And it's a tale I'd far more gladly tell you than this sorry life of mine. But I cannot. That I did kill a dragon I remember clearly—the hot gush of blood, its bleak scream of despair—but beyond that nothing. The events leading to and from that instant of horror and—strangely—guilt are gone from me entirely, like so much else that happened since I left the Bridge, lost in mist and forgetfulness.

Look at our shadows, like giants, nodding their heads in sympathy.

WHAT THEN? I remember scrambling across the steep slate rooftops, leaping and slipping in a way that seems quite mad to me now. Corwin the glover's boy and I were stringing the feast-day banners across the street to honor the procession below. The canvases smelled of mildew. They were stored in the Dragon Gate in that little room above the portcullis, the one with the murder hole in the floor. Jon and Corwin and I used to crouch over it betimes and take turns spitting, vying to be the first to hit the head of an unsuspecting merchant.

Winds gusted over the roofs, cold and invigorating. Jumping the gaps between buildings, I fancied myself to be dancing with the clouds. I crouched to lash a rope through an iron ring set into the wall just beneath the eaves. Cor had gone back to the gateroom for more banners. I looked up to see if he were in place yet and realized that I could see right into Becky's garret chamber.

There was nothing in the room but a pallet and a chest, a small table and a washbasin. Becky stood with her back to the window, brushing her hair.

I was put in mind of those stories we boys told each other of wanton women similarly observed. Who, somehow sensing their audience, would put on a lewd show, using first their fingers and then their hairbrushes. We had none of us ever encountered such sirens, but our faith in them was boundless. Somewhere, we knew, were women depraved enough to mate with apes, donkeys, mountain trolls—and possibly even the likes of us.

Becky, of course, did nothing of the sort. She stood in a chaste woolen night-gown, head raised slightly, stroking her long, coppery tresses in time to the faint elven music that rose from the street. A slant of sunlight touched her hair and struck fire.

All this in an instant. Then Cor came bounding over her roof making a clatter like ten goats. He shifted the bundle of banners 'neath one arm and extended the other. "Ho, Will!" he bellowed. "Stop daydreaming and toss me that rope-end!"

Becky whirled and saw me gawking. With a most unloving shriek of outrage, she slammed the shutters.

ALL THE WAY BACK to the tavern, my mind was filled with thoughts of Becky and her hairbrush. As I entered, my littlest cousin, Thistle, danced past me, chanting, "elves-elves-elves," spinning and twirling as if she need never stop. She loved elves and old stories with talking animals and all things bright and magical. They tell me she died of the whitepox not six years later. But in my mind's eye she still laughs and spins, evergreen, immortal.

The common room was empty of boarders and the table planks had been taken down. Aunt Kate, Dolly, and my eldest sister, Eleanor, were cleaning up. Kate swept the breakfast trash toward the trap. "It comes of keeping bad company," she said grimly. "That Corwin Glover and his merry band of rowdies. Ale does not brew overnight—he's been building toward this outrage for a long time."

I froze in the doorway vestibule, sure that Becky's people had reported my Tom-Peepery. And how could I protest my innocence? I'd've done as much and worse long ago, had I known such was possible.

A breeze leapt into the room when Eleanor opened the trap, ruffling her hair and making the dust dance. "They gather by the smokehouse every sennight to drink themselves sick and plot mischief," Dolly observed. "May Chandler's Anne saw one atop the wall there, making water into the river, not three nights ago."

"Oh, fie!" The trash went tumbling toward the river and Eleanor slammed the trap. Some involuntary motion on my part alerted them to my presence then. They turned and confronted me.

A strange delusion came over me then, and I imagined that these three gossips were part of a single mechanism, a twittering machine going through predetermined motions, as if an unseen hand turned a crank that made them sweep and clean and talk.

Karl Whitesmith's boy has broken his indenture, I thought.

"Karl Whitesmith's boy has broken his indenture," Dolly said. He's run off to sea.

"He's run off to sea," Kate added accusingly.

"What?" I felt my mouth move, heard the words come out independent of me. "Jon, you mean? Not Jon!"

How many 'prentices does Karl have? Of course Jon.

"How many 'prentices does Karl have? Of course Jon."

"Karl spoiled him," Kate said (and her words were echoed in my head before she spoke them). "A lad his age is like a walnut tree which suffers not but rather benefits from thrashings." She shook her besom at me. "Something the likes of you would do well to keep in mind."

Gram Birch amazed us all then by emerging from the back kitchen.

Delicate as a twig, she bent to put a plate by the hearth. It held two refried fish, leftovers from the night before, and a clutch of pickled roe. She was slimmer than your little finger and her hair was white as an aged dandelion's. This was the first time I'd seen her out of bed in weeks; the passage of the elves, or perhaps some livening property of their music, had brought fresh life to her. But her eye was as flinty as ever. "Leave the boy alone," she said.

My delusion went away, like a mist in the morning breeze from the Awen.

"You don't understand!"

"We were only—"

"This saucy lad—"

"The kitchen tub is empty," Gram Birch told me. She drew a schooner of ale and set it down by the plate. Her voice was warm with sympathy, for I was always her favorite, and there was a kindly tilt to her chin. "Go and check your trots. The head will have subsided by the time you're back."

My head in a whirl, I ran upbridge to the narrow stairway that gyred down the interior of Tinker's Leg. It filled me with wonder that Jon—gentle, laughing Jon—had shipped away. We all of us claimed to be off to sea someday; it was the second or third most common topic on our nighttime eeling trips upriver. But that it should be Jon, and that he should leave without word of farewell!

A horrible thing happened to me then: With the sureness of prophecy I knew that Jon would not come back. That he would die in the western isles. That he would be slain and eaten by a creature out of the sea such as none on the Bridge had ever imagined.

I came out at the narrow dock at the high-water mark. Thoughts elsewhere, I pulled in my lines and threw back a bass for being shorter than my forearm. Its less fortunate comrades I slung over my shoulder.

But as I was standing there on the dark and slippery stones, I saw something immense and silent move beneath the water. I thought it a monstrous tortoise at first, such as that which had taken ten strong men with ropes and grappling hooks to pull from the bay at Mermaid Head. But as it approached I could see it was too large for that. I did not move. I could not breathe. I stared down at the approaching creature.

The surface of the river exploded. A head emerged, shedding water. Each of its nostrils was large enough for a man to crawl into. Its hair and beard were dark, like the bushes and small trees that line the banks upriver and drown in every spring flood. Its eyes were larger than cartwheels and lusterless, like stone.

The giant fixed his gaze upon me, and he spoke.

WHAT DID HE SAY, YOU ASK? I wonder that myself. In this regard, I am
like the victim of brigands who finds himself lying by the wayside, and
then scrabbles in the dust for such small coppers as they may have left
behind. What little I possess, I will share with you, and you may guess
from it how much I have lost. One moment I stood before the giant and
the next I found myself tumbled into the river. It was late afternoon and
I was splashing naked with the knackery boys.

I had spent most of that day mucking out the stables in the
Approach, part of an arrangement Black Gabe had made whereby the
Pike and Barrel got a half a penny for each guest who quartered a horse
there. I was as sweaty and filthy as any of the horses by the time I was
done, and had gladly fallen in with the butcher's apprentices who would
cleanse themselves of the blood and gore their own labors had
besmirched them with.

This was on the south side of the river, below the Ogre Gate. I was
scrubbing off the last traces of ordure when I saw the elven lady staring
down at me from the esplanade.

She was small with distance, her mask a white oval. In one hand she
carried a wicker cage of finches. I found her steady gaze both discon-
certing and arousing. It went through me like a spear. My manhood
began of its own accord to lift.

That was my first sight of Ratanavivicta.

It lasted only an instant, that vision. The light of her eyes filled and
blinded me. And then one of my fellow bathers—Hodge the tanner's
son it was, whom we in our innocence considered quite the wildling—
leaped upon my back, forcing me under the water. By the time I
emerged, choking and sputtering, the elf-woman was gone.

I shoved Hodge away, and turned my gaze over the river. I squinted
at the rafts floating downstream, sweepsmen standing with their oars
up, and the carracks making harbor from their voyages across the sea.
On the far bank, pier crowded upon shack and shanty upon warehouse.
Stone buildings rose up behind, rank after rank fading blue into the distance, with here and there a spire or tower rising up from the general
ruck.

Long snakelike necks burst from the water, two river lizards fight-

ing over a salmon. A strange elation filled me then and I laughed with
joy at the sight.

AT SUNSET THE ELF-HOST was still crossing the Bridge. Their numbers
were that great. All through the night they marched, lighting their way
with lanterns carried on poles. I sat in the high window of a room we
had not let that evening, watching their procession, as changing-
unchanging as the Awen itself. They were going to the mountains of
the uttermost north, people said, through lands no living man had seen.
I sat yearning, yearning after them, until my heart could take no more.

Heavily I started down the stairs to bed.

To my astonishment the common room was filled with elves. A little wicker cage hung from a ceiling hook. In it were five yellow finches.
I looked down from it to the eyes of a white-masked woman. She crooked
a finger beckoningly, then touched the bench to her left. I sat beside her.

An elven lord whose manner and voice are gone from me, a pillar
of shadow, Cakaravartin himself, stood by the fireplace with one fingertip lazily tracing the shells and coiled serpents embedded in the stone.
"I remember," he said in a dreamy voice, "when there was no ford across
the Awenasamaga and these stones were part of Great Asura, the city
of the giants."

"But how could you—?" I blurted. Masked faces turned to look at
me. I bit my tongue in embarrassment.

"I was here when this bridge was built," the speaker continued
unheedingly. "To expiate their sins, the last of the giants were compelled
to dismantle their capital and with its stones build to the benefit of men.
They were a noble race once, and I have paused here in our quest for
parikasaya because I would see them once more."

Dolly swept in, yawning, with a platter of raw salmon and another
holding a stacked pyramid of ten mugs of ale. "Who's to pay?" she asked.
Then, seeing me, she frowned. "Will. You have chores in the morning.
Ought not you be abed?"

Reddening, I said, "I'm old enough to bide my own judgment."

An elf proferred a gold coin which, had it been silver, would have paid for the service ten times over, and asked, "Is this enough?"

Dolly smiled and nodded. Starting to my feet, I said, "I'll wake the coin-merchant and break change for you." Ignoring the exasperation that swept aside my sister's look of avaricious innocence.

But the elf-woman at my side stilled me with a touch. "Stay. The coin is not important, and there is much I would have you learn."

As the coin touched Dolly's hand she changed, for the merest instant, growing old and fat. I gawked and then she was herself again. With a flip of her skirts she disappeared with the coin so completely I was not to see her for another twenty years. One of the elves turned to the wall, lifting her mask for a quick sip of ale, restoring it with nothing exposed.

The finch-bearer brought out a leather wallet and opened it, revealing dried herbs within. Someone took a long-stemmed clay tavern pipe from the fireplace rack and gave her it. As Ratanavivicta filled the bowl, she said, "This is *margakasaya,* which in your language means 'the path to extinction.' It is rare beyond your knowing, for it grows nowhere in the world now that we have given up our gardens in the south. Chewed, it is a mild soporific. Worked into a balm it can heal minor wounds. Smoked, it forms a bridge through the years, so that one's thoughts may walk in past times or future, at will."

"How can that be?" I asked. "The past is gone, and the future—who is to say what will happen? Our every action changes it, else our deeds were for naught."

She did not answer, but instead passed the pipe to me. With a pair of tongs she lifted a coal from the fire to light it. I put the stem to my lips, exhaled nervously, inhaled. I drew the smoke deep into my lungs, and a whirring and buzzing sensation rose up from my chest to fill my head, first blinding me and then opening my eyes:

It was night, and Cakaravartin's raiders were crying out in anger and despair, for the enemy had stolen a march on us and we were caught by the edge of the marshes, lightly armed and afoot.

Screaming, crazy, we danced ourselves into a frenzy. At a sign from Cakaravartin, we loosed the bundles from our backs and unfolded a dozen horsehides. We pulled out knives and slashed ourselves across arms and chests. Where the blood fell across the hides, the black loam filled them, lending them form, billowing upward to become steeds of earth, forelegs flailing, nostrils wild, eyes cold and unblinking stars.

Then we were leaping onto our mounts, drawing our swords, galloping toward the east. Where hoof touched sod, fresh earth flowed up into the necromantic beasts, and down again through the rearmost leg.

"Tirathika!"

On hearing my adoptive name, I turned to see Krodasparasa riding maskless alongside me, his markings shining silver on his face. His eyes were gleeful and fey. Krodasparasa gestured, and I tore free of my own mask. I felt my cock stiffen with excitement.

Krodasparasa saw and laughed. Our rivalry, our hatred of each other was as nothing compared to this comradeship. Riding side by side, we traded fierce grins compounded of mockery and understanding, and urged our steeds to greater efforts.

"It's a good day to die," Krodasparasa cried. "Are you ready to die, little brother?" He shifted his sword to his far side so we could clasp hands briefly at full gallop, and then swung it around in a short, fast chop that took all of my skill to evade.

I exhaled.

The common room wrapped itself about me again. I found myself staring up at the aurochs horns nailed as a trophy to the west wall, at the fat-bellied withy baskets hanging from the whale-rib rafters. Overhead, a carved and painted wooden mermaid with elk's antlers sweeping back from her head to hold candles, turned with excruciating slowness.

The elf-woman took the pipe from my nerveless fingers. She slid the long stem under her mask so skillfully that not a fingertip's worth of her face showed. Slowly, she inhaled. The coal burned brighter, a wee orange bonfire that sucked in all the light in the room. "That was not what I wished to see," she murmured. She drew in a second time and then handed the pipe on.

Slowly the pipe passed around the room again, coming last of all to me. Clumsily, I accepted it and put the end, now hot, to my lips. I drew the magic in:

I stood on an empty plain, the silk tents of the encampment to my back. Frost rimed the ground in crisscross starbursts. My blood was pounding.

It was a festival night, and we had cut the center-poles for our conical tents twice as high as usual. Small lanterns hung from their tips like stars. All was still. For the *am'rta skandayaksa,* venturing out on a festival night was a great impiety.

Tortured with indecision I turned away and then back again, away and back. I could be killed for what I intended, but that bothered me less than the possibility that I had misread the signs, that I was not wanted. I stood before one particular tent, glaring at it until it glowed like the sun. Finally I ducked within.

Ratanavivicta was waiting for me.

Throwing aside my mask, I knelt before her. Slowly, lingeringly, I slid my fingers beneath her mask and drew it off. Her face was scarred, like the moon, and like the moon it was beautiful and cold. My hand was black on her breast. A pale nipple peeked between my fingers like the first star of twilight.

"Ahhh," she sighed voicelessly, and the pipe passed to the next hand.

EVERYTHING HAD CHANGED.

You cannot imagine how it felt, after twenty years of wandering, to return at last to Long Bridge. My heart was so bitter I could taste it in my mouth. Two decades of my life were gone, turned to nothing. My memory of those years was but mists and phantoms, stolen away by those I had trusted most. The Dragon Gate was smaller than I remembered it being, and nowhere near so grand. The stone buildings whose spires had combed the passing clouds were a mere three and four stories high. The roadway between them was scarce wide enough to let two carts pass.

My face felt tight and dry. I slid a finger under my mask to scratch at the scar tissue where it touched one corner of my mouth.

Even the air smelled different. The smoky haze of my boyhood, oak and cedar from the chimneys of the rich, driftwood and dried dung from the roofholes of the poor, was changed utterly, compounded now of charcoal and quarry-dug coal with always a sharp tang of sulfur pinching at the nose. Wondrous odors still spilled from the cookshop where old Hal Baldpate was always ready with a scowl and a sugar-bun, but the peppery admixture of hams curing next door was missing, and the smokehouse itself converted to a lens-grinder's shop.

The narrow gap between the two buildings remained, though—do you young ones still call it the Gullet?—and through it rose a light breeze from the Awen. I halted and leaned on my spear. It was exactly here one long-ago evening that Becky had showed me her freckled breasts and then fleered at me for being shocked. Here Jon and I would kneel to divvy up the eggs we'd stolen from the cotes of Bankside, which, being off the Bridge, was considered fair game by all good river-brats—I see you smiling! Here I crouched in ambush for a weaver's prentice whose name and face and sin are gone from me now, though that folly cost me a broken arm and all of Becky's hard-won sympathy.

Somebody bumped into me, cursed, and was gone before I could turn and crave pardon. I squeezed into the Gullet so others could pass, and stared out over the sun-dazzled river.

Down the Awen, a pyroscaph struggled toward the bay, smoke billowing from its stack, paddles flashing in unison, as if it were a water-beetle enchanted beyond natural size. The merchanters entering and leaving the harbor were larger than I remembered, and the cut of their sails was unfamiliar. Along the banks the city's chimneys had multiplied, pillaring smoke into the darkened heavens. It was a changed world, and one that held no place for such as me.

The ghosts of my youth thronged so thickly about me then that I could not distinguish past from present, memory from desire. It was as if I had turned away for an instant and on turning back discovered myself two decades older.

Fill the bowl again. One last time I would hear the dawn-music of my youth, the sound of lodgers clumping sleepily down the stairs, the clink and rattle of plates and pewter in the kitchen. The quick step of Eleanor returning from the cookshop with her arms full of fresh-smelling bread. The background grumbles of Black Gabe standing just out of sight, finding fault with my work.

What a cruel contrast to this morning! When I turned away from the Awen, the Bridge was thick with scurrying city-folk, shopkeepers and craftsmen in fussy, lace-trimmed clothes. The air was full of the clicking of their heels. Men and women alike, their faces were set and grim. For an instant my spirit quailed at the thought of rejoining human company. I had spent too many years in the company of owls and wolves, alone in the solitudes of the north, to be comfortable here. But I squared my shoulders and went on.

The old Pike and Barrel stood where it has always stood, midway down the Bridge. From a distance it seemed unbearably small and insignificant, though every stone and timber of it was burned forever into my heart. The tavern-placard swung lazily on its rod. That same laughing fish leaped from that same barrel that a wandering scholar had executed in trade for a night's stay when Aunt Kate was young. I know, for she spoke of him often.

Below the sign a crowd had formed, an angry eddy in the flow of passers-by. A hogshead had been upended by the door and atop it a stout man with a sheriff's feather in his cap was reading from a parchment scroll. By him stood a scarecrow underling with a handbell and behind him a dozen bravos with oaken staves, all in a row.

It was an eviction.

Kate was there, crying with rage and miraculously unchanged. I stared, disbelieving, and then, with a pain like a blow to the heart, realized my mistake. This worn, heavy woman must be my sister Dolly, turned horribly, horribly old. The sight of her made me want to turn away. The painted pike mocked me with its silent laughter. But I mastered my unease and bulled my way through the crowd.

Without meaning to, I caused a sensation. Murmuring, the bystanders made way. The sheriff stopped reading. His bravos stirred unhappily, and the scrawny bell-man cringed. The center of all eyes, I realized that there must be some faint touch of the elven glamour that clung to me yet.

"What is happening here?" My voice was deep, unfamiliar, and the words came hesitantly from my mouth, like water from a pump grown stiff with disuse.

The sheriff blusteringly shook his parchment at me. "Don't inter-fere! This is a legal turning-out, and I've the stavesmen to back me up."

"You're a coward, Tom Huddle, and an evil man indeed to do this to folk who were once your friends!" Dolly shouted. "You're the rich man's lickspittle now! A hireling to miscreants and usurers, and naught more!"

A mutter of agreement went up from the crowd.

The sheriff ducked his massive head and without turning to meet her eye, grumbled, "By damn, Dolly, I'm only doing my—"

"I'll pay," I said.

Tom Huddle gaped. "Eh? What's that?"

I shrugged off my backsack, of thick dwarven cloth embroidered with silk orchids in a woods-elf stitch, and handed my spear to a gangly youth, who almost dropped it in astonishment. That was you, wasn't it? I thought so. The haft is ebony, and heavier than might be thought.

Lashed to the frame, alongside my quiver and the broken shards of what had once been my father's sword, was a leather purse. After such long commerce with elves I no longer clearly knew the value of one coin over another. But there would be enough, that much I knew. The elvenkind are generous enough with things that do not matter. I handed it to my sister, saying, "Take as much as you need."

Dolly stood with the purse in her outstretched hand, making no move to open it. "Who are you?" she asked fearfully. "What manner of man hides his features behind a mask?"

My hand rose involuntarily—I'd forgotten the mask was there. Now, since it no longer served a purpose, I took it off. Fresh air touched my face. I felt dizzy almost to sickness, standing exposed before so many people.

Dolly stared at me.

"Will?" she said at last. "Is it really you?"

WHEN THE MONEY had been counted over thrice and the sprig of broom the sheriff had nailed over the doorsill had been torn down and trampled underfoot, the house and neighbors all crowded about me and bore me into the Pike and Barrel's common room and gave me the honored place by the fire. The air was close and stuffy—I could not think. But nobody noticed. They tumbled question upon question so that I had but little chance to answer, and vied to reintroduce themselves, crying, "Here's one you're not expecting!" and "Did you ever guess little Sam would turn out such a garish big gassoon?" and roaring with laughter. Somebody put a child on my knee, a boy, they said his name was Pip. Somebody else brought down the lute from its peg by the loft and struck up a song.

Suddenly the room was awhirl with dancers. Unmoved, I watched them, these dark people, these strangers, all sweaty and imperfect flesh. After my years with the pale folk, they all seemed heavy and earthbound. Heat radiated from their bodies like steam.

A woman with wrinkles at the corners of her eyes and mischief within them, drew me up from the stool, and suddenly I was dancing too. The fire cast an ogreish shadow upon the wall behind me and it danced as well, mocking my clumsy steps.

Everything felt so familiar and yet so alien, all the faces of my youth made strange by age, and yet dear to me in an odd, aching way, as if both tavern and Bridge were but clever simulacra of the real thing, lacking the power to convince and yet still able to rend the heart. My childhood was preternaturally clear, as close to me now as the room in which I sat. It was as if I had never left. All the years between seemed a dream.

"You don't know who I am, do you?" my dancing partner said.

"Of course I do," I lied.

"Who, then?" She released me and stood back, hands on hips.

Challenged, I actually *looked* at her for the first time. She moved loosely within her blouse, a plump woman with big brown freckles on her face and forearms. She crossed her arms in a way that caused her breasts to balloon upward, and laughed when I flushed in embarrassment.

Her laughter struck me like the clapper of a great bell.

"Becky!" I cried. "By the Seven, it's you! I never expected—"

"You never expected I'd grow so fat, eh?"

"No, no!" I protested. "It's not—"

"You're a fool, Will Taverner. But that's not totally unbecoming in a man." She drew me into the shadow of the stairway where there was privacy, and a small bench as well. We talked for a long time. And at the end of that conversation I thought she looked dissatisfied. Nor could I account for it until she reached between my legs to feel what was there. My cod, though, was a wiser man than I and stood up to greet her. "Well," she said, "that's a beginning. Cold dishes aren't brought back to a boil in a minute."

She left me.

You look unhappy. Becky's your mam, isn't she? Now that I come to think of it, there's that glint in your eye and a hint at that same diabolus that hides at the edge of her mouth. Well she's a widow now, which means she can do as she pleases. But I will horrify you with no more details of what we said.

Where's my pipe? What happened to that pouch of weed? Thank you. I'd be long asleep by now if not for its aid. This is the last trace of the *margakasaya* left in all the world. With me will die even the memory of it, for there are no elves abroad in the realms of men anymore. They have found *parikasaya*, "final extinction" you would say, or perhaps "the end of all." Did you know that *am'rta skandayaksa* means "deathless elfgroup?" There's irony there, knew we only how to decipher it.

Maybe I was wrong to kill the dragon.

Maybe he was all that kept them from oblivion.

When we had all shared Cakaravartin's vision of Great Asura and of the giants at labor, their faces stolid and accepting of both their guilt and their punishment, and spoken with Boramohanagarahant, their king, it was almost dawn. Cakaravartin passed around the pipe one more time. "I see that you are determined to come with us," he said to me, "and that is your decision to make. But first you should know the consequences."

Ratanavivicta's mask tilted in a way that I would later learn indicated displeasure. But Cakaravartin drew in deeply and passed the pipe around again. I was trembling when it came to me. The mouthpiece was slick with elf-spit. I put it between my lips.

I inhaled.

At first I thought nothing had happened. The common room was exactly as before, the fire dying low in the hearth, the elkmaid slowly quartering out the air as ever she had done. Then I looked around me. The elves were gone. I was alone, save for one slim youth of about my own age, whom I did not recognize.

That youth was you.

Do I frighten you? I frighten myself far more, for I have reached that moment when I see all with doubled sight and apprehend with divided heart. Pray such possession never seizes you. This—now—is what I was shown all these many years ago, and this is the only chance I will ever have to voice my anger and regret to that younger self, who I know will not listen. How could he? A raggedy taverner's boy with small prospects and a head stuffed full of half-shaped ambitions. What could I say to make him understand how much he is giving up?

By rights you should have been my child. There's the bitter nub of the thing, that Becky, who had all but pledged her heart to me, had her get by someone else. A good man, perhaps—they say half the Bridge turned out to launch his fire-boat when he was taken by the dropsy— but not me.

I have lost more than years. I have lost the life I was meant to have, children on my knee and a goodwife growing old and fat with me as we sank into our dotage. Someone to carry my memory a few paces beyond the emptiness of the grave, and grandchildren to see sights I will not. These were my birthright, and I have them not. In his callowness and ignorance, my younger self has undone me.

I can see him, even now, running madly after the elves, as he will in the shadowy hour before dawn. Heart pounding with fear that he will not catch up, lungs agonized with effort. Furious to be a hero, to see strange lands, to know the love of a lady of the *am'rta skandayaksa*. They are fickle and cruel, are the elves. Ratanavivicta snatched me from my life on a whim, as casually as she might pick up a bright pebble from the roadside. She cast me aside as easily as she would a gemstone of which she had wearied. There is no faith in her kind.

Ah, it is a dreadful night! The winds prowl the rooftops like cats, bringing in the winter. There'll be frost by morning, and no mistake.

Is the story over, you ask? Have you not been listening? There is no story. Or else it all—your life and mine and Krodasparasa's alike—is one story and that story always ending and never coming to a conclusion. But my telling ends now, with my younger self starting from his dream of age and defeat and finding himself abandoned, the sole mortal awake on all the Bridge, with the last of the elf horde gone into the sleeping streets of the city beyond the Dragon Gate.

He will leap to his feet and snatch up his father's sword from its place over the hearth—there, where my spear hangs now. He will grab a blanket for a cloak and a handful of jerked meat to eat along the road, and nothing more, so great will be his dread of being left behind.

I would not stop him if I could. Run, lad, run! What do you care what becomes of me? Twenty years of glory lie at your feet. The dream is already fading from your head.

You feel the breeze from the river as you burst out the door.

Your heart *sings*.

The moment is past. I have been left behind.

Only now can I admit this. Through all this telling, I have been haunted by a ghost and the name of that ghost was Hope. So long as I had not passed beyond that ancient vision, there was yet the chance that I was not my older self at all, but he who was destined to shake off his doubts and leap out that door. In the innermost reaches of my head, I was still young. The dragon was not slain, the road untraveled, the elves alive, the adventures ahead, the magic not yet passed out of the world.

And now, well. I'm home.

Midnight Express

EXCUSE ME. THIS CAN'T BE RIGHT.

Yes?

According to this schedule, we arrive at Elf Hill Station at 8:23 PM and after a half-hour layover, the train departs exactly two hundred years later.

Quite right.

But that can't be!

Is this your first time on this route?

Yes, my company is expanding into new markets. I'm a commercial traveler. I used to cover Indiana and Illinois.

Well, that explains it. I take it this is your first visit to Faerie? No previous travel experience in the Noncontiguous Territories—Grammarie, Brocielande, Arcadia, et cetera?

Well ... no, but I've done a lot of traveling, and I've got an excellent record. I won the Daniel L. Houseman Sales Cup three years running.

Most impressive. An obviously intelligent man such as yourself, then, should have no trouble comprehending the chronologically liberated nature of the *night lands,* as we like to call them.

I beg your pardon. Chronologically liberated?

That's what I said. You'll have noticed that physical travel here is particularly dreamlike, that an hour can be spent rushing furiously past a small pond, that a hundred miles can go by in the wink of an eye. That's because you journey not only physically but temporally—back, forth, sideways in time. Much of the governance of the Territories is managed in that way. Which is a good thing, given how fey most of the officials of Oberon's court are. I doubt they could deal with matters in a more straightforward manner.

Phew! You'll pardon me for feeling dizzied. Things don't work that way where I come from.

That's not entirely true. There are owls.

Owls?

Owls are continuously flying back and forth through time. It's their nature. That's why they have that short labyrinthine name: the circle, the recomplication, the straight line. It's also why they're nocturnal. Ambichronology is so much easier when nobody's looking.

Then that's why it's still night, even though we've been traveling so long?

I said that you were intelligent! To differing degrees, it's always night here. Don't worry about Elf Hill. You'll make up the time later. Or earlier—fourth-dimensional grammar is so boring, don't you think? I trust you have a Baedeker. You'll want to study it carefully.

I see I will. Well. That clears things up quite a bit. Thank you.

You're welcome. Do you like my breasts?

I—yes, they're quite lovely.

You may touch them if you wish. Yes, like that. Mmmmm. Both hands, please.

They're amazingly soft and ... warm, aren't they?

It's the fur. You haven't said anything about my nipples.

They're beautiful too. And pink. Startlingly so.

All my leathers are pink. Look at the pads of my paws. Exactly the same.

Wow! Those are some claws.

Three inches long. Needle sharp. Retractable. They can slice through steel. They can gut a man from crotch to sternum in less time than it takes to say it. You took your hands away.

I wouldn't want to get, ah, overly familiar with you.

I'll let you know if you're getting fresh. You're not entirely unattractive, you know. For a mortal.

Really, I'm nothing much. Just a commercial traveler. Nobody special.

I feel myself strangely drawn to you.

I can't imagine why.

A woman—well, a female, at least—has certain needs. Desires. No, needs.

I'm sure I don't know what you're talking about.

You have noticed that I'm female, haven't you? And beautiful. God's own lioness, a poet called me once. Isn't that lovely? It's a pity what happened to him.

I think I'd better leave.

I think you'd better not. I think you'd be well advised to stay. In fact, I don't believe you'd be able to leave if you wanted to. If you get my meaning.

I—I'm afraid I do.

Good. You should take off your suit.

Yes. Perhaps I should.

I'll lock the door. So we're not disturbed.

Who—what—would dare disturb *you?*

You'd be surprised. Slowly, little mouthful, slowly! Don't just throw off those clothes. We've got all the time we need; night lasts forever here, remember. Oh, now that's quite nice. You must work out every day. Now the trousers. My! You're a big one. I hope that's not painful to you. I promise to take good care of it. Afterwards I'll ask you a riddle.

Why?

It's just my nature, I'm afraid. I'd spare you if I could. But let's not think about that now. What would you like to do first?

I'm not sure I should.

I beg your pardon.

It's just that it ... well, it would be bestiality. Wouldn't it?

It's only bestiality if *I* am a beast. Do you think me a beast?

I ... I don't know.

Good. That's the way it should be. It would be impertinent for you to presume one way or the other. Now let's see, how shall I begin? I think I'll just—mmmm. And then—ahhhh. You like that, don't you?

Well ...

There's no need to be coy. Nobody's taking notes; this is completely off the record. Bring your mouth here. Kiss me. Yes. Now lower. Lower. There. Yes. The other one too. Oh, that's quite nice—what you do with your hands. Yes, I like that. Lower.

My God, you're so ...

Yes, I'm a hairy bitch all right. Keep doing that. I'll just stretch around like this and ...

Watch it with those claws!

Sorry. I'm passionate by nature—Mediterranean, you understand. Here, I'll lick away the blood. Now isn't that better?

Yes.

Oh, my! I feel quite carried away. I think I'd like to—

None of that, now!

Tsk. What's life without a little risk? Here. I'll just run my tongue up the side, and then ... You liked that, eh? The way I closed my lips about the tip?

My God, yes.

Let's see how much of that monster I can take in my mouth at once.

That's ... oh yes, that's fine, that's ... *Whoah!*

Did I hurt you?

No, I, I'm just startled is all. I wasn't expecting—

What use are such fine sharp teeth as mine if they're never used? I didn't actually break the skin anywhere, did I? No, I didn't think I had. It's not the sort of thing I'd do by accident. Come up here, you. Yes, bring your face to mine. Now we kiss. So you can taste yourself in my mouth and I can taste myself in yours. Let the flavors mingle. That's what's called the alchemical marriage. It can be harnessed to work magics.

Like what?

Well, I'll admit I've never actually done it myself. There was never anything I wanted at that particular moment more than what I could easily arrange for myself with materials on hand.

I could think of a few things.

Really? Then tell me, what would you like to have *right now?* Be honest. What is it you really want most? Diamonds? A gold Rolex? A mission-style hacienda with central air, in-ground heated pool, and a tennis court?

I'd ... like your mouth again. You know. What you were doing before.

Oh, wise little monkey! And here's your reward for choosing so well.

Ahhh. This is wonderful. This is so good. I could do this all night.

Be careful what you wish for. Remember where we are.

What do you mean?

Time is malleable in the night lands. Here, desire is a primal force—it's entirely possible to be so caught up in some action that it lasts all night. And remember, night here lasts forever. Literally.

Oh.

I like how hairless you are. It's so perverse. I'm going to crouch over you. Like this. With my front paws on your shoulders. It's exactly the posture a lion takes before tearing open its prey. Do I frighten you?

A little.

Good. You should be frightened. I'm not at all human, you know. Do you enjoy what I'm doing with my tail?

Very much.

How gallant. Now I'll just drag the tips of my breasts across your ... Sir! What an impetuous creature you are. Not that I dislike it, mind you, I—yes, that's good. That's nice. But just lean back down for a moment and let me place you inside me. There! Ahh. Yes. You can continue what you were doing now.

What I was doing? Do you mean you want my mouth *here?* Or maybe you'd like my hands to squeeze you *here?* Or would you like me to place my fingers ... *here* and do ... *this?*

Oh my. So many decisions to make. Demonstrate those choices for me again, would you? Ahhh. Mmm. Oh! Well, I must say they're all ... diverting. I believe I'll take the lot.

You'll have to choose. I can't possibly do them all at the same time.

You can't? How tiresome. In that case, I'll just . . . *throw you down!* And ravish you! Yes! You're helpless now. I can do anything I want with you.

I'm not as helpless as all that, you know. I'm not helpless at all. Let me show you a hold I learned in varsity wrestling. I just place one hand here and the other there, and—voila!

Yes, yes, tumble me around! Tumble me around! Take me from behind now. Here, I'll crouch down low and raise my haunches high. Do you like this? Do you think it's sexy?

More than words can express. Sexier than anything I've ever imagined. What are those lights?

Fata morganas. Ignore them. Just keep—ahhh, yes. Like that. They're just excess magic grounding itself. Our passion creates little eddies in the time-flow. Ooh. Harder. You don't need to be delicate with me. I admit they're pretty to look at, though. The lights, I mean.

Lights? What lights?

I forget. I—ah! Oh, but you're—ah!

You like this, eh? You do? You want me to keep going?

I'll kill you if you stop. Ah! Oh, but that's—ah!—nice.

Then I'll continue. It wouldn't be very gentlemanly of me to refuse a lady what she wants.

Ah! Ah! Ah! Ah! Slam it home! Slam it home! Ahhhhhh, ahhhhhh. Oh, what a sweet little monkey you are.

Hey—the cushions!

Hmmmm? Did I do *that?* Well, no matter, we'll just flip them over. And you. Poor thing, you're not finished yet.

Well . . .

Here. Let me just roll you over, and—comfy? Good. Now I'll run my tongue down your abdomen, and . . . Oh, are my breasts in your way? No, I can see that they're not. That's very nice, by the way. I'll put one paw here, and the other here, and then I'll bring my mouth up to . . .

Ahhh. That's so . . .

Hush. Let me just . . . mmmmm. And . . . mmmmm. You're a lot closer to coming than I thought you were. Here—I'm going to shift myself around, and guide you inside me. Ahh. Isn't that better? Don't try to answer me. I'd be terribly insulted if you could.

I, I . . .

That's more like it. Incoherent with passion. Now. Long, even strokes. I want you deep inside me when you—oh, my.

Oh god, oh god, oh god, oh god.

There. There, it's done. Are you happy, sweetmeats? Was it good for you?

My god, yes.

Good. Because now I have to ask my riddle.

Why are you putting your paws there? Don't you think you should retract your claws?

It's only a technicality. First I ask the riddle. Then you answer it. Correctly, I hope. Because if you answer it wrong, I'll rip the family jewels right off that precious little bod of yours.

But that's terrible! I'd be a . . . I'd bleed to death!

Well, yes, but I'd like to think I'm worth it. Are you ready?

No!

I'm going to ask you a second time, and it won't matter what you say. But the third time, if you say no . . . well, remember what I said about some things lasting forever. Not all primal experiences are pleasant, after all. Are you ready?

Can't we just—?

No. Third time's the charm, now. Ready?

I suppose so. As ready as I'll ever be.

Here's the riddle: What walks on two legs and enters four-legs with his third leg to make a beast with six legs and—sometimes—two backs?

Oh, but that . . . it's . . . you're talking about the two of us. What we just did.

There. You see? That wasn't so difficult after all, was it? Of course, *I* get to choose which riddle to ask, and I'm feeling particularly fond of you at the moment. So I'll just retract my claws and . . . Why, you bad thing! You're hard again. So you like a taste of danger, do you?

Well, that and . . . how shall I put it?

Delicately, I trust.

A certain … a touch of … perfume in the air.

Oh, that! Well, I am feline in nature, after all. When I'm in heat, I stink of it. But right now, I'd better see to your needs. That looks so terribly, terribly swollen. Would you like me to take care of it?

Oh, yes.

Then I will. And afterwards, I'll ask you another riddle. You'd like that, wouldn't you?

Mmmmm.

This could take all night.

The Wisdom of Old Earth

Judith Seize-the-Day was, quite simply, the best of her kind. Many another had aspired to the clarity of posthuman thought, and several might claim some rude mastery of its essentials, but she alone came to understand it as completely as any offworlder.

Such understanding did not come easily. The human mind is slow to generalize and even slower to integrate. It lacks the quicksilver apprehension of the posthuman. The simplest truth must be repeated often to imprint even the most primitive understanding of what comes naturally and without effort to the space-faring children of humanity. She had grown up in Pole Star City, where the shuttles slant down through the zone of permanent depletion in order to avoid further damage to the fragile ozone layer, and thus from childhood had associated extensively with the highly evolved. It was only natural that as a woman she would elect to turn her back on her own brutish kind and strive to boot-strap herself into a higher order.

Yet even then she was like an ape trying to pass as a philosopher. For all her laborious ponderings, she did not yet comprehend the core wisdom of posthumanity, which was that thought and action must be as one. Being a human, however, when she did comprehend, she

244

understood it more deeply and thoroughly than the posthumans themselves. As a Canadian, she could tap into the ancient and chthonic wisdoms of her race. Where her thought went, the civilized mind could not follow.

It would be expecting too much of such a woman that she would entirely hide her contempt for her own kind. She cursed the two trollish Ninglanders who were sweating and chopping a way through the lush tangles of kudzu, and drove them onward with the lash of her tongue.

"Unevolved bastard pigs!" she spat. "Inbred degenerates! If you ever want to get home to molest your dogs and baby sisters again, you'll put your backs into it!"

The larger of the creatures looked back at her with an angry gleam in his eye, and his knuckles whitened on the hilt of his machete. She only grinned humorlessly, and patted the holster of her *ankh.* Such weapons were rarely allowed humans. Her possession of it was a mark of the great respect in which she was held.

The brute returned to his labor.

It was deepest winter and the jungle tracts of what had once been the mid-Atlantic coastlands were traversable. Traversable, that is, if one had a good guide. Judith was among the best. She had brought her party alive to the Flying Hills of southern Pennsylvania, and not many could have done that. Her client had come in search of the fabled bell of liberty, which many another party had sought in vain. She did not believe he would find it either. But that did not concern her.

All that concerned her was their survival.

So she cursed and drove the savage Ninglanders before her until all at once they broke through the vines and brush out of shadow and into a clearing.

All three stood unmoving for an instant, staring out over the clumps and hillocks of grass that covered the foundations of what had once been factories, perhaps, or workers' housing, gasoline distribution stations, grist mills, shopping malls ... Even the skyline was uneven. Mystery beckoned from every ambiguous lump.

It was almost noon. They had been walking since sundown.

Judith slipped on her goggles and scanned the grey skies for navigation satellites. She found three radar beacons within range. A utility accepted their input and calculated her position: less than a hundred miles from Philadelphia. They'd made more distance than she'd expected. The empathic function mapped for her the locations of her party: three including herself, then one, then two, then one, strung over a mile and a half of trail. That was wrong.

Very wrong indeed.

"Pop the tents," she ordered, letting the goggles fall around her neck. "Stay out of the food."

The Ninglanders dropped their packs. One lifted a refrigeration stick over his head like a spear and slammed it into the ground. A wash of cool air swept over them all. His lips curled with pleasure, revealing broken yellow teeth.

She knew that if she lingered, she would not be able to face the oppressive jungle heat again. So, turning, Judith strode back the way she'd come. Rats scattered at her approach, disappearing into hot green shadow.

The first of her party she encountered was Harry Work-to-Death. His face was pale and he shivered uncontrollably. But he kept walking, because to stop was to die. They passed each other without a word. Judith doubted he would live out the trip. He had picked up something after their disastrous spill in the Hudson. There were opiates enough in what survived of the medical kit to put him out of his misery, but she did not make him the offer.

She could not bring herself to.

Half a mile later came Leeza Child-of-Scorn and Maria Triumph-of-the-Will, chattering and laughing together. They stopped when they saw her. Judith raised her *ankh* in the air, and shook it so that they could feel its aura scrape ever so lightly against their nervous systems.

"Where is the offworlder?" The women shrank from her anger. "You abandoned him. You *dared*. Did you think you could get away with it? You were fools if you did."

Wheedlingly, Leeza said, "The sky man knew he was endangering the rest of us, so he asked to be left behind." She and Maria were full-blooded Canadians, like Judith, free of the taint of Southern genes. They had been hired for their intelligence, and intelligence they had—a low sort of animal cunning that made them dangerously unreliable when the going got hard. "He insisted."

"It was very noble of him," Maria said piously.

"I'll give you something to be noble about if you don't turn around and lead me back to where you left him." She holstered her *ankh,* but did not lock it down. "Now!" With blows of her fists, she forced them down the trail. Judith was short, stocky, all muscle. She drove them before her like the curs that they were.

The offworlder lay in the weeds where he had been dropped, one leg twisted at an odd angle. The litter that Judith had lashed together for him had been flung into the bushes.

His clothes were bedraggled, and the netting had pulled away from his collar. But weak as he was, he smiled to see her. "I knew you would return for me." His hands fluttered up in a gesture indicating absolute confidence. "So I was careful to avoid moving. The fracture will have to be reset. But that's well within your capabilities, I'm sure."

"I haven't lost a client yet." Judith unlaced his splint and carefully straightened the leg. Posthumans, spending so much of their time in microgravity environments, were significantly less robust than their ancestral stock. Their bones broke easily. Yet when she reset the femur and tied up the splint again with lengths of nylon cord, he didn't make a sound. His kind had conscious control over their endorphin production. Judith checked his neck for ticks and chiggers, then tucked in his netting. "Be more careful with this. There are a lot of ugly diseases loose out here."

"My immune system is stronger than you'd suspect. If the rest of me were as strong, I wouldn't be holding you back like this."

As a rule, she liked the posthuman women better than their men. The men were hothouse flowers—flighty, elliptical, full of fancies and elaboration. Their beauty was the beauty of a statue; all sculptured features and chill affect. The offworlder, however, was not like that. His look was direct. He was as solid and straightforward as a woman.

"While I was lying here, I almost prayed for a rescue party."

To God, she thought he meant. Then saw how his eyes lifted briefly, involuntarily, to the clouds and the satellites beyond. Much that for humans required machines a posthuman could accomplish with precisely tailored neural implants.

"They would've turned you down." This Judith knew for a fact. Her mother, Ellen To-the-Manner-Born, had died in the jungles of Wisconsin, eaten away with gangrene and cursing the wardens over an open circuit.

"Yes, of course, one life is nothing compared to the health of the planet." His mouth twisted wryly. "Yet still, I confess I was tempted."

"Put him back in the litter," she told the women. "Carry him gently." In the Quebeçois dialect, which she was certain her client did not know, she added, "Do this again, and I'll kill you."

She lagged behind, letting the others advance out of sight, so she could think. In theory she could simply keep the party together. In practice, the women could not both carry the offworlder and keep up with the men. And if she did not stay with the Ninglanders, they would not work. There were only so many days of winter left. Speed was essential.

An unexpected peal of laughter floated back to her, then silence.

Wearily, she trudged on. Already they had forgotten her, and her *ankh.* Almost she could envy them. Her responsibilities weighed heavily upon her. She had not laughed since the Hudson.

According to her goggles, there was a supply cache in Philadelphia. Once there, they could go back on full rations again.

THE TENTS WERE BRIGHT mushrooms in the clearing. Work-to-Death lay dying within one of them. The women had gone off with the men into the bush. Even in this ungodly heat and humidity they were unable or unwilling to curb their bestial lusts.

Judith sat outside with the offworlder, the refrigeration stick turned up just enough to take the edge off the afternoon heat. To get him talking, she asked, "Why did you come to Earth? There is nothing here worth all your suffering. Were I you, I'd've turned back long ago."

For a long moment the offworlder struggled to gear down his

complex thoughts into terms Judith could comprehend. At last he said, "Consider evolution. Things do not evolve from lower states to higher, as the ancients believed, with their charts which began with a fish crawling up upon the land and progressed on to mammals, apes, Neanderthals, and finally men. Rather, an organism evolves to fit its environment. An ape cannot live in the ocean. A human cannot brachiate. Each thrives in its own niche.

"Now consider posthumanity. Our environment is entirely artificial—floating cities, the Martian subsurface, the Venusian and Jovian bubbles. Such habitats require social integration of a high order. A human could survive within them, possibly, but she would not thrive. Our surround is self-defined and therefore within it we are the pinnacle of evolution."

As he spoke, his hands twitched with the suppressed urge to amplify and clarify his words with the secondary emotive language offworlders employed in parallel with the spoken. Thinking, of course, that she did not savvy handsign. But as her facility with it was minimal, Judith did not enlighten him.

"Now imagine a being with more-than-human strength and greater-than-posthuman intellect. Such a creature would be at a disadvantage in the posthuman environment. She would be an evolutionary dead end. How then could she get any sense of herself, what she could do, and what she could not?"

"How does all apply to you personally?"

"I wanted to find the measure of myself, not as a product of an environment that caters to my strengths and coddles my weaknesses. I wanted to discover what I am in the natural state."

"You won't find the natural state here. We're living in the aftermath."

"No," he agreed. "The natural state is lost, shattered like an eggshell. Even if—when—we finally manage to restore it, gather up all the shards and glue them together, it will no longer be natural, but something we have decided to maintain and preserve, like a garden. It will be only an extension of our culture."

"Nature is dead," Judith said. It was a concept she had picked up from other posthumans.

His teeth flashed with pleasure at her quick apprehension. "Indeed. Even off Earth, where conditions are more extreme, its effects are muted by technology. I suspect that nature can only exist where our all-devouring culture has not yet reached. Still ... here on Earth, in the regions where all but the simplest technologies are prohibited, and it's still possible to suffer pain and even death ... This is as close to an authentic state as can be achieved." He patted the ground by his side. "The past is palpable here, century upon century, and under that the strength of the soil." His hands involuntarily leapt. *This is so difficult,* they said. *This language is so clumsy.* "I am afraid I have not expressed myself very well."

He smiled apologetically then, and she saw how exhausted he was. But still she could not resist asking, "What is it like, to think as you do?" It was a question which she had asked many times, of many posthumans. Many answers had she received, and no two of them alike.

The offworlder's face grew very still. At last he said, "Lao-tzu put it best. 'The way that can be named is not the true way. The name that can be spoken is not the eternal name.' The higher thought is ineffable, a mystery which can be experienced but never explained."

His arms and shoulders moved in a gesture that was the evolved descendant of a shrug. His weariness was palpable.

"You need rest," she said, and, standing, "let me help you into your tent."

"Dearest Judith. What would I ever do without you?"

Ever so slightly, she flushed.

THE NEXT SUNDOWN their maps, though recently downloaded, proved to be incomplete. The improbably named Skookle River had wandered, throwing off swamps that her goggles' topographical functions could not distinguish from solid land. For two nights the party struggled southward, moving far to the west and then back again so many times that Judith would have been entirely lost without the navsats.

Then the rains began.

There was no choice but to leave the offworlder behind. Neither he nor Harry Work-to-Death could travel under such conditions. Judith put Maria and Leeza in charge of them both. After a few choice words of warning, she left them her spare goggles and instructions to break camp and follow as soon as the rains let up.

"Why do you treat us like dogs?" a Ninglander asked her when they were underway again. The rain poured down over his plastic poncho.

"Because you are no better than dogs."

He puffed himself up. "I am large and shapely. I have a fine mustache. I can give you many orgasms."

His comrade was pretending not to listen. But it was obvious to Judith that the two men had a bet going as to whether she could be seduced or not.

"Not without my participation."

Insulted, he thumped his chest. Water droplets flew. "I am as good as any of your Canadian men!"

"Yes," she agreed, "unhappily that's true."

When the rains finally let up, Judith had just crested a small hillock that her topographics identified as an outlier of the Welsh Mountains. Spread out before her was a broad expanse of overgrown twenty-first-century ruins. She did not bother accessing the city's name. In her experience, all lost cities were alike; she didn't care if she never saw another. "Take ten," she said, and the Ninglanders shrugged out of their packs.

Idly, she donned her goggles to make sure that Leeza and Maria were breaking camp, as they had been instructed to do.

And screamed with rage.

THE GOGGLES JUDITH had left behind had been hung, unused, upon the flap-pole of one of the tents. Though the two women did not know it, it was slaved to hers, and she could spy upon their actions. She kept her goggles on all the way back to their camp.

When she arrived, they were sitting by their refrigeration stick, surrounded by the discarded wrappings of half the party's food and all of its opiates. The stick was turned up so high that the grass about it was white with frost. Already there was an inch of ash at its tip.

Harry Work-to-Death lay on the ground by the women, grinning loopily, face frozen to the stick. Dead.

Outside the circle, only partially visible to the goggles, lay the offworlder, still strapped to his litter. He chuckled and sang to himself. The women had been generous with the drugs.

"Pathetic weakling," Child-of-Scorn said to the offworlder, "I don't know why you didn't drown in the rain. But I am going to leave you out in the heat until you are dead and then I am going to piss on your corpse."

"I am not going to wait," Triumph-of-the-Will bragged. She tried to stand and could not. "In just—just a moment."

The whoops of laughter died as Judith strode into the camp. The Ninglanders stumbled to a halt behind her, and stood looking uncertainly from her to the women and back. In their simple way, they were shocked by what they saw.

Judith went to the offworlder and slapped him hard to get his attention. He gazed up confusedly at the patch she held up before his face.

"This is a detoxifier. It's going to remove those drugs from your system. Unfortunately, as a side effect, it will also depress your endorphin production. I'm afraid this is going to hurt."

She locked it onto his arm, and then said to the Ninglanders, "Take him up the trail. I'll be along."

They obeyed. The offworlder screamed once as the detoxifier took effect, and then fell silent again. Judith turned to the traitors. "You chose to disobey me. Very well. I can use the extra food."

She drew her *ankh*.

Child-of-Scorn clenched her fists angrily. "So could we! Half-rations so your little pet could eat his fill. Work us to death carrying him about. You think I'm stupid. I'm not stupid. I know what you want with him."

"He's the client. He pays the bills."

"What are you to him but an ugly little ape? He'd sooner fuck a cow than you!"

Triumph-of-the-Will fell over laughing. "A cow!" she cried. "A fuh-fucking cow! Moo!"

Child-of-Scorn's eyes blazed. "You know what the sky people call the likes of you and me? Mud-women! Sometimes they come to the cribs outside Pole Star City to get good and dirty. But they always go back to their nice clean habitats afterwards. Five minutes after he climbs back into the sky, he'll have forgotten your name."

"Moooo! Moooo!"

"You cannot make me angry," Judith said, "for you are only animals."

"I am not an animal!" Child-of-Scorn shook her fist at Judith. "I refuse to be treated like one."

"One does not blame an animal for being what it is. But neither does one trust an animal that has proved unreliable. You were given two chances."

"If I'm an animal, then what does that make you? Huh? What the fuck does that make you, goddamnit?" The woman's face was red with rage. Her friend stared blankly up at her from the ground.

"Animals," Judith said through gritted teeth, "should be killed without emotion."

She fired twice.

WITH HER PARTY THUS diminished, Judith could not hope to return to Canada afoot. But there were abundant ruins nearby, and they were a virtual reservoir of chemical poisons from the days when humans ruled the Earth. If she set the *ankh* to its hottest setting, she could start a blaze that would set off a hundred alarms in Pole Star City. The wardens would have to come to contain it. She would be imprisoned, of course, but her client would live.

Then Judith heard the thunder of engines.

High in the sky a great light appeared, so bright it was haloed with black. She held a hand to lessen the intensity and saw within the dazzle a small dark speck. A shuttle, falling from orbit.

She ran crashing through the brush as hard and fast as she could.

Nightmarish minutes later, she topped a small rise and found the Ning-landers standing there, the offworlder between them. They were watching the shuttle come to a soft landing in the clearing its thrusters had burned in the vegetation.

"You summoned it," she accused the offworlder.

He looked up with tears in his eyes. The detoxifier had left him in a state of pitiless lucidity, with nothing to concentrate on but his own suffering. "I had to, yes." His voice was distant, his attention turned inward, on the neural device that allowed him to communicate with the ship's crew. "The pain—you can't imagine what it's like. How it feels."

A lifetime of lies roared in Judith's ears. Her mother had died for lack of the aid that came at this man's thought.

"I killed two women just now."

"Did you?" He looked away. "I'm sure you had good reasons. I'll have it listed as death by accident." Without his conscious volition, his hands moved, saying, *It's a trivial matter, let it be.*

A hatch opened in the shuttle's side. Slim figures clambered down, white med-kits on their belts. The offworlder smiled through his tears and stretched out welcoming arms to them.

Judith stepped back and into the shadow of his disregard. She was just another native now.

Two women were dead.

And her reasons for killing them mattered to no one.

She threw her head back and laughed, freely and without reserve. In that instant Judith Seize-the-Day was as fully and completely alive as any of the unworldly folk who walk the airless planets and work in the prosperous and incomprehensible habitats of deep space.

In that instant, had any been looking, she would have seemed not human at all.

Radio Waves

I WAS WALKING THE telephone wires upside down, the sky underfoot cold and flat with a few hard bright stars sparsely scattered about it, when I thought how it would take only an instant's weakness to step off to the side and fall up forever into the night. A kind of wildness entered me then and I began to run.

I made the wires sing. They leapt and bulged above me as I raced past Ricky's Luncheonette and up the hill. Past the old chocolate factory and the IDI Advertising Display plant. Past the body shops, past A.J. LaCourse Electric Motors-Controls-Parts. Then, where the slope steepened, along the curving snake of row houses that went the full quarter-mile up to the Ridge. Twice I overtook pedestrians, hunched and bundled, heads doggedly down, out on incomprehensible errands. They didn't notice me, of course. They never do.

The antenna farm was visible from here. I could see the Seven Sisters spangled with red lights, dependent on the Earth like stalactites. "Where are you running to, little one?" one tower whispered in a crackling, staticky voice. I think it was Hegemone.

"Fuck off," I said without slackening my pace, and they all chuckled.

Cars mumbled by. This was ravine country, however built-up, and the far side of the road, too steep and rocky for development, was given over to trees and garbage. Hamburger wrappings and white plastic trash bags rustled in their wake. I was running full-out now.

About a block or so from the Ridge, I stumbled and almost fell. I slapped an arm across a telephone pole and just managed to catch myself in time. Aghast at my own carelessness, I hung there, dizzy and alarmed.

The ground overhead was black as black, an iron roof that somehow was yet as anxious as a hound to leap upon me, crush me flat, smear me to nothingness. I stared up at it, horrified.

Somebody screamed my name.

I turned. A faint blue figure clung to a television antenna atop a small, stuccoed brick duplex. Charlie's Widow. She pointed an arm that flickered with silver fire down Ripka Street. I slewed about to see what was coming after me.

It was the Corpsegrinder.

When it saw that I'd spotted it, it put out several more legs, extended a quilled head, and raised a howl that bounced off the Heaviside layer. My nonexistent blood chilled.

In a panic, I scrambled up and ran toward the Ridge and safety. I had a squat in the old Roxy, and once I was through the wall, the Corpsegrinder would not follow. Why this should be so, I did not know. But you learn the rules if you want to survive.

I ran. In the back of my head I could hear the Seven Sisters clucking and gossiping to each other, radiating television and radio over a few dozen frequencies. Indifferent to my plight.

The Corpsegrinder churned up the wires on a hundred needle-sharp legs. I could feel the ion surge it kicked up pushing against me as I reached the intersection of Ridge and Leverington. Cars were pulling up to the pumps at the Atlantic station. Teenagers stood in front of the A-Plus Mini Market, flicking half-smoked cigarettes into the street, stamping their feet like colts, and waiting for something to happen. I couldn't help feeling a great longing disdain for them. Every last one worried about grades and drugs and zits, and all the while snugly barricaded within hulking fortresses of flesh.

I was scant yards from home. The Roxy was a big old movie palace, fallen into disrepair and semiconverted to a skateboarding rink which had gone out of business almost immediately. But it had been a wonderful place once, and the terra cotta trim was still there: ribbons and river gods, great puffing faces with panpipes, guitars, flowers, wyverns. I crossed the Ridge on a dead telephone wire, spider-web delicate but still usable.

Almost there.

Then the creature was upon me, with a howl of electromagnetic rage that silenced even the Sisters for an instant. It slammed into my side, a storm of razors and diamond-edged fury, hooks and claws extended.

I grabbed at a rusty flange on the side of the Roxy.

Too late! Pain exploded within me, a sheet of white nausea. All in an instant I lost the name of my second daughter, an April morning when the world was new and I was five, a smoky string of all-nighters in Rensselaer Polytech, the jowly grin of Old Whatsisface the German who lived on LaFountain Street, the fresh pain of a sprained ankle out back of a Banana Republic warehouse, fishing off a yellow rubber raft with my old man on Lake Champlain. All gone, these and a thousand things more, sucked away, crushed to nothing, beyond retrieval.

Furious as any wounded animal, I fought back. Foul bits of substance splattered under my fist. The Corpsegrinder reared up to smash me down, and I scrabbled desperately away. Something tore and gave.

Then I was through the wall and safe among the bats and the gloom.

"*Cobb!*" the Corpsegrinder shouted. It lashed wildly back and forth, scouring the brick walls with limbs and teeth, as restless as a March wind, as unpredictable as ball lightning.

For the moment I was safe. But it had seized a part of me, tortured it, and made it a part of itself. I could no longer delude myself into thinking it was simply going to go away. "Cahawahawbb!" It broke my name down to a chord of overlapping tones. It had an ugly, muddy voice. I felt dirtied just listening to it. "Caw——" A pause. "——awbb!"

In a horrified daze I stumbled up the Roxy's curving patterned-tin roof until I found a section free of bats. Exhausted and dispirited, I slumped down.

"Caw aw aw awb buh buh!"

How had the thing found me? I'd thought I'd left it behind in Manhattan. Had my flight across the high-tension lines left a trail of some kind? Maybe. Then again, it might have some special connection with me. To follow me here it must have passed by easier prey. Which implied it had a grudge against me. Maybe I'd known the Corpsegrinder back when it was human. We could once have been important to each other. We might have been lovers. It was possible. The world is a stranger place than I used to believe.

The horror of my existence overtook me then, an acute awareness of the squalor in which I dwelt, the danger which surrounded me, and the dark mystery informing my universe.

I wept for all that I had lost.

Eventually, the sun rose up like God's own Peterbilt and with a triumphant blare of chromed trumpets, gently sent all of us creatures of the night to sleep.

WHEN YOU DIE, the first thing that happens is that the world turns upside down. You feel an overwhelming disorientation and a strange sensation that's not quite pain as the last strands connecting you to your body part, and then you slip out of physical being and fall from the planet.

As you fall, you attenuate. Your substance expands and thins, glowing more and more faintly as you pick up speed. So far as can be told, it's a process that doesn't ever stop. Fainter, thinner, colder ... until you've merged into the substance of everyone else who's ever died, spread perfectly uniformly through the universal vacuum, forever moving toward but never arriving at absolute zero.

Look hard, and the sky is full of the Dead.

Not everyone falls away. Some few are fast-thinking or lucky enough to maintain a tenuous hold on earthly existence. I was one of the lucky ones. I was working late one night on a proposal when I had my heart attack. The office was empty. The ceiling had a wire mesh within the plaster, and that's what saved me.

The first response to death is denial. *This can't be happening,* I thought. I gaped up at the floor where my body had fallen, and would lie undiscovered until morning. My own corpse, pale and bloodless, wearing a corporate tie and sleeveless grey Angora sweater. Gold Rolex, Sharper Image desk accessories, and of course I also thought: *I died for THIS?*

By which of course I meant my entire life.

So it was in a state of both personal and ontological crisis that I wandered across the ceiling to the location of an old pneumatic message tube, removed and casually plastered over some fifty years before. I fell from the seventeenth to the twenty-fifth floor, and I learned a lot in the process.

Shaken, startled, and already beginning to assume the wariness that the afterlife requires, I went to a window to get a glimpse of the outer world. When I tried to touch the glass, my hand went right through. I jerked back. Cautiously, I leaned forward, so that my head stuck out into the night.

What a wonderful experience Times Square is when you're dead! There is ten times the light a living being sees. All metal things vibrate with inner life. Electric wires are thin blue scratches in the air. Neon *sings.* The world is filled with strange sights and cries. Everything shifts from beauty to beauty.

Something that looked like a cross between a dragon and a wisp of smoke was feeding in the Square. But it was lost among so many wonders that I gave it no particular thought.

NIGHT AGAIN. I awoke with Led Zeppelin playing in the back of my head. "Stairway to Heaven." Again. It can be a long wait between Dead Milkmen cuts.

"Wakey-risey, little man," crooned one of the Sisters. It was funny how sometimes they took a close personal interest in our doings, and other times ignored us completely. "This is Euphrosyne with the red-eye weather report. The outlook is moody with a chance of existential despair. You won't be going outside tonight if you know what's good for you. There'll be lightning within the hour."

"It's too late in the year for lightning," I said.

"Oh dear. Should I inform the weather?"

By now I was beginning to realize that what I had taken on awakening to be the pressure of the Corpsegrinder's dark aura was actually the high-pressure front of an advancing storm. The first drops of rain pattered on the roof. Wind skirled and the rain grew stronger. Thunder growled in the distance. "Why don't you just go fuck your—"

A light laugh that trilled up into the supersonic, and she was gone.

I was listening to the rain underfoot when a lightning bolt screamed into existence, turning me inside out for the briefest instant then cartwheeling gleefully into oblivion. In the femtosecond of restoration following the bolt, the walls were transparent and all the world made of glass, its secrets available to be snooped out. But before comprehension was possible, the walls opaqued again and the lightning's malevolent aftermath faded like a madman's smile in the night.

Through it all the Seven Sisters were laughing and singing, screaming with joy whenever a lightning bolt flashed, and making up nonsense poems from howls, whistles, and static. During a momentary lull, the flat hum of a carrier wave filled my head. Phaenna, by the feel of her. But instead of her voice, I heard only the sound of fearful sobs.

"Widow?" I said. "Is that you?"

"She can't hear you," Phaenna purred. "You're lucky I'm here to bring you up to speed. A lightning bolt hit the transformer outside her house. It was bound to happen sooner or later. Your Nemesis—the one you call the Corpsegrinder, such a cute nickname, by the way—has her trapped."

This was making no sense at all. "Why would the Corpsegrinder be after her?"

"Why why why why?" Phaenna sang, a snatch of some pop ballad or other. "You didn't get answers when you were alive, what made you think you'd get any *now?*"

The sobbing went on and on. "She can sit it out," I said. "The Corpsegrinder can't—hey, wait. Didn't they just wire her house for cable? I'm trying to picture it. Phone lines on one side, electricity on the other, cable. She can slip out on his blind side."

The sobs lessened and then rose in a most unWidowlike wail of despair.

"Typical," Phaenna said. "You haven't the slightest notion of what you're talking about. The lightning stroke has altered your little pet. Go out and see for yourself."

My hackles rose. "You know damned good and well that I can't—"

Phaenna's attention shifted and the carrier beam died. The Seven Sisters are fickle that way. This time, though, it was just as well. No way was I going out there to face that monstrosity. I couldn't. And I was grateful not to have to admit it.

For a long while I sat thinking about the Corpsegrinder. Even here, protected by the strong walls of the Roxy, the mere thought of it was paralyzing. I tried to imagine what Charlie's Widow was going through, separated from this monster by only a thin curtain of brick and stucco. Feeling the hard radiation of its malice and need ... It was beyond my powers of visualization. Eventually I gave up and thought instead about my first meeting with the Widow.

She was coming down the hill from Roxborough with her arms out, the inverted image of a child playing at tightrope walker. Placing one foot ahead of the other with deliberate concentration, scanning the wire before her so cautiously that she was less than a block away when she saw me.

She screamed.

Then she was running straight at me. My back was to the transformer station—there was no place to flee. I shrank away as she stumbled to a halt.

"It's you!" she cried. "Oh God, Charlie, I knew you'd come back for me, I waited so long, but I never doubted you, never, we can—" She lunged forward as if to hug me. Our eyes met.

All the joy in her died.

"Oh," she said. "It's not you."

I was fresh off the high-tension lines, still vibrating with energy and fear. My mind was a blaze of contradictions. I could remember almost nothing of my post-death existence. Fragments, bits of advice from the old dead, a horrifying confrontation with ... something, some creature or phenomenon that had driven me to flee Manhattan. Whether it was this event or the fearsome voltage of that radiant highway that had scoured me of experience, I did not know. "It's me," I protested.

"No, it's not." Her gaze was unflatteringly frank. "You're not Charlie and you never were. You're—just the sad remnant of what once was a man, and not a very good one at that." She turned away. She was leaving me! In my confusion, I felt such a despair as I had never known before.

"Please . . ." I said.

She stopped.

A long silence. Then what in a living woman would have been a sigh. "You'd think that I—well, never mind." She offered her hand, and when I would not take it, simply said, "This way."

I followed her down Main Street, through the shallow canyon of the business district to a diner at the edge of town. It was across from Hubcap Heaven and an automotive junkyard bordered it on two sides. The diner was closed. We settled down on the ceiling.

"That's where the car ended up after I died," she said, gesturing toward the junkyard. "It was right after I got the call about Charlie. I stayed up drinking and after a while it occurred to me that maybe they were wrong, they'd made some sort of horrible mistake and he wasn't really dead, you know? Like maybe he was in a coma or something, some horrible kind of misdiagnosis, they'd gotten him confused with somebody else, who knows? Terrible things happen in hospitals. They make mistakes.

"I decided I had to go and straighten things out. There wasn't time to make coffee so I went to the medicine cabinet and gulped down a bunch of pills at random, figuring *something* among them would keep me awake. Then I jumped into the car and started off for Colorado."

"My God."

"I have no idea how fast I was going—everything was a blur when I crashed. At least I didn't take anybody with me, thank the Lord. There was this one horrible moment of confusion and pain and rage and then I found myself lying on the floor of the car with my corpse just inches beneath me on the underside of the roof." She was silent for a moment. "My first impulse was to crawl out the window. Lucky for me I didn't."

Another pause. "It took me most of a night to work my way out of the yard. I had to go from wreck to wreck. There were these gaps to jump. It was a nightmare."

"I'm amazed you had the presence of mind to stay in the car."

"Dying sobers you up fast."

I laughed. I couldn't help it. And without the slightest hesitation, she joined right in with me. It was a fine warm moment, the first I'd had since I didn't know when. The two of us set each other off, laughing louder and louder, our merriment heterodyning until it filled every television screen for a mile around with snow.

My defenses were down. She reached out and took my hand.

Memory flooded me. It was her first date with Charlie. He was an electrician. The people next door were having the place rehabbed. She'd been working in the back yard and he struck up a conversation. Then he asked her out. They went to a disco in the Adam's Mark over on City Line Avenue.

She wasn't eager to get involved with somebody just then. She was still recovering from a hellish affair with a married man who'd thought that since he wasn't available for anything permanent, that made her his property. But when Charlie suggested they go out to the car for some coke—it was the Seventies—she'd said sure. He was going to put the moves on her sooner or later. Might as well get this settled early so they'd have more time for dancing.

But after they'd done up the lines, Charlie had shocked her by taking her hands in his and kissing them. She worked for a Bucks County pottery in those days and her hands were rough and red. She was very sensitive about them.

"Beautiful hands," he murmured. "Such beautiful, beautiful hands."

"You're making fun of me," she protested, hurt.

"No! These are hands that *do* things, and they've been shaped by the things they've done. The way stones in a stream are shaped by the water that passes over them. The way tools are shaped by their work. A hammer is beautiful, if it's a good hammer, and your hands are too."

He could have been scamming her. But something in his voice, his manner, said no, he really meant it. She squeezed his hands and saw that they were beautiful too. Suddenly she was glad she hadn't gone off the pill when she broke up with Daniel. She started to cry. Her date looked alarmed and baffled. But she couldn't stop. All the tears she hadn't cried in the past two years came pouring out of her, unstoppable.

Charlie-boy, she thought, you just got lucky.

ALL THIS IN AN INSTANT. I snatched my hands away, breaking contact. "*Don't do that!*" I cried. "Don't you *ever* touch me again!"

With flat disdain, the Widow said, "It wasn't pleasant for me either. But I had to see how much of your life you remember."

It was naive of me, but I was shocked to realize that the passage of memories had gone both ways. But before I could voice my outrage, she said, "There's not much left of you. You're only a fragment of a man, shreds and tatters, hardly anything. No wonder you're so frightened. You've got what Charlie calls a low signal-to-noise ratio. What happened in New York City almost destroyed you."

"That doesn't give you the right to—"

"Oh be still. You need to know this. Living is simple, you just keep going. But death is complex. It's so hard to hang on and so easy to let go. The temptation is always there. Believe me, I know. There used to be five of us in Roxborough, and where are the others now? Two came through Manayunk last spring and camped out under the El for a season and they're gone too. Holding it together is hard work. One day the stars start singing to you, and the next you begin to listen to them. A week later they start to make sense. You're just reacting to events—that's not good enough. If you mean to hold on, you've got to know why you're doing it."

"So why are *you?*"

"I'm waiting for Charlie," she said simply.

It occurred to me to wonder exactly how many years she had been waiting. Three? Fifteen? Just how long was it possible to hold on? Even in my confused and emotional state, though, I knew better than to ask. Deep inside she must've known as well as I did that Charlie wasn't coming. "My name's Cobb," I said. "What's yours?"

She hesitated and then, with an odd sidelong look, said, "I'm Charlie's widow. That's all that matters." It was all the name she ever gave, and Charlie's Widow she was to me from then onward.

I ROLLED ONTO MY BACK on the tin ceiling and spread out my arms and legs, a phantom starfish among the bats. A fragment, she had called me, shreds and tatters. No wonder you're so frightened! In all the months since I'd been washed into this backwater of the power grid, she'd never treated me with anything but a condescension bordering on contempt.

So I went out into the storm after all.

The rain was nothing. It passed right through me. But there were ion-heavy gusts of wind that threatened to knock me right off the lines, and the transformer outside the Widow's house was burning a fierce actinic blue. It was a gusher of energy, a flare star brought to earth, dazzling. A bolt of lightning unzipped me, turned me inside out, and restored me before I had a chance to react.

The Corpsegrinder was visible from the Roxy, but between the burning transformer and the creature's metamorphosis, I was within a block of the monster before I understood exactly what it was I was seeing.

It was feeding off the dying transformer, sucking in energy so greedily that it pulsed like a mosquito engorged with blood. Enormous plasma wings warped to either side, hot blue and transparent. They curved entirely around the Widow's house in an unbroken and circular wall. At the resonance points they extruded less detailed versions of the Corpsegrinder itself, like sentinels, all facing the Widow.

Surrounding her with a prickly ring of electricity and malice.

I retreated a block, though the transformer fire apparently hid me from the Corpsegrinder, for it stayed where it was, eyelessly staring inward. Three times I circled the house from a distance, looking for a way in. An unguarded cable, a wrought-iron fence, any unbroken stretch of metal too high or too low for the Corpsegrinder to reach.

Nothing.

Finally, because there was no alternative, I entered the house across the street from the Widow's, the one that was best shielded by the spouting and stuttering transformer. A power line took me into the attic crawl space. From there I scaled the electrical system down through the second and first floors and so to the basement. I had a brief glimpse of a man asleep on a couch before the television. The set was off but it still held a residual charge. It sat quiescent, smug, bloated with stolen energies. If the poor bastard on the couch could have seen what I saw, he'd've never turned on the TV again.

In the basement I hand-over-handed myself from the washing machine to the main water inlet. Straddling the pipe, I summoned all my courage and plunged my head underground.

It was black as pitch. I inched forward on the pipe in a kind of panic. I could see nothing, hear nothing, smell nothing, taste nothing. All I could feel was the iron pipe beneath my hands. Just beyond the wall the pipe ended in a T-joint where it hooked into a branch line under the drive. I followed it to the street.

It was awful: Like suffocation infinitely prolonged. Like being wrapped in black cloth. Like being drowned in ink. Like strangling noiselessly in the void between the stars.

To distract myself, I thought about my old man.

When my father was young, he navigated between cities by radio. Driving dark and usually empty highways, he'd twist the dial back and forth, back and forth, until he hit a station. Then he'd withdraw his hand and wait for the station ID. That would give him his rough location—that he was somewhere outside of Albany, say. A sudden signal coming in strong and then abruptly dissolving in groans and eerie whistles was a fluke of the ionosphere, impossibly distant and easily disregarded. One that faded in and immediately out meant he had grazed the edge of a station's range. But then a signal would grow and strengthen as he penetrated its field, crescendo, fade, and collapse into static and silence. That left him north of Troy, let's say, and making good time. He would begin the search for the next station.

You could drive across the continent in this way, passed from hand to hand by local radio, and tuned in to the geography of the night.

I went over that memory three times, polishing and refining it, before the branch line abruptly ended. One hand groped forward and closed upon nothing.

I had reached the main conduit. For a panicked moment I had feared that it would be concrete or brick or even one of the cedar pipes the city laid down in the 19th century, remnants of which still linger here and there beneath the pavement. But by sheer blind luck, the system had been installed during that narrow window of time when the pipes were cast iron. I crawled along its underside first one way and then the other, searching for the branch line to the Widow's. There was a lot of crap under the street. Several times I was blocked by gas lines or by the high-pressure pipes for the fire hydrants and had to awkwardly clamber around them.

At last I found the line and began the painful journey out from the street again.

When I emerged in the Widow's basement, I was a nervous wreck. It came to me then that I could no longer remember my father's name. A thing of rags and shreds indeed!

I worked my way up the electrical system, searching every room and unintentionally spying on the family who had bought the house after the Widow's death. In the kitchen a puffy man stood with his sleeves rolled up, elbow-deep in the sink, angrily washing dishes by candlelight. A woman who was surely his wife expressively smoked a cigarette at his stiff back, drawing in the smoke with bitter intensity and exhaling it in puffs of hatred. On the second floor a preadolescent girl clutched a tortoise-shell cat so tightly it struggled to escape, and cried into its fur. In the next room a younger boy sat on his bed in earphones, Walkman on his lap, staring sightlessly out the window at the burning transformer. No Widow on either floor.

How, I wondered, could she have endured staying in this entropic oven of a blue-collar row house, forever the voyeur at the banquet, watching the living squander what she had already spent? Her trace was everywhere, her presence elusive. I was beginning to think she'd despaired and given herself up to the sky when I found her in the attic, clutching the wire that led to the antenna. She looked up, silenced and amazed by my unexpected appearance.

"Come on," I said. "I know a way out."

RETURNING, HOWEVER, I couldn't retrace the route I'd taken in. It wasn't so much the difficulty of navigating the twisting maze of pipes under the street, though that was bad enough, as the fact that the Widow wouldn't hazard the passage unless I led her by the hand.

"You don't know how difficult this is for me," I said.

"It's the only way I'd dare." A nervous, humorless laugh. "I have such a lousy sense of direction."

So, steeling myself, I seized her hand and plunged through the wall.

It took all my concentration to keep from sliding off the water pipes, I was so distracted by the violence of her thoughts. We crawled through a hundred memories, all of her married lover, all alike.

Here's one:

Daniel snapped on the car radio. Sad music—something classical—flooded the car. "That's bullshit, babe. You know how much I have invested in you?" He jabbed a blunt finger at her dress. "I could buy two good whores for what that thing cost."

Then why don't you, she thought. Get back on your Metroliner and go home to New York City and your wife and your money and your two good whores. Aloud, reasonably, she said, "It's over, Danny, can't you see that?"

"Look, babe. Let's not argue here, okay? Not in the parking lot, with people walking by and everybody listening. Drive us to your place, we can sit down and talk it over like civilized human beings."

She clutched the wheel, staring straight ahead. "No. We're going to settle this here and now."

"Christ." One-handed he wrangled a pack of Kents from a jacket pocket and knocked out a cigarette. Put the end in his lips and drew it out. Punched the lighter. "So talk."

A wash of hopelessness swept over her. Married men were supposed to be easy to get rid of. That was the whole point. "Let me go, Danny," she pleaded. Then, lying, "We can still be friends."

He made a disgusted noise.

"I've tried, Danny, I really have. You don't know how hard I've tried. But it's just not working."

"All right, I've listened. Now let's go." Reaching over her, Daniel threw the gearshift into reverse. He stepped on her foot, mashing it down on the accelerator.

The car leapt backwards. She shrieked and in a flurry of panic swung the wheel about and slammed on the brake with her free foot.

With a jolt and a crunch, the car stopped. There was the tinkle of broken plastic. They'd hit a lime-green Hyundai.

"Oh, that's just perfect!" Daniel said. The lighter popped out. He lit his cigarette and then swung open the door. "I'll check the damage."

Over her shoulder, she saw Daniel tug at his trousers' knees as he crouched to examine the Hyundai. She had a sudden impulse to slew the car around and escape. Step on the gas and never look back. Watch his face, dismayed and dwindling, in the rear-view mirror. Eyes flooded with tears, she began quietly to laugh.

Then Daniel was back. "It's all right, let's go."

"I heard something break."

"It was just a taillight, okay?" He gave her a funny look. "What the hell are you laughing about?"

She shook her head hopelessly, unable to sort out the tears from the laughter. Then somehow they were on the Expressway, the car humming down the indistinct and warping road. She was driving but Daniel was still in control.

WE WERE COMPLETELY lost now and had been for some time. I had taken what I was certain had to be a branch line and it had led nowhere. We'd been tracing its twisty passage for blocks. I stopped and pulled my hand away. I couldn't concentrate. Not with the caustics and poisons of the Widow's past churning through me. "Listen," I said. "We've got to get something straight between us."

Her voice came out of nowhere, small and wary. "What?"

How to say it? The horror of those memories lay not in their brutality but in their particularity. They nestled into empty spaces where memories of my own should have been. They were as familiar as old shoes. They *fit*.

"If I could remember any of this crap," I said, "I'd apologize. Hell, I can't blame you for how you feel. Of course you're angry. But it's gone, can't you see that, it's over. You've got to let go. You can't hold me accountable for things I can't even remember, okay? All that shit happened decades ago. I was young. I've changed." The absurdity of the thing swept over me. I'd have laughed if I'd been able. "I'm dead, for pity's sake!"

A long silence. Then, "So you've figured it out."

"You've known all along," I said bitterly. "Ever since I came off of the high-tension lines in Manayunk."

She didn't deny it. "I suppose I should be flattered that when you were in trouble you came to me," she said in a way that indicated she was not.

"Why didn't you tell me then? Why drag it out?"

"Danny—"

"Don't call me that!"

"It's your name. Daniel. Daniel Cobb."

All the emotions I'd been holding back by sheer force of denial closed about me. I flung myself down and clutched the pipe tight, crushing myself against its unforgiving surface. Trapped in the friendless wastes of night, I weighed my fear of letting go against my fear of holding on.

"Cobb?"

I said nothing.

The Widow's voice took on an edgy quality. "Cobb, we can't stay here. You've got to lead me out. I don't have the slightest idea which way to go. I'm lost without your help."

I still could not speak.

"*Cobb!*" She was close to panic. "I put my own feelings aside. Back in Manayunk. You needed help and I did what I could. Now it's your turn."

Silently, invisibly, I shook my head.

"God damn you, Danny," she said furiously. "I won't let you do this to me again! So you're unhappy with what a jerk you were—that's not my problem. You can't redeem your manliness on me any more. I am not your fucking salvation. I am not some kind of cosmic last chance and it's not my job to talk you down from the ledge."

That stung. "I wasn't asking you to," I mumbled.

"So you're still there! Take my hand and lead us out."

I pulled myself together. "You'll have to follow my voice, babe. Your memories are too intense for me."

We resumed our slow progress. I was sick of crawling, sick of the dark, sick of this lightless horrid existence, disgusted to the pit of my soul with who and what I was. Was there no end to this labyrinth of pipes?

"Wait." I'd brushed by something. Something metal buried in the earth.

"What is it?"

"I think it's—" I groped about, trying to get a sense of the thing's shape. "I think it's a cast-iron gatepost. Here. Wait. Let me climb up and take a look."

Relinquishing my grip on the pipe, I seized hold of the object and stuck my head out of the ground. I emerged at the gate of an iron fence framing the minuscule front yard of a house on Ripka Street. I could see again! It was so good to feel the clear breath of the world once more that I closed my eyes briefly to savor the sensation.

"How ironic," Euphrosyne said.

"After being so heroic," Thalia said.

"Overcoming his fears," Aglaia said.

"Rescuing the fair maid from terror and durance vile," Cleta said.

"Realizing at last who he is," Phaenna said.

"Beginning that long and difficult road to recovery by finally getting in touch with his innermost feelings," Auxo said.

Hegemone giggled.

"What?" I opened my eyes.

That was when the Corpsegrinder struck. It leapt upon me with stunning force, driving spear-long talons through my head and body. The talons were barbed so that they couldn't be pulled free and they burned like molten metal. "Ahhhh, Cobb," the Corpsegrinder crooned. "Now this is *sweet.*"

I screamed and it drank in those screams, so that only silence escaped into the outside world. I struggled and it made those struggles its own, leaving me to kick myself deeper and deeper into the drowning pools of its identity. With all my will I resisted. It was not enough. I experienced the languorous pleasure of surrender as that very will and resistance were sucked down into my attacker's substance. The distinction between *me* and *it* weakened, strained, dissolved. I was transformed.

I was the Corpsegrinder now.

MANHATTAN IS A VIRTUAL SCHOOL for the dead. Enough people die there every day to keep any number of monsters fed. From the store of memories the Corpsegrinder had stolen from me, I recalled a quiet moment sitting cross-legged on the tin ceiling of a sleaze joint while table dancers entertained Japanese tourists on the floor above and a kobold instructed me on some of the finer points of survival. "The worst thing you can be hunted by," he said, "is yourself."

"Very aphoristic."

"Fuck you. I used to be human too."

"Sorry."

"Apology accepted. Look, I told you about Salamanders. That's a shitty way to go, but at least it's final. When they're done with you, nothing remains. But a Corpsegrinder is a parasite. It has no true identity of its own, so it constructs one from bits and pieces of everything that's unpleasant within you. Your basic greeds and lusts. It gives you a particularly nasty sort of immortality. Remember that old cartoon? This hideous toad saying 'Kiss me and live forever—you'll be a toad, but you'll live forever.'" He grimaced. "If you get the choice, go with the Salamander."

"So what's this business about hunting myself?"

"Sometimes a Corpsegrinder will rip you in two and let half escape. For a while."

"Why?"

"I dunno. Maybe it likes to play with its food. Ever watch a cat torture a mouse? Maybe it thinks it's fun."

From a million miles away, I thought: So now I know what's happened to me. I'd made quite a run of it, but now it was over. It didn't matter. All that mattered was the hoard of memories, glorious memories, into which I'd been dumped. I wallowed in them, picking out here a winter sunset and there the pain of a jellyfish sting when I was nine. So what if I was already beginning to dissolve? I was intoxicated, drunk, stoned with the raw stuff of experience. I was high on life.

Then the Widow climbed up the gatepost looking for me.

"Cobb?"

The Corpsegrinder had moved up the fence to a more comfortable spot in which to digest me. When it saw the Widow, it reflexively parked me in a memory of a grey drizzly day in a Ford Fiesta outside of 30th Street Station. The engine was going and the heater and the windshield wiper too, so I snapped on the radio to mask their noise. Beethoven filled the car, the Moonlight Sonata.

"That's bullshit, babe," I said. "You know how much I have invested in you? I could buy two good whores for what that dress cost."

She refused to meet my eyes. In a whine that set my teeth on edge, she said, "Danny, can't you see that it's over between us?"

"Look, babe, let's not argue in the parking lot, okay?" I was trying hard to be reasonable. "Not with people walking by and listening. We'll go someplace private where we can talk this over calmly, like two civilized human beings."

She shifted slightly in the seat and adjusted her skirt with a little tug. Drawing attention to her long legs and fine ass. Making it hard for me to think straight. The bitch really knew how to twist the knife. Even now, crying and begging, she was aware of how it turned me on. And even though I hated being aroused by her little act, I was. The sex was always best after an argument; it made her sluttish.

I clenched my anger in one hand and fisted my pocket with it. Thinking how much I'd like to up and give her a shot. She was begging for it.

Secretly, maybe, it was what she wanted; I'd often suspected she'd enjoy being hit. It was too late to act on the impulse, though. The memory was playing out like a tape, immutable, unstoppable.

All the while, like a hallucination or the screen of a television set receiving conflicting signals, I could see the Widow, frozen with fear half in and half out of the ground. She quivered like an acetylene flame. In the memory she was saying something, but with the shift in my emotions came a corresponding warping-away of perception. The train station, car, the windshield wipers and music, all faded to a murmur in my consciousness.

Tentacles whipped around the Widow. She was caught. She struggled helplessly, deliciously. The Corpsegrinder's emotions pulsed through me and to my remote horror I found that they were identical to my own. I *wanted* the Widow, wanted her so bad there were no words for it. I wanted to clutch her to me so tightly her ribs would splinter and for just this once she'd know it was real. I wanted to own her. To possess her. To put an end to all her little games. To know her every thought and secret, down to the very bottom of her being.

No more lies, babe, I thought, no more evasions. You're mine now.

So perfectly in synch was I with the Corpsegrinder's desires that it shifted its primary consciousness back into the liquid sphere of memory, where it hung smug and lazy, watching, a voyeur with a willing agent. I was in control of the autonomous functions now. I reshaped the tentacles, merging and recombining them into two strong arms. The claws and talons that clutched the fence I made legs again. The exterior of the Corpsegrinder I morphed into human semblance, save for that great mass of memories sprouting from our back like a bloated spidersack. Last of all I made the head.

I gave it my own face.

"Surprised to see me again, babe?" I leered.

Her expression was not so much fearful as disappointed. "No," she said wearily. "Deep down, I guess I always knew you'd be back."

As I drew the Widow closer, I distantly knew that all that held me to the Corpsegrinder in that instant was our common store of memories and my determination not to lose them again. That was enough, though. I pushed my face into hers, forcing open her mouth. Energies flowed between us like a feast of tongues.

I prepared to drink her in.

There were no barriers between us. This was an experience as intense as when, making love, you lose all track of which body is your own and thought dissolves into the animal moment. For a giddy instant I was no less her than I was myself. I was the Widow staring fascinated into the filthy depths of my psyche. She was myself witnessing her astonishment as she realized exactly how little I had ever known her. We both saw her freeze still to the core with horror. Horror not of what I was doing.

But of what I was.

I can't take any credit for what happened then. It was only an impulse, a spasm of the emotions, a sudden and unexpected clarity of vision. Can a single flash of decency redeem a life like mine? I don't believe it. I refuse to believe it.

Had there been time for second thoughts, things might well have gone differently. But there was no time to think. There was only time enough to feel an upwelling of revulsion, a visceral desire to be anybody or anything but my own loathsome self, a profound and total yearning to be quit of the burden of such memories as were mine. An aching need to *just once* do the moral thing.

I let go.

Bobbing gently, the swollen corpus of my past floated up and away, carrying with it the parasitic Corpsegrinder. Everything I had spent all my life accumulating fled from me. It went up like a balloon, spinning, dwindling ... gone. Leaving me only what few flat memories I have narrated here.

I screamed.

And then I cried.

I don't know how long I clung to the fence, mourning my loss. But when I gathered myself together, the Widow was still there.

"Danny," the Widow said. She didn't touch me. "Danny, I'm sorry."

I'd almost rather that she had abandoned me. How do you apologize for sins you can no longer remember? For having been someone who, however reprehensible, is gone forever? How can you expect forgiveness from somebody you have forgotten so completely you don't even know her name? I felt twisted with shame and misery. "Look," I said. "I know I've behaved badly. More than badly. But there ought to be some way to make it up to you. For, you know, everything. Somehow. I mean—"

What do you say to somebody who's seen to the bottom of your wretched and inadequate soul?

"I want to apologize," I said.

With something very close to compassion, the Widow said, "It's too late for that, Danny. It's over. Everything's over. You and I only ever had the one trait in common. We neither of us could ever let go of anything. Small wonder we're back together again. But don't you see, it doesn't matter what you want or don't want—you're not going to get it. Not now. You had your chance. It's too late to make things right." Then she stopped, aghast at what she had just said.

But we both knew she had spoken the truth.

"Widow," I said as gently as I could, "I'm sure Charlie—"

"Shut up."

I shut up.

The Widow closed her eyes and swayed, as if in a wind. A ripple ran through her and when it was gone her features were simpler, more schematic, less recognizably human. She was already beginning to surrender the anthropomorphic.

I tried again. "Widow …" Reaching out my guilty hand to her.

She stiffened but did not draw away. Our fingers touched, twined, mated. "Elizabeth," she said at last. "My name is Elizabeth Connelly."

We huddled together on the ceiling of the Roxy through the dawn and the blank horror that is day. When sunset brought us conscious again, we talked through half the night before making the one decision we knew all along that we'd have to make.

It took us almost an hour to reach the Seven Sisters and climb down to the highest point of Thalia.

We stood holding hands at the top of the mast. Radio waves were gushing out from under us like a great wind. It was all we could do to keep from being blown away.

Underfoot, Thalia was happily chatting with her sisters. Typically, at our moment of greatest resolve, they gave us not the slightest indication of interest. But they were all listening to us. Don't ask me how I knew.

"Cobb?" Elizabeth said. "I'm afraid."

"Yeah, me too."

A long silence, and then she said, "Let me go first. If you go first, I won't have the nerve."

"Okay."

She took a deep breath—funny, if you think about it—and then she let go, and fell into the sky.

First she was like a kite, and then a scrap of paper, and finally she was a rapidly tumbling speck. I stood for a long time watching her falling, dwindling, until she was lost in the background flicker of the universe, just one more spark in infinity.

She was gone and I couldn't help wondering if she had ever really been there at all. Had the Widow truly been Elizabeth Connelly? Or was she just another fragment of my shattered self, a bundle of related memories that I had to come to terms with before I could bring myself to finally let go?

A vast emptiness seemed to spread itself through all of existence. I clutched the mast spasmodically then, and thought: *I can't!*

But the moment passed. I've got a lot of questions, and there aren't any answers here. In just another instant, I'll let go and follow Elizabeth (if Elizabeth she was) into the night. I will fall forever and I will be converted to background radiation, smeared ever thinner and cooler across the universe, a smooth, uniform, and universal message that has only one decode. Let Thalia carry my story to whoever cares to listen. I won't be here for it.

It's time to go now. Time and then some to leave. I'm frightened, and I'm going.

Now.